I0768402

the Raven's Cry

the Raven's Cry

ARCHIVES OF THE WARDEN
Book Three

V. K. DIXON

The Raven's Cry
Copyright © 2024 by Victoria Dixon

All rights reserved. This book or parts thereof may not be reproduced in any form, stored in any retrieval system, or transmitted in any form by any means — electronic, mechanical, photocopy, recording, or otherwise — without prior written permission of the publisher.

Contact Info: www.xeniahousepress.com

Cover Design by : Maria Spada
Sigil Illustrations by : Hannah Fogarty
Map Illustration by : V.K. Dixon
Editor : Brittany Howard

This book is a work of fiction. Names, characters, business, organizations, places, events, and incidents are either the product of the author's imagination or are used fictitiously. Any resemblance to actual persons, living or dead, events, or locales is entirely coincidental.

ISBN: 979-8-9868452-5-8

First Edition: September 2024

*For the creators of Cabot Cove, ME.
Because of you, I'll forever dream
of living by the sea like J.B.*

Porthaven Township

The salt-swept shores of serenity

Table of Contents

Author's Note

The spirit world referenced in this novel is inspired by the truth.
It is not, however, the real truth.
In making the truth fantastic, it is my hope to stir up questions within reality.

Two years ago . . .

Upon an unexpected inheritance, brothers and co-authors Peter and Spencer Collins moved to the small town of DeVerre, WA, to accept the grand estate of their estranged great-aunt, Diane Larkin, and pursue their lifelong dream of being full-time authors. Along with their inheritance of a new house, two dogs, and the townspeople's suspicions, they found themselves drawn into the mysterious past of their great-aunt and the reason for her move to DeVerre over thirty years ago.

Through the town librarian, Ava Bernard, the brothers learned that the home they'd inherited from Diane—the House of Occasus—was once owned by the principal founding family of DeVerre: the Varons. The old Varon estate was rumored to hold a vault that held the town's greatest secrets. She explained to them that it was for this reason that the townspeople didn't like Diane and remained wary of the brothers.

In their early exploration of the town's history and Diane's decision to make DeVerre her home, the news of a string of animal attacks reached them. Peter became suspicious of the attacks, though Spencer tried to ignore them altogether.

With the help of Diane's closest friend, Cassandra Clement—who, to their surprise, was an attractive woman their own age—the brothers discovered that they were not biological Collinses as they believed. Their ancestors originated from DeVerre. Diane and her brother, Phillip, the brothers' grandfather, had been born in DeVerre and adopted by the Collins family on less than legal terms. Cassandra taught them about Diane's search for the parents she'd lost and introduced them to the spirit world that the two women had discovered together. A world filled with ghosts, phantoms, and beasts. One such phantom was Gerard Alarie, whom Cassandra had tethered to their home in exchange for his knowledge about the history of DeVerre.

Together, the three of them sought out the truth about their family's past and the secrets held in the town. Their pursuit of answers led them to Owen Bernard, a Wielder of the spirit world and agent of the Warden sent to DeVerre to ensure its safety. Owen taught them about the Warden—an organization dedicated to protecting the spirit world from the machinations of the Druids—and about the Veil hidden within DeVerre— a space where the line between the spirit world and physical world is thinnest.

As a team of four, Peter, Spencer, Cassandra, and Owen discovered the presence of Druids within the town, working to take over the Veil. Their investigation led them to the discovery that Cassandra's cousin, Debbie Mercier, was one of these Druids intent on taking control of the Veil and that the cult had orchestrated the "animal" attacks. When Debbie attacked the brothers, Cassandra came to their rescue, shattering Debbie's soul with an arc of the spirit world's essence.

In the wake of their battle, Peter, Spencer, and Cassandra worked to figure out their next move. They knew the Druids wouldn't take lightly the damage inflicted on Debbie. But they also knew they were in too deep to back out. They needed to find the truth behind their ancestry and keep the Druids from claiming control of the spirit world.

With Owen's continued help, they worked to find the vault hidden in their home and to uncover the identity of the Druids. They also continued their research on the Warden, the Druids, and the spirit world, hoping to find any information that might give them an edge in protecting the town. While Owen continued to explain more of the Warden's history, he told them of a Warden town—Porthaven, ME—regarded as a cautionary tale due to a devastating incident eight years prior.

Through weeks of trial and error and a near-death run-in with the Druids, they finally found Occasus's vault and the secrets they were so desperate to uncover. The brothers learned that they were Varons. Their great-grandparents had secretly worked to bring down the Druids, which led to the sacrifice of their lives. They also learned the names of the Druids within DeVerre, arming them with the knowledge they needed to take the cult down and reclaim their rightful inheritance as protectors of the spirit world.

But before they could enact their plan and rid the town of the Druids, the cultists attacked their home, twenty against four. Only through a feat of extreme, unknown power did Cassandra drive the Druids back, saving their lives. Now, the team faces the remaining threat of Druids in their town and the desperate need to earn the townspeople's trust.

However, before they could convince the town of anything, Peter stumbled upon a meeting with Gerard Alarie and Alexander Frossard—the town doctor recently named as the Druid leader—discussing the failure of the attack on Occasus and the impending arrival of "the Vessel." Unable to get away in time, Alexander caught Peter and took him captive, leaving Spencer unaware of his brother's plight.

Now, our story continues, taking us to Porthaven, ME, and the woman whose sacrifice will save them all . . .

Cait

Present Day

"What are you drawing now?" Rese asked, resting her arms on the counter between them.

Without looking up from her sketchbook, Cait answered, "It's a blue-sting scylla."

Her sister let out a cynical snort. "Genni would be thrilled."

Cait couldn't help smirking as she shaded around the sucker-like protrusions on the tentacled beast. This one was softer, with a more ancient curve to its bulbous frame. Unlike the more familiar variety of scylla, this one didn't have quite the same horrifying characteristics. It was, in Cait's opinion, rather cute in its octopod-esque way.

Dropping her pencil, Cait flexed her right hand. She'd been sketching and making notes at the coffee shop all morning, and even with all her exercises, her fingers were growing tired. She stretched her fingers and sat back. The oversized locket around her neck landed heavily against her clavicle. Her hand went to it instinctively, the memories attached threatening to surface.

The subtle shift of Ludus at her feet drew Cait's attention away from the locket. She looked down at the dog. Not that you could really call him a "dog." He was more like a wolf—massive with a narrow snout, fluffy black and gray fur, and intelligent amber eyes.

Giving his shoulder a playful tap with the toe of her boot, Cait turned back to her sister. "Could you get another tea for me?" she asked, nudging the porcelain cup toward her.

Readily, Rese snatched it up, but she didn't move. She held the cup between them as if in a desperate plea. "Why don't you let me make you something coffee-based for a change?" she begged. "You know, something fun and creamy and maybe a little chocolatey?"

Cait smiled. "I'll stick with the tea."

With a good-humored huff, Rese stood back up. "You're very boring."

"I've had enough excitement for a lifetime, thank you."

At her feet, Ludus snorted as though amused. Cait nudged him again, and his long snout nudged her foot back.

Soft folk music filled the coffee shop, adding to its calm mood. Five years ago, Rese had purchased the shop after working in it since right out of high school. As Porthaven's only coffee shop, it had thrived, particularly after she'd renovated and begun roasting in-house. Like everything Rese touched, the shop was sophisticated, lovely, and modern. Muted floral wallpaper and white wainscoting covered the walls. Customers lounged pleasantly on the plush velvet couches, reading books, working on laptops, or simply chatting. Others clustered at the marble and gold tables, craft coffees in hand. The bright late morning sunlight streamed through the windows, casting a white-yellow glow over the room.

Being in the coffee shop felt equal parts comforting and inconsistent to Cait. She liked being in an atmosphere so beautiful and soothing. But it also gave her a sense that she'd betrayed her old sketching spot— reminding her that she'd not returned there for almost ten years.

Smoothing the front of her loosely fitted, navy button down, Cait forced herself to smile as Rese returned with the fresh cup of tea, the cream still swirling in the whiskey-colored liquid. Cait thanked her sister and picked her pencil back up.

"You gonna send that to Matt when you're done with it?" Rese asked.

Cait had barely put pencil to paper, but the comment drew her eyes back to her sister's face. "When don't I send them to Matt?" she returned.

Rese failed to play it casual as she pursed her lips and shrugged. "Oh, well, you never know." She twisted a finger through her golden waves. "How is he?"

Drawing the charcoal pencil across the page, Cait let the question hang. She knew why her sister was asking. What she couldn't figure out was how she'd come to the conclusion that anything had changed. "Last we talked, he's doing well," she replied flatly.

Rese didn't take the hint. "He's still at the university?"

"He works at the university."

"Right, you mentioned that. Does he miss Porthaven?"

Rolling her eyes, Cait looked up at her sister. "Stop."

"What?" she asked innocently. "I'm just curious. It's been years since I've talked to Mattie."

"Then why don't *you* give him a call?"

Rese huffed. "*I'm* not the one he's in love with."

Cait glared at her.

"He's still single, isn't he?" Rese pestered.

"Technically," Cait admitted. "I think so, at least. He *was* seeing someone last I knew, so there's a chance he's gotten engaged."

Rese pursed her lips in disappointment. "I thought he'd wait for you."

"He'd be waiting for eternity."

The lift of Rese's immaculately sculpted eyebrow said that she thought Cait was being ridiculous. But really, it was Rese who was intentionally ignoring the facts. Even if Cait wanted to move on, she couldn't. She'd made promises she couldn't break as much as she'd made mistakes she couldn't correct.

The merry *tinkle* of the bell over the door rang out, breaking their exchange.

Then it happened.

Cait dropped her pencil, her heart lurching as the rumble started at the base of her skull. For the first time in a decade, it welled up, spreading to her chest and down her arms. All the sound in the coffee shop faded to a subtle whisper as Cait's skin tingled, and the soft growl thrummed in her head. Her eyes flew to Ludus at her feet, the dog's pointed ears alert and his head raised.

Hands shaking, Cait's gaze shot up to confirm her suspicions.

Her heart jolted as the door swung shut behind the man who'd entered the shop. He strode forward to the counter. His attractively disheveled dark hair brushed over the tops of his ears, a thin scruff covering his jawline as though he'd forgotten to shave that morning—or maybe the last two mornings. But even ten years hadn't changed that much. He looked the same as he ever had. Steady, rich brown eyes. Expressive face. Lopsided grin.

Cait thought she might be sick.

He was back.

"Not that one," the Wolf whispered. *"A different Varon."*

"What—that's not—" Cait was going to say that it wasn't possible. That this man looked too much like him, too perfectly identical, for it to be anyone else. But as he stepped up to the register less than three feet from her seat at the bar, she realized that wasn't quite true.

In expectation of a customer, Rese had spun around at the bell, but her welcoming persona dropped entirely as she saw the man. She scanned him with a scowl as he smiled kindly at her.

"Hi there," he said, even his voice shockingly similar.

Her thoughts fuzzed by the hum still radiating through her body and the stranger's likeness, Cait couldn't find her voice to warn her sister.

"What are you doing here?" Rese demanded.

The man hesitated, his brow quirking up. "Uh. . . ." He glanced at Cait for the first time, no glimmer of recognition in his eyes.

Of course he didn't recognize her, she reminded herself. He wasn't *him*.

A nervous chuckle escaped the stranger as he turned back to Rese. He drew a hand along his jaw, highlighting the notable absence of two distinctive freckles that *should* have been on his left cheek. "I was looking to get some coffee," he said.

"Is that so?" Rese retorted, her arms crossed. "Well, I'm afraid we don't serve backstabbing pricks—"

"Rese," Cait interrupted, finally managing a single word.

They both turned to look at her, the man now wide-eyed and clearly confused while Rese's expression pinched in annoyance.

Holding her sister's stare, Cait gave a firm shake of her head.

Skepticism, then horror, flashed across Rese's face. Her jaw dropped. "Oh, my—I—I am *so* sorry!" she said, whirling to face the customer. "I thought you were someone else."

The stranger nodded, his dark eyes flickering between Rese and Cait. "No problem," he muttered, though he sounded completely baffled. He scratched the back of his neck, the flash of a familiar gold ring reflecting in the light.

Not the same Varon, but a Varon, nonetheless.

"Must be a particularly strong resemblance," he remarked lightly.

"Shockingly so," Cait heard herself say.

"Huh." He tugged on the collar of his brown leather jacket. "Resemblance to a backstabbing prick doesn't preclude a guy from getting a coffee, does it?"

Rese gaped at him. "No, of course not! What would you like? It's on the house. Anything at all."

He let out a thin laugh. "Nah, that's cool. I don't mind—"

"Please!" she insisted. "As an apology."

Accepting the offer, the stranger gave his order. Rese hurried to prepare his drink, leaving him to stand at the register alone with Cait. Her heart hadn't slowed, her hands still shaking as she stared at him. The hum had settled, though it still reverberated in her chest and skull. It always did this. But it hadn't happened for over a decade. Not since *him*.

In the silence, the man's gaze drifted to her. Sure that her expression gave away the panic roaring through her system, Cait tried to offer him a polite smile.

He laughed again at her clear failure. "That strong of a resemblance, huh?"

Tipping her head to the side, Cait continued to study him. "I'm probably the only one who would have known."

He appeared both amused and wary at the suggestion. "You spend a lot of time with unscrupulous guys?"

"I did once," she admitted. "I learned my lesson."

"It only takes one, I guess." He smiled then, warm, friendly, and completely unaffected. "I'm Peter."

Accepting the handshake he offered to her, Cait raised her brow. "Peter Varon?"

His smile dipped at the corner. "How'd you know that?"

Cait's gaze flickered down toward the dog at her feet. "A friend told me."

His eyebrows rising, Peter understood the intonation of her words. "I didn't catch your name," he prompted.

"Cait Lewan," she offered.

With a nod, Peter's smile returned in full. "In that case—" He moved to the empty seat on the other side of her and sat down. "Do you believe in coincidences, Cait?"

Cait turned to him, shutting the notebook in front of her. "Absolutely."

"Good." He shrugged off his jacket as Rese arrived with his drink. "Because coincidentally, I was sent here to find you."

CHAPTER ONE

Cait

Ten years ago . . .

This was always Cait's least favorite day: the first day of the new school year.

Often, she wondered if she disliked the building, with its pen-like structure, or the people within it more. Not that she disliked people in general. In fact, she refused to dislike anyone on principle. The students and teachers of Porthaven High were simply a constant reminder to Cait of who she was: an outsider.

Cait and her sisters hadn't chosen to live in Porthaven. No one ever asked them what they wanted. No one thought to see what would make the three girls feel cared for after enduring one of the most dreadful thing that could happen to a child.

Instead, they'd been gathered up, brought to the seaside town, and placed under protective custody.

Almost twelve years later, Cait had grown no more comfortable in their new home.

Of course, her older sister, Rese, had made the most of it. With her silky waves, dazzling smile, and charming personality, she'd clawed her way to the top of the high school's popular kids list. No matter what lingering side effects came with being one of the three Lewan girls, Rese had managed to flourish, growing out of "reject" status.

While their younger sister, Genni, had a bubbly, cheerful personality, she'd only managed two friends in her time. Though Genni insisted that Alexis and Jared were all the friends she needed, Cait couldn't help fearing that she and her sister were still at the bottom of the heap, inevitably destined to remain there.

Sometimes, Cait thought it was her fault. She hadn't really tried to make friends. Considering her quiet, lackluster personality, she knew it wouldn't work—even if the rumors about their family suddenly stopped circulating. And after more than a decade in the Porthaven school system, she knew if she hadn't made a friend by the start of her senior year, it wasn't likely she ever would.

Fifty-some years ago, Mayor Simon, the second of his family line, built Porthaven High onto the already existing Porthaven School, separating the elementary from the junior and senior high students. Until four years ago, the school hadn't changed much. Then, the current Mayor Simon—the fourth generation to take office—had chosen to make the long-needed updates. On the peninsula, as they were, the ever-unoriginal school council chose the most obvious theme for their school's redesign: the ocean.

Cait liked the seaside. The salt air and constant *hush* of waves that followed her around town settled happily in her senses. But she couldn't understand why the leaders of Porthaven felt the need to be so on the nose with all their decisions.

Now, crisp white and aqua-blue tiles covered the floors of the school. Dark-blue lockers lined the halls. Brand new desks and navy blue chairs outfitted the classrooms. They'd even put in a professional-style gym for the athletes. The sports teams themselves had been revamped with new uniforms, updated gear, and a new mascot—Poseidon.

Mayor William Simon claimed the expensive revamp was for the betterment of all future generations. But many townspeople called it favoritism, swearing it was simply because the mayor's son had started high school that year. It wouldn't do to make the mayor's son spend the next four years of his life in the salt-encrusted halls of the school.

Cait didn't have an opinion, and she truly didn't care.

She'd attended the school before William's renovation initiative. The bland halls and outdated decor had made the already narrow corridors and low ceilings feel even more like a cage. At least with the freshly painted walls, newly tiled ceilings, and refreshed window treatments, it felt brighter.

Still, Cait didn't think she'd ever see the school as anything but a pen, the students shepherded from classroom to classroom, stuck in those uncomfortable blue chairs behind those cramped, wooden desks.

First to class, as always, Cait sat at the back corner of the room. Porthaven was a small town, which meant the high school was small as well. Her graduating class included the same kids she'd gone through the school system with—all the kids she'd shared classes with every day since she'd arrived in town.

Each classroom was equipped to hold twenty-five students. Cait's class only numbered twenty-one. Desks sat in five-by-five rows, and every student knew their unofficially assigned seat. Regardless of the room, they sat in the same arrangement in every class. It was the way things went. The first four rows were reserved for the normal kids, while Cait sat in the back row alone.

At the front of the class, the teacher stood writing on the chalkboard. She was new to town. A pretty, middle-aged woman with wavy brown hair and a rosy complexion. She wore the typical teacher look—slacks, button up, and cardigan.

It surprised Cait to have a new teacher. Porthaven often got visitors, but they rarely had new residents. Due to the response to their own family's relocation to the seaside township, she'd always assumed the town's leadership intentionally discouraged new citizens.

A mass of other students filtered into the room. She'd spent the entire summer successfully avoiding these kids. The seniors chattered and laughed, goofing off, their moods were strategically languorous and blasé. They *were* seniors, after all. Why should they take this school year seriously? They could coast through school as they coasted through life.

Quickly, the students filled the desks, the seats beside Cait remaining purposefully empty.

Notebook open on her desktop, Cait sketched in the margins. She was careful with her sketches at school. She didn't need anyone thinking her any weirder than they already did. Keeping a hand nonchalantly resting on the page to block any accidental peeks, she drew the beginnings of a cat-like creature with two tails. The constant ramble of students droned in the background as Cait added whiskers. Her lips lifted as she imagined the creature's black nose twitching, whiskers tickling as it sniffed pockets for dried fruit. She was so caught up in her drawing that she failed to realize the peculiarity of a presence nearing until someone took the seat beside her.

Sure that she must be mistaken—who would sit next to her?—Cait's hand froze over the notebook. Had someone noticed her sketching and walked over to make fun of her for it? Slowly, she turned to survey the interloper.

A boy with messy brown curls sat there, lips pressed together in a bashful and boyish grin. He wore a red and black buffalo check flannel open over a white tee. His small, round nose and full yet defined cheeks gave him an additional boyish flair. Cait imagined that if he were fifteen or twenty-five, you'd never know the difference.

"Hey," he said, his reedy voice soft.

At a loss for who this boy was, Cait blinked. "Hi," she murmured.

Reaching across his book-laden desk, the boy held out his hand. "I'm Matt," he said.

Cait's eyes flickered toward the rest of the class. Sure enough, several students were looking over their shoulders at this new kid, muttering amongst themselves. With nothing else to do, Cait accepted the handshake, giving him her own name.

"It's nice to meet you, Cait," he said, that broad, thin-lipped smile causing his cheeks to almost pucker with friendliness. "I'm new, as you probably noticed. This town is pretty small, huh?"

Unaccustomed to such ready conversation, Cait found herself lamely replying, "Uh-huh."

"How long have you lived here?"

Playing with her pencil, Cait wondered if she should warn him that he'd chosen the wrong person to befriend. Being new, he didn't have a choice other than to sit in the back row, but that didn't mean he had to sit next to her. In fact, it'd be better for him if he didn't.

Instead of giving her warning, Cait answered, "Almost twelve years."

"Really? That's cool." He sighed as though relieved. "I'm glad I'm not the only non-native, ya know? I've only been here, like, a week, but it seems like this place is pretty tight-knit. Where did you live before?"

A flush of pride swept through Cait, grateful she'd spoken smoothly enough to keep him from hearing any accent. Over the years, she'd worked hard to lose her native accent to help people forget that she was different.

Feeling somewhat more confident, Cait replied, "Ireland."

"Oh!" Matt's grin grew in excitement. "That's legit! Why did your family move here? Like, are your parents from Ireland, or were they in the military and stationed there or something? Does the military even have a station in Ireland?"

The rapid-fire questions caused Cait's mind to stall. "Do you always ask this many questions?"

Matt scratched his nose. "Uh, yeah, kind of. My sister says that I never know when to shut up."

"I see."

"I—I can leave you alone if you want," he offered. "I don't mean to pry. I just—I like to be friendly, ya know?"

Cait didn't know.

"That's all right," she promised. "I don't know the answer to your questions about the military, but no, my parents weren't in it. My dad was from Ireland, and my mom from France."

"Neat. You must've been really young when you moved here, huh? Are you seventeen too?"

"Yes," Cait replied to both questions. Then she thought his kindhearted question deserved a more in-depth answer. "I'll be eighteen next month, though."

"That's cool. It'll be March for me." Matt flipped one of his floppy curls off his forehead, opening his mouth to ask another question when all sound in the room faded to a drone.

Whatever Matt had begun to ask, Cait didn't hear it. The world around her settled into a hum, her ears filling with the sound. Everything faded as Cait looked toward the front of the class.

From books and movies, Cait knew that other girls got butterflies in their stomachs. Not her. Butterflies didn't even begin to describe the sensation that overcame her when he was near.

A low hum filled her head, causing the hairs on the back of her neck to stand on end. Her senses kicked up, fully alert. She struggled to process anything but that sound, the familiarity of it a near comfort to her. It was inevitable, this thrumming under her skin—this awareness of him. She'd know that presence anywhere.

Three boys strode in, heads and spirits high as they greeted their other classmates. As always, Garrett and Brady made their entrance first, sweeping through the room as though preparing it. Aside from their lumbering builds and Maine-pale skin, they were near opposites. Sandy-haired and cocksure, Garrett was the enforcer. Brown-headed and sensible, Brady was the trusted adviser. With their fathers serving as sheriff and reverend, respectively, their status was unsurprising.

But Cait looked past their tall stature to the boy behind them.

There, on the far side of the room, with his dark brown hair mussed to perfection, Desmond Simon walked into the class.

Well, Cait thought to herself, it was more of a saunter than a walk.

With the ease of being the mayor's son, Desmond wore confidence like the backpack coolly draped over his shoulder. As always, he dressed in an impossible blend of laziness and pulled-togetherness. Dark jeans, long-sleeved tee, and boots, all name brands. All more expensive than anything Cait had ever owned in her life.

Practically every other student beamed over at Desmond, his lackeys basking in the light of his glory. Sydney, one of his ever-obsessed devotees, batted her heavily mascaraed lashes at him. Indifferent to their admiration, Desmond slipped easily into his desk chair on the far side of the room, dropping his black and brown backpack at his feet. He said something to Garrett under his breath, to which his friend sniggered.

Desmond had given his friends their seating assignments, Cait knew. Brady sat directly to his right in the second row so Desmond could easily make some snide remark during class. Garrett sat behind his counterpart like a bodyguard. The pair followed him around everywhere. Unless, of course, he didn't want them to. Then, they made themselves immediately scarce.

"Who's that?" Matt asked, his voice lower than before as the teacher cleared her throat to settle the students down.

"He's the mayor's son," Cait answered.

As though he'd heard her, Desmond looked over his shoulder, like he always did when he spoke to Garrett, but his eyes went straight to Cait. They flickered to Matt, then back to her. He smirked before turning around once more.

"Oh." Matt scratched his smooth jaw. "Do you, uh—are you friends with him?"

"What?" Cait frowned, gripping her pencil more tightly than she should. "No. No, he's—he's the *mayor's* son," she reiterated, sure that Matt should quickly learn of the Simons' prestige.

Matt looked as if he was about ready to ask another question when the teacher spoke up. "Good morning, everyone," she said, her voice kind yet authoritative. "I'm Mrs. Davis. And as I'm sure you're aware, I'm the new teacher this year."

She smiled cheerfully at the twenty-two students. Their muttering had died down as they slouched in their seats, listening with blatant boredom. "However, I actually grew up here," she continued. "As an alumnus of Porthaven High, I'm happy to return as a teacher. Of course, I'll start by calling roll today, but hopefully, I'll learn your names and faces well enough to mark attendance myself in the future. Sound good? Let's get started."

Mrs. Davis picked up a sheet from her desk, calling out the first name, Bryan Abbey. In the front row, directly in front of Desmond, the teen raised his hand. The teacher continued through the list, marking Jesse Beauxmont behind Desmond and Sydney Bellerose on the other side of Brady.

Pausing to look up with a grin, Mrs. Davis looked to the back of the classroom. "Mattie," she called with a sly grin. "Present, I see."

The whole class turned to stare at Matt. His lips twisted in an embarrassed frown as he slumped in his seat. "Yeah," he muttered.

While several students snickered at the pet name, Cait realized that it was Matt *Davis*, making him their teacher's son.

With one stern look, Mrs. Davis silenced the scoffers. Next up were the Edgars cousins, Garrett and Scott, who, despite their family ties, hated each other. It was a good day when Scott didn't taunt Garrett into an outburst.

Continuing to call roll, Mrs. Davis made it through several names before pausing. "Ca—oh, I'm sorry, I think I'm going to mispronounce this," she warned, then attempted, "Caitriona Lewan?"

More quiet, mocking laughter swept through the classroom. Even Desmond let out a little amused scoff. She'd pronounced it "Cat-re-oh-na," as most people did when they saw Cait's full name. After almost twelve years of the reoccurring procedure, she'd grown used to it.

Kindly, Cait corrected with the phonetic "Katrina" before adding, "People call me Cait."

"Right." Mrs. Davis smiled gratefully. "'Cait' it is."

On the list went, but Mrs. Davis was destined for as difficult a first day as Cait expected for herself.

"William Simon," she called, eliciting the entire class to whip their heads toward the far left seat on the second row.

Lounging in his chair, a bored look on his face, he corrected, "It's Desmond."

As Mrs. Davis blinked at him, Garrett—loudmouth that he was—scoffed. "I thought you were from Porthaven," he mouthed off. "Seems you should know the mayor's son."

Though the teacher opened her mouth to rebuke her student, Desmond beat her to it. "She's new, you idiot," he retorted. "Give her a break."

An irritated expression still on his face, Desmond turned back to Mrs. Davis. "Sorry about him. He's not smart enough to know when to shut up." He rested his arms on his desktop. "William is my dad," he explained. "I go by my middle name: Desmond."

Mrs. Davis appeared befuddled by this exchange, her eyes flickering between Desmond and the now-subdued Garrett. "Oh," she muttered, then cleared her throat. "I'm sorry for the mistake."

"You didn't know," Desmond replied.

"I'll make sure to mark it," she returned with a grateful smile.

Cait tapped her pencil against her fingers while Mrs. Davis went on. Her eyes kept flickering across the classroom. She couldn't help herself. It was like the hum; if he was in the room, her gaze found its way to Desmond. Mayor's son, star of the sports teams, honors student, most-popular-boy-in-school, spoiled brat, snide narcissist, smart-mouth, rebellious prick; all the names the town called him. They never were quite right in Cait's mind. Be them all true, he was also far more than those titles gave him credit for.

Sure, he could be an arrogant jerk. But then he did stuff like that—standing up for a teacher when he really had no reason to. Desmond could get away with anything. Cait had seen him skip out on class for a week straight without their teachers saying a word to him or his parents. And still, he got straight A's. He ignored the "unpopular" students, he carried himself with marked conceit, and he never let anyone tell him what to do.

Yet he also did stuff like *that*.

After calling the last two names—Hunter Varon and Miranda Yates—Mrs. Davis set her list down, scribbling a few notes on its face. She brushed her bangs out of her eyes before smiling at the class. "Now, I know you're all my seniors," she began. "And I'm sure you're looking forward to an easy final year. However, I'm not an easy teacher. I don't accept slack or lazy work. I will demand the best you have to give.

"As your first period, I'll get you all bright and early each morning," she eyed them knowingly, "so we'll make sure to start our days out right, okay? Let's overview what you can expect to learn this year."

While Mrs. Davis went over her syllabus, Cait settled in, her eyes regularly drifting to the far desk in the second row even as she took notes. The cat creature took shape in her notebook over the course of the class. History—Mrs. Davis's subject—had always been her best. What was there to study? The past read like a story; read it enough times, and you could memorize the tiny details teachers were so fond of putting on tests.

Mrs. Davis was a decently interesting teacher. First period passed with a gratefully non-boring pace. The early September sun rose higher as the students barreled out of the classroom. Hunter and Desmond shared their usual hostile glance—sharp blue eyes meeting dark brown. The Varons and Simons were always at odds. Something to do with usurped rights. Cait hadn't lived in Porthaven when the feud began, but she knew it was unending.

Taking her time, Cait lingered at her desk, carefully placing her supplies into her worn, tan canvas backpack. She tucked some of her hair behind her ear. Such a colorless blonde, she always thought, and stick straight, as unremarkable as her.

Cait prepared to slip an arm into the backpack's strap when she saw Matt still standing by his desk. His gray backpack hung on his shoulders, his thumbs looping through the bottom of the straps. He gave her that lips-pressed-together smile of his. Shifting from foot to foot, he waited on her.

"Uh—" Cait scanned the almost empty room. "You—you didn't have to wait for me."

"That's cool," he replied cheerfully. "No reason not to, right?"

She thought of plenty of reasons not to. "Thanks," she muttered anyway.

While Cait moved for the door, Matt followed behind, starting up his flurry of conversation. "What's your next class? Mine's chemistry."

"We have—there's only one senior class," she explained as they stepped out into the hall. Hundreds of students wove in and out of each other's paths, their voices reverberating off the lockers. "We have all the same classes."

"Oh, nice!" Matt sounded genuinely thrilled. "So, all those kids in history, they're gonna be the people we spend all our time with?"

Though Cait knew she should educate him on the proper etiquette of Porthaven sociability, she didn't know how. She'd never had to explain it to anyone before. Even Genni had grasped the concept well enough on her own. Having to teach someone who or who not to befriend was as odd as having someone try to befriend her in the first place.

"Yeah, pretty much," Cait replied.

Matt followed her steadily down the hall. "Obviously, that Desmond's the cool kid," he prattled. "He seemed kind of decent, I guess."

Cait didn't share her opinion.

"Did you, uh—did you figure out that our teacher's my mom?" Matt asked.

Giving him a compassionate glance, Cait noted, "I think most people did."

"I was worried about that," he grumbled. "You know, she just doesn't get it. She says that I should be happy to have a mom for a teacher. Like it's some major benefit. But how am I supposed to make friends when she calls me 'Mattie'? Everyone will think I'm lame."

Cait intentionally didn't look at him as she turned the corner.

"Do *you* think I'm lame?"

Coming to a stop outside the chemistry lab, Cait stared at Matt's sneakers. The once-white toes were smudged to near blackness. "I dunno," she admitted, forcing herself to meet his anxious gaze. "I just met you."

Matt pursed his lips, quirking his mouth to the side. He looked so much like a cartoon character, so animated in all his expressions, that she almost laughed. "You think I'm lame," he determined.

Unsure whether to roll her eyes or comfort him, Cait shrugged. "I think you shouldn't be so worried about what I think," she said.

His thin eyebrows pulled together. "You're saying I shouldn't care about other people's opinions?"

Cait immediately shook her head. "No, that's not what I'm saying at all."

Matt scratched behind one of his overly large ears, clearly confused.

"You should *definitely* care what the other students think about you," Cait insisted. "Their opinions matter. Particularly Desmond's. Then probably Hunter's. The rest of them will follow whatever they think. Which is my point—"

Cait drew her backpack's strap farther onto her shoulder as Matt listened, brown eyes wide. "If you'd like to make friends here, let me warn you: You should care what the others think."

A glimmer of disappointment lit Matt's eyes, his lips turning down. "I'm not sure that's . . . good."

"It isn't," she admitted. "But it's the way things are in Porthaven."

Matt stared at his scuffed trainers, considering her words for several long seconds. Cait thought about leaving him during that time. It would be for his best if no one saw them together anymore. After that first class, he had a lot of making up to do as it was. And she didn't want anyone else to experience even a single school year of the isolation she faced.

In the hesitation of her indecision, Matt looked back up at her. "Why doesn't your opinion matter?" he asked.

Cait blinked. Had anyone ever asked her that? She didn't think so.

"Because I'm cursed," she said, then turned to enter the chemistry lab.

CHAPTER TWO

Cait

"What do you mean you're cursed?"

Shaking her head at Matt's persistence, Cait watched the replay of history class take place in the chemistry lab. They sat in the back corner at the tall desk, their backpacks at their feet. In walked all the same students who headed to all their same seats. Hunter Varon and his girlfriend, Elizabeth Greene, took their seats in the front row, always punctual and orderly. She'd never felt quite as negatively toward them as the rest of the students. If anything, she admired the couple. Whatever bad blood the Simons and Varons held between them, at least Hunter carried himself with dignity. And neither of the pair had picked on her, so that made them nicer than the rest of the class.

Cait turned back to Matt, not in the mood to explain the catastrophe that was her life. "Listen, we don't have long until class starts, so I think it'd be best to warn you now." She straightened her shoulders to show him how serious she was. "You shouldn't be friends with me. And you definitely shouldn't sit next to me in classes."

Mouth hanging open, Matt scratched his temple in thought. "Uh, I—well, I mean, if you don't want me to sit with you, that's fine," he murmured, a tinge of hurt in his voice. "I get it. I can come on kind of strong. Like I said, my sister regularly tells me that my mouth doesn't have an off-switch, so I know I can be kind of annoying—"

Lifting a hand to stop him, Cait didn't have any interest in listening to his insecurities unfold. "It isn't that I don't like you or that I find you annoying," she insisted. "I'm sincerely trying to help you out. If you sit with me—if you *talk* to me, you are accepting the black mark of Porthaven High."

"I don't understand—"

"You don't need to," she said. "All you need to know is that being friends with me takes away your chances of becoming friends with anyone else."

Matt's big brown eyes reminded Cait of their terrier, Red. Anytime the dog got scared, his round eyes took on that exact sad look that Matt wore now. "You don't have any friends?" he asked almost in a whisper.

Straightening the collar of her tee, Cait turned away. "No," she said, more to her closed notebook than to him.

He remained silent as more students piled into class. Sterling Faulk ambled across the room, the cord of his headphones dangling down his front, his long, thick black-brown hair covering the earbuds. He was always listening to something—music, Cait assumed. The Faulk family had their own stigma in Porthaven; something about their family history of which she'd never gotten the full story. Yet somehow, his parents had still managed to garner the respect of all the Warden members in town.

As he passed the front row, Sterling shared an offhanded nod with Hunter. Despite his more reclusive nature, Sterling's friendship with Hunter was his saving grace. After being paired up in a school project together in second grade, the two became lifelong friends. And a friendship with Hunter was almost as good as one with Desmond.

The rustle of Matt shifting in the seat next to her reminded Cait that he still sat there, puzzling through her words. "I think," he muttered, a nervous tremor to the words, "that everyone deserves to have a friend. And so, if it'd be okay with you, I'd be happy to be yours."

Unsure how to tell him "no," even for his own good, Cait stared at Matt. He clearly didn't understand how Porthaven worked. And she doubted that once he figured it out, he'd want to stick around. But this was the first time someone had offered to be her friend. She wasn't sure she had the heart to refuse it.

A small, embarrassed smile pulled Matt's lips into a thin line. "You can think about it if you'd like."

"I think *you're* the one who should think about it," Cait returned even as the corner of her mouth lifted. "But in the meantime, you were gonna be stuck with me as a lab partner anyway. I'm the only one who didn't have one."

"They didn't make you sit with the other kids?"

Cait shrugged off the idea. "Mr. Belanger doesn't like me much. And I do well enough on my own."

"The *teacher* doesn't like you?"

"No one likes me."

Matt shook his head, a look of wonder on his face. "The people here must be really stupid."

Suddenly, Cait found herself laughing. She didn't know the last time she'd laughed in school. In everyday life, she laughed and enjoyed herself just fine. But in school? The halls of Porthaven High were a cage of isolation for her. Laughter was as impossible here as finding a friend.

The hum returned to Cait's mind, cutting off her good humor. Desmond waltzed into the room with Garrett and Brady once more. The seating arrangement was thrown off a tad within the lab, with each desk holding a pair of students. Desmond sat with Garrett—less because he preferred Garrett's company and more because Desmond did all the work while Garrett got a passable grade. A deal that kept the brute on the sports team.

Cait knew all the ins and outs of Porthaven's drama like that. It was one of the benefits of being the outcast—no one noticed when you were watching. No one saw what you saw. And with all her gleaned knowledge, Cait knew everything about her classmates. Like the fact that no one in the school had higher grades than Desmond Simon, even when he skipped class at least once a week. Or that Monica Robertson, one of Desmond's cousins, had a major crush on his best friend, Brady Lavigne, who seemed truly oblivious to her presence. Or that the only reason Desmond hadn't chosen Scott Edgars over Garrett Edgars for his posse was because Scott had already been friends with Hunter Varon. Or the way that all the girls in class who weren't related to Desmond were all helplessly in love with him, including Melissa, who was dating Scott, and Whitney, who was in a perpetual on-again-off-again relationship with Garrett. Even Hunter's girlfriend, Elizabeth, had a strange affection for Desmond.

Seeing all the ridiculous behavior of her peers, sometimes Cait was grateful to be on the outside. Other times, it made her sad, as though she was missing out on a vital experience in life. Because no matter how stupid all the drama was, her classmates had each other. They lamented their situations together, drawing them closer to one another. They had friends. They had camaraderie.

Cait had none of that. And while sometimes, she was thankful for an unbroken heart and unfractured relationships, there were other times that it made her feel unbearably alone.

~

"So, about that curse thing," Matt was saying as he traded out books from his locker. "Is that like a funny way of saying you don't have luck in the friend department? Or do you really believe that you're cursed?"

Cait didn't know why she'd followed Matt to his locker. She knew she should give him space. The poor kid's first day was going to ruin him if he wasn't careful. "It doesn't matter if I believe it or not," she returned. "Everyone else does."

Matt's animated forehead wrinkled with exasperation. "Why?"

She adjusted her backpack. "Probably because it's true."

"You're not very good at explaining things," he lamented.

Cait almost laughed. "I've never had to explain it before. Everyone in Porthaven already knows."

"Well, I'm not from Porthaven."

"I noticed."

Matt sighed, shutting his locker door. "I know we just met and all that, but I'd like to understand if I can. I mean, it's just super weird, ya know? You seem like a pretty nice person, and if you weren't so quiet, I think you could be really fun to talk to. It doesn't make sense for no one to like you."

Thinking that she ought to give the poor kid some context, Cait struggled to form the words. Knowing your own seedy background was different from explaining it. Aside from talking with Rese, Genni, and their nan from time to time, the discussion was off the table.

Cait chewed on the inside of her lip, working up the courage to speak. She didn't want to go into the whole ordeal here in the hallway between periods. But she could give him something that would tide him over until they could have a more in-depth conversation.

Without warning, someone bumped into Cait, knocking her against the lockers. She bit through the flesh she'd been chewing on, an instant bead of blood burnishing her tongue.

A couple of jocks in their junior year passed false apologies her way, snickering as they hurried down the hall, likely having completed some stupid dare. Matt glared at them in shock before turning back to Cait with worry in his eyes. "Are you okay?"

Hand to her cheek, Cait tried to ignore the stinging pain as she waved him off. "I'm fine."

Matt looked ready to press when he was interrupted by the arrival of a tall, lithe figure right beside them. They both looked up at Sydney Bellerose, a sickly-sweet smile on her glossy lips. Cait always thought of Sydney as beautiful in the most unappealing way. Oh, her makeup was perfect, her outfit stylish, and her nails manicured. But Cait could always see the flash of nerves in the girl's light gaze. Her short skirts and high heels subtly told Cait the truth about her haughty demeanor—she felt like a fraud.

Completely ignoring Cait's presence, Sydney gave her brightest, most beguiling smile to Matt. "Hi there," she said, holding out her hand. Matt reluctantly accepted the handshake. "I'm Sydney, head of the student council. As such, I wanted to officially welcome you to Porthaven High. Go, Tridents." She chuckled at her overbright school spirit.

Matt glanced at Cait.

Sydney caught the surreptitious look. Clearing her throat, she rose to the full extent of height the heels would give her. "Anyway," she continued, her attention wholly on Matt, "if you have any questions or need someone to show you around the school, just let me know. I have a couple of assistants who would be absolutely fantastic at giving you a full tour."

"Uh. . . ." Matt's ever-expressive face didn't hide his bewilderment at her pep. "That's—that's cool. Cait has actually been helping me find my way around."

An immediate scowl of distaste flickered across Sydney's face. "Yes." She shot a sidelong glance at Cait. "I noticed you were getting to know one another, and that's . . . great."

Cait pressed her lips together at the snide comment.

Sydney continued to ignore her. "But I was thinking, Mattie—"

"It's Matt," he corrected.

"Oh, right. Well, I was thinking—" Coyly, she played with the lace hem of her blouse. "If I were new to the school, I'd want to find some friends right away. Find where I fit in and all that. And the best way for me to do that would be with a girl, right? I'd want to make the friends who would last me a lifetime. You know what I mean?"

Matt scratched his temple. "I'm not sure I do."

"Well, like," Sydney held out her hands as she attempted to explain, "you're a guy. So, I have several guys in the student council who'd be more than happy to show you around and help you find where you belong." She paused, spared a dismissive glance toward Cait, then turned back to Matt. "And to help you find the sort of friends you *should* be making."

Though Cait would have liked to take a pair of scissors to Sydney's lovely rose-gold waves, she held still as though the girl wasn't blatantly insulting her. Cait knew better than to stand up for herself. It would only wind up making her more of a villain to them anyway. Instead, she sucked on the still bleeding cut on the inside of her lip.

Matt didn't get the "suffer in silence" memo. His thin eyebrows pulled low over his eyes, and he glowered at Sydney. "You know, school councils are supposed to advocate for *all* students, right? Seems like if you're the head of the council, you aren't doing a very good job."

A flicker of irritation crossed Sydney's face, but she tamped her emotions down as she gave him a placating smile. "It sounds like you're a very loyal person, Matt," she returned. "And that's commendable. But you're putting it in the wrong place. I'd be happy to assign someone to help enlighten you about our—" she gave Cait a side-eye, "more questionable students so that you don't get yourself into something you didn't sign up for."

Distracted by Sydney's harassment and fear that Matt would make the situation worse, Cait hadn't noticed the return of that familiar hum until it was right on top of her. It crept up her spine, tingling into her skull. The slap of a hand against metal rang out behind her, jarring her senses and making her jump. Cedar and musk overwhelmed her in an alluring cloud. She longed to lean back and fall into the scent, letting it embrace her in the warmth of its promise.

Heart thundering, Cait whirled around to see Desmond Simon practically hovering over her. She slumped against the lockers under the hand he had propped there a few inches from her head. His dark gaze was fixed on Sydney. Garrett and Brady stood by, waiting in case they were needed.

With his signature indifferent manner, Desmond grinned. "Hey, Syd," he practically purred.

Smoothing down her too-short floral skirt, Sydney beamed at him. Her blue eyes almost twinkled even in the dim hall lighting. "Hi, Desmond." She breathed his name like it was sacred. "How are you today?"

He cast an indifferent glance toward Cait, still cowering under his arm, before giving a single scan to Matt. He turned his superior, heart-melting smile on Sydney. "I'd be a whole lot better if you'd stop scaring the new kid."

"I was only—"

"I know what you were doing," he interrupted, his tone a commanding calm. "But let the kid make his own choices, huh? If he wants to be friends with the outcasts, let him. It's not your call."

Drawing her shoulders back, Sydney tried to reclaim some of her dignity. Her apologetic smile didn't reach her eyes. "Surely, he deserves to have all the information before he makes his choice."

A knowing glint came to Desmond's eyes. "Bullying isn't an attractive look for you, Syd. It clashes with your god complex."

Sydney blanched. Matt's eyebrows shot onto his forehead. Garrett sniggered, and Brady smirked. Cait just watched.

Desmond pushed off the locker, adjusting his canvas bomber jacket as he straightened. His eyes darted over Cait disinterestedly. "Lewan," he greeted flatly.

She slumped another inch.

Without another word, Desmond moved off, around Sydney and down the hall, his posse at his back.

Face white as a sheet, Sydney glared at Cait as though *she* was the reason Desmond had scolded her. The girl curled her elegant fingers into fists, then muttered something resembling "have a good day" to Matt before stomping off.

Matt stared at Cait, dumbfounded. "What the heck is this place?" he gasped.

The idea of shoving *herself* into a locker had a sudden high appeal to Cait. "I'll explain later," she mumbled. Then she pushed away from the lockers, the cold metal stinging her hands.

~

The cafeteria was Cait's least favorite place in the school. As all the students congregated, their voices rose to a near-deafening howl of sound. Noise vibrated off every wall. The raucous laughter and chatter, the pounding footsteps as students rushed to get the seats they wanted, and the clatter of plates and utensils—it all blended into a chaotic chorus that caused Cait's head to pound.

She could hardly even hear the soft thrum of Desmond's presence at the far end of the room, where he sat eating with his troupe. Brady sat at his side during lunch, Garrett and Whitney—currently a couple—across from them. Each table held enough seats for six students, so another of Desmond's cousins, Gabrielle, and her boyfriend, Jesse Beauxmont, joined them.

Most of the students had the aqua-blue lunch trays in front of them, eating from the cafeteria's lackluster menu. Cait, however, opened her lunch bag. Her nan, Maeve, didn't approve of spending the extra money on the school's lunches. Their thin budget didn't allow for such frivolities.

White and aqua banners hung through the room, cheering on the school with things like Sydney's earlier "Go, Tridents" and "2012-2013 State Champions," denoting their victory in both the state basketball and baseball tournaments. The victory was, of course, achieved under the headship of Desmond's captaincy.

Matt sat across from Cait, his tray filled with the cafeteria's offerings for the day: something resembling lasagna with a side of green beans. He picked at his food, watching as Cait unwrapped her sandwich. "Do I have to ask you a third time?" he prompted.

Double-checking her sandwich for a tomato, Cait grimaced. It was notably present. "Hang on," she told him, turning to scan the room. "Why is she always late to everything?"

"Who?" Matt asked, curiosity tipping up his tone.

Catching sight of the trio, Cait sighed. Following her friends through the food line, Genni held her own paper bag dangling at her side. She languidly let Alexis and Jared take their time gathering their meals as she unwittingly held Cait's lunch hostage.

Genni was Cait's near double. Bright blonde hair, willowy frame, unembellished features. She sometimes felt like apologizing to her little sister for their lack of striking genes. It was like Rese inherited them all while Cait and Genni were stuck with the simple, understated looks that made someone say, "yeah, I guess she's kind of pretty" rather than, "wow, she's beautiful."

Turning around, Cait gestured to Matt's untouched plate. "Go ahead and start," she said. "It'll be a minute for me."

"What do you mean?" he asked.

"Oh, my nan got my and my sister's lunches mixed up," she explained.

"You have a sister?"

"I have two sisters."

"Cool!" Matt's enthusiasm seemed genuine. He scanned the remainder of the empty seats at their table. "Do they sit with you at lunch?"

"Well, Rese graduated last year," Cait explained, scooting Genni's sandwich in front of the seat at her side. "And while she let me sit with her if I wanted, I didn't really like her friends, so I didn't often choose to. But Genni always sits with me."

"What about her friends?"

"They sit with their own siblings and cousins."

"That's nice." He surveyed the lunch line. "I guess they're all younger?"

Cait nodded.

"What year?"

"Sophomore. Genni turned fifteen a couple of months ago."

"So, you're the middle kid?"

"Mm-hmm."

Matt picked at his food some more but didn't eat anything. "It's just me and my older sister. She's a junior in college now, though. Is your older sister in college?"

"No." Cait didn't care to explain why, so she worked up something else to talk about. "Why did your family move to Porthaven?"

"Oh, uh—well, like my mom mentioned, she grew up here," he said. "My grandpa—her dad—he still lives here, so we moved in with him."

"Where does he live on the peninsula?"

Matt considered it, tapping his fork on the rim of his lunch tray. "You know the neighborhood where all the streets are named in fishing terms?" he asked.

Cait got a funny feeling in her gut. "Yeah."

"We live on Sinker Street," Matt explained.

"Oh." The coincidence was almost annoying. Cait forced herself to smile. "Us too."

Matt's mouth dropped open. "We're neighbors?"

"Seems like it."

Before either of them got time to speak more, fierce arms wrapped around Cait's neck, nearly choking her with affection. "I'm so proud of you!" Genni exclaimed, her lunch bag coming inches within smacking Cait in the face. "You made a friend!"

Ripping her sister's arms apart, Cait coughed. "And you're yelling," she grumbled.

Genni dropped into the seat next to Cait, ignoring her to beam at Matt. She thrust a hand across the table. "I'm Genni."

"Matt," he replied, accepting the handshake.

"It's nice to meet you, Matt." Genni started unloading her lunch bag over the sandwich Cait had placed before her, totally oblivious. "Are you new to Porthaven?"

"Yep. We just moved in a week ago."

"That's great. You'll love it here." Genni cheerfully began unwrapping the tomato-free sandwich.

"Uh, Genni—" Cait began, but Genni kept going.

"Where did you live before Porthaven?"

Matt watched as Cait tried to halt Genni's process. "Um, Florida."

"Wow!" Genni swatted Cait's hand away. "From Florida to Maine? I hope you like the cold because it gets *freezing* here in the winter."

"Genni—"

"What?" Her sister stared at her wide-eyed, then took a bite of the sandwich.

Cait sighed. "That's *my* sandwich."

"Huh? Oh!" Genni mumbled around the mouthful. She set the sandwich down, found the one hidden under her paper bag, and bashfully made the exchange. "Sorry."

"It's fine," Cait assured her.

Matt was grinning, unable to hide his amusement. That was the thing about Genni. She could make anyone smile. She was so innocent, blunt, and carefree that people found it endearing.

Genni turned back to Matt. "Are you a senior too?"

"Yep," he replied, happily digging into his meal.

"And you're friends with Cait?"

"Why wouldn't I be?"

Genni looked at Cait. "He doesn't know, does he?" she asked.

Cait shrugged. "I haven't exactly had the time to tell him."

Matt leaned heavily on the table in anticipation. "Are you finally going to explain this whole 'curse' business?"

Genni rolled her eyes. "We aren't cursed."

"We?" Matt gasped. "I thought you said that *you* were cursed."

Cait shrugged nonchalantly. "My family is included."

"But," he pointed to Genni with his sauce-covered fork, "she's got friends."

"Alexis and Jared don't listen to stupid rumors," Genni said imperiously.

"And what do those rumors say?"

Ready to get the whole thing over with, Cait set her sandwich down. "I told you that my family moved to Porthaven almost twelve years ago," she reminded him. "And as the people here aren't fans of outsiders, to begin with, the circumstances of our move were . . . troublesome."

"What circumstances?"

Genni's chewing slowed as she glanced at Cait.

Cait shoved down her feelings, rushing to explain. "Our parents were killed, and we were brought to Porthaven to ensure that their murderers wouldn't have the chance to kill us too."

Matt's mouth hung open, a bite of lasagna suspended in the air on his fork. His jaw clamped shut. "That's the curse you're talking about? You're—what, you're in protective custody or something?"

"No," Cait corrected. "The curse has nothing to do with us being protected. It has to do with *why* our parents were killed in the first place."

"Which is?"

Cait swallowed down the discomfort the story always brought to her. "They were witches."

"Well," Genni cut in, "they were accused of being witches. Though I always thought that was pretty stupid because Da couldn't have been a witch. He'd have been a warlock or a wizard, right?"

"Witches can be guys too," Cait muttered.

"Mm. Either way—" Genni waved a chip through the air. "Nan says that it isn't true. They weren't witches, and whatever the town says is wrong. There's no curse, there's no demon, and no one is trying to kill us."

Matt's swallow was audible. "Hold on—did you say *demon*?"

"That's the curse," Cait said, voice low.

"*Supposed* curse," Genni corrected.

Cait continued, "It's said that our da sold his soul to the devil, granting him vast power in exchange for allowing himself to be possessed by a demon, cursing our bloodline. They say he was killed because of that power."

"Which is total baloney," Genni exclaimed. "Da was the nicest person in the world. He never would have had anything to do with a demon."

"You don't remember Da," Cait countered, even though she knew Genni was right. She remembered everything about their da. Owen Lewan never would have dealt in the occult. He prayed with them nightly, kneeling next to her and her sisters each bedtime. They went to chapel every Sunday. He taught them to read their Bibles, be kind to everyone, and remember that, no matter what, God was good.

The very idea of him being a witch was a profoundly absurd claim.

But that didn't change the fact that Cait knew something was wrong. Something had happened in Ireland that caused her parents' brutal deaths. Someone had wanted their whole family dead. Matt was right. She and her sisters had been brought to Porthaven to be placed under protective custody. But Cait also knew that it was equally for the safety of others as it was for their own.

William Simon, the mayor of Porthaven, was in regular contact with their nan, Maeve. He called weekly to check in. He supervised their case personally, granting them allotments from the town's funding to keep them afloat. He visited their house once a year with the reverend, Benjamin Lavigne, to talk with Cait and her sisters. During that time, Ben would always set a hand on each of their heads and pronounce a short benediction over them as though banishing the demons of their father's past.

Genni staunchly refused to believe in the curse. Rese treated it as though it were nonexistent. Cait wasn't so sure. All the strange behavior of the adults in their lives told her that *something* was terribly wrong. And whatever it was, she was convinced that there was a perfectly viable reason the people of Porthaven feared them.

CHAPTER THREE

Desmond

The Varon men were cursed; Desmond was convinced of it.

With a *thwack*, he depressed the aluminum bar handle to exit Porthaven's town hall. He strode across the lush green lawn to the parking lot. The sun hung lazily in the afternoon sky, a contradiction to his grumbling, rushed mood.

Well, he determined, "cursed" was a bit melodramatic. But he couldn't understand how it was that all the other guys in his class were pushing six feet while his body had just given up months ago, deciding that, yes, five foot, nine inches was a perfectly reasonable height. It didn't matter that his mom stood at five-eight and her dad at six-three. Desmond had inherited those stupid Varon genes that permeated their line.

Of course, no one would believe him if he touted his theory. After all, Hunter-freakin'-Varon was six foot himself. And Desmond was a Simon. According to Hunter, "that didn't count."

Sometimes, Desmond wanted to shove Hunter's face into his desk and ask if it counted then.

But then, sometimes, Desmond wanted to tell the whole town that Hunter was right. It *didn't* count. Or, at least, it shouldn't.

They weren't Varons anymore. Who in their right mind would consider his family the legitimate heirs to the leadership of their town?

Whoever believed in that stupid inheritance of the Varon ring, that's who.

The Varon line lost their rights to the ring over a century ago. Desmond's dad wore the signet now. William Simon had inherited the Varon ring from his father, Charles Simon, who inherited it from his father, Martin Simon, who inherited it from his father, Lyndon Simon, who inherited it from his father-in-law, Christopher Varon, after his retirement without a biological male heir. And thus, the blood feud began.

Christopher's son, Martin Varon, had died an early death. Martin's best friend, Lyndon Simon, had married Martin's sister, Marivel, making him a second son to Christopher. But Christopher's brother, Timothy Varon, felt the inheritance belonged to him, not to some outsider named Simon. There were arguments. There was outrage. There was usurpation. And now, the Simons ran Porthaven under their claim as the "true Varons" of the town.

Desmond found it all to be a bit much.

Still, he played along by hating Hunter, interning for the Warden, and maintaining his claim to the Varon lineage. Which really wasn't hard, considering how much the Simons *looked* like Varons. They had the same deep brown hair, hooded eyes, sharp jawlines, strong cheekbones, and mediocre height. Desmond had all those things in spades. What he hadn't gotten so lucky to inherit was the brute strength of a Varon.

Maybe it was just Desmond who was cursed and not the whole of the Varon bloodline. After all, *he* was the one who'd inherited their traditionally short height along with his mother's narrow frame. The sort of build that refused to bulk up like the other guys in school. No matter how hard he worked out or how much he ate, his muscles stayed lean and his figure trim. He could spend hours in the gym—which he did—and he was convinced he'd never wind up earning the buff physique of his father or any of the other Varon men.

Though that wasn't to say that Desmond wasn't damn proud of the hard-earned muscle he *had* gained. It might not be bulk, but he was as toned as a Spartan soldier. And if he'd learned anything from the movies, women liked a man with six-pack abs regardless of whether he had broad shoulders or not.

One more reason for the girls of Porthaven High to obsess over him, he supposed. His devilish smirk and dark hair gave him that mysterious "bad boy" vibe that said he was dangerous. The type that a girl would absolutely die to help "change" by "overcoming his insecurities." The morally gray archetype that made desperate girls with stupid delusions wish they could be the ones he'd want to be good for.

The whole of his social standing in Porthaven was dumb—and sometimes downright irritating—but it made it easy for Desmond to put in minimal effort and get maximum results. No one questioned if he was the irreverent bad boy. He just had to flash that cynical smile in the direction of those airheaded girls, and everyone knew—that's what he was.

And that meant no one expected anything out of him.

No one except his father.

William Simon held no sympathy for Desmond's "insecurities." He didn't care about Desmond's disinterest in the Warden or that he found the whole thing to be an annoying, bureaucratic social club. Whatever his son wanted was moot. As the heir to the Varon lineage and the Warden leadership, Desmond's future was laid out for him, wanted or not.

Consequently, his predetermined future was the source of those insecurities that girls were so convinced they could help him heal from.

Desmond didn't need their help with that, though. He leaned into the bad boy persona, accepting the ire it often earned him from William. It wasn't like his dad did anything about it anyway. If Desmond wound up getting caught in his irreverent behavior, it earned him a slap on the wrist at best and more time at his internship at worst.

Which was why Desmond was running late today. William had caught Desmond sneaking a bottle of whiskey out of Councilman Moyer's office last week. Subsequently, his dad added an extra hour to his after-school internship schedule to teach him "responsibility."

Now, Desmond slipped into his shiny black Dodge Challenger, enjoying the roaring rumble of the engine when it turned over. He liked how loud it was, knowing it annoyed the pissants that worked for his dad inside the town hall. They all stared at him and his muscle car like he was some upstart kid in great need of being taught the ways of the world.

Desmond didn't really care. He was just ready to be done with his final week of extra hours so that he could return to his normal life.

Desmond knew he was playing into the stereotype with his irreverent attitude, underage drinking, petty theft, and routine lies. In the end, that was the reason he did it. His dad wanted him to be the responsible, elitist heir of this salt-encrusted peninsula. Desmond wanted to be a kid. So, in little ways, like with booze, he rebelled.

It wasn't like he was on drugs. He didn't even fraternize with the girls at school. Not that he didn't have an interest. He simply didn't have time for them. Between family-imposed social engagements, his internship, the sports his dad required him to participate in, his time at the gym, and making sure he got straight A's, scheduling time to meet up with a girl for a secret, forbidden rendezvous wasn't possible.

Well . . . that wasn't wholly true.

Desmond turned off the main road to speed down the coastline. The ocean waves crashed languidly against the rocky, tree-studded cliffs. Autumnal burgundy, amber, and emerald leaves clung to the trees. He'd always liked the fall season. Beyond the crisp sting that permeated the salt air, the colors had a way of lifting his usually disagreeable mood.

The low sun shone off the cerulean waves, flashing in Desmond's eyes. He squinted as he careened at an unreasonable pace toward the abandoned factory at the edge of town. He'd been visiting the property since he was a kid. Boarded up and dilapidated, he'd never been brave enough to enter the massive brick building. More than fifty years back, there'd been a fire in the factory. Once a canning facility for all the fish the town exported, it had helped put Porthaven on the map. The fire had put a temporary hold on their growth. Then they'd rebuilt a bigger, better, more-code-acceptable factory closer to town. There had been petitions for the old factory to be torn down and others for it to be revitalized for another purpose. No mayor had had the guts to make a decision one way or the other, so it remained a crispy relic of their past.

Desmond parked his car at the back of the vacant lot. He hopped out, grabbing his backpack from the front seat. Jacket hanging open even in the cool breeze of the late afternoon, he headed into the forest that surrounded the old building. After over a decade of three-plus trips a week, he'd worn down a clear path in the underbrush. Sometimes, he thought he ought to try covering up such blatant evidence, but he liked living on the edge.

Or maybe he hoped he *would* get caught.

The walk through the pines, oaks, and aspens took Desmond fifteen minutes. He knew the path so well that it felt like five. The sound of the waves kissing the pebbled shoreline greeted him well before the beach came into view. Late as it was, the sky had already turned a rusty orange as he reached the break in the trees.

The hill sloped down, revealing the rest of the beach. Light gray sand and charcoal rocks stretched out in a crescent, the slate-blue waves softly rolling in. Large, craggy cliffs rose on either side of the beach, blocking it from the view of the rest of the world. The only way in or out of the cove was through the forest or by sea. Wholly isolated as it was, no one ever came here.

Except for Desmond and the girl who waited for him.

The setting sun gilded her in light, her blonde hair glinting silver instead of gold. She sat on a faded, striped blanket. They kept it stashed in a plastic bag inside the hollow of the log she now rested against. They'd moved that log out there eight years ago. Huffing and puffing, they finally managed to get it exactly where they wanted, in the perfect spot to watch the waves as the sun disappeared beyond the horizon.

Desmond bounded down the slope, his boots slipping on the sandy hillside. A scruffy, ginger-furred terrier roamed the sand, its nose rising into the air at the sound of his arrival. The dog let out a singular, jovial "bark" in greeting before returning to peruse the seaside.

Sauntering to the log, Desmond slipped his backpack off his shoulder and plopped down next to Cait. "Hey," he said, leaning over to scan the page of her journal. "The bird one again, huh?"

Cait hardly glanced over at him as her dainty, controlled hand continued to shape the feathered creature. "Yeah," she admitted. "It was in my dream last night."

"Figured as much," he remarked, eyes locked on the sketch. He tried not to enjoy the way their arms pressed together as he surveyed her work. Humanoid and hulking, the creature's body was frighteningly powerful. Feather-like fur covered its torso, two massive wings hanging at its sides, attached to its arms. Taloned fingers hovered in the air, ready to leap off the page and tear into flesh. Its whole face was a beak with intelligent hollows for eyes that stared creepily at him.

"Adorable," Desmond muttered, sitting back away from her.

Cait merely smirked.

The whole journal was full of monsters like that—the exact opposite of the girl who drew them. Cait was the last person in the world to take an interest in monsters. Not only was she too freaking innocent for such things, too soft-spoken and dignified, she didn't match the vibe. Her straight, silver-blonde hair drifted around her face like an elegant curtain. Her simple white tee, hunter-green jacket, and gray jeans marked her as the easygoing wallflower she was.

She was simply too cute for such occultic nonsense. Her pale skin almost glowed with how pearly-white it was. Elegant freckles dotted her skin, one on her right cheek, another right beside her nose, two on her forehead, and a smattering of them along her neck and collarbone. And she had a button nose, for goodness' sake!

Yet, she dreamed of these hideous, horrifying monsters every night.

Well, they weren't all hideous and horrifying. Some were actually pretty freakin' cool.

Which reminded Desmond. . . .

With a snap of his fingers, a black cat manifested onto the blanket between them. It sat immediately, its neon yellow eyes glowing in the sunset. Desmond smiled, reaching out to scratch its ear. "Hey, bud," he greeted.

The cat purred, nuzzling into his hand, its two tails happily twitching behind him. Desmond had begun to summon the beast from the spirit world when he was six. He'd heard his dad talking about the Clerics within the Warden, and, as he'd always wanted a pet, he'd decided to try creating one himself.

Thus, Hades was born. Two tails, insanely sharp incisors, and an ever-present shimmer of ivory around its blue-black fur.

Desmond took great pains to be sure that no one else learned of Hades's existence. Beasts—even tame ones—weren't just taboo; they were dangerously suspect creatures. No one in the Warden fully understood them or the consequences of summoning them. There was no telling if the Wielder—an individual like Desmond who could wield the spirit world—ever had full control over the beasts. And in Porthaven, any utilization of the spirit world was strictly prohibited, the powers that be working endlessly to protect the town . . . and the Warden's secrets.

Cait reached over to pat Hades's head. She'd never questioned Desmond's ability to summon the cat-beast. Growing up in Bushmills, Ireland—another Warden-run town, though vastly less restrictive—she knew the basics well enough. And what she didn't know, she didn't want to know. A consequence of her parents' deaths.

Desmond leaned back, resting his elbows on the log behind him. He watched as Hades nudged Cait's jacket pocket with his nose, looking for snacks. "So," he began, "seems like you've got yourself a friend at school."

The cat prematurely began to lick Cait's fingers as she pulled a small baggie of dried fruit from her pocket, his purr almost as loud as the engine of Desmond's car. Red, the terrier, bounded over at the crumple of the plastic bag.

"For now," Cait replied, the beast and dog taking their snacks in turn. Then, she looked over at Desmond, a small smile on her lips. "I have something for you."

"What's the occasion?" he asked, enjoying the chance to freely hold her gaze. Her eyes were such a pretty color. Blue-gray; the sea if it froze over.

"Call it a 'start of the school year' present," she teased, reaching into the backpack on her other side.

Desmond watched, amused, as she readily found her gift. "And here, I didn't get you anything."

"You never get me anything," she replied.

"Yeah, well, we never have anything to celebrate."

Cait responded by holding out a slip of paper clearly torn from her notebook.

Taking it, Desmond looked down at the sketch. He let out a snort, then showed the picture to Hades. "Look, it's you."

Hades ignored him, happily chewing on the dried date.

Chuckling, Desmond turned the paper back around to take a longer look at the drawing. Cait had always been an incredible artist. Every image was lifelike with a nearly romantic line to them, as though she was trying to make the monsters somehow less monstrous.

"You know," Desmond said, brushing his fingers over the paper's edge, "it's too bad we aren't friends." He looked up at her. "Because you make a pretty good one."

The immediate tinge of pink that came to Cait's cheeks caused a surge in his chest, like a wave crashing against the cliffside. "Thanks," she murmured, turning away. She picked up her pencil again, returning to her sketch.

Pulling a science fiction novel from his backpack, Desmond tucked the drawing between the pages, replacing the random slip he'd been using as a bookmark. As Cait drew, Desmond started to read. Hades curled up between them as Red sat, wagging his tail, hoping for another date.

Desmond settled in, the fantastically wrought prose of the novel working in tandem with Cait's presence to draw him into an escape from reality. This was why he didn't have time for girls. Desmond met up with Cait at least three times a week. And while there was nothing illicit about their time together, his father would be furious if he found out about it. Which was part of what made whatever his relationship with Cait was so enticing in the first place.

They weren't really friends. Cait and he were more like indifferent acquaintances who happened to understand one another better than anyone else. She never got mad at him for being a selfish prick, and he never took issue with her being a purported demon-cursed witch child. They spent their afternoons together in contended solitude, hidden away from the rest of Porthaven, free of the expectations and fears of others.

Desmond knew it couldn't last forever. The ten and half years it had already gone on were impressive enough. One day, he would inherit the role of "true Varon," and all of this would end. He'd have to take up the leadership of Porthaven—both the town and the Warden members within it. He'd have to meet every expectation his father set out for him. He'd be forced to choose a wife and have a kid or two, ensuring the family line.

Desmond thought about that looming future with increasing frequency. Any girl in school would be thrilled for him to choose her. Yet, no matter how vast his options were, they felt so limited. None of the girls in his year were viable candidates. Those who weren't his cousins were either already in a relationship, way too weird, or Sydney—and she was a bigger drama queen than Cleopatra. The girls younger than him were just as ridiculous, and the women older than him were either already married or single for a reason.

If asked what kind of woman he was looking for, Desmond often wound up describing Elizabeth Greene—more out of habit than anything. Whether or not she was dating Hunter, she was the only one with a brain. Not only was she beautiful in an abnormally timeless way, she knew what she wanted, and she got it. Maybe it came from being the doctor's daughter, but Elizabeth didn't put up with nonsense.

Red trotted out to the driest patches of sand, drawing Desmond's already-distracted attention away from his book. He watched as the terrier began to dig out a piece of driftwood.

If Desmond were honest with himself, he wasn't so sure he wanted a woman like Elizabeth anyway. If he were forced to describe the true type of wife he wanted, he'd illustrate a very different sort of girl. One with a quiet, steady personality. One who laughed easily, smiled often, and exuded a strangely contagious peace. One who knew him better than anyone else. One who didn't make him feel like he needed to be anything more than he was—insecurities and all.

In the list of potential options, there was always one girl in Porthaven Desmond left out. It was easier to ignore Cait's presence in general than to risk drawing attention to her. No one knew about them or their weird relationship in the first place. And even if he wanted to consider it, it could never happen anyway.

As much as Desmond liked Cait—and he did *like* her, he freely admitted to himself—they had no future together. He was the mayor's son. She was the witch's daughter. Even if everything went right and the creature never chose her or managed to break through the Warden-placed block on her spirit, any romance between them was impossible. It would be his job to control Cait and her sisters for the rest of their lives. That wasn't a foundation for a happy marriage.

But that didn't stop Desmond from thinking about it from time to time.

Glancing over at Cait as she finished up some details on her dream monster, Desmond remembered hearing her laugh at the school today. He couldn't help how jealous it made him. She never laughed at school. She laughed with him but not at school.

"Is the new kid nice?" he found himself asking.

Cait tossed him a sideways glance at the sudden question. "He didn't run away when I told him about my family's curse, so I'd say he's nicer than most people in Porthaven."

"It isn't hard to be nicer than most people in Porthaven," he returned, setting his book aside. "You seriously told him about your family?"

"He kept asking."

"Yeah, but . . . he's a stranger, Caity. Do you really think you should be sharing that kind of information with him?"

Tucking some hair behind her ear, Cait abandoned her sketch. "It isn't like he wouldn't have heard about it soon enough anyway. Sydney was about to tell him in the hallway this morning."

"You're welcome, by the way."

"I didn't ask you to step in."

Desmond scowled. "Sydney's a bitch."

Now, Cait scowled. "Do you have to swear?"

"No," he replied with a smirk. "I just enjoy making your nose wrinkle."

Agitated, Cait's nose remained wrinkled. "Why do I hang out with you?"

"Because I'm charming," Desmond said, pleased with how irritated she was growing. He draped his arm over the log behind her, tapping her arm on the other side. "And because while I can't really do much, I *can* keep you safe."

The warmth of Cait burned into his arm. Desmond would have scooted closer if Hades wasn't contentedly lounging between them. He reminded himself to thank the cat for his interference later. He wasn't sure if the beast could understand when he talked to it. He just liked to show the cat gratitude when it kept him from doing something unfathomably stupid.

A slow, reluctant smile came to Cait's lips. She dropped her head back, sucking in an annoyed breath. "Why are you like this?"

"Hilarious? Handsome? Heroic?"

"Obnoxious."

Desmond reached around to tap her adorable nose. "Chalk it up to destiny."

Slapping his hand away, Cait snarled at him. "I don't believe in destiny."

"Why not?"

"Because if there's such a thing as destiny, then my parents were *destined* to be murdered." Cait's frosty blue eyes bored into him, making his heart sink. "I don't believe in destiny because I know that wasn't what God wanted for them. Or for me."

Desmond didn't like it when Cait took things theological on him. He attended the church to appease his parents. And while he believed in God, he didn't care to change his life to fit some rhetoric.

"If your parents hadn't died," he replied, voice low, "you wouldn't have come to Porthaven."

Cait turned to the sea, her hair tickling the back of his hand where it rested by her shoulder. She remained silent, but Desmond could hear her response in his head. She would have been happier back in Ireland. Not only would she have had her parents alive and well, but she also wouldn't be the victim of vicious rumors. She wouldn't be afraid of ridicule and scorn. She wouldn't be lonely.

Allowing himself to rub his thumb against her shoulder blade, Desmond told himself it was just to comfort her. "I wish we could change it," he whispered.

Cait dipped her head, leaning into his touch. He knew, of course. He knew how she felt about him. Like every other girl in school, she secretly hoped to be the one who filled that space at his side. The one who soothed the wounds that made him act like the spoiled jerk that he was. He knew that as he knew that Cait was the only one who *could* make him better. After all, she was better than everyone else in the entire world.

But there was nothing he could do about it.

The sun's coppery rays glinted off Cait's face as she watched it dip its toes into the water on the horizon. "Me too," she whispered back.

Desmond really did wish there was something—*anything*—that he could do about it. He would give the leadership back to the Varons if he thought that would change anything.

Cait shut her notebook with a *snap*. "I've got to get going," she muttered, carefully stowing the book and pencil.

Frowning, Desmond retracted his arm. "But I just got here."

Cait tossed him a smirk, her good nature returning. "Yeah, well, you were late. Tonight's my night to help with dinner. You know how Nan is about punctuality."

"I don't, actually," Desmond teased. "I've only met your nan, like, once."

Shifting to her knees, Cait slung her backpack over one shoulder. "Sorry," she replied. "I won't be inviting you over for dinner anytime soon."

"I'm devastated."

Cait slugged his arm, and he feigned a whimper. "See you tomorrow?" she asked, rising.

Staring up at her, Desmond squinted into the halo of sunlight that surrounded her. "I've got practice tomorrow," he reminded her. "Gotta find out what the damage is this year."

"Right, captaincy calls." She nudged his foot with hers. "Maybe Friday?"

"No good," he sighed, sitting forward. "Mom organized some big shindig for the start of the school year. All the stuffy usuals will be at my place, and I gotta make a showing."

Cait's eyes narrowed as she started drifting backward from the blanket. "Don't drink anything," she ordered.

Desmond raised his eyebrows. "Caity, I gotta stay hydrated somehow."

"You're seventeen, Des," she returned.

He smiled at the nickname he only let her use. "Only for another month."

"Eighteen is still underage."

Desmond sighed dramatically, draping his arms on either side of the log. "You're such a Goody Two-Shoes," he lamented.

"One of us ought to be," she replied, then pointed at him. "Don't forget to put the blanket away this time."

"I won't."

"And seal it properly."

"I got it, Caity," he promised.

Cait smiled at him, and Desmond knew it was the most pure, beautiful smile he'd ever seen. She whistled, and Red jerked up, alert, before trotting to her side. "See you later, Simon," she said, turning for the far side of the beach.

"See you later, Lewan," Desmond called back, watching her walk away from him well after she was out of sight.

CHAPTER FOUR

Cait

Cait reached the edge of the forest after the short hike with Red trotting happily at her side. He shook out his sandy fur as she uncovered her bike from the brush. Giving the terrier a quick scratch behind the ear, she attached his long leash and began the five-minute bike ride home. Living on the edge of town gave her more freedom than if they lived in its heart. Built onto the peninsula, much of the forest surrounded the outskirts of Porthaven. She liked how secluded it felt, separate and hidden from the rest of the townspeople.

Wind in her hair, Cait sailed down the road past the half-dozen houses on Sinker Street. Another benefit of living away from everyone else— large lawns and clusters of trees kept the houses spaced out and private. At lunch, Genni had gotten Matt to tell them about his grandfather and exactly where they lived. Now, she tossed a glance at Howard DeGarmo's house, its faded seafoam-green siding and tchotchke-covered yard detailing the once-solitary life of the old man.

Before she'd come to a complete stop, Cait began to swing off the bike, careening into her driveway. Red padded next to her, headed for the detached garage. The houses out this way were some of the oldest in Porthaven and, therefore, some of the most in need of repair. When they'd moved to town almost twelve years ago, William Simon had gifted them the home with the promise of fixing it up as needed.

It was a strange arrangement, the mayor being their not-quite-landlord. He used the government money to finance them, which meant he couldn't be overly generous. The Lewan residence was a charity case, something that made the townspeople feel good about themselves. But half of the house still begged repair, and Cait regularly found herself as the one making them.

After stowing her bike, Cait padded up the back porch. She'd tamped down the high of meeting with Desmond on the trip home. Even after ten years, she couldn't help the way her mood improved when she was around him. It was as though the humming sensation that his presence brought on gave her life. And the more she experienced it, the happier she was.

Beyond that, Desmond's attention—be it out of rebellion or not—made her gloriously, and a tad smugly, euphoric. She had managed what none of the other girls in school could. Not that they were dating. Obviously, Desmond would never have any interest in *her*. They weren't even friends. But he did value her; she knew that. He shared his secrets with her. He shared his hopes and dreams, his fears and frustrations. And no one could take that away from her.

Cait stepped through the back door, straight into the kitchen. The dated, floral wallpaper peeled at the edges, the table and chairs were mismatched, and the front right burner on the stove didn't work. But the lace curtains, embroidered tablecloth, and porcelain kettle made it feel like home.

Her grandmother, Maeve, stood at the counter, already at work with the dinner. She'd pulled her soft, gingered hair into a clip, her wispy bangs perfectly bouncy over her forehead. In her sixties, Maeve Lewan's petite frame and sharp features didn't match her granddaughters in the slightest.

Cait and her sisters were all blonde, taller than average, and their faces rounded. If it wasn't for her matching blue-gray eyes, Cait might've thought her an imposter.

"Hello, *a leanbh*," Maeve called over her shoulder. Her fierce Irish accent filtered every word she spoke. Sometimes, she even slipped back into Gaelic—often when she was emotional or angry. But she always called her granddaughters *"a leanbh,"* Gaelic for "my child," and said "uh lan-uv," unlike its spelling would suggest.

Cait darted over to kiss her nan's cheek before slipping off her jacket. "What's my job?" she asked, hanging the jacket on the hooks by the door.

"Fish," Maeve instructed, gesturing to the pan on the stove with her masher. Then she went back to the bowl of potatoes. "Did yeh have a good walk?"

The gas burner let out a *snap, snap, snap* as Cait lit it. "Yeah, it was nice."

Her nan never minded Cait's long bike rides to walk through the woods. As the only granddaughter who enjoyed taking Red on a walk, Maeve readily approved of them. There was little danger of wildlife or strangers in their small town, allowing Cait to be gone for hours at a time with no questions.

The walks had started as a way of remembering her da. Every day, Owen Lewan would take long, languid walks with his own faithful companion—a massive, black, Irish Wolfhound named Conroy. Cait had asked to join once when she was four. When she'd returned with aching feet well after the sun had set, she'd determined never to ask again.

Now, Cait found herself desperate for her solitary walks—and subsequent meetings with Desmond.

Dropping a quarter stick of butter into the pan, Cait swirled it across the bottom.

Maeve glanced at her, a curious glimmer in her eyes. "Genni said yeh made a friend today," she remarked.

Desperately wanting to roll her eyes, Cait kept herself in check. "I suppose," she admitted.

"And he lives in the neighborhood?"

She nodded. "His grandfather is Mr. DeGarmo."

Maeve nodded. "He's always been a kindly old man."

Cait chose not to remark on Howard DeGarmo's likely mutual age with her nan.

"Would yeh tell me about yer friend?" Maeve prodded.

Hearing the implication in her nan's tone, Cait casually went about her work. She couldn't let Maeve think there was anything special about Matt. She didn't need her nan keeping a closer eye on her than normal.

Pulling the plate of filleted fish from the fridge, Cait began her careful description. "His name is Matt, and he's a very nice boy. He reminds me of Genni in some ways. They both like to talk too much."

Maeve chuckled at that. "Is he cute?" she pressed.

The fillets sizzled as they hit the buttery pan. "I guess. He's not really my type, I don't think."

Pausing in her work, Maeve looked at Cait, eyebrows raised. "Yeh have a type?"

Cait certainly did; snarky, messy-haired, and too smart for anyone's good. "Probably," she deflected. "Doesn't everyone have 'a type'?"

Straightening the Claddagh ring on her left ring finger, Maeve gave Cait a tiny smile. "Not especially, *a leanbh*," she said, her motherly tone enacted. "Yeh may find yeh prefer certain things over others, but, all in all, a man is a man. Yeh'll learn that looks aren't all they're said to be."

Flipping the fish, Cait doubted that. While she knew looks weren't *everything*, she couldn't help thinking that Desmond would be a whole lot less appealing if he wasn't so roguishly handsome. Though Rese always said he looked like a scruffy-headed beanpole, so she guessed he wasn't everyone's type.

The thought of her sister—or perhaps it was the smell of dinner— brought Rese into the room. Her burnished blonde hair bounced pleasantly as she strode to the cabinet. "I see you're back," she said, scanning Cait as she drew four plates down. She smirked. "Your new boyfriend go with you?"

Cait glared at her older sister. "I have absolutely no interest in Matt that way," she insisted.

"Oh!" Genni exclaimed, bounding into the kitchen. "Why not? He's so nice!"

"Gen says he's cute too," Rese added with a snide grin as she began to set the table.

Heaving a sigh, Cait stared at her family. All three women watched her with suspicion like it was inevitable that she'd catch feelings for the first boy who showed her any attention. Which Cait supposed was sort of true. After all, whatever had happened to her when she first met Desmond Simon, she'd fallen hard and forever. It didn't matter that he would never feel anything resembling love for her. She was convinced that she would never feel the same for any other man. How could she when his very presence brought that soothing hum to her whole being?

Determined not to give them any reason to distrust her surety, Cait turned back to the fish. "Then why doesn't Genni date him?"

"Ew, he's, like, totally not my type," Genni proclaimed, dropping into a dining chair.

"What is it with yeh girls and 'types'?" Maeve lamented. She set the bowl of mashed potatoes onto the table. "Besides, Genni is too young for a boyfriend."

"I'm fifteen," Genni argued.

Maeve shot her a fierce stare. "Which is too young. I've told yeh all: sixteen and no earlier. Even that I'm not thrilled about."

"Speaking of—" Rese folded a napkin, glancing up at her nan between her lashes. "Ryan asked if I'd go with him to the Festival next month. As his, like, official girlfriend."

Cait nearly gagged. Ryan Greene—older brother of Elizabeth from her class—was once the golden boy of Porthaven High. She'd always found him to be the most obnoxiously airheaded jock there could ever be. If not for Desmond, Ryan would have gone down in Porthaven history as their brightest star in track, basketball, *and* baseball. And that was about all that could recommend the towheaded dolt. But Rese was obsessed.

With a proud smile, Maeve brushed a hand over Rese's arm. "Ah, I'm very happy for yeh, *a leanbh*," she crooned. "Jest bring 'im over for dinner before I approve quite yet, huh?"

A grimace tugged up the corner of Rese's mouth, her sapphire-blue eyes darting around their dilapidated kitchen. Cait couldn't blame her for not wanting to bring Ryan here. As the doctor's son, he was used to a certain standard of living. One that wouldn't understand their rundown, vintage house.

But this was their life. And Cait thought that if a man couldn't accept their current status in Porthaven, he didn't deserve to raise them out of the status, to begin with.

Besides, it wasn't such a bad little house. Each of them had their own rooms, though they shared one bathroom, and Cait had made significant improvements to the overall shape of the place. If the mayor could find a little more wiggle room in the budget for things like paint and unblemished furnishings, she thought it would be downright charming.

Once the table had been set and the food plated, Cait sat down with her family at the rickety table. She scanned her nan and sisters. Yes, she was happy enough living in their old house with them. She'd be even happier once she graduated high school. And that was good, as this would be her home for the rest of her life.

No matter what silly jokes her sisters made, no matter the hopes Cait harbored, she knew the truth—the curse of the Lewan family wouldn't let her be free. Something was wrong with her, innately. And until she could find a way to break whatever evil charm it was that had wormed itself into her blood, twisting her dreams into those strange nightmares, Cait would have no future beyond these peeling walls. There would be no boys asking her to the annual Fisher's Festival, no making their relationship "official," no introductory approval dinners. She would remain as she was—cursed and alone.

~

The dreams always started the same way. That was how Cait knew, beyond a shadow of a doubt, that they were dreams and not reality. If it wasn't for the exact replication of each and every dream, the visceral, lifelike sensation would have driven her crazy, questioning what was real and what was dream.

They always began with darkness and a knowing—an awareness that something was there with her.

Cait opened her eyes to find herself in the room. It was a small, cozy space, just big enough for two twin beds and a tiny bassinet along the far wall. Hand-quilted comforters dressed the beds, pillows with ditsy floral cases resting at the heads. A soft green knitted blanket draped over the bassinet's side. Antique furnishings of rich oak pressed against the walls—a dresser, a nightstand, a rocking chair. Childish artwork hung, pinned to the walls, crayon and colored pencil scrawls of all variations.

The ceiling sloped with a steep pitch, wood beams protruding from its cream plaster. A dormer window hovered behind Cait, letting in the glowing, silver moonlight like a spotlight. It metalized everything with its white-gray gleam, sapping almost all color from the room.

Every time, the dream started here. Every time, Cait stood in the center of her memories, the room she'd shared with her sisters back in Ireland. Every time she opened her eyes, the moonlight pressed against her back as she stared at the locked door. Cait knew it was locked because, in every dream, she followed the same routine.

Cait stepped to the door. Her fingers found the metal knob, loose in its fitting. But it didn't turn. There was no keyhole and no means for her to unlock it.

She could hear movement on the other side of the door. Always a low, pacing sound, footsteps padding back and forth. A slow, anticipatory breath rumbled through the wood. Someone—or some *thing*—was waiting out there.

The metal doorknob warmed under her touch, signaling the next stage of the dream.

Cait took a single step back. Silvery light bled through the crack under the door, a shadow shifting as the being paced.

Watching the movement, Cait saw the first wisps curl from under the crack. Her heartbeat rose, and she took hurried steps backward. Smoke whispered into the room, tracing the baseboards, crawling over the floors, scaling the walls.

Throat constricting, Cait worked to keep her breathing steady. The smoke coiled from every crevice of the door, the pacing on the other side never slowing. It wanted in, whatever was on the other side. It wanted in, and it wanted her.

A sudden cry split the air, a wail of piercing agony.

Tears sprang to Cait's eyes. She knew that sound. It had woken Cait all those years ago, in this very room, to the smoke and the horror. It haunted her like nothing else—the heartbroken cry of a woman having watched her husband murdered in front of her eyes. The sob of her mother just before her life was taken too.

Smoke tendrilled around Cait's knees now, pressing in on her. It rose rapidly, hungrily. The thing on the other side of the door continued to pace.

Cait knew she should try to open the window. If she could get it open, the smoke would escape. She could escape. But she couldn't bring herself to turn—she knew what waited on the other side.

Panic welled, squeezing her throat tighter. Cait backed farther from the door. Something rumbled out there, the sound of determined aggravation.

A sudden *thud* banged against the door, and Cait jumped.

The smoke clouded around her waist.

Another *crash* on the door, but it held.

Cait blinked, and he was there.

A presence—or perhaps just a concept—existed in Cait's dreams. Not a person but a thing. The feeling of some strange barrier hovering between her and the door. She always gave it the face of William Simon. Whatever the thing was, it represented him; that she could feel.

Whorls of smoke wrapped around Cait's shoulders as she stared back at the image of William. She'd decided long ago that he looked very little like his son despite the family resemblance. They shared dark hair, hooded eyes, and that stubborn set to their jawlines. But there was a withholding in William's brown stare that didn't reside in Desmond's.

The door rattled under a third attack. William stood between her and the thing on the other side. Somehow, Cait knew he was protecting her. He wouldn't let that being on the other side break through.

As the smoke clawed its way to her mouth and nose, Cait's eyes stung. She took in the burning fumes with her next intake of air, eliciting a cough. William stood there unaffected by the vapor, his indifferent gaze shadowed under his heavy brow. He held his arms crossed over his broad chest as though unworried about the thing slamming ferociously against the door at his back.

Vision clouding, Cait tried to keep her breathing steady. The more rapid her breath grew, the more smoke she inhaled. The moonlight filtered through the smog, broken lines of light catching in the tendrils that stole inside her and seared her lungs.

Another impact banged against the door, and through her teary eyes, Cait could have sworn she saw a hairline fracture snap along the hinges.

The smoke became too much. Cait couldn't stop herself from breathing it in anymore. It stung and burned and scalded her insides. She coughed, choking on the air as she tried to get a clear breath over and over again.

Hand to her mouth, Cait's heart thudded with fright. She didn't want to turn around. She didn't want to try the window. It wouldn't open anyway. She would die here as she always did, each night smothered by the smoke.

But she had to try.

Whirling around, Cait lunged for the window. The cold casing sent icy tingles through her fingers as she fumbled with the latch. It wouldn't budge. No matter how hard she tried, her hand only grew slick with the condensation on the panes.

Her throat raw from coughing, more smoke clouded Cait's lungs. She abandoned the latch to bang on the windowpanes, desperate to get free. Absentmindedly, she realized she was sobbing. Her breaths were growing shallow, and she dropped to her knees. She pressed her forehead to the window, the horrible image of her childhood lawn lying before her.

The moon's spotlight bleached the scene. Her parents' bodies lay strewn on the lawn, torn and glinting in the night. This was the scene she'd woken to twelve years ago. This was the memory that haunted her every night. Her mother and father sprawled out, their limbs at unnatural angles and blood staining their torn flesh and clothes.

A silent scream of agony pulled itself through Cait's throat. She couldn't breathe to give the cry any sound, but she felt it tearing through her chest anyway.

Shadows pressed in around Cait, the smoke finally taking shape. It always did this. Each time, the smoke thickened and took on form. Sometimes, the forms were beautiful, built of the same silvery substance as the moonlight. Most times, they were monstrous, figments wrought of shadow and terror.

Tonight, they were darkness, monsters with flashing neon eyes, slavering jowls, and murderous intent—reflections of the demon that cursed her family's bloodline.

Cait slipped to the floor, her body beginning to shake in desperation for air. She let herself tremble as the monsters pressed in. Darkness slipped into the corners of her vision. That was good, she thought. She was about to black out.

Laying on the hard, wooden floor, Cait stared up at the monsters. She knew their shadowy forms; she called them the devil-horses. Though, really, it was Desmond who'd named them after he'd seen her sketches portraying their serrated hooves, spiked spines, and curving horns rather than ears.

"You really ought to dream about nicer stuff, Caity," he'd said.

Something like a laugh coughed out of Cait. The being slammed into the door again, William watching her unflinchingly. The devil-horses tossed their shadow manes, tearing at the floors impatiently with their hooves as though preparing to stampede. But they held their place, yellow eyes locked on her, waiting.

Yes, Cait thought, she really ought to dream of nicer things.

Then she suffocated on the smoke clouding her throat.

CHAPTER FIVE

Desmond

"*This party is boring.*" Desmond knew he shouldn't be texting her. He was asking for trouble, with his parents and all the rest of Porthaven's elite families gathered around him. The whole gang was here: Simons, Lavignes, Greenes, Edgarses, even the Varons. Over fifty people crammed into the oversized house in the center of town. And he was texting the one person he shouldn't be caught talking to.

Desmond's phone vibrated less than five minutes later. He snuck into the kitchen for a refill before surreptitiously slipping his phone from his pocket. Closed off from the rest of the house, he could easily hide as he read her message: *"Aren't Garrett and Brady there?"*

Desmond smirked to himself, tapping in his reply. *"With their parents. They have to BEHAVE when they're around."*

He refilled his cup as he waited—one of those clear plastic types you use when you want to be "fancy" but don't want to wash a million dishes. Despite his natural tendency, he'd listened to Cait's command; he hadn't touched the liquor so prevalent at the party. Of course, the adults weren't likely to get plastered for the heck of it. And the teens were too scared of getting caught to try.

On a normal day, Desmond would have done it anyway. But he kept hearing Cait's voice in his head each time he considered it, so he decided to stick with mixing himself a plain old Arnold Palmer.

His phone buzzed again.

"I thought Brady always behaved."

"You have a point. He's almost as bad as you." He didn't wait before sending the next message. *"But the reverend is here. And Brady's got a particular holier-than-thou vibe when his dad is around."*

He watched the bubble come up, its three dots pulsing to tell him she was typing. Taking a sip of his tea and lemonade mixture, it seemed she was writing a book before the short message popped up.

"Maybe you should learn from his example."

Desmond shook his head, a light chuckle escaping him. She *would* take Brady's side.

Preparing to text back, Desmond jumped when his mother suddenly walked into the room. The large kitchen practically burned the eyes with the starkness of its white cabinets and marble countertops. They'd renovated last year, bringing it from the nineties into the twenty-teens.

Robin Simon caught sight of her son instantly, her sharp blue eyes scanning him—another thing he hadn't inherited from her. She dressed like she was the first lady in a light blue pencil skirt and white silk blouse. "What are you doing in here, sweetheart?" she asked, a slight tilt to her voice as she headed for the fridge.

Desmond raised his drink in response.

"Ah." Robin grinned, her broad smile thinning out her lips. Desmond sometimes wondered how they could be related, considering how little alike they looked. However, the Varon genes overrode everything else, so he supposed it made sense.

Pulling a backup tray of meats and cheeses from the fridge, his mother continued to stall his response to Cait. Her steady gaze swept over him knowingly. "It's a little hectic out there, isn't it?" she remarked, then set the tray on the island across from Desmond. "I could use a minute of quiet myself."

"Mom," Desmond replied with just enough sarcasm in his tone to let her know he appreciated her understanding. "You're kind of ruining my quiet time."

Robin instantly chuckled. Sense of humor he *had* inherited from his mom. While William Simon was perpetually stoic, Robin enjoyed a good joke or witty retort as much as Desmond. "I am sorry, little seabird," her eyes twinkled at the use of his childhood nickname, "but it's a mother's prerogative to interrupt her child's solitude."

Dropping his phone onto the island, Desmond realized he wouldn't get to reply to Cait for a while longer. He leaned forward, resting his arms on the counter. "Who're you escaping this time?" he asked, content to accept his mother's company.

Robin scowled dramatically. "Your aunt."

"Which one? Priscilla?"

She didn't need to confirm it; her eye roll said enough. "Who names their daughter Priscilla?" she whispered her favorite line about his dad's sister. "It's a recipe for a prissy woman."

"At least she makes good chip dip," he offered.

The humor that sparkled in Robin's eyes bled into her retort. "Why do you think I keep inviting her to things?"

Desmond pursed his lips. "Well, I assumed it was because she's dad's sister, but I guess dip can cover a multitude of sins."

His mother's low laughter made Desmond's chest swell. Many times, he questioned how his dad had managed to marry such a wonderful woman.

He reached across the island to snatch a strip of what he hoped was Gouda. His mom watched him, tilting her head to the side. "What about you?" she prompted. "Why are you hiding?"

Desmond shrugged, hoping she'd read the move as indifferent. "No real reason. Just bored."

"So, you decided to come to the kitchen alone? Yes, that's a great way to liven things up."

"You're the one who always tells me that I'm marvelous company."

"The best." Robin winked at him. Then she nudged her chin at his phone. "Who were you texting?"

Working to keep his expression placid, Desmond's heart stuttered. His mom always was too observant. "No one," he said blandly. "Just a school thing."

One of her light brown eyebrows tipped up. "If it's a girl, I won't be mad," she assured him. "I've been waiting for you to bring someone home."

"I'm seventeen."

"And most of your peers have been dating for years."

Desmond frowned playfully at his mom. "Seriously? You want to use my classmates as examples of healthy romantic relationships?"

"I didn't say they had healthy relationships," she retorted. "Just that they *had* them."

"There's no one to date, Mom."

"Isn't there?"

"Not really."

Her light eyes drifted to his phone. "So, it isn't a girl."

"I told you, it's a school thing."

"Doesn't mean it isn't a girl."

Desmond shifted as lazily as he could. He didn't like when either of his parents brought up relationships. Not only was it weird, but it also often led to conversations about his future and the responsibilities he bore as the town's eventual leader.

"Mom," Desmond began, "when I find a girl worth dating, I'll tell you."

Robin studied his face, her clear blue eyes piercing through him the way she'd always been able to. Perhaps it was a perk of being a mother. Or maybe his mom was just more insightful than others. But he knew she could read him and the lies he was telling.

Lifting the tray, Robin gave him a nod. "All right, seabird," she said affectionately. "Just know, whoever she is . . . I trust you."

If anyone else had said those words, Desmond would have scoffed. But his heart felt heavy as his mother held his gaze. "You'll make the right choice," she continued. "And I very much look forward to meeting her."

"Mom," he replied, hoping his sarcasm covered his nerves. "You know literally everyone in Porthaven. I couldn't introduce you to anybody."

She didn't reply, just dipped her chin in acceptance, then walked out.

Desmond stared at his phone on the island. He took a sip of his drink, jaw tight as he swallowed. His mother's goodwill was nearly as oppressive as his father's expectations. She trusted him—which meant she trusted that he wouldn't choose the wrong woman. That he wouldn't let his heart get involved with someone so impossibly unsuitable for him.

Seabird, she called him, because she always said: *"You may fly away, but you always come back. The shore always calls you home."*

She had no idea.

Every rebellion, every assertion of his independence, it was all a joke. Desmond simultaneously hated and obsessed over his inheritance. It stifled him. It excited him. He feared it. He longed for it. The power, the responsibility—it called to him. Inexplicably, the Varon blood that ran through his veins *wanted* to lead. It was why his grades were immaculate, why he worked out at least an hour every day, and why he excelled at sports. It was why he kept his relationship with Cait a secret.

If he were a true rebel, he wouldn't be such a coward. If he really didn't care what his parents thought, he'd spend time with her in the open. If he actually wanted to reject his future, he would date her.

Desmond flicked the corner of his phone, sending it spinning on the smooth counter. It whirred, round and round.

So many times, Desmond had told himself to stop seeing Cait. Stop talking to her. Stop giving either of them hope that anything could change.

He hated himself for the way he treated her, ignoring her in public and adoring her in secret. It was wrong; it was cruel. But he couldn't stop himself.

Every time he tried to call it off, he talked himself out of it.

Cait wasn't just some girl he had a crush on. She was his best friend. Brady would be offended, but that was the truth of it. She knew him better than anyone; he knew her better than anyone. And he couldn't imagine life without her.

He was only delaying the inevitable, he told himself daily. He'd have to break it off sooner or later. Better do it now and save them any further heartbreak.

Desmond rolled his eyes at himself, slipping the phone back into his pocket. He was being stupid. There was nothing to break off. They weren't dating. They were simply meeting up a handful of times a week— sitting there chatting or reading and sketching. They weren't in love; they were seventeen. And whatever came, they'd always known their fun couldn't last.

~

Porthaven Chapel didn't live up to its name. Chapels were small and quaint. The one in Porthaven was more like a cathedral.

Desmond wasn't sure who'd decided the town needed something so opulent. Probably the same Varon mayor who'd decided the town hall should be a columned tribute to the Grecian pavilions. But in the chapel's case, they'd taken their cues from Victorian London with its characteristic arches and columns, gothic buttresses, domed ceilings, and stained glass windows.

Running a hand over his mouth to hide his yawn, Desmond tried to listen to Reverend Benjamin Lavigne. He really did try. He just couldn't get his brain to focus.

He sat in the uncomfortable antique pew with his parents, Brady, and the rest of the Lavigne family. At least with Brady at his side, he could whisper occasional remarks. Though his friend often let out near-silent snorts at his sarcasm, he immediately returned to his diligent notetaking.

Like every family in Porthaven, Brady was lined up to inherit his father's job. And he took his future job seriously.

That was how all Warden towns worked as far as Desmond knew. Families passed roles on from one generation to the next. Your dad was a cop? Well, you get to be a cop. Your dad was an accountant? Hope you like numbers, buddy.

Desmond thought the whole thing was stupid. Who decided "family" businesses were a beneficial concept? What if you had a kid who didn't care about the business? What if, instead of growing up to inherit the leadership of an entire town, your kid wanted to be . . . oh, a writer or something? Maybe an astronaut. Perhaps a distiller; that seemed like a pretty awesome job.

Desmond had once asked Brady and Garrett if they ever thought about doing something other than what their family did. They'd both stared at him in utter confusion. Though, to be fair, that's how Garrett looked most of the time.

Smirking at the thought, Desmond reminded himself that he was in church. He was *supposed* to be learning about the Bible. He was in the front row, after all. Of all the people in the chapel, they ought to be taking in every detail of Ben's sermon.

Desmond stared up at his friend's dad. Ben and Brady looked a decent amount alike. Dark hair, action-hero jawlines, naturally muscular builds. Not the sort you'd peg for a reverend. If it wasn't for Desmond, he was pretty sure Brady would be the schoolgirls' obsession. But that was part of what was so ridiculous about their town. Desmond was only the "hot guy" because he was a Simon. His title earned him their attention—not *him*. You give Brady the last name Simon, and every girl would go stark raving mad over him.

Maybe that was why Desmond kept Brady around, as a reminder of just how inadequate he was. Not only was Brady the obnoxious epitome of masculinity, but he was also everything that Desmond *should* be. He was dedicated to his faith, he was intelligent and rational, and he kept his emotions tempered. Even his moral compass was true north. The only reason Brady ever drank or did anything "bad" was because Desmond wouldn't leave him alone until he joined in on the "debauchery." And that was probably just so Desmond didn't feel *completely* inferior to his friend.

In reality, Desmond knew he'd be friends with Brady either way. It didn't matter that he liked his company; they were destined to be best friends. After all, William and Ben were best friends, as all the mayors and reverends of Porthaven had been since its start.

Finally, Ben asked that the congregation rise for the closing prayer. "Draw us to the heart of your Son," the reverend led, the townspeople joining in, "inspire us by your Holy Spirit, and teach us to see the unseen. Amen."

A tingle raced down Desmond's spine as it did each time they prayed that prayer. The smallest tug in his chest urged him to mean it next time, to truly desire those things.

Desmond could see the unseen, of course. That ability came naturally and powerfully to the Simons—another Varon inheritance they'd usurped. He was better equipped than any other in Porthaven to connect with the spirit world. It was why Hades was such an easy thing for him to summon. Not that he had ever let his parents know that. Summoning a beast at six years old wasn't exactly common *or* acceptable—not even for the "true Varon" heir.

Turning to Brady to start up a conversation, Desmond didn't get his mouth open before he felt a tug on his arm. The unmistakable, firm grip of his father caused him to whirl around, eyebrows raised. "What?" he asked, staring unflinchingly into William's fierce brown eyes.

Desmond always thought his dad looked like the poster child for the Marine Corps. He just had that sort of face—square, serious, and downright aggressive. It didn't match the fine button down and tie he wore.

"We have new residents," he said, deep voice forceful, as though expecting a fight. "As the leadership of the town, it's our job to welcome them."

Working hard to keep from heaving a sigh, Desmond pressed his lips together. Thankfully, Porthaven rarely gained new citizens, so he'd only had to attend his father on a meet and greet a handful of times before. He still didn't understand the point of it. They were at the chapel; it seemed to Desmond that it was Ben and Brady's job to be welcoming.

This time, already knowing who the new residents were, Desmond's desire to greet them was nonexistent. "She's my teacher, Dad," he reminded him. "I've already met Mrs. Davis and her son."

"You met her as her student," William countered. "Now, you'll meet her as an individual and the future leader of this town."

Desmond drew in a long breath to keep from spitting out a sharp retort. He knew it wouldn't do any good. His dad would drag him along anyway.

With a thoughtless nod, Desmond acquiesced. William turned on his heel, walking up the center aisle. He waved and smiled at the many congregants who greeted him in passing. Desmond shoved his hands into his pockets, tipping his chin up in acknowledgment when it would be otherwise rude to ignore the person.

It was when they were only a handful of pews away that Desmond found his heart sinking. Mrs. Davis and her son, Matt, stood in one of the back rows, happily talking with four women. His eyes locked on Cait first, her soft blonde hair hanging like a shimmering curtain around her face. She wore a white blouse with blue and yellow flowers embroidered all over it. He recognized it as a hand-me-down from her older sister, Therese. It looked far less suggestive on Cait than it had on her sister. It could have been their different body types—Therese's being more voluptuous and Cait's daintier. But Desmond remembered seeing Therese wear that blouse into school one day, its neckline matching the demure cut Cait now wore, then noticing when that same blouse seemed to have dipped into a lower V after the girl exited the bathroom.

Desmond had never liked the eldest Lewan girl. She was snooty, ambitious, and a hint salacious. When Cait and he started high school, Therese had been so busy working her way up the social ladder that she'd all but ignored her little sister.

Not that Desmond was much better. If he really cared about Cait, he would have let their friendship be known.

Hardening his jaw, Desmond forced himself to look away from Cait. Her younger sister, Genevieve, stood on one side, Matt on the other. Mrs. Davis was merrily chatting with Maeve Lewan, the grandmother who somehow still managed to look barely older than his own mom. Maybe it was her red hair. Or maybe it was the luck of the Irish.

Cait saw them coming first. Her sea-like blue-gray eyes met his, and he saw the visible shift in her posture. She always did that when he came around; he didn't think she even realized she was doing it. Her shoulders slumped, and her head dipped. He assumed it was a subconscious attempt at making herself smaller, as though telling people she feared his presence. To him, it looked like she was zeroing in, drawing low like a wolf stalking its prey.

"Good morning," William called as they came to a stop a respectful distance away from the group. Desmond hung behind his father, an unwilling shadow as the women and Matt turned to them.

Maeve let out a good-natured "oh" before turning to Mrs. Davis. "Penny, this is Mayor Simon," she said to the woman, her lilting accent so thick that Desmond had to pay attention to catch all the words. "And I'm sure yeh know his son, Desmond."

Mrs. Davis—Penny—gave them both a kind smile. She was pretty for a forty-something woman. Her auburn-brown hair hung around her shoulders today; she usually wore it in a ponytail or bun at school. "Yes, good morning, Desmond," she said.

Lifting a hand in passive greeting, Desmond muttered, "Morning."

William took over. "Mrs. Davis, it's a pleasure to meet you," he said with a lift of respectability in his tone. "Desmond and I just wanted to come over and welcome you and your son to Porthaven."

"She lived here before, Dad," Desmond corrected before realizing his mistake.

William shot a tense look his way. Then his expression softened as he turned back to Penny. "Is that so?"

"Yes, I grew up here, actually." She smiled. "I believe your wife and I were in the same class together."

Knowing his father would find this tidbit to be a sign of his failure—not remembering some woman who'd lived in Porthaven decades ago—Desmond wanted to smirk. Instead, he kept his face impassive and refused to look at Cait.

"Well, isn't that a coincidence," William said, his attempt at a lighthearted chuckle failing. "In that case, we're happy to have you back."

He turned to Matt then, holding out his hand as he asked, "And you are?"

Mouth hanging ajar, Matt accepted the handshake, muttering his name. Desmond fought down a scoff. The kid was a total catastrophe. A senior and he was even shorter than Desmond. Worse, the boy was all skin and bones; his ears were too big for his head, and his lips practically disappeared when he smiled.

Yet *he* was the one standing next to Cait.

Desmond rolled his shoulders, turning to indifferently scan the emptying chapel.

"It's a pleasure to meet you, Matt," William said, mayoral dignity returned. He turned back to Penny. "If there is anything you need, Mrs. Davis, please let me know. As you know, we like to keep Porthaven a strong, tight-knit community. Our numbers have grown over the years, but we'd like to be sure that everyone feels at home and cared for."

Penny nodded knowingly. "It's one of the reasons I chose to return.

And I truly appreciate it, Mayor Simon." She draped an arm over Matt's shoulders and squeezed. "Mattie and I are excited to be here."

Matt squirmed under his mother's arm, but she seemed to enjoy making her son uncomfortable as she grinned, tightening her grip.

Desmond decided then that he liked Penny Davis.

William began to step back. "Mrs. Lewan, girls," he said, overviewing them for the first time. "I hope you all have a pleasant Sunday."

Therese and Genevieve looked bored, the first surveying her nails and the other staring blankly at them. Maeve graciously returned the mayor's farewell. Cait's eyes kept flickering to Desmond.

A smug sense of satisfaction welled in Desmond's chest. As his father began to turn, Desmond smirked at the stick figure of a boy. "Mattie," he said with a dismissive nod.

Then, like an idiot, he winked at Cait. "Lewan."

Before any of them could say anything, Desmond turned and followed in his father's path. He could have sworn he heard Therese muttering something about "such a prick" and her grandmother scolding her. His smirk grew.

Good, he thought. If they regarded him as an arrogant snob, they'd have no reason to suspect that his regard for Cait was anything but contempt.

The thought sent an immediate tinge of regret through Desmond. His behavior left him feeling hollow—this need to ignore and belittle Cait in public. To make people think he didn't feel anything for her, that he viewed her as dust beneath his feet.

It made him feel like the worst sort of person.

Lost in his self-contempt, Desmond failed to notice his father's altered gait. It allowed him to catch up and then overtake William just as they approached the front row once more. At which point, his dad covertly latched onto his arm, keeping him moving.

Desmond didn't need to ask where they were going. His dad marched him across the front of the chapel carefully so that anyone might think they were nonchalantly going to the back where the choir kept their robes. As if anyone would ever go there to have a casual chat.

Mind rolling through the last few minutes, Desmond tried to figure out what he'd done wrong. Had his dad caught the wink directed to Cait? Had he figured it out? Was this finally going to be the end of their secret meetups? Was he about to lose Cait because of his stupid jealousy?

William ushered Desmond into the small room, flicked on the light, and shut the door. "You didn't care to tell me your teacher was a Porthavenian?"

A sigh of blended relief and irritation huffed out of Desmond. He shrugged, hands slapping his thighs as they dropped back down. "Didn't really cross my mind, to be honest. Figured you'd already know."

"Don't be a smart-ass," William shot back. "You know I have plenty on my plate right now with the Festival coming up. We have hundreds of people lined up to come to town. I don't have time to notice whether or not our newest resident was in my wife's graduating class."

"Not sure how that's my fault," Desmond replied dryly.

William's gaze darkened. He took a step closer, his broad frame threatening. His dad had never hit him. Not even when he deserved it. William Simon would never get violent; he was too above that. But Desmond would almost have preferred that he would. Then, there would be something to fight back against. Instead, he was only faced with insurmountable expectations and disappointment.

"It is our job to make these people feel cared for, Desmond," his father preached. "They need to know that we're here for them. And forgetting one of our own makes me look careless."

The ridiculousness of his assertion made Desmond want to scoff. Smartly, he held the reaction in. "There are fifteen hundred people in this town, Dad. And, like, a hundred thousand more that have come and gone. It's impossible to remember them all."

"It is our *job* to remember them all," William commanded. Though he and his father were the same height, Desmond couldn't help feeling like a small child under his weighty presence. "I taught you to remember them all."

"And yet you forgot one," Desmond returned. "Who cares? Mrs. Davis didn't."

"When will you ever understand?" he murmured. His tone suggested exhaustion rather than anger. A long-running disappointment overflowed into his words.

Desmond felt his shoulders instinctively slump even as he hardened his jaw.

William held up a finger, pointing first to his own chest, then tapping it forcefully to Desmond's. "We are leaders. And leaders don't fall to the status quo. We rise above it. We are better because that is the responsibility set upon our shoulders. Every person in this town—all one thousand seven hundred and twenty-three of them—rely on *us*." He lifted the finger to point at Desmond's nose. "It is up to *you* to be the one who keeps them safe—the one who makes them *feel* safe."

Barely managing to swallow down the tension that constricted his throat, Desmond kept his expression as deadpan as he could. "I'm seventeen," he muttered.

"Youth is not an excuse for negligence."

That was one of William's favorite lines. And the one that made Desmond feel immeasurably lacking.

William drew back, releasing a long sigh. "Tell me about this boy, Matt."

The switch from scolding father to instructive mentor was a whiplash to which Desmond had grown numb. "I don't know much," he admitted. "He's not really in my 'crowd.'"

"He's friends with the Lewan girls?"

Desmond licked his lips. "Yeah. At least with—with the middle one."

"Does he know?"

With a reflexive eye roll, Desmond lifted his shoulders in a half-assed shrug. "I mean, he knows what most of the town knows, I'm sure. It was inevitable. Everyone gossips about Lewan."

William narrowed his eyes. That was always what Desmond called Cait in public. Pretending they weren't on a first-name basis made it appear as though he viewed her as someone without a name, without humanity. But over the years, it had become a strange term of endearment for him. *Lewan.* Different and unique and wholly removed from everything in Porthaven.

"You should be kinder to her," William said, his mayoral voice in place. "She's one of us too."

They'd had this argument before; his dad liked to pretend he was some benefactor to the Lewans. Just like he pretended to be with the Faulks. It was all a show. And Desmond knew that if his father found out just how close he was with Caitriona Lewan, extra hours at his internship would be the least of his worries.

"She's a Vessel," Desmond replied.

William shot a look over his shoulder as though he'd find the door suddenly flung wide open. "Be careful where you use that term."

"What does it matter? No one knows what it means beyond the Warden."

William glared at him. "Names have power, Desmond. When you have a name, you can call forth answers."

"How mystical of you," Desmond murmured. "I don't think the kid knows anything serious. Like you said, he's friends with Lewan. And I doubt she's gonna tell him that she's harboring a spirit."

His father eyed him curiously. "We don't know which daughter inherited it."

Desmond tipped his head in admittance. "No, but you have a theory, don't you?"

"I don't speculate on things when I have no way of knowing the answer."

He scoffed. "Whatever Matt knows, it's likely the drivel the town has concocted over the years, thanks to you and Grandpa."

William's eyes flared with frustration, but Desmond waved it off. "I know, I know. Respect my elders." He held out his hand, hoping to ease his dad's worries. "Look, even *if* Lewan told him about her dad, you made damn sure she doesn't know half of the truth. At most, she thinks what the rest of the town thinks: Her father was a witch possessed by a demon. Why Grandpa chose that bull—"

"We're in church," his father scolded.

"Yet you can call me a smart-ass?"

"Watch it."

Desmond blew it off. "I don't understand what the big deal is. Why don't we just tell her and her sisters the truth? The Faulks know."

"The Faulks have over two hundred years of relationship with the Warden," William said. "They have proven themselves and their willingness to cooperate. There is nothing to fear from them. They are happy to accept the block and keep the creature smothered."

"You're not even giving Cait and her sisters a chance," Desmond argued. "You're treating them like prisoners. They don't even know they've got a block on them in the first place. How is that acceptable to you? How do you rationalize that with your Biblical morality?"

"We are *protecting* them!" William growled, his fury making the words blunt like a barrier. "The Lewan line is unpredictable. They ran roughshod in Bushmills. There were no checks, and that *thing* attached to their father had total control."

"He never hurt anyone," Desmond objected.

"It's what got him killed," William retorted. "We don't know what they're capable of—the Lewan girls or their burden. Until we know more, it is safer to keep them subdued. That's our job."

"Everything is our job," Desmond grumbled. "Fine. Whatever. Do what you want. Oppress and lie to three young girls whose parents were murdered. Sounds like a great plan to me."

"They are not oppressed," he argued. "We care for them as best we can. Our town provides everything they have."

"And yet we live in a newly renovated house while they pass down their clothes."

William raised his chin, silent.

Feeling dangerously gratified, Desmond smirked. "Guess it's our job to be hypocrites too."

Without waiting for his father's reply, he skirted around him and pushed out of the room.

CHAPTER SIX

Cait

After the weekend, a part of Cait questioned if Matt would have given up. Would he have noticed the separation from their peers brought on by a friendship with her? And a small part of her worried that he'd try to distance himself from her at the start of the new school week.

But after Cait took her isolated seat in the corner, Matt slipped in next to her only minutes later. "So, I'm curious," he began without preamble. "Why don't you ride on the bus?"

Cait looked at him in surprise. "Why *do* you ride on the bus?"

"I don't have a car."

"Neither do I."

His slim eyebrows pulled together. "How do you get to school then?"

"Genni and I bike here," she explained. "Why don't you just ride with your mom?"

"Are you kidding?" Matt exclaimed as though she'd suggested something particularly heinous. "First of all, Mom has gotta be here *way* too early in the morning. Second, it's bad enough that everyone's calling me 'Mattie.' I don't need them seeing me coming and leaving with my mom every day."

"Mm." Cait opened her notebook.

Matt watched, his eyes paying more attention than she'd like. "Do you, uh—I noticed that you kinda doodle a lot. Is that just, like, a hobby, or is that what you want to do?"

"Doodle?"

"Draw. Be an artist."

Playing with the string attached to the collar of her blouse, Cait shrugged. She didn't know why she'd chosen to wear the rose-colored shirt today. It belonged to Rese until a couple of months ago when she handed it down. Cait had never intended to wear something so feminine and bright, but when she saw it in her closet, she couldn't help remembering the way Desmond had looked at her in church yesterday morning.

It was so seldom they interacted in public, especially in the church, that she wasn't sure she'd ever realized that he paid attention to how she dressed. After the way he'd given her an extra-long scan, she wanted to see if she could elicit that same sort of reaction from him again.

Realizing Matt was still waiting for her response, Cait dropped the string. "Uh, no, not particularly," she said. "I like to draw, but I'm not really an artist."

"What do you want to do?"

Cait blinked. "I don't know."

Matt scratched his cheek. "Yeah, me either. Are you thinking of going to college somewhere?"

The hum of Desmond's arrival warmed through Cait, and she fought to hold her focus on Matt. "No, there aren't any universities in Porthaven," she said.

"Well, no," Matt accepted, his slim frame slouched. "But there's a community college not far in Calais. And then there's always the University of Maine, and that's less than three hours away. Trust me,

Mom has been shoving the applications down my throat for the past two months."

Rather than explaining that she had neither the money nor the ability to leave Porthaven, Cait chose to distract Matt with her own questions. "What do you plan to major in?" she asked, allowing herself to glance at Desmond.

He was already lounging at his desk, chatting coolly with Garrett.

"I dunno," Matt sighed. "Mom keeps trying to get me to decide, but I just can't get excited about anything. Dad told me there's no reason to declare a major, though. He said the first couple of years are wasted on Gen Ed anyway. What do you think?"

Cait forced herself to look away from Desmond and meet Matt's steady gaze. "About what?"

"I mean, do you really think it's necessary to make a choice on a major right away? Or should I just feel it out and get my mandatory credits out of the way."

Completely unaccustomed to these conversations, Cait said honestly, "I don't know."

At that moment, Penny Davis called the class to order. The school day passed in its rote, replicated manner. The students moved from room to room, stopping in the halls to exchange books at their lockers or linger with their friends.

For the first time in her life, Cait actually had someone to stop with her at her locker. Matt hung by her side while she switched out her textbooks and homework. He kept up his usual commentary, asking her endless questions. She preferred the ones about the town over the ones about herself. Even though she was becoming more comfortable with Matt, she still wasn't used to sharing who she was with people.

When they entered the cafeteria, Cait moved toward their usual table as Matt got in line. She took her seat, facing the rest of the room. A smattering of students filled the blue seats, chatting while they ate. However, most of the teens were still in line for food, leaving a clear view of Desmond's table at the far end.

Though it was still empty, Cait scanned the seat that awaited his arrival. Then she slipped her phone out of her pocket. Holding her phone under the table, she tried not to smile.

"You should wear pink more often," Desmond's text read.

Her fingers kept flickering to the keyboard, attempting multiple false starts at a reply. She couldn't figure out what to say. A "thank you" seemed too simple. Desmond liked it when she teased him back, she knew, but everything she started felt wrong.

Cait glanced around the cafeteria. Matt was slowly shuffling through the line, Desmond not far behind him, both nearing the end. She had to move quickly. And she had to be careful. Texting Desmond was always a mission of stealth. Neither of them did it when there was any chance of getting caught.

Bagged lunch spread out in preparation before her, Cait turned back to her phone. She'd begun and subsequently deleted so many messages that the same ones were starting to pop back up. What was so difficult about a text anyway? She had no problem talking to him on a normal basis. Why did this feel different?

Beginning another likely failed attempt, Cait panicked as she saw Matt making his approach. Hastily, she typed, *"Really? Why?"* and hit send.

She internally grimaced at such a lame reply.

Dropping into the seat across from her, Matt gave her that big, thin-lipped grin of his. "You didn't have to wait for me," he said.

Cait slipped her phone under her leg. "I didn't mind."

"Should we wait for Genni too?"

She waved a hand through the air. "You never know how long she'll take."

Accepting her permission, Matt dug into the tuna casserole on his plate while she opened the plastic container of chilled soup from home. Most of the time, Cait didn't mind not eating off the cafeteria menu. Her nan's cooking gave her a sense of comfort in the reverberating chaos of the school.

Savoring the hearty flavors of the broth and the snap of carrots, leeks, and potatoes, Cait let Matt control the conversation. He was good at that, she'd come to learn. Though his chatter and questions could sometimes veer into being annoying, she appreciated that there was no demand on her to keep the conversation going.

"You know, I was thinking," he said after swallowing his previous bite. "Maybe—if it'd be okay, that is—I have a bike—well, it's my mom's old bike. But maybe I could ride to school with you and Genni? Rather than taking the bus, I mean."

Cait smiled at him. "That'd be fine with me."

"Really?"

"Sure. And Genni will be more than happy to have someone come with us. I'm not great at conversation in the morning."

Matt laughed. "You're not a morning person?"

"Not really."

"Believe it or not, me either," he admitted. "Mom is the talker of the two of us in the morning. Most of the time, I'm still half asleep."

Cait couldn't help but chuckle with him.

"Another thought I had," Matt said, braver now that she'd responded well to his first suggestion. "I've been wanting to see the town. Mom and I have spent so much time at home settling in and stuff that I've not really gotten to explore downtown. And . . . well, I thought it'd be cool to get a tour from a local."

"Your mom's a local," she reminded him.

"She *used* to be a local," he corrected. "Besides, she's not as fun to hang out with as you."

A slight blush came to Cait's cheeks. She wasn't used to compliments.

Her phone vibrated under her thigh as though scolding her for forgetting Desmond. He complimented her. Usually infused with sarcasm, but they were compliments all the same.

Itching to check the text, Cait forced herself not to look. She didn't want Matt to catch her texting someone.

The sudden and unexpected arrival of Hunter Varon made Cait jump in her seat. "Hey," he said, a friendly tilt to his voice. With wavy light brown hair and the charming, signature Varon grin, he was one of the more attractive boys in Cait's class. His bright blue eyes helped add to the overall appeal.

Hunter smiled at them both, his demeanor easy and relaxed. Cait had always secretly liked Hunter. She knew it would appall Desmond to hear it. But out of all the students, Hunter had never been mean to her. Sure, he'd ignored her, but it was more out of indifference than the fear the rest of the students displayed. Even if he was distant, he was surprisingly nice for all the bluster that went on between him and Desmond.

"How's it going?" Hunter asked, resting his hands on the table as he leaned down toward the two of them. He gave Cait a cordial nod before turning to Matt in full. "So, I know that it's kind of delayed, but . . . I just wanted to come over and welcome you to Porthaven."

Matt stared up at Hunter, his brown eyes wide as he gaped at him. "Oh, uh—thanks," he replied.

"Yeah, sure," Hunter returned. His expression turned sheepish. "Sorry that I didn't do it last week. My girlfriend, Liz, reminded me that I can kind of get caught up in my own world." He added a self-deprecating chuckle at the end.

Matt continued to stare at him in confusion.

Hunter cleared his throat, adjusting the collar on his denim button up. "Anyway, I wanted to be sure you knew that we're all happy to have you here."

"What about Cait?" Matt asked instantly.

Cait blanched as Hunter dumbly replied, "Huh?"

Panic swarmed through Cait. Why was Matt bringing *her* into this?

The usual puppy dog look in Matt's eyes hardened into a glare. "Are you happy to have Cait here?" he demanded.

"Uh—" Hunter glanced at Cait as though asking for help.

Everything in Cait wanted to slip down her chair and hide under the table. Her shoulders slumped as she met Hunter's nervous stare with her own shell-shocked one.

Hunter scratched his neck, turning back to Matt. "I mean, yeah," he said. "I've never had a problem with Cait."

"How come you're not friends with her then?" Matt asked with an acerbic inflection to his words.

With another glance at Cait, Hunter drew back from the table. He looked utterly baffled, lips smashed together as he tried to puzzle out Matt's accusation. "I, uh—we've just never hung out," he offered.

"Why? 'Cause she's supposedly cursed?"

"Matt, please," Cait heard herself murmur.

He looked over to her, face softening as he caught the horror in her expression. "I just—it isn't right, Cait," he said, almost desperately. "They all treat you like you're invisible when you're the nicest person I've ever met."

Blinking back the stinging tears of frustration, Cait gave a single shake of her head. "It isn't worth it."

Matt's whole face scrunched up in disbelief. "Yeah, you are," he insisted.

The kind sentiment refused to take root in Cait. Not as she noticed how shockingly quiet the room was. Hunter still stood there, though he'd begun to slowly drift away while the rest of the cafeteria muttered amongst themselves. They were watching them, listening in to the conversation as Matt confronted Hunter on her behalf.

While he humiliated her even as he tried to be nice.

This was the reason Cait didn't stand up for herself. If she tried, she became the subject of even more ridicule. It wasn't worth it.

Tentatively, Cait raised her eyes to look beyond Matt's shoulder. In an instant, across the length of the cafeteria, she caught Desmond's dark gaze. They always sat facing each other like this, occasionally sharing silent communication at opposite ends of the room. And in this moment, she could read his thoughts exactly: *"Disappear."*

Without waiting, Cait pushed back from the table, the metal legs of her chair squealing against the tiles. She whirled around the chair, fingers finding the handle of her backpack as she rushed for the door, passing a wide-eyed Genni on the way.

Tears brimming over, Cait refused to slow down as she barreled through the halls. She wound past the trophy case, shining with medals won by Simons and Varons over the years. She tore through hall after hall of bright blue lockers, cheerful banners, and cluttered poster boards.

Her phone vibrated in her hand again as she pushed into the stairwell. She scaled the steps two at a time until she reached the top. Facing the gray metal door that led to the rooftop access, she swiped her hand under the fire extinguisher hanging on the wall. Her fingers tugged on the hidden key, pulling it free of the tape that held it there.

Cait unlocked the door, its handle unlatching with a metallic *slap* as she shoved it open. Another short staircase awaited her, dim emergency lighting guiding her up to the rooftop entrance. She pushed through, out into the brightness of the sunshine.

Blinking both the sun's rays and the tears out of her eyes, Cait heaved the heavy breath she'd held in her lungs through the school. It came out almost as a sob. Her chest burned with unspent emotion.

After slipping the key into the side pocket of her backpack, Cait dropped it by the door. She ambled over to the small, shadowy alcove created by the HVAC and the high rim of the cafeteria skylight. She crossed her legs, tucking herself under its shade to finally look at her phone.

Two messages waited for her: *"It suits you."* and *"Ten minutes."*

Though hidden under the HVAC's shade, Cait soon began to sweat. She stared out at the town of Porthaven, surveying the old, white brick town hall, the brightly painted shops, the weather-worn docks. Located in the middle of downtown, the school gave her a plain view all the way to the sea. Seagulls swooped over the waves, their pleading cries an echo of Cait's desperation.

The sunlight glittered on the water, fishing boats bobbing with the tide. Cait always liked watching the boats float around the peninsula. It gave her hope that if bits of wood and plastic could withstand a turbulent sea, perhaps she could survive the battering of her own life.

A sharp *click* broke the quiet, bringing the hum with it. Cait didn't look away from the water even as Desmond rounded the corner and slipped into the alcove next to her. Their knees pressed against each other as they sat cross-legged.

"You know," he said simply, "I'm starting to really dislike this Matt kid."

Cait twisted the hem of her blouse between her fingers. "People are going to notice that you disappeared after I did," she said.

"Nah," he replied, rolling up the long sleeves of his tee. "They'll all be too busy gossiping about how Mattie chewed out Hunter, then went looking for you."

A sigh escaped Cait, and she dropped her head into her hands. She fought against the tears that threatened to return. Her throat and chest burned, but she refused to cry over something as simple as an embarrassing encounter.

Desmond's elbow bumped hers. "I'm sorry," he muttered.

Looking up at him, Cait felt her heart jolt at the tenderness in his warm gaze. "I shouldn't be upset," she whispered. "He was just trying to be a good friend."

A flicker of irritation flashed across his face as he turned to the sea. "He doesn't have a clue." He dug his nail into the leather of his boots. "He's known you for all of what? Five days? And he thinks he knows how to take care of you?"

At the tension in his tone, Cait studied Desmond's profile, searching for the source of his frustration. It couldn't be jealousy. Desmond wasn't jealous of anyone.

Unable to deduce what he was thinking, Cait followed his gaze, watching as a boat pulled into port. "He's not from here," she reminded them both. "There's no way he could understand why. . . ."

She drifted off, letting the unspoken hang between them.

After a long pause, Desmond adjusted to stretch his legs out in front of him. As he set his hands behind him, his arm brushed hers. "You need to be careful with him, Caity." He practically whispered the warning.

Out of her peripheral, she saw Desmond wet his lips. Cait decided that she'd sat under the HVAC for an appropriately long enough time to require her own adjustments. She shifted so that her knee rested against the side of his leg.

Desmond didn't flinch, but she caught the subtle twitch of his lips. The faintest hint of his smirk before he buried it. He was good at that—burying his emotions. Pretending that he didn't feel anything strongly or deeply.

Cait knew it was all a lie, just like the act they put on for the town. Desmond was good at pretending. She was good at it too.

"You don't have to worry about Matt," she promised, knowing he would hear the double meaning.

He didn't have to worry because she would no more let Matt hurt her than she would let him replace Desmond.

However nice Matt was, he was not the person she trusted. He wasn't the one who caused her heart to stir and set her mind to humming with his very presence. He wasn't the one she wanted.

Desmond did smirk then. He looked over at Cait, one eyebrow cocked teasingly. "Trust me," he bumped his shoulder forward into hers, "I'm not worried about Mattie."

Staring up into his eyes, the hum pressed in on Cait's senses. Her skin crawled with gooseflesh, the hairs on her arms rising as though he wore an electrical field around him. She couldn't help her slight lean in his direction, like some invisible force was drawing her into him.

His brown eyes dropped from her face for a fraction of a second. Then he reached across and grabbed one of the strings hanging from Cait's collar. "Pink really is a good color for you, Lewan," he said, twisting the string around his finger. It lifted the collar from her clavicle the smallest fraction. In his proximity, her senses were sharper than usual, and she could feel the slight breeze that brushed through. "It shows off how easily you blush."

Cait felt her cheeks flush, and he grinned. "Just like that," he teased.

Desmond released the string and tapped her cheek with two of his fingers. "Come on, Caity," he said, beginning to push himself off the ground. "We've got classes to get to."

Watching him rise, Cait waited for her heart to still. Small touches. That was all she had. Small, innocent flirtations that wouldn't ever amount to anything and a furious rumble in her chest that demanded more.

Cait rose, passed the key off to Desmond, and left first. They always came and went from the rooftop separately. Everything between them was handled with great care. Their meetings. Their messages. Their conversation. Their connection.

Small moments, small exchanges, and small touches. That was all Cait would ever have with Desmond. And as with everything else, she pretended that it was enough.

Cait

Matt apologized over and over for the rest of the school day. While he plainly didn't understand why standing up for her had made her so upset, he insisted that he had to make it up to her. "Could I—well, are you still okay to show me around town this afternoon?" he asked.

"Of course I am," Cait promised. Though she hadn't fully gotten over the embarrassment he'd caused her, she couldn't hold it against him.

Matt sighed in relief. "Well, in that case, would it be okay if I bought you something? Like ice cream or chocolate or something. I mean, if you like dessert. Do you like ice cream?"

With a small smile, Cait nodded. "I love ice cream."

"Good," Matt replied. "I'll buy you ice cream then. To make up for it."

"You don't have to do that, Matt."

"I want to," he said, that puppy dog look of his making him pitifully impossible to say no to.

Cait acquiesced.

"Awesome! Well, I've got to take the bus home so that I can get my bike," he said. "Do you want to ride back with me?"

"What would I do with my bike, then?" Cait asked.

"Oh, good point." Matt frowned, trying to work through the predicament.

Cait took care of it for him. She told him to ride the bus home, get his bike, and then meet her at Seahorse Park, the tiny, sea-themed playground on the edge of town. Though Matt looked disappointed at this option, she promised she didn't mind waiting for him, brandishing her sketchbook as proof.

After the final bell rang, they split paths. He headed for the bright yellow buses, and she went toward the bike rack. Cait had just bent to unlock her bike when she heard her name called. Looking over her shoulder in surprise, she felt her breath catch as Hunter Varon jogged across the paved entryway. His typical posse of Elizabeth, Scott, Melissa, and Sterling continued walking toward the parking lot, sending Cait cautious glances.

Straightening, Cait watched Hunter approach. He brushed a hand through his waves, pushing them away from his face. That nervous smile was back on his face. "Hey, do you have a second?" he asked.

Cait gave a quick look at his friends, now nearly to their cars. No one else was around; the majority of the students were either on the buses or on their way home. Genni's bike was already gone, too, off to spend the afternoon with Jared and Alexis, leaving Cait with no hope of escaping the conversation.

"What's up?" she said, bike lock hanging from her hand.

Scratching his scruffy jawline, Hunter appraised Cait. "It's just—" He scoffed in an almost apologetic way. "I'm sorry about lunch. I really didn't mean to cause trouble. I just wanted to make sure the new kid felt welcome."

Cait shifted her stance. "I know."

"Yeah?"

She nodded.

"Okay, cool," he said, though his tone was still tight. "Also, I—I want you to know that we *are* happy to have you here too. I was thrown off by his question, but . . . well, it isn't like we believe the rumors, Liz and I. And if you wanted, we'd be happy to be your friends. We just never tried before because we always assumed you preferred to be alone."

Perhaps it was how forced the offer felt or how he couldn't quite meet her gaze while he made it, but Cait found herself growing annoyed. "Why would you think that?" she almost demanded.

Hunter looked caught off guard. "Well . . . I mean, you've—you've always been quiet and—and distant, so—well, it was just kind of the natural thing to assume."

Cait didn't think it was natural at all. "Maybe I was distant because no one ever talked to me," she countered.

Shame crossed Hunter's expression as he swallowed. "Yeah, I see your point. It's just—" He paused to glance around them, then took a step closer and dropped his voice. "I mean, you know I'm Warden, right?"

Understanding dawned in an instant.

Cait raised her chin defensively. "Yes."

Hunter nodded as though they were sharing some newfound connection. "It's my family's job to protect the spirit world," he said.

Cait wanted to roll her eyes. It was the *Simon* family's job to protect the spirit world. The Varons in Porthaven had lost that privilege over a century ago.

He continued, unaware of the issue she took with his claim. "So, it's difficult—knowing about your past in a way others don't," he said. His shoulders drew back with a lift of pride like he was the most enlightened member of Porthaven. "I know about everything that happened in Ireland, and . . . well, it isn't a coincidence, you having been brought here."

That was the wrong thing to say.

With a snarl, Cait glared up at Hunter. "*Everything* is a coincidence," she shot back, her Irish accent slipping in. Even as she tried to shove it down, it affected several of her words. "My sisters and I are in Porthaven because, by some remarkable concurrence of events, the Warden decided *this* was the safest place for us. That's a coincidence. You even talking to me is a coincidence."

Hunter began to shake his head, opening his mouth in rebuttal, but Cait kept going. "You're only out here because Matt said something, coincidentally making you feel guilty," she accused. "*Coincidentally—remarkably*—leading you to talk to me for the first time in twelve years."

The flare of her anger blazed within Cait's cheeks. Her ears roared with boiling-over emotion as Hunter gaped at her.

A sudden cooling tingle raced up Cait's spine, the hum sending a cascade of emotion coursing down her body. Desmond was there, Brady at his side. "Everything all right over here?" he asked, a tinge of protectiveness in his tone.

Cait began to shake. Whether it was from the anger she felt or the suddenness of his presence, she couldn't tell.

Pressing his lips together, Hunter drew back a step. "Yeah, Simon, everything is fine," he grumbled.

"I wasn't asking you," Desmond returned, then looked to Cait. She felt her shoulders draw in as he scanned her. "You setting up a pattern, Lewan? How many times am I gonna have to stand up to bullies for you this year?"

"It's fine," Cait muttered, doing her best to avoid Desmond's gaze. It was always so difficult to make the switch from who they were in private to who they were supposed to be in public. It was even harder when she'd lost control of her emotions. "Hunter was just apologizing."

"Wow." Desmond huffed. "This the first time you've ever admitted to being wrong, Hunter?"

"Sometimes it pays to be humble, Simon," Hunter retorted. He turned to Cait. "I meant what I said. You're welcome to sit with Liz and me in the future."

"Thanks," Cait mumbled just before Hunter pushed past Desmond, their shoulders connecting in a threatening shove.

Desmond held his ground, hardly even shifting at the impact. "See you tomorrow, Hunt," he called with a thread of sarcasm.

Hunter didn't look back but raised a hand to flip Desmond off.

With a snort of humor, Desmond glanced at Brady over his shoulder. "I think that's his way of saying he'll miss me."

Brady nodded, an even-tempered grin on his face. "Most definitely."

Chuckling, Desmond turned back to Cait. "Moving up in the world, Lewan?"

Still working to tame her anger, Cait kept her steely glare on her backpack, shoving in the bike lock. She didn't know why he kept doing this. He was playing a dangerous game for both of them, inserting himself into her life. It wasn't like he'd stepped up in the past. People would figure it out if he kept coming to her defense.

"Lewan," he prodded.

"I'm late," she mumbled, pulling her bike from the rack as she prepared to leave.

Desmond set a hand on the center of the handle, holding her in place. He dipped his head down, angling his body so that Brady couldn't see the concerned expression on his face even as he kept his voice at a normal volume. His dark eyes locked with hers, pleading. "Seriously, I can't keep interfering for you," he said. "You're either gonna have to stand up for yourself, or I'm gonna have to let it happen."

Shooting a nervous look Brady's way, Cait tightened her jaw. "I get it. Can I go, please?"

A flash of something—was that hurt or simply confusion?—pulled at Desmond's expression before he regained his composure. He released her bike, and Cait immediately pushed off. She had to get away from him and the hum howling through her head. She kept such a tight leash on her emotions, working so hard to avoid upsetting the balance of her life. With all the secrets, with all the rumors, with all the horrors of her dreams and memories, Cait knew one thing she could count on to be steady in her life: If she remained invisible, she remained in control.

No one could push her into those wild reactions. No one could fault her for her tame manner. No one could name her as the bearer of her father's curse.

The hum receded, the waves of emotion steadying as she peddled toward the center of town. The salty-fish air cooled her face as the late summer sun warmed her back. The farther from Desmond she got, the more control she regained. And as she coasted up to the park, she took her first clear breath.

Cait walked her bike to the public rack, caging the remainder of her anger and all those other unruly feelings with it.

~

By the time Matt rode into town, Cait was back to her usual docile self.

She sat on the bench, charcoal pencil in hand, pleasantly sketching the horns of the lizard-like monster from her dream last night. At the approaching *whiz* of Matt's bike, she shut the book and returned it to her backpack. Once he'd locked his bike alongside hers, he turned to her. "So, I guess we just start here?" he asked.

Cait looked across the short distance between the playground and the streets of Porthaven proper. Sea-weathered roofs and brightly painted businesses lay to their left. On the far side of the road was the more sophisticated side of downtown. Flower boxes and trees lined both sides of the street, giving the town a homey quality.

"It's as good a start as any," Cait supposed.

As she slung her backpack over one shoulder, Matt eyed her nervously. "Oh, uh—I could, uh—I could carry that for you if you like? I should have offered to take it home with me, but I didn't think about it."

"That's okay," Cait replied, her grip firm on the strap. "I keep it light."

Matt pressed his lips into a line, a strange set coming into his jaw. Even after only a few days of knowing him, Cait had learned what that look of his meant: He wanted to say something but felt he couldn't. Or possibly shouldn't.

In this case, he was right.

Moving for the main road, Cait intentionally left the conversation behind them. "This is Lawrence Avenue," she explained. They stepped onto the concrete sidewalks, little pebbles and seashells embedded in their surface. "The highway leads here, and the rest of downtown branches off of the avenue. So, most people will give you directions in relation to Lawrence Ave."

Cait's phone buzzed in her jacket pocket, distracting her as Matt asked, "Does the name Lawrence have any significance?"

Attempting a nonchalant glance at her phone, Cait read the text notification on the screen: *"You okay?"*

Throat going dry, Cait felt immediately guilty. She shouldn't have gotten so upset with Desmond. What reason did she have to be angry with him anyway? He'd been trying to help her out. And now, he was checking on her.

"Cait?" Matt prodded, an unsure lift to his voice.

"Huh? Oh, sorry." Cait slipped the phone back into her pocket. She was smart enough not to have explicitly named Desmond on her phone. She'd simply saved his contact as "S" for Simon and left it at that. But she didn't want Matt to see and ask about it.

"I don't actually know," she answered, deflecting from the text. "From what I've heard, there's never been anyone with the name Lawrence in Porthaven—as a first or last name."

Matt appeared more interested in asking about her distraction than the town, but he did that funny thing with his jaw and moved on. "Mkay, so Lawrence Avenue is the true north of Porthaven," he summarized. "What are all these buildings on it?"

"Well, that—" Cait pointed to the largest building several yards ahead on their right, "is the town hall." The white brick and columned façade stood out starkly against the more cottage-like shops and offices around it. Its large parking lot held dozens of vehicles, most notably a shiny, black muscle car.

"The rest are different shops and businesses," she explained. "If you follow the avenue all the way to the end, you'll run into Warf Way, which is how you get to the docks."

"That's sort of on the nose, isn't it?" Matt said with a grin.

Cait smiled. "Our town has a knack for cheesy street names and slogans."

"Like 'the salt-swept shores of serenity'?" Matt offered.

Laughing at the ridiculous town motto, Cait nodded. "Exactly like that."

As they continued their tour, Cait led Matt all through Porthaven's downtown. Fluffy clouds drifted across the blue sky, the sunshine keeping them warm as they explored. They went to the right first, through the officious side of town. It held the church and the school, the post office and the clinic, as well as the most luxurious neighborhood in town.

Vintage-style black streetlamps lined the sidewalk. Every house had a white picket fence, a lush front lawn filled with flowering bushes and delicate lawn ornaments, and a columned porch with elegant furnishings. There were less than twenty homes in all. Only the oldest and most prestigious families lived on Osprey Street.

"These houses are . . ." Matt paused, marveling at their old yet immaculate edifices. "They're beautiful!"

Cait ran her fingers over the metal house number on the fence post at her side. "Yeah," she murmured with a small smile. "This one's the mayor's house."

Ever dramatic as his expressions were, Matt stared up at the building wide-eyed. The mayor's home had always been Cait's favorite in town. Though similar to the other houses on Osprey, something about the Simon home felt different. Perhaps the ferns hung from the covered porch gave its colonial design that distinctly homey feel. Or maybe the white-painted swing hung off to the side, light blue pillows resting against each arm, lent it an especially inviting presence. It could have been the charming blue hydrangea bushes that lined the front like large poofs.

Cait told herself it wasn't because of Desmond.

Above the black door, a wooden lintel bore the etching of a V superimposed over a large, multi-point star, a heraldic hound emblazed in its center. The Latin words *"Omnes pro Christo"* rested under the sigil. For her whole life here in Porthaven, she'd wondered what it looked like beyond that door and those hurricane shutters. She imagined magazine-worthy rooms filled with lavishly beautiful decorations and amazingly comfortable furnishings. She knew she'd never know for sure.

"What's with the V?" Matt asked, his voice quiet as though worried they'd be overheard by the residents.

Knowing that no one was home, Cait moved on anyway. Her fingers caught on each spoke of the fence as they walked. "Well, the founders of Porthaven were Varons, like Hunter's family."

Matt nodded in understanding.

"And they built that house." She gestured back toward the front gate. "It's why the house number is 1775. That's when they built Porthaven."

"That's when the Revolutionary War started," Matt remarked, an awed glimmer in his eyes. "They were building a town in the midst of that?"

Cait shrugged. She didn't know much more about the history, only the little snippets she'd picked up from Desmond and the rest of the townspeople. "I guess they were," she said. "Though the house wasn't built at that time. I think that was a decade or so later. But it *was* the first mayor's house. And they've passed it down from generation to generation since."

"And they became Simons along the way?" Matt surmised. "Makes sense, I guess."

Continuing the walk back out of the neighborhood, Cait did her best to deviate away from the history of the town. "This is sort of the lame part of town, so that's why I started with it. The other half is filled with cool shops and restaurants and other, much more interesting things."

Matt followed Cait's lead happily, hands tucked into his jeans pockets. A light breeze followed them through the streets, ruffling their hair. She pointed out Aster Island in the distance, the white lighthouse standing tall, the sunlight glinting off the glass of the lantern room. Next, she guided him through the streets, showing him the library, the pharmacy, which still held a traditional soda fountain, the old-fashioned diner, the confectionary shop, the bookstore, the butcher and charcuterie shop, the fromagerie, and all the other little businesses that she liked best.

"Do you ever get used to the fish smell?" Matt asked as they crossed the street.

"What do you mean?" Cait asked.

"I *mean*—" He raised his eyebrows. "It smells like fish. *Everywhere*."

Cait sniffed the air instinctively. She supposed it did hold a particularly pungent tang of fish. "I guess I've never noticed," she admitted.

That answer didn't appease Matt, but the next shop they came across distracted him. Short and squat, plant life covered the rich green siding. Its casement windows were open; a pungent aroma of herbs and incense drifted out onto the street. Windchimes hung all over the front, each plinking out their individual, merry, discordant tunes.

Attempting to speed up her pace, Cait kept going while Matt slowed down. "What's this?" he asked.

Determined not to be drawn into the shop, Cait unwillingly slowed with him. "Hm? Oh, it's nothing. Just a—a tea shop."

"Tea?" Matt furrowed his brow. "Are people that into tea in Porthaven?"

Cait shrugged, inching backward in hopes that Matt would follow. "I think she sells other things too. I wouldn't know. I've never been inside."

"Why not? It looks kind of cool." He gave the building another once-over. "Kinda creepy, but cool."

Growing desperate, Cait tried taking another step away. "I suppose. Did you still want to get that ice cream?"

Matt caught her discomfort then. His face screwed up in surprise, but he began walking toward her. "What is it?" he almost whispered as they moved away from the shop. "Why don't you like that place?"

Cait swallowed, trying to appear nonchalant. "Nothing. I just—I don't really care to go inside."

"What's wrong with tea?"

"Nothing," she repeated. "It's only—there are some rumors about the owner. I haven't met her personally or anything, so I don't know if they're true, but . . . well, I know that you can't take rumors at face value, but I also know that people like to talk, and . . ."

Cait looked back over her shoulder at the building. "I don't think it'd be a good idea for me to go in."

Matt tugged on the hem of his graphic tee. "For you specifically?"

"And my sisters."

"Because . . . ?"

"Because they claim that the owner is a witch," she explained.

Matt gaped at her. "What is it with this town and witches? Do you really believe they're real?"

Cait shrugged. "I'm not sure it matters if I think they're real or not," she said. "The people of Porthaven believe that my da was a witch, and they believe that Lilith—the owner of that shop—is a witch. If I or any of my sisters went into her shop, it'd be as good as confirming that they're right."

"That seems . . . wrong."

Cait didn't respond.

Matt scratched his head, tousling his mop of hair. "So . . . do you believe in witches?"

Keeping her gaze on the sidewalk beneath their feet, Cait avoided the cracks out of sentiment more than superstition. "I don't know," she murmured. "I mean, I know there are people out there who claim that they're witches, but . . . I don't know if I believe they can actually do magic."

"Hm." Matt looked back over his shoulder, keeping stride with her. "Well, I don't. I think it's like most of the spooky stuff in the world, ya know? Made up to explain the weird stuff that happens."

"What do you mean?"

"Like, random stuff. We always think everything has some major meaning, but . . . what if it doesn't? What if shadows that seem to move are just our imagination or a trick of light? What if all the unexplained stuff in the world has no explanation?" Matt pressed his lips together as his shoulders rose in a self-conscious shrug. "I dunno. It just seems to me that stuff happens all the time without a greater reason."

Thinking of her conversation with Hunter earlier, Cait played with the strap of her backpack. "You mean like coincidences?"

Matt kicked a loose pebble on the sidewalk. "I guess." He opened his mouth to say more, then shook his head.

"What?" Cait prodded.

"Nah, it's—you won't wanna hear about it."

"Why not?"

Matt's chin nearly brushed his chest with how low it dropped. "It—it's personal."

"Oh." Cait felt an inexplicable blend of relief and curiosity from his silence. She gave him a sidelong glance. "Do you *want* to tell me about it?"

"I don't wanna bug you with it," he muttered.

"That's okay," she promised. "I've bugged you with my family's curse."

"Rumored curse," he corrected.

She nodded in assent.

Matt sighed, shoving his hands back into his pockets. "Okay, well . . .

if I wind up annoying you, tell me to shut up, all right? I kinda want to talk about it, but I don't want to dump on you or anything."

"All right," Cait assured him.

After one final nervous glance, Matt began. "So, the reason my mom and I moved to Porthaven is because my parents got a divorce," he explained. "My dad's in the Air Force, and well, he wasn't around a ton. But when he was, it was always great. Or at least, *I* thought it was.

"Anyway, when my parents told Kelly and me that they were getting a divorce—" He scowled as though hearing it for the first time again. "I couldn't believe it. I thought we were happy. And it just seemed so . . . pointless. Like, Mom and Dad were perfect for each other. Everyone said so."

Cait watched carefully as Matt scrubbed a hand over his face. "They'd been together since college," he went on. "The story was always 'love at first sight.' Dad saw Mom, and the stars aligned. They'd been married for almost twenty-three years. So, what was the point, ya know? What was the point of any of it if the stars that aligned all those years ago suddenly unaligned twenty years later?"

Without an answer for him, Cait just walked silently at his side. She knew better than to apologize. People liked to apologize for things that weren't their fault. It made them feel better—like they were doing something. But it never helped the person who was hurting.

It never made the pain easier to handle.

Coming to the corner of the street, Cait paused to look over at Matt. "I think you're right," she said. "I think there are some things in life that have no explanation. And other things that—that may have a form of explanation to them but no real reason."

Sheepishly, Matt met her gaze. "Like your parents' deaths?"

Unable to form words, Cait simply nodded.

Matt mimicked her somberly, lips pressed together.

Aware of the dark mood that had found them, Cait nudged Matt's elbow. "I have one last place to show you," she said.

His puppy dog eyes scanned her. "Oh, yeah?"

"This way," Cait summoned, heading off toward the docks. She led him down the street to the very edge of town. A small shack sat at the end of the road, its aged wood covered in peeling, banana-yellow paint. Over the singular opening at the front of the shack hung a sign that read, "Salty's Scoops."

Matt chuckled, surveying the tiny ice cream hut. "A deal's a deal, huh?" he said.

Cait smiled. "I'll never turn down ice cream."

CHAPTER EIGHT

Desmond

All afternoon at his internship, Desmond kept checking his phone. He truly was worried about Cait. There had been bad days in the past, days when the kids at school said cruel things or made their dislike abnormally blatant. But she knew how to handle that sort of offhanded bullying: Smother it, bury it, and forget it.

Desmond had watched Cait for the past eleven years, ten months, and twenty-two days. He'd watched from a distance at first and then from the strange vantage of her secret confidant. He'd learned how quietly strong and brave she was and the stoic way she handled the misery that filled her life. Her meekness, her self-containment, her isolation—it was self-inflicted. Even Therese and Genevieve had made friends, the elder catching the eye of Ryan Greene and the younger living carefree of their family's stigma.

Only Cait held onto the curse like it was a lifeline. Only she kept herself solitary and excluded. No matter the bad behavior of the Porthaven townspeople, Cait worsened the situation by intentionally distancing herself from them.

And after a decade of listening to the real voice of Caitriona Lewan, Desmond knew it was because she was afraid of herself. She was afraid to make friends and build a life because what would happen if it was all taken away from her again? What would happen if she proved the rumors right? What if she really was cursed?

A phantom vibration in Desmond's pocket had him slipping his phone out again. He pressed his lips together, realizing that it was only his imagination. This Matt kid was ruining everything. If it wasn't for him, Cait wouldn't have been thrust into the spotlight today. She would have been able to keep to the shadows as she liked, protected from the social demands she found so frightening.

Desmond shoved his phone back in his pocket, internally grumbling to himself. He could still see the way Cait looked, contending with Hunter, cheeks blazing red, her lips curled into a snarl. Her anger had leaped through the air, snapping taut. And he knew she'd been mortified by it.

He didn't care that she'd snapped at him too. She deserved to be angry. At Matt, at Hunter, and at him. He shouldn't have stepped in. He shouldn't have gotten involved. The more he put himself in Cait's presence, the more likely he'd draw attention to them. To her. And she didn't want that.

There'd been a time at the start of high school when Desmond had considered bringing Cait into his friend group. He'd thought it would be good for her to have people around her. And it would have been another jab at his father, which would have been good for him.

He hadn't done it, all for one reason: Cait would hate it.

Being part of Desmond's crew meant popularity. It meant limelight and attention. It meant that everyone would be looking at her even more than they already were. Cait could hide in solitude; Desmond's presence brought her to center stage. And he wouldn't do that to her, no matter how much he wanted to stick it to his father. No matter how much he wanted to keep her around.

It did worry Desmond that she hadn't responded to his text message. She never ghosted him like this. It could take him hours to break free to reply to her. But Cait? She didn't have near the social life that he did. He was always surrounded by people. She could readily escape to reply in secret.

The school day had ended two hours ago. Now, Desmond was finishing up his internship, and still nothing. He checked his phone again just to be sure. The only notifications were a text from his mom reminding him about some social obligation and a handful of memes that Brady and Garrett had sent him on social media.

Desmond pulled up his text messenger, double-checking to be sure his message went through. He'd named her contact "school project girl." That way, if anyone asked him who he was texting or saw his phone, he could say, "Oh, just this girl from school that I'm working on a project with." Thankfully, in the mere handful of times he'd been caught, no one had ever bothered to ask him her name.

As Desmond resigned himself to the fact that Cait simply hadn't replied to his text, the door to the clerk's office opened, and his father walked in. Desmond did most of his internship here, organizing files and entering data for the clerk. Records that his dad didn't want the regular government workers handling. Things that dealt with the Warden.

William held the door open and halted just over the threshold. He caught Desmond's gaze and raised a hand to beckon to him.

"My shift just ended," Desmond said, slinging his backpack over his shoulder.

"Something's come up," William replied cryptically.

Desmond sighed. "Should I clock back in?" He didn't get paid for his time working for the government. It all went toward his school record, earning him credit with the potential universities his dad might send him to.

"No," he said, tone flat and dull. "This doesn't have to do with your internship."

Certain he was in for a scolding, Desmond racked his brain for what sins he'd committed recently. It was getting harder to filch liquor these days—the government workers were getting wise to his schemes. However, he'd snuck out a half-full bottle of gin at the end of last week, but no one seemed to notice. Maybe they'd finally discovered the graffiti he'd left under the table in the council chamber three years ago: *"Property of Mayor Buttmon."* Fourteen-year-old Desmond had been particularly proud of that one. Seventeen-year-old Desmond found the comedic creativity lacking but the overall execution impressive. It'd taken them this long to find it, after all.

Following his dad out of the clerk's office, they passed into the town hall's foyer. Men and women in business casual suits moved for the front door, calling their farewells at the closing of the typical workday. Going against the crowd toward the second floor, they headed for the mayor's office.

William's dress shoes and Desmond's boots gave off contradictory clacks and slaps to the tiled floors. They continued down the hall, rows of windows keeping the space bright and cheery. The large, lacquered wood door of the mayor's office was original to the first iteration of the town hall. Over the years, they'd renovated the building, adding the second and third floors and expanding onto the back. But this door, hewn from the black cherry trees of the Porthaven forests, had passed from mayor to mayor. Varon to Simon.

Desmond stepped into the well-known office. He'd been inside these white walls—decorated by molding, photos, and certificates—nearly as much as the school. At the massive partner desk—made of the same cherry wood as the door—a gray-bearded man sat in one of the visitors' chairs.

In an instant, Desmond recognized the grizzled face of Fischer Lavigne, the lightkeeper of Porthaven. More commonly known as "Fish," the man lived in a small cottage on Aster Island. Brady's Great-Uncle Fish had inherited the care of the lighthouse from his father. His weathered, sun-tanned skin, burly and imposing frame, and thick, silver-streaked, shoulder-length hair gave him the unkempt, crazed look that Desmond thought any lightkeeper worth his salt should have.

Fish rose from his seat as the men entered, his flannel shirt bunching under the fleece-lined jacket he wore. He turned his fearsome blue glare on Desmond, overgrown salt-and-pepper eyebrows low. "You're looking skinny, boy," he charged.

With a smirk, Desmond returned the man's inspection. "You're looking fat, old man."

Fish's hearty, raspy laugh filled the room as William moved around the desk to his tufted leather chair. Fish clasped one of Desmond's shoulders in his decidedly bear-like hands—or paws, if you were following the metaphor, Desmond supposed. "Always a pleasure, kid," the lightkeeper said.

"Likewise," Desmond returned. He'd always had a soft spot for the lightkeeper. He and Brady used to visit the island regularly, helping the man tend to the grounds. It was his unofficial internship when he'd been too young to have a real one.

"You said you have news, Fischer," William said, calling the meeting to order.

Both Fish and Desmond took the two visitors' seats.

"It's not good," Fish said. The lightkeeper's voice carried a pleasant growl despite his ominous words. Desmond always thought he'd been born to tell stories with that voice. And he was awfully good at them—particularly when they involved ghosts and beasts.

"What *is* it?" William prodded.

The slant of Fish's gaze said he didn't appreciate the impatient prompting. "It's suspicious activity; that's what it is," he replied. "At first, I thought it was some animals stirring before hibernation. A last-minute effort to prepare. But then I realized: They were too big."

"The animals?"

Fish nodded. "The markings, the tracks they left behind—all too big to be the island's furbearers. We don't have anything bigger than a coyote on occasion. The island's too small. And for that matter," he went on, leaning forward in his chair, "the wildlife's been acting up. The birds left earlier than normal, but I chalked it up to early migration. However, the furbearers are behaving strangely too—like they're cowering from something."

A faint tension seeped into the room at the news, and Desmond looked at his dad. William sat upright in his chair, hand running along his smooth jawline. "Beasts?" he asked.

"That's my guess," Fish said.

"Have you seen any?"

"Not yet."

Desmond furrowed his brow. "How do you know it's beasts then? What if it's just another animal coming in and stirring up the others?"

Fish fixed him with a wry stare. "Think about it, kid," he charged. "A creature that big would have had to work its way through town, then trek across the rock bridge or through the sea. What large animal do you know that could make that journey without getting spotted at least once?"

An almost annoyed sigh escaped William. "It has to be a beast."

"Or multiple of 'em," Fish added.

Desmond shook his head in awe. "That would mean someone's summoning them."

Fish gave him a singular, cynical nod.

"Have you had any visitors to the island recently?" William asked.

"Nope," Fish assured him immediately. "I've not seen anyone come or go from the island in weeks. Granted, I'm not there 100% of the time. Occasionally, I visit my boys or Ben and his family. But I've seen no signs of trespassers on the grounds of the lighthouse or in the woods."

William looked toward Desmond, a question plain in his stare.

"Everyone at school knows better than to go to the island," he told his dad. "Most of the elementary kids are too scared of Fish to even consider it, while the high schoolers know there's nothing to see there anyway."

"You haven't heard of any secret meetups?" William pressed.

"Trust me," he returned. "We delinquents find better, easier places to sneak off to on the mainland."

Fish snorted. "It isn't foolhardy teens, William. It's a Wielder."

Watching his dad carefully, Desmond worked not to flinch at the term. It was so rare to hear. Nearly as rare as actually seeing someone wield the spirit world itself—in any form, be that interaction with ghosts, controlling beasts, or conjuring its very essence. In Porthaven, they took great pains not to speak of the spirit world. It was their job to protect it, and they did that by keeping it quiet.

Only a small fraction of the town knew of its existence to begin with. The Warden had started Porthaven with the Varons, Lavignes, Edgars, Greenes, Abbeys, Toussaints, and Faulks. These days, the Abbeys and Toussaints had fallen out of the loop, and the Simons had earned their place at the head.

The Warden's presence in Porthaven focused on one thing: containment. How best could they keep the spirit world from affecting the lives of the innocent? How did they protect it from misuse? The safest method was to forbid dabbling in the spirit world at all. They'd concluded that only the most devout were to be trusted, leaving the wielding of the spirit world to the Lavignes as the religious leaders of the town. Not even the Varons got a pass.

Desmond flexed his hand, thinking about how he regularly summoned Hades—a beast, albeit a tame one. Though he supposed all beasts were tame if their summoner required them to be. But that was why he had to keep Hades a secret. He didn't want to imagine the consequences that he'd earn if his dad found out that he was wielding.

"Are you accusing a member of your own family, Fischer?" William asked.

"I don't have enough evidence to accuse anyone, William," Fish countered. "All I know is that there are beasts on my island, and we know that isn't possible unless someone is summoning them."

As William considered this predicament, Desmond tried to puzzle out who could possibly be at fault. There was, of course, the chance that one of the other Warden members was secretly wielding like him. Maybe one of the kids at school *was* sneaking over to the island to practice.

Desmond shook off the ridiculous idea. The only options were Brady, Garrett, Hunter, Elizabeth, Scott, or one of their younger siblings—and none of them made sense. Brady and his younger sister were Lavignes, so they could wield all they wanted and not get in trouble. Garrett was, honestly, too stupid to care about wielding. Hunter and his sister were too sanctimonious, Elizabeth too holier-than-thou, and Scott . . . well, Scott *might* do it, just for fun. But even that seemed far-fetched.

Then the thought struck Desmond: There were two other options.

"Do you think—it couldn't be one of the Faulks or Lewans, right?" Desmond asked, a sense of dread crawling over his shoulders at the thought.

Fish looked at William for an answer.

"Doubtful," the mayor finally said, his deep voice thick with consideration. "Their blocks are too strong. Regardless, the Faulks have always been compliant. I don't see why they'd change now. And the Lewans. . . ."

Desmond didn't like how his father paused there, as though there was more to consider with the Lewans.

William shook his head. "We were intentional. The Lewans' blocks are secure, and their knowledge is limited. Whatever they know, it isn't enough to be summoning beasts."

"What about the witch?" Fish asked.

Desmond raised his brow. He hadn't thought about Lilith Drake.

"She isn't a witch," William said, a flat edge to his words. "She's an ex-Druid. That's quite different."

"Makes her a good suspect, though, doesn't it?" Fish suggested.

Desmond thought the lightkeeper had a point. The once-Druid had come to Porthaven fifteen years ago, begging for sanctuary in exchange for information regarding the cult's dealings. She'd claimed to have been raised within Druidism, and she'd finally grown the strength to leave her family and the cult in fear for her life. She knew that the Warden fought against the Druids, so she'd come to Porthaven and offered to tell them everything she knew if they'd let her live within their borders and under their protective banner.

A great debate sprang up amongst the Warden members. Many of them didn't want to allow any Druid into their town, be she reformed or not. But Brady's grandfather, Thomas, spoke in Lilith's favor. *"Is it not our call to forgive?"* he'd charged, according to the story. *"Does Christ not offer the undeserving mercy?"*

So, the town had allowed Lilith Drake sanctuary. However, they hadn't taken her up on her offer of information. It had been Desmond's own grandfather, Charles, who'd stated, *"Mercy does not mean trust. You may live amongst us, but you will never be one of us."*

Once Charles Simon had retired, passing the mayoral position to William, there had been a shift in the agreement. While Desmond's dad didn't trust Lilith any more than his father, neither was he as cruelly hardheaded. William had met with Lilith, apologizing for his father's nasty remarks, and assured her that she was a valued member of their community. There would be no exchange of information, but neither would they treat her as an outcast.

Desmond didn't think the rest of the town had gotten the memo on that one.

And if there was anyone summoning beasts, Desmond thought the ex-Druid was likely the best place to start.

William didn't seem to agree. "I don't think it's wise to go around accusing anyone just yet," he said. "First, I will contact Sheriff Edgars and have him open an investigation. Tomorrow, he, Desmond, and I will join you on the island to see what we can find."

A wave of shock rolled through Desmond. "I—I'm going?"

"Yes," his dad said with little emotion. "It will be good for you to get some firsthand experience at what it means to protect this town. Perhaps it will give you a sense of purpose for once."

"I doubt that," Desmond retorted, then added, "I have school tomorrow," as though he didn't skip at least a handful of times a month.

"I'll handle that."

"You might want to bring Ben as well," Fish suggested. "Just 'cause it's daylight doesn't mean the beasts won't come out in the cover of the forest. And I don't care to be the only one fighting off a potential horde of scylla."

Desmond smirked at the lightkeeper. "You pick scylla for any particular reason?"

"We're holding the Leviathan captive, kid," he replied, a lighthearted tilt to his growl. "It's only natural to assume that's what we're facing, right?"

William didn't share Desmond's amusement. "Very well," the mayor said. "I'll get with Ben and Rick tonight, and the four of us will be on the island first thing tomorrow morning."

Fish gave one of his sharp nods before pushing out of his chair with a grunt. He adjusted his corduroy jacket, its hem fraying. He muttered his pleasantries, slapped Desmond on the back of the head, and walked out of the office.

Brushing down his ruffled hair, Desmond turned to his dad. William's dark eyes were trained on the desktop, his hand back on his jaw.

"Why are you really including me in this?" Desmond found himself asking.

William's gaze flashed up, locking with his. "You're nearly eighteen, Desmond."

"Sure, but I've still got at least twenty more years until you retire, right?" He shrugged. "Why rush it?"

A strange expression came to his dad's face at that, some unreadable emotion that made Desmond squirm in his seat.

Drawing in a deep breath, William's hand dropped to the arm of his chair. "I know I'm not the most . . . affectionate father. I'm aware that you and I have had our differences." His thick eyebrows pulled together with earnest intensity. "But what's between us—this is child's play, Desmond. My father was cruel. He was vindictive. He was harsh and calculating, and he was ruthless because the Varons were trying to steal our lineage from us."

William adjusted the Varon ring on his right ring finger. "I understood his reasons, but I hated him, nonetheless. I don't want you to say the same of me."

Unable to hold his dad's gaze any longer, Desmond stared at his hands clasped between his knees.

"Whatever you think of me now," William continued despite his silence, "I am not satisfied to remain your adversary. I want the best for you, Desmond. And if I'm hard on you, it's because I know you can be better. I know you aren't giving your life all that you have to offer."

Slouching in his chair, Desmond worked to keep from fidgeting.

"I want our relationship to be different than the one I had with my father," William concluded. "I want to work *with* you for the whole of my career. I consider this the start of that."

A fist clamped over Desmond's heart as though to tear it up his chest, through his throat, and out his mouth. He didn't think he could speak for fear that he'd say something caustic. His dad wanted to work *with* him, did he? He wanted to see Desmond be his best? Maybe he should have remembered that Desmond was still a kid. Maybe he should have cut his child some slack for not reaching his "full potential."

Swallowing around his agitation, Desmond managed to grind out, "Can I go?"

Though he didn't look at his dad, he could feel disappointment flowing through the charged atmosphere. "Yes," William replied, his tone deadpan.

"Great." Desmond shoved himself up from the chair and pushed through the door.

CHAPTER NINE

Cait

The first thing Cait did the next morning was pick up her phone. She'd unintentionally left Desmond's text unanswered, distracted by showing Matt around Porthaven, dinner with her family, and the subsequent chores and homework she'd needed to do. By the time she had a free moment last night, Cait realized she didn't even know what she'd say.

Staring at the unanswered text in the dim morning light of her room, Cait still didn't know how to reply. She read it over and over: *"You okay?"*

Was she okay?

Cait didn't know.

With a sigh, Cait typed in the only thing she could think of. *"I'm fine. See you at school?"* Then she shoved the phone in her backpack, refusing to look at it again as she got ready to leave.

With one bathroom to split between four women, the Lewan mornings were always chaotic. Maeve worked part-time as a bookkeeper for a few businesses around town, her flexible schedule allowing her to give up the bathroom to the girls as she prepared their lunches downstairs. Though Rese was no longer in school herself, she worked at the local coffee shop, requiring her to be up and out the door around the same time as her sisters. She often hogged the bathroom with her long routine, squealing with rage whenever Cait or Genni would try to interrupt.

Such was the occasion that Cait stumbled upon when she exited her room that morning.

Genni stood in the hall furiously pounding on the bathroom door as Rese shouted back at her, "It's occupied!"

"We *all* have to get ready, you know," Genni yelled, still banging her fist against the door.

"The longer you annoy me, the longer it'll take," Rese noted.

Seeing that her routine would have to wait, Cait immediately turned around, leaving her bedroom door hanging open to use the restroom the first chance she got. She'd learned long ago not to rely on a free bathroom, so she kept her minuscule beauty products in the bottom drawer of her desk. She tied her stick-straight hair back into a ponytail—there would be no time to shower this morning—before applying the small amount of makeup she liked to wear. Rese always wore a full face of makeup, her cheekbones perfectly highlighted and lips glossed, but Cait hadn't mastered those skills. Instead, she settled for filling in her brows, darkening her lashes, and adding enough bronzer and blush to make her pale skin a little less deathly. While she would rather look like Rese and Sydney and all those other girls at school who appeared beautifully refined, she felt intimidated by the whole process. As though the idea of applying eyeshadow would instantly draw attention to the fact that she didn't know what she was doing.

Even after Rese abdicated her claim to the bathroom, Genni instantly took over. However, she was gracious enough to let Cait temporarily borrow the space for the use of the toilet.

Cait often felt sorry for her nan having to put up with three teenage girls, all within four years of each other. If it wasn't bad enough losing her husband, then her son and daughter-in-law, having a curse attributed to their names, and little financial security to count on, she also had to raise granddaughters who couldn't get through one day without some argument.

While Rese left for the coffee shop, Cait and Genni finished their breakfasts with Maeve. "I plan to take Red on a walk this afternoon, Nan," Cait informed her.

"That's jest fine, *a leanbh*," Maeve assured.

The girls grabbed their lunches and headed out the door to retrieve their bikes. They met Matt on the road, his rusty old bike in worse shape than either of theirs. "It was my mom's when she was a kid," he said sheepishly. "She promised to buy me a new one as soon as we get settled in."

"I like it," Genni said cheerfully. "And at least it's red. It could have been pink like Rese's."

Pushing off, the trio started down the street. The red maples and yellow birches lining the road showed off their autumn colors. Even as far inland as they were, the ocean air still tickled their noses as they headed downtown. Used to Genni's chatter on their morning commute, Cait found herself strangely accustomed to Matt's voice chiming in. It felt almost natural, having him join them.

There had been a time in her life when Cait wondered what it would be like to have a brother. Around the ages of eight to ten, she'd wondered if that's what Desmond might be to her. She'd quickly realized that whatever caused that humming sensation in her body only happened in his presence. No other boy caused her senses to alight like that. As she couldn't talk to anyone else about the feeling, she'd concluded on her own that their relationship must be something altogether different.

Now, with Matt, Cait thought she might be getting a glimpse at what it really looked like to have a brother. Someone kind and caring, protective and loyal, but who didn't draw on any sense of special affection or attraction within her. Despite the minimal male relationships she'd had in her life, Cait now saw the clear difference between platonic and romantic. No matter the true ties between her and Desmond, no matter that they would never have anything but an ending, there was a distinction between the way he looked at her and the way Matt looked at her. And Cait would always have that, even when their end finally came.

As Genni and Matt shared their happy, ambling conversations, Cait let her mind wander all the way to town. In their rush to leave, she'd forgotten to see if Desmond had texted her back. She hoped he wouldn't be too upset that she'd taken so long to respond. She'd never had to face his disappointment in her. They'd never had so much as an argument in the past. She dreaded what that would feel like, being at odds with Desmond.

They let their bikes coast up to the bike rack. After securing their locks, they headed into the building. Genni broke off from them, hurrying to her first class while Matt and Cait headed straight for history. "Your sister's really goofy," Matt remarked, an amused look on his face.

Cait grinned, thinking it ironic that *he* would consider anyone goofy. "Yes, she is," she confirmed. "I think that's why people like her so much. She's so honest and genuine that it catches people off guard."

"She's definitely honest," Matt said, eyebrows raised. He pointed to his shirt. "Do *you* think this green is a bad color for me?"

Unable to help her laugh, Cait led the way into their classroom. Penny Davis stood at the chalkboard, writing out the day's lesson notes. She paused to greet them, winking teasingly at her son.

Once they reached their desks and dropped into their seats, Cait answered Matt. "Not really," she admitted. "Genni just has this thing about people's coloring. She's convinced that your undertone determines what you should or shouldn't wear."

"And you don't agree?" Matt asked.

Cait shrugged as she unzipped her backpack. "I can't say I pay enough attention to that sort of thing," she replied.

As she pulled out her notebook, Cait's eyes caught on her phone. She glanced at Matt out of her peripheral. He was also unloading his supplies. Taking his distraction as an opportunity, she checked her phone, her heart stuttering as she saw a singular text notification on the screen.

Cait didn't get the chance to read it as Matt chose that moment to turn back to her. "I've got a kind of . . . sensitive question," he began, picking at the cover of his textbook.

Stifling the irritation at having to wait to see what Desmond said, Cait set her phone face down on her desk. "Go ahead."

"How, uh—how old were you? When your parents . . . ?"

Though such a question should draw up sorrow and pain, Cait had grown numb to such sentiments concerning her parents' deaths. While a dull ache lingered in her chest at the thought of them, she couldn't quite feel its effect on her emotions. "I was six. Well," she corrected, "I was five, but I turned six three weeks after."

"Oh." Matt nodded as though he should have done the math himself. "So, Genni was . . . three or four?"

"Three. Her birthday isn't until April."

Another nod. "Do you remember them? Either of you?"

"Genni likes to say she does, but . . . I don't think she does," Cait admitted. "She always asks too pointed of questions for her to truly remember anything."

"Mm."

Tapping her pencil on her notebook, Cait tried not to mind having the discussion in class. She could have told him they'd talk about it another time. She could have refused to talk about it altogether. And yet, she'd allowed herself to get dragged into it.

"I remember everything," she concluded, not interested in giving him any more information.

Matt grasped that the subject was closed and pressed his lips together in an apologetic grin. "I hope you don't mind me asking," he muttered.

"I don't," she assured, though she wasn't sure that was true. She'd talked to her sisters and to her nan, but she'd only ever told one person the true depth of her feelings and memories of Ireland. And she didn't care to bear her soul to anyone else.

As the final few students funneled into the class, Penny Davis called them to order. Cait furrowed her brow, noting that Desmond's desk remained empty. Had he chosen to skip today? He typically texted when he did that.

Remembering her unread notification, Cait cautiously and silently flipped her phone face up. She glanced down at the text: *"Not today. Special internship business."*

Even as she stared at the screen, another text popped up: *"Free this afternoon."*

A small smile pulled at Cait's lips. He always kept his texts short and abrupt, intentionally sarcastic or dispassionate in case anyone saw them. But she could read his meaning: He'd meet her at the cove after school.

~

The school day passed without incident. After the chaos of the previous day, Cait appreciated its blandness. No one messed with them as Genni joined them in the cafeteria. And no one stopped them as they grabbed their bikes to return home together.

Despite being early in the fall season, a cold wind swept off the ocean, sending a chill through the air. Matt shivered, looking up at the cloudy sky. "It's September," he lamented. "It shouldn't be this cold yet."

"Welcome to Maine," Genni teased. "If you think it's cold now, wait until the snow hits. Which could be anytime, by the way."

Matt looked somewhere between intrigued and horrified. "We won't be able to ride our bikes through the snow, will we?" he asked.

"No," Genni confirmed. "But we can typically make it through a couple of snowfalls."

"What then? Do you just ride the bus?"

"We used to," she replied, glancing at Cait. "But that didn't go so well."

"Nan takes us now," Cait explained. "Or she lets us use the car."

Matt considered this. "We could ride the bus together," he offered. "Maybe it wouldn't be so bad now that, ya know—now that you have a friend."

"I've always had friends," Genni said.

Cait didn't take offense at her sister's comment. She knew Genni didn't intend it to sound backhanded; she simply didn't think about how her words might have double meanings.

The bike ride home took about thirty minutes, an easy jaunt that left their cheeks flushed and their pulses slightly elevated. Their tires buzzed over the macadam as they skirted potholes and rocks. Despite their path along the main road of Porthaven, there weren't many cars. However, Cait kept her eyes out for a black Dodge that rumbled with particular fury. While she didn't see it, she stuck to her plan to pick up Red and head for the cove.

Genni picked up speed, splitting off toward their driveway. Continuing at a slower pace with Matt still at her side, Cait felt a tiny bead of anticipation rising with the expectation of returning to the cove. It wasn't just the place where she met up with Desmond; it was the place she loved most. The place where she could sit and think wholly undisturbed. The cove was her escape. Being there always made her happy.

"Are you going on a bike ride today?" Matt asked.

"Huh?" Cait replied, completely caught off guard.

Matt looked sheepish as he reached up to scratch his eyebrow, quickly gripping the handle again as the bike wobbled. "Not to be weird or anything, but—I noticed you go on a bike ride with your dog after school most days."

Cait didn't know what to say. Was it weird for him to notice? He'd gotten home from school before her every day last week, having taken the bus. For him to notice, he'd have had to see her riding past his grandpa's house. Did that mean he was watching for her?

The nervous expression hadn't left Matt's face. "I was hoping—I mean, you can totally tell me no, but I thought . . . would it be okay if I come with you?"

Slowing their bikes as they neared her house, Cait's tongue felt swollen. How did she say no? She *had* to say no. She was going to meet with Desmond. Bringing Matt along wasn't an option. "Oh, uh—well, I don't really—I just take Red on a walk through the woods," she said, hoping he'd get the hint.

Matt's eyes lit up. "Like, you go hiking?"

Certain that she was failing herself, Cait muttered, "Kind of."

"I love hiking!" Matt exclaimed.

Cait needed to tell him no. She needed to say that she wanted to be alone. But she couldn't form the words. It terrified her to tell him no. This was the only person at school who would talk to her. What if she refused his company and he got angry? She'd never had a friend before; was it that easy to upset one? If she said no, would he refuse to be friends with her anymore?

"I tend to stay out for a long time," Cait said, attempting to let him down easily again.

Matt finally sensed her hesitation. "I—I mean, I don't have to come if you don't want me to. I just—I thought, you know, we could keep hanging out, and maybe you could show me your favorite places to hike or—or whatever."

Sensing his disappointment, Cait began to panic. She *was* upsetting him. "It isn't that I don't want to hang out more," she assured him. "It's just that no one ever comes with me."

His brow furrowed. "Your nan is okay with that?"

"Yeah."

"Wow, she must be super chill. Mom never lets me go out by myself."

"Was it that dangerous in Florida?" Cait asked, bemused by the idea.

"Nah, not really," Matt said with a shrug. "Just, like, ya know, stranger danger and stuff. She's always been kind of overprotective, I guess."

Cait nodded, though she couldn't say she shared the experience. Her nan never worried about them like that. Cait sometimes found it strange—after losing so much of her family, how could she not worry? But in the end, she'd concluded that Maeve needed the solitude as much as the girls did. She needed a break from the constant reminders of her dead son.

"So," Matt looked up at her with those puppy dog eyes, "do you mind if I join?"

With absolutely no means to refuse him, Cait simply shook her head.

"Great! Thanks," Matt said cheerfully.

"Sure," Cait managed to reply. But her heart wasn't in it. In fact, as she went in to retrieve Red, she spent the whole time thinking of ways she could tell him that she'd changed her mind. She considered telling him that he couldn't come with her because she wanted to be alone. Which wasn't true. She *wanted* to be with Desmond.

Desmond.

A cold sweat broke over Cait's neck as she and Matt began the ride toward the woods. She needed to text Desmond to warn him. She needed to tell him that she couldn't meet after all. But her phone was in her backpack. She couldn't stop without drawing Matt's attention.

"I bet there are a ton of cool places to hike around here," Matt remarked as they rode. "Florida was kind of lame in that regard. But we lived in North Carolina before that, and there were some super legit spots out there."

"Does your whole family like to hike?" Cait asked half-heartedly.

"Not really," he said regretfully. "Kelly, my sister, hates it. She's sort of the worst if I'm being honest. We've never gotten along."

Cait wondered who couldn't get along with Matt. But then she remembered the way he scolded Hunter, and she thought she understood.

"Anyway," Matt went on. "Dad and I used to hike together a ton. It was sort of our thing. That and Boy Scouts."

"You were a Boy Scout?"

"An Eagle Scout, actually," he said, a proud lift to his smile. "I earned my rank last summer. It was a lot of work, but I really enjoyed it. I started volunteering with the younger Scouts, but then we moved here, and, well, you guys don't have a troop."

Cait raised her chin as though in understanding, though she didn't understand at all. She knew of the Boy Scouts but had no clue what they did beyond survival stuff like tying knots and first aid. She thought they might go camping a lot.

Matt looked at her with a glimmer of hope in his eyes. "Do you think they might let me help start a troop here?" he asked. "Like, with my experience and stuff, we could probably get a few troops together for all different ages too."

"You could ask," she suggested, though she didn't think anyone would take him up on it. Most of the kids already had their extracurricular time taken up by various social clubs and sports teams.

Not knowing what else to do, Cait led Matt to the woods that led to the cove. She intended to simply walk through the woods for a while before claiming she was tired and suggesting they go home. They settled their bikes on the inside of the tree line—Cait promised no one would steal them—and then headed through the pines, birches, and maples. Red tugged on the leash, ready to go straight to the cove, but she kept a firm grip, forcing him to stay at her side. He looked up at her with confused brown eyes that looked far too much like Matt's.

The cool air hit harder under the shade of the trees, and Matt bristled against it. "I should have grabbed my jacket," he mumbled.

A sprig of hope budded within Cait. "If it's too cold, we can always do this another day," she offered.

With a pleasant smile, Matt shook his head. "Nah, that's cool. Once we get going, I'm sure I'll warm up." He turned to scan the woods, then gasped in excitement. "Oh, nice, there's a trail!"

Cait's heart sank. Why hadn't she thought about that? After ten years of traipsing through the woods, she'd carved a path that led straight to the cove. If Matt followed it, it would lead him directly to her and Desmond's secret spot. "Uh, it's—it's not that great of a trail," Cait said. "We could forge our own path."

"It's not safe to go off the trails," Matt said, his expression growing thoughtful. "I should have brought my bear spray."

Cait wanted to tell him that there weren't any bears on the peninsula, but she was too baffled that he had bear spray in the first place.

With a definitive set to his jaw, Matt made his decision. "No, we shouldn't stray from the path. Especially not unprepared like we are today. We'll need to make lots of noise so the bears and all the other woodland creatures stay well away from us."

Cait gaped as he began down the path, Red moving happily to follow until the leash grew taut. This was a disaster. And there was nothing she could do about it. She *had* to text Desmond.

But as she began to shift her backpack to retrieve her phone, Matt started another conversation, waiting for her to join him on the path. "I bet you've seen a lot of cool animals living here," he prompted.

"Uh, I guess," she replied, reluctantly abandoning her mission to walk at his side.

"What's your favorite?"

"Well, I've seen a few foxes, and I really like them."

"Whoa, that is amazing! Have you seen any bears?"

"I don't think we have bears on the peninsula."

"Hm." Matt scanned the trees surrounding them. "That would be nice. It's always a little sketchy to be out knowing they could be around. Have you ever gone hunting?"

Cait raised her eyebrows. "No."

Matt tucked his hands into the pockets of his jeans, his backpack bouncing as they walked. "Me either. I've always thought it would be kind of fun, but—I dunno. I'm not sure I could kill an animal, ya know?"

Having learned that Matt asked if "she knew" quite a lot, Cait couldn't help smirking. "Yeah, I don't know that I could either."

During the rest of their hike along the narrow path Cait had carved out over the past decade, Matt talked about the various animals he'd studied and the tracking skills he'd picked up from Scouts and further developed on his own. He told her his favorite animals were wolves because they were so loyal and intelligent. When Cait informed him that there were no longer any wolves left in Maine, he frowned and said, "That's too bad."

As they began to near the cove with Matt in the lead, Cait fumbled to work up some excuse for them to turn back. She didn't want to bring him there. They'd only been friends for a week now. She wasn't ready to let him see the place that meant the most to her. And she was terrified that Desmond was already there, waiting for her. Her fingers itched constantly to reach for her phone, but Matt was too attentive. He'd have noticed if she was texting.

The tang of salt grew, and Matt's eyes went wide. "I think we're nearing the ocean!" he exclaimed, picking up his pace. Red reacted to his excitement, loping along readily.

Cait's heart raced, and her gut twisted. She followed him, a hollowness carving its way through her. Matt didn't notice her discomfort, whether because she was doing a good job of hiding it or simply because he couldn't read her well enough.

They broke through the tree line; the cove lay open before them. Light gray sands and variegated pebbles led to the slate-blue ocean, the clouds a thick blanket above them. If she wasn't so distracted by the sense of betrayal weighing down her stomach, she'd have thought to tell Matt that it might rain and they should return home.

"Wow!" Matt gasped, surveying the area. "This is so cool! Have you ever been here before?"

Cait couldn't speak past the tension in her throat, so she merely lied with a shake of her head.

"Why haven't you followed the path?" he asked, utterly confused.

Cait shrugged. "I, uh—" She cleared her throat and started again. "I typically just make sure Red gets a good walk, then pick a place and sketch for a while."

"Huh, I guess that makes sense." Matt headed down the slope to the beach.

Cait wanted desperately to yell at him to stop. She wanted to grab his arm, jerk him back up the bank, and shove him all the way back through the forest. He didn't belong here. She never should have let him come.

Instead, she followed mutely, horrified as he ranged across her and Desmond's hideaway. Red tugged against his leash, used to freely roaming the beach. She released him absentmindedly.

Matt walked straight up to the log, kicking the toe of his boot against it. "It's perfectly solid," he observed, pleased. The joy on his face was palpable as he turned around and took a seat. "This is seriously the best."

Though she didn't want to encourage him, Cait hurried to the far side of the log to sit down. She couldn't let Matt get anywhere near the stash she and Desmond kept in the log's hollow. If he discovered the blanket, rain jackets, and emergency supplies they kept there, he'd know something was up.

"Ya know," Matt said, slipping his backpack from his shoulders. He smiled at her. "I'd say this is a perfect place to sketch."

Cait tried to return the smile. "Yeah, I think you're right."

Seeing no way around it, Cait joined Matt in getting comfortable. Red was already busy digging in the sand, and she needed to send a message to Desmond before it was too late. She dropped her backpack between her legs and drew out her sketchbook, trying to be nonchalant as she scrounged for her phone at the bottom of the bag. Matt wasn't paying attention, though, as he pulled out some homework.

But as Cait hurriedly opened the text app, she saw that she'd failed. Desmond had texted her already: *"Tell him to go away."*

Attempting a casual look over her shoulder, Cait searched the spot where Desmond always broke through the trees. Her heart pounded, the slightest rumble of his presence meeting her brain. Yet all she could see was Hades, his sharp ears folded back as his tails twitched in agitation. Cait could have sworn the cat's golden eyes were glaring at Matt.

Matt was saying something about his mom and unreasonable amounts of homework, but Cait couldn't process it. Not as she was sure that Desmond stood on the other side of the trees, catching her in the midst of her betrayal. A powerful wave of fear and anger welled up inside of Cait.

"Hey, Matt?" she said, cutting off whatever he'd been saying with more aggression than necessary.

His overly animated face showed every ounce of his surprise and concern as he looked over at her. "What?"

"I think we ought to go home."

Matt's forehead scrunched in confusion. "We just got here."

"Yeah, but. . . ." Cait scanned the cove, desperate for an excuse. She noticed the gray clouds and latched on to the one she should have used minutes ago. "I think it's going to rain. And we don't want to get caught out in it."

With his mouth pressed into a disappointed line, Matt stared up at the sky. "Ah, yeah, I think you're right. Those do look like nimbostratus clouds."

Cait blinked. Of course he knew the scientific name of rain clouds. "Exactly," she affirmed, shoving her sketchbook back into her bag. She stood before she'd even fully zipped it up. "We should get going."

"Yeah," Matt lamented. "It's too bad. This place is legit."

Cait gave him an apologetic grin that she didn't feel as she hurried to reattach Red's leash. The dog looked up at her as though she'd lost her mind, gray sand matted in the gingery fur of his snout.

"Maybe we can come back," Matt suggested, joining her.

"Maybe," Cait lied.

She would *never* bring him back here.

Without giving Matt any chance to change his mind, Cait headed straight for the path. Red reluctantly followed, occasionally pulling on the leash as though begging to stay. She glanced once at where Hades hid in the shadows. As covertly as she could, she held her phone before her, typing quickly. *"I'm sorry! He wouldn't leave me alone."*

CHAPTER TEN

Desmond

Desmond suppressed a yawn, his eyes squinting against the bright morning light that reflected off the rolling gray sea around Aster Island. On any normal day, he'd be happy to miss out on school. But joining his dad, Ben, and Uncle Rick to visit the island had meant waking up at an ungodly hour and having his dad shuffle him out of the house with hardly any chance for breakfast.

Fish greeted the four of them at the edge of his property. Desmond stood between his dad and Ben, his Uncle Rick—Garrett's dad—on William's other side. The large white lighthouse tore into the cloudy sky above them as they surveyed the beautiful island.

Aster Island had a definitive kidney bean shape to it. On the front half nearest the peninsula sat the lighthouse and the small cottage that Fish lived in with his wife, Laurel. The couple had raised their three sons on the island, and now the men lived on the mainland with their own families. Rumor had it that Fish's youngest son was set to inherit the role of lightkeeper rather than the traditional eldest. Something about personality differences between the father and his older sons.

All in all, Desmond wished he'd been born as Fish's son. He could easily imagine growing up on the idyllic island, its tall reeds and green grass swaying in the near-perpetual wind. The whole island spanned just under a square mile, most of the grounds covered by the dense woods of various pines, colorful poplars, and hearty oaks. Blue wood aster flowers dotted the entire island, their soft blue petals creating a mystical atmosphere amongst the thick forest. Many wild woodland creatures made their home on the island, having made their way across the land bridge that revealed itself at the lowest tides. Otherwise, the only entrance on or off the island was by boat or the slippery rock bridge that stretched the quarter-mile gap between shorelines.

Every time Desmond set foot on the island, he found an unusual sense of calm settle over him, as though that mere jaunt across the rock bridge shut out the weight of responsibility that Porthaven carried. The peaceful, craggy beach and the gentle hum of the waves brought a peace the mainland couldn't. It felt like the cove on a grander scale.

Thinking of the cove, Desmond checked his phone. Cait had texted him that morning—finally: *"I'm fine. See you at school?"* He couldn't tell whether that was her way of forgiving him or if he still had apologizing to do. Either way, Desmond knew he wouldn't feel settled until he could see her again and ask her forgiveness for the whole situation yesterday.

Not that he'd really done anything wrong, he supposed. He'd stood up for her. Wasn't that what friends were supposed to do?

But they weren't friends, and that was the problem. They were supposed to be nothing to one another, and he'd made the mistake of inserting himself into her life. He'd cast light on her, and he worried that he'd caused her even more problems.

It was for the best that he wasn't at school today. Let people forget the fact that he'd challenged Hunter Varon over Cait Lewan. The absence of his presence would give her the chance to fade into the background once again.

A chilly breeze cut through Desmond's bomber jacket as he walked under the heavy morning shadow of the lighthouse. Fish led the way past his quaint home. Desmond could see Laurel tending her garden in the backyard, a cream cardigan wrapped around her trim shoulders. She gave them all a wave as they passed, promising lunch and fresh baked goods when they returned.

"So," Rick began, his lighthearted voice not matching the officious nature of the silver badge attached to his tan and black sheriff's uniform. Rick looked a lot like his sister Robin—Desmond's mom—with their piercing blue eyes, sharp features, and that impossible height the Edgars family boasted of. The cop slicked back his gray-streaked light brown hair as he scanned the tree line. "What're we looking at here?"

"There are a few burrows that I've discovered close to the forest's edge," Fish explained as he guided them. "None have breached its borders yet, but I wouldn't count on that for long."

Ben kept pace at Desmond's side. Out of church, he dressed like any civilian in jeans and a thick cable-knit sweater. "What do you think they're doing out here?" the reverend asked. "Aren't beasts summoned for specific tasks."

Fish gave his nephew a pointed look. "You know better than to rely on the Warden's knowledge alone," he replied. "We've still got a great deal to learn."

"We *do* know they can't breach the spirit world on their own," William countered. "Someone summoned these monsters."

"Well, sure," Fish allowed, turning his weather-worn face to look over his shoulder at them. "But that doesn't mean they gave them any purpose beyond roaming free."

"Why would anyone do that?" Desmond asked.

"Practice?" Fish suggested. "Boredom? Pure, idiotic curiosity?"

None of that sounded right to Desmond. Though he'd never been around a beast aside from Hades, his dad had forced him to study them enough to know that they were servant creatures called forth for a specific task. Even *he* had a reason for summoning Hades as a boy looking for a companion.

So, what was this Wielder's reason?

"Preparation?" Rick added, stopping them all in their tracks.

They all turned to the sheriff, the proposition unnerving.

"Preparation for what?" William demanded.

Rick shrugged. Not only did he look like Robin Simon, but Desmond also found that Uncle Rick acted a lot like her too. Unlike his bumbling, hotheaded son, the sheriff had an easygoing disposition that sometimes didn't quite fit the station he held. "I dunno, Will," he replied. "It's my job to think of all the angles, and if someone's out here summoning a whole bunch of beasts, it makes me think: What for? Sure, it could be as innocent as a kid who doesn't know what they're doing. But it could be a Druid who's slowly building an army to attack the town."

Desmond scanned the men around him, knowing they were all thinking of the singular ex-Druid in their town.

"We can't accuse someone until we have evidence," Ben reminded them.

"Which is why we're here, right?" Rick returned. "Gathering evidence."

Fish let out a grunt. "Come on."

The lightkeeper led them under the fall-thinning canopy of trees. Between the cloud cover and the thick branches above, a heavy shadow fell over them despite the blanket of leaves that littered the forest floor. Scarlet and amber surrounded them as the evergreen trees remained— well, ever-green. The dainty blue asters clung to the base of the trees, making their final display in the early autumn before they'd wilt into winter. Shafts of light filtered through the gaps in the clouds, but the woods still carried a washed-out dimness that sent a chill down Desmond's spine.

They were hunting beasts in a shadowy forest. Every Warden member knew that the monsters thrived in darkness. The darker it was, the stronger the creatures were. They'd chosen to explore in the early morning for that very reason. The likelihood of a beast coming out in the daytime was slim. With an almost vampire-like aversion to the sun, these monsters couldn't survive in the light.

That didn't mean they were safe, though. They were poking around the beasts' hiding places—whatever those looked like. If they stumbled upon a nest or a den or whatever groups of beasts were called, there was no guarantee they wouldn't have to fight their way out. Which was why they needed Fish and Ben with them.

Desmond knew that he and his dad had power enough to fight the beasts off too. But only in the direst circumstances were they allowed to access their power. Yet another special rule of the Porthavenian Warden that he found mindbogglingly stupid. What was the point of protecting the spirit world if you never used it?

Over the next couple of hours, Fish took them to the various sites he'd mentioned the previous day. There were unnatural gouges in the trees and strange mounds dug from the earth. An entire oak tree was knocked over, with jagged cuts all along its bark. Massive prints were embedded into the softer dirt. Whatever had left these tracks, they found no fur, splinters of claws, or scat. A sure sign that the creatures weren't of this world.

Rick remained hunched over the final burrow they were inspecting as Ben turned to Fish. "I haven't seen a single animal the entire time we've been out here," he remarked. "Are they all hiding?"

"That's my guess," Fish said, his arms crossed. "Typically, I cross paths, or at least hear them when I take my walks. Recently, it's been quiet."

Desmond raised his brow. "You think they're still out there?"

A wry tilt lifted Fish's lips. "You mean, do I think the beasts have eaten them all?"

Desmond held his stare, waiting for the answer.

"Not sure," Fish admitted. "Can't say I've ever known a beast to eat an animal. Might be that the furbearers are just afraid and hiding. Could be that they're gone or hibernating. As I said, the birds have already migrated."

In the notably hushed woods, Desmond didn't have any trouble imagining that Fish was correct. Whatever animals remained on the island weren't stirring from their hiding places.

"What now?" Rick asked, rising. "We've confirmed there are beasts, more or less. How do we figure out who's summoning them?"

William ran a hand over his jaw in thought. He stared out into the depths of the forest. "There's one more place we need to check," he said.

"I've already been there," Fish countered. "There's no sign of trouble."

The mayor wasn't dissuaded. "If someone is coming out here, there's a reason. Could be for privacy, but I want to ensure it's safe. Personally."

Fish shrugged in reluctant agreement, then turned and led them farther into the trees. They grew thicker as the group traversed deeper. Roots twisted into winding spirals across the ground. A stream burbled, cutting across their path. The farther they went, the stiller the forest grew. Not in the usual sense; the wind still blew, causing the branches and leaves to tremble at its cold touch. Even the muffled crash of the ocean against the island's rocky edge reached their ears.

No, it was a different kind of stillness. The same sort that Desmond felt the moment he stepped onto the island. A stillness of the soul. One that made you feel an inexplicable sense of reverence.

A sudden, small clearing opened in the heart of the forest. Desmond knew they were near the back of the island, one of the farthest spots from town. A great sycamore stood in the center of a perfect, grassy ring as though all the other trees of the forest had gathered to watch it. It stretched at least five stories high, the trunk a massive chunk of moss-mottled, light gray bark. Two giant arms twisted out of the trunk, reaching up with their innumerable branches. The tree's leaves had turned gold in the autumn, shining brightly even in the dim light.

William had brought Desmond here for the first time five years ago on his thirteenth birthday. *"This is our inheritance,"* his dad had told him. *"This is why we're here. And we must protect it till our last breaths."*

The Veil of Porthaven.

Desmond hardened his jaw, staring at the giant tree. Finding a single, nearly extirpated sycamore on a random island in northeastern Maine was odd enough. But he never could quite understand how a natural formation of earth could be a link to the supernatural. It didn't make sense to him. Then again, there was a lot about the spirit world that didn't make sense. It wasn't their job to know the answers—it was their job to protect it.

The five men stood on the cusp of the grassy ring surrounding the Veil. They all hesitated to approach, a healthy sense of respect for something so unknown embedded in each of them. No one went near the Veil as a matter of principle. From the formation of Porthaven, the Warden made it law that only the Varons—now the Simons—were allowed to approach.

"What are we doing here again?" Rick asked, his voice hushed.

Ben stared at the tree like he wanted to cross himself and start muttering a prayer. Fish simply held his arms crossed in a lazy manner, eyeing the tree in disapproval and waiting for William's reply.

"I need to be sure it's safe," the mayor repeated.

Rick glanced down at Desmond, nudging his nephew's arm. "Seems safe enough to me," the cop muttered.

Desmond smirked, but William didn't appreciate the jest. "I'm going to get closer," he said even as he took his first step forward.

Wide-eyed, the other four watched as William thoughtfully approached the tree.

"Desmond," his dad beckoned in that no-nonsense tone of his that demanded rather than requested.

Bolstering his courage, Desmond followed in his dad's steps. The dry grass and leaves crunched under his boots. As he drew closer to the sycamore, he began to see it more clearly. Such a monstrosity of a tree bore intricacies that you couldn't imagine from a distance. Its bark resembled a Jackson Pollock painting, speckled in muted grays, greens, creams, and browns. Heavy branches drooped, and he had to duck under a few as they approached the trunk.

Desmond came to a halt an arm's length from the tree. There were no roots above the ground. It looked like the tree had simply shot out of the ground like a daisy. "What are we looking for?" he asked, sure they shouldn't stand so close to the curtain of the spirit world.

With his dark eyes locked on the tree, William pointed to where the two parent limbs split from the trunk. "Do you see that?"

Squinting, Desmond shifted to his right, trying to get a better view. "What am I—oh." He gaped, moving around his dad, entranced by the sight.

Just below the branching arms was a shadow of . . . *something*. It curved farther back to the other side of the trunk. Desmond followed its path, William right behind him.

"You find something?" Fish called from the tree line.

"Maybe," William replied as Desmond came to a halt at the back of the tree.

"Uhhhh." Desmond spared a worried glance at his dad before turning back to the sycamore. "What is *that*?"

A large crack marred the trunk, the bark split open as though it had burst from the inside out. A jagged tear stretched a good five feet along the side and ran almost too high up for Desmond to view.

Despite his better judgment, Desmond leaned in to get a good look under the ruptured bark. Without clear light, he couldn't pick out all the details, but he could see that something lurked under the crack in the tree. "Is it supposed to do that?" he asked.

"No," William replied, a dangerous edge to his voice.

"What *is* it?"

William glared at the rip. "I don't know."

Turning back to the tree, Desmond tilted his head, still trying to get a clear view. He wanted to know what was causing the rupture. He could have sworn it looked like something was inside the tree, trying to get out. A slight bulge under the cracking bark caught his eye. Icy white gleamed within the minimal rays of light. It held the same general texture as the rest of the wood, but it was smoother, less mottled, and streaked with black, like soot.

William grabbed Desmond's arm, drawing him away from the tree. "We need to return," he ordered.

"What—what's happening to it?" Desmond asked.

"I don't know," William replied, eerily calm.

Knowing better than to ask questions, Desmond jerked out of his dad's grip but stayed at his side. He gave the sycamore one more look over his shoulder. Something was wrong with the Veil. Something or someone had tampered with it. Likely, it was whoever was summoning these beasts.

A trickle of dread dripped down Desmond's spine. Something was wrong with the Veil, and that meant. . . .

Desmond curled his hands into fists. He needed to check on Cait. If something was going wrong in the spirit world, it might cause problems for her. He'd always known those dreams of hers were more than simple oddities. She dreamed of beasts every night. That wasn't a coincidence, no matter how much she wanted to believe in them.

If there was something going wrong with the Veil, there was a chance that the danger would come to her too. And Desmond wouldn't let that happen.

~

After the time it took to trek through the forest, have lunch at Fish and Laurel's, and endure the adults' hours of discussion on what they'd seen at the Veil, Desmond didn't get home until after school had already let out. He immediately got in his car, promising to be home for dinner, and rushed to his meetup with Cait.

He couldn't remember the last time they'd gone this long without being at the cove together. Despite his family and their busy schedule, he always found a way. And after the summer, when they met up almost every day, this felt like an eternity.

Pulling off Lawrence Avenue, Desmond veered to the right onto the highway that stretched all the way to where the peninsula met the rest of Maine. He tossed a momentary glance to the left at the fork that led to the Lewan residence. He'd never actually been to her house, but he knew the address. He entered the receipts detailing exactly how much the Warden provided for the Lewan family.

Knowing the neighborhood, Desmond imagined Cait's home regularly. She'd described their house in Ireland to him once, and he couldn't help melding his imagination of their cottage with the place they lived in now: a quaint but outdated sort of place, probably with lots of lace curtains and floral wallpaper.

Desmond didn't like thinking of Cait in Ireland. He knew she'd be happier there, but it made him sad to imagine her anywhere but in Porthaven. Anywhere that kept them more than a handful of miles apart made him antsy.

The car's engine growled as he drove down the coastline. The sky remained overcast, the clouds thick with the promise of rain. He didn't worry that it would hinder their meetup. If it rained, they would put on their rain jackets and sit on the log under the blanket. They'd spent many afternoons at the cove in inclement weather.

Desmond parked at the old factory and hurried for the path, summoning Hades the second he was under the cover of the forest canopy. The cat-beast trotted at his side, pointy blue-black ears alert. The cat was large, standing at Desmond's mid-calf, with paws that could nearly cover Cait's palm. At a passing glance, someone might think Hades was a small dog rather than of the feline persuasion.

Hurrying through the woods, Hades kept up with Desmond's pace easily. He was late again. He hoped Cait wasn't on kitchen duty today. They hadn't been together enough recently, and he needed plenty of time to work up to his apology.

Walking down the path, Desmond thought through what he would say to her. He couldn't just jump in with the apology first. He had to check on her, see how she was, ask after school, lull her into a good mood, and *then* beg for her forgiveness. And when he did, he'd be as genuine as possible with no aimless wandering and no pandering. A simple, honest apology always worked best.

"Cait," he'd say. "I'm sorry. I butted in when I should have let you handle the situation. You don't need me to take care of you, and I know that. It won't happen again."

She'd smile, pat his arm—though he knew she'd secretly want to hug him—and accept his apology. Desmond would probably consider doing something stupid, like putting his arm around her. And he'd probably act on the impulse. He'd never done anything truly and irrevocably stupid with Cait, but he knew that even those little stupid actions made the next few years impossibly difficult. Yet he couldn't seem to stop himself.

Caught up in his thoughts, Desmond almost didn't recognize the sound of voices until he was about to break through the trees. Not voices—one voice of a decidedly male nature.

At the last second, Desmond slipped behind a tree, hoping that his approach hadn't been seen or heard. His heartbeat kicked up, and he held his breath. Then he peeked around the tree.

Something between fury and horror spread from Desmond's crown down his neck and over his chest. He couldn't believe it. She'd brought that boy to their cove.

Gaping at the scene, Desmond felt Hades brush against his leg, the heavy weight of the cat pressing into him. There on the beach, sitting on the log they'd dragged out there eight years ago, Matt-freaking-Davis prattled away. His stupid curly brown hair and lanky frame sat in Desmond's spot while Cait slouched on the far end.

At least she had the good sense to look ashamed to have brought the whelp to their cove.

Before he fully thought it through, Desmond yanked his phone from his pocket. Hades padded into view as he sent the text. He saw Cait pull her phone out of her backpack, watching carefully as she stared at the screen. He saw the exact moment she read the text. Her expression went slack as she dropped the phone to her side.

Cautiously, Cait lifted her chin, glancing beyond Matt straight to where Desmond stood, hidden in the shadows. He didn't know if she could see him, but if she could, he knew she'd see the flat, irritated expression he wore.

How could she bring that kid here? Of all places. They'd agreed to meet, and she'd brought him along with her. Why?

Desmond watched, his heartbeat thudding in his ears as he tried not to allow rage to overcome him. Cait was corralling Red, guiding Matt away from the cove. With desperate yet deft action, she managed to get them moving. Desmond's phone buzzed in his hand.

"I'm sorry! He wouldn't leave me alone."

Tightening his jaw, Desmond shoved down his irritation. He couldn't be mad at Cait. Not when he'd done something equally dumb the previous day. That was the difficult part of their relationship—or whatever it was they shared. He had to constantly stifle that urge to care for her, completely unable to behave as a friend should in public. And she had to pretend indifference, if not fear, toward him when he was the only person she opened up to.

Looking down at the phone in his hands, Desmond let go of his anger. *"Tomorrow?"* he asked, then turned and left the cove.

"Come on, bud," he muttered to Hades.

The cat looked up at him, walking by his side.

"You can help me with homework when we get home."

Hades looked thrilled.

Tomorrow, Desmond told himself. He only had to wait one more day, and he could see her again. He'd make his apology, tell her about the odd discovery, and ensure her safety. It would all be fine tomorrow.

~

"Tomorrow," he'd said. And yet here he was in tomorrow, and he was no closer to seeing Cait than before. For one thing, he'd forgotten about basketball practice, and Coach would have killed him if he skipped. Beyond that, Cait had already informed him that Matt asked to go on another hike that afternoon. When he'd asked about after their hike and his practice, she'd said, *"It'll be too late. Nan will want me home."*

So, meeting up was removed from the agenda.

Desmond supposed it was for the best. It wasn't like he could tell her all that much about the situation anyway. After all, the information was classified. She didn't know about the Veil in the first place. Explaining to her that the island harbored a secret link to the spirit world wouldn't be easy.

He really had nothing more interesting to say than, "Hey, you know those spirit world beasts I told you about? Well, they're popping up at random. But don't ask anything more—I can't tell you."

No, until the Warden got more information, Desmond wouldn't tell Cait. Hopefully, it wouldn't take long for them to find their answers anyway. The Lavignes were signed up to clear the island of beasts over the next several nights. Then, the rest of the Warden would join them, keeping vigil to see who was summoning the creatures.

Until the investigation was complete and Desmond had something real to share, he'd keep his mouth shut.

After a typical basketball practice, Desmond stayed to work out in the gym. He'd heard it wasn't usual for high schools to have gyms so well outfitted, but it had been put in during the renovation project four years back. Some people complained about the misuse of funds. But when both their basketball and baseball teams won the state championship last year, they'd changed their tunes.

Since he started high school, Desmond found himself in the gym regularly. It was the place he went to be alone. The place where he ignored the demands of everyone else, blasting music on his headphones and enjoying the pain of tearing his muscles until they gave out from pure fatigue. Even if someone else was in the gym, no one messed with him here.

Until today.

As he added another set of plates to his barbell, Hunter Varon stepped up to his mat. He leaned against the mirrored wall, *chalantly* nonchalant.

Already irritated, Desmond pulled an earbud out and let it hang onto his sweat-soaked tee. "You need something, Hunt?" he asked.

Hunter clenched his jaw at the nickname. Then he tempered his expression. "I realized something the other day," he said.

Moving to close the barbell clips, Desmond didn't look up at him. "What's that?"

"Cait doesn't know, does she?"

Desmond's hands stilled. He glanced at Hunter. "Excuse me?"

Arms crossed, Hunter appeared completely at ease. He'd changed back into his street clothes, his casual button up hanging absurdly open to the third button like he was some suave lady-killer. "Cait," he said her name again as though Desmond wouldn't recognize it. "She doesn't know about . . . well, any of it, I'm guessing."

Standing up straight, Desmond glared at Hunter. "First of all," he infused his voice with all the snark he could muster, "you're not a member of the Warden. Therefore, you don't know what you're talking about."

Hunter rolled his obnoxiously blue eyes. "Yeah, well, you're not a Warden member either," he countered. "And your dad tells you stuff, doesn't he?"

Desmond narrowed his eyes. Technically, an individual had to be eighteen to join the Warden. The organization had made an exception for Desmond when he was thirteen, and his dad wanted to bring him aboard for training. But still, the title was honorary.

"Are you saying that your dad is breaking Warden policy?" Desmond asked.

Hunter didn't flinch. "What's your dad's excuse? That he's the mayor?"

"I'd say it has more to do with the ring he wears," he retorted. "You know the one: a massive gold monstrosity of a thing. Big V on the front. Hard to miss."

Jaw tightening once more, Hunter returned Desmond's irritated stare. Of course, he knew the ring. It was the thing that marked William Simon as leader over all the Varons within Edmond Varon's line. A fact that the Porthaven Varons would never forgive him for.

"Look," Hunter ground out. "I'm just concerned for her, that's all. And I don't think it's right—keeping that from her or her sisters."

"Aren't you the social justice warrior?"

"Their parents died because of it," he argued. "Don't you think they deserve to know that?"

"I think that's not my call," Desmond returned, ignoring the twinge of curiosity at Hunter's choice of words. How did he know why her parents died? From Desmond's knowledge, the Warden hadn't deduced that for themselves yet.

Hunter shook his head as though disappointed. "Fine. Whatever. Keep playing the douchebag, and I'll actually give a crap about people. Then, when we're adults, and it *is* your call, people will listen to me over you."

Unable to help himself, Desmond chuckled. "So, that's what this is about? You're trying to figure out how easy it'll be to stage a coup when it comes time for me to take over?"

"No," Hunter said, exasperation lining his voice. "No, I'm—I'm actually kind of worried about her. I mean, don't you think it's dangerous? What if she's the Vessel?"

Desmond frowned. "You're not supposed to know about that."

"I'm not supposed to know about a lot of things."

"Then you should probably forget them all."

"You do realize you need her to cooperate with you, right?" Hunter challenged. "Whether it's her or one of her sisters, the prophecy says we *need* them."

Now, Desmond's gut churned. "You're *definitely* not supposed to know about that."

"Neither are you," he returned.

"I'm the heir."

Hunter's expression made it clear that he didn't think he should be. "And I'm a Varon too."

"Doesn't give your dad the right to reveal the Warden's secrets."

"If it keeps us safe—if it helps us defeat the Druids—isn't it better that we all know?"

Setting his hands on his hips, Desmond noted his heart rate's return to its normal rhythm. "You've effectively ruined my workout," he said. "Anything else you'd like to screw up for me before I head home?"

Hunter didn't appreciate his sarcasm. "It's dangerous, Desmond."

Raising his chin, Desmond paused at the use of his given name. Hunter only ever called him by his last name in a derogatory manner.

"Whichever sister it chose," he continued, "*they* are dangerous. And if we don't take the prophecy seriously, we not only risk losing control of them but also losing this whole war."

Desmond found himself furrowing his brow before he could catch himself.

Hunter noticed. He stood up straighter. "You didn't know?"

"Of course I did," he lied.

Hunter didn't buy it. "Huh," he murmured, scanning Desmond with a knowing glint in his eyes. A sly smile tugged at the corner of his mouth.

"Guess being an honorary council member doesn't mean you know everything, does it?"

"I've *read* the prophecy," Desmond countered. "You've heard it secondhand."

That wasn't a lie. He had read the prophecy. At least, the lines about the Lewan family coming under the guardianship of Porthaven. It was one of his dad's favorite teaching points: *"We were selected to protect the Warden's greatest asset."*

What Desmond hadn't realized until now was that his dad had only allowed him to read *part of* the prophecy.

"Well," Hunter began to move away, "if you ever want to discuss it, I'd be happy to brainstorm the best way to ensure the Warden's success. After all, if we want the Wolf's help, we'll need his allegiance."

The Wolf. A war. A risk of losing control of the Vessel.

Three things that Desmond hadn't known. Three things his father had kept from him.

Smirking, Desmond scanned Hunter. "I keep my own counsel, thanks."

Hunter dipped his head, that knowing grin still on his lips. Then he turned and left.

Desmond glared at the mirror in front of him. His dad was keeping things from him. Important things. Things that the Varons were sharing amongst themselves.

With a different sort of adrenaline now running through his veins, Desmond stepped up to the barbell. He completed the lift and let it slam back to the mat. The furious clang of plates reverberated through him, mimicking his internal aggression.

So, his dad was keeping secrets.

Well, that just meant Desmond would have to uncover them.

CHAPTER ELEVEN

Cait

A week. One whole week since Cait and Desmond had last met up. Well, Cait supposed it wasn't quite that melodramatic. They'd met on the roof of the school on Monday. But that was different from meeting at the cove. It was wholly different from being able to spend time together, talking freely and sharing each other's company.

As much as it irritated Cait, she couldn't figure out what else to do. The idea of telling Matt that she didn't want to spend time with him made her throat dry up. She didn't want to lose the one friend she'd finally made. And she couldn't lie to him either. Knowing that he'd seen her riding past all those days ago meant it wasn't safe to say she was busy only to ride past his house a few moments later.

Yesterday, Matt had asked to join Cait on her bike ride-slash-hike with Red again. Unable to deny him, Cait had intentionally taken him farther up the peninsula to distract him from the cove. They'd spent the whole afternoon hiking along the coastline, much to Desmond's annoyance. He'd been especially short when he'd responded to her text, letting him know that she wouldn't be able to make it to the cove after all.

And today, Desmond had practice and his internship, so there'd be no meeting up as it was.

However, Cait had decided that spending three afternoons in a row with Matt was enough. He was a wonderful friend, but she saw him all day at school, and then he wanted to spend the rest of their free time together. She needed a break.

So, she'd lied, telling him she couldn't hang out because she had a ton of homework to catch up on.

Matt took it well, glancing ahead toward his house with a grimace. "Yeah, same here," he'd admitted, then sighed. "Well, I guess we can't put it off forever."

Cait smiled and said her goodbyes, pulling into the drive behind Genni. And while it wasn't totally a lie—she really did have homework to do—it wasn't entirely the truth either. She didn't have to catch up on anything. Every night, Cait managed to get her homework done before bed. She'd always been fast with her schoolwork. Perhaps because she spent her free period at school *actually* doing work rather than goofing off with friends. So, Cait spent a rare afternoon in her bedroom sketching the monsters from her dreams the previous night.

At dinner, both Genni and Rese teased Cait about how much time she was spending with Matt. To which Cait informed them that that was why she was home today. "I need some time to myself," she explained. "He's nice, but he can be a bit much."

Rese didn't look convinced. Genni looked disappointed. Maeve looked concerned.

"Is he bothering yeh, *a leanbh*?" her nan asked warily.

"No," Cait assured her. "Nothing like that. Like I said, he's nice, and I do like him, but not like that. And sometimes you just need time to be alone, ya know?"

Hearing herself use Matt's trademark line convinced Cait that the separation was good. If she started adding "ya know" to the end of every sentence, she'd seriously consider sewing her mouth shut.

After helping to wash up the dishes, Cait headed for the stairs. Rese had disappeared into her room after dinner, likely talking with Ryan on the phone. Maeve invited Cait to stay and watch a movie; their nan and Genni were already bundled under a blanket together on the couch, fresh stovetop popcorn in a bowl between them. She turned them down, repeating her homework excuse.

The evening passed in quiet productivity for Cait. She set her phone on the desktop, letting her favorite music stream as she dealt with the ads that came with the free service. Eventually, her homework was complete, and she bundled it all together in the folders she kept organized in her backpack. She'd never understood why other students—like Genni—were sloppy with their work. It made life vastly easier to take the extra minute to put things in order.

Cait completed her nighttime routine, washing her face and brushing her teeth in the bathroom. She pulled her curtains, then changed into her pajamas. She was grabbing her sketchbook from the desk when she heard a sudden rapping on her window. Had it begun to rain?

But no, the sound had stopped shortly after it started. In addition, it had only sounded at the far double window at the back of her room.

Cait gripped her sketchbook closer, staring at the drawn lilac curtains. The room was eerily silent. Then, with one step toward the window, she heard it. The low hum permeated her skull, tingling over her skin as another rap came at the window.

Tossing her sketchbook onto the bed, Cait rushed forward. She drew the curtain back to see Desmond crouched on her roof. "What—" She stopped, pushed the curtain all the way open, and knelt on the tiny window seat. "What are you doing here?"

Desmond's eyes were wide with expectation as she stared at him. "Are you gonna let me in or what?" he asked, his voice heavily muffled by the glass between them.

Despite her better judgment, Cait unlatched the casement window and cautiously opened it. The windows creaked sometimes, and she didn't want anyone in the house to hear. Given the cold night air, there'd be no reason for her to open a window.

The second the opening was wide enough, Desmond barreled his way through without giving her the chance to refuse him entrance. He wore his black bomber jacket open over a black shirt and black jeans like some undercover spy. Only his dark brown leather boots broke the pattern.

Pushing off the bench seat, Desmond turned to shut the window quietly.

"You can't stay," Cait objected, reaching to stop him.

"Caity—" He leveled her with a determined stare as the last puff of cold air seeped through. "I just walked two miles to talk to you. You're not throwing me out."

In her surprise, Cait let him latch the window. "You walked here?"

"Well, yeah," he replied, his voice as hushed as hers. "I couldn't exactly pull up in your driveway and say, 'Hey, Nana Lewan, I'd like to have a little chat with your granddaughter.'"

"I call her Nan," Cait corrected for no reason other than that she didn't know what else to say.

Desmond ignored the reply, giving Cait a single glance before scanning her room. Never before had she noticed every detail of her space. The purple walls seemed entirely too girly, the sketches that hung on her walls too childish, and the clothes pouring out of the hamper too personal. She hoped nothing embarrassing was sticking out anywhere.

"Huh," Desmond muttered as he inspected the space. "Can't say this is what I pictured."

"You pictured my room?" Cait asked in a whisper.

He smirked even as he continued his study. "Once or twice," he said, then turned to her. His eyes drifted down, and she suddenly realized she was in her pajamas, her very old, very pink, and very skimpy pajamas with frills on the hem of the shorts.

Desmond's smirk grew.

An immediate wash of embarrassment drove Cait to cross her arms, granting herself a false sense of modesty. "What are you doing here?" she demanded, keeping her voice low. With him so near, the hum had risen to a full-on rumble in her chest, causing her emotions to rise with it as a blend of shock, elation, annoyance, and nervousness muddled her senses.

Desmond scoffed. "Your boyfriend is really annoying."

"He's not my boyfriend," was all Cait could think to say as heat flared to her cheeks from both embarrassment and irritation.

"You should probably tell him that," he replied with a hint of irritation in his tone too.

Cait rolled her eyes, averting her gaze. "What's the real reason you walked here?"

With his signature irreverence, Desmond shrugged. "Well, I wanted to talk to you, and people would have heard my car if I drove."

"That's because you have a stupid car," she deflected, trying not to allow her heart to warm.

He stared at her in mock offense. "Clarisse is beautiful."

Cait raised an eyebrow. "It's impractical."

"That's the point."

Unable to stop her smile, Cait punched his arm. She wanted to tell him that she'd missed him, that she was happy he had walked two miles to sneak into her room just so he could talk to her. But she didn't, because not only did she have to make him leave, but she also couldn't admit to feeling those things for him either.

"Those are pretty cute pj's, Caity," he teased, giving a gentle tug to one of the spaghetti straps of her tank.

The reminder of just how undressed she was drew heat to her cheeks again. "You can't stay, Des," she insisted.

"Why not?"

"This is my *room*," she said, making sure her inflection said what she didn't want to say aloud.

Desmond's wry grin returned as he held her gaze. "As fun as it would be, I'm not here for *that*."

"That's—well, I—I know *that*. That's beside the point," she whispered, face aflame. She struggled to hold his gaze, crossing her arms self-consciously once more.

Desmond wet his lips. "That's not helping anything, Caity."

Confused, Cait caught Desmond's pointed downward glance. She followed his gaze, noticing the cleavage she'd created in an attempt to cover up. With a gasp, she whirled around, the sound of Desmond's low chuckle following her.

Casting about the room for help, Cait grabbed the long sweater draped over the back of her desk chair. She pulled it on, wrapping it around herself. It didn't do much to cover her legs, but considering how pale and pathetic they were, she didn't think they were much to look at anyway.

When she turned back to Desmond, he'd made himself comfortable on the window seat. "You don't have to worry," he teased, settling against the wall. "I'm not that depraved."

"You still can't stay," Cait returned, voice thin.

"Again, I ask: Why not?"

"Desmond—" She took a step closer to the bench. "This is my house. My nan or one of my sisters could hear us. Or worse, they could come into the room and catch you here."

He shrugged as though it were a nonissue. "Lock the door."

"We're not allowed."

His eyebrows rose. "You're 'not allowed'? What is this some sort of rehab center where they do random sweeps of the rooms to be sure you aren't hiding drugs?"

"It's a matter of principle. We keep our doors unlocked to show we have nothing to hide."

"What if you simply want to be left alone?"

"Then we tell each other." Though more likely, Rese or Genni would yell it at each other.

Desmond narrowed his eyes. "Your family is weird."

With a sigh, Cait took another step closer. "Desmond, you *have* to go," she pleaded. "The longer you're here, the more likely they'll hear us."

"We're whispering," he countered.

"These walls are thin."

Desmond leaned forward, his arms crossed. "So, what? I'm not allowed to see you anymore?"

"That's—that's not—"

"It's been a week, Caity." He glared at her, a look of indignation in his rich brown gaze. "A whole freakin' week since I've gotten to talk to you. And things have happened that I'd like to tell you about."

"I know," Cait promised. She found herself taking the seat next to him as though drawn to his side. Her knee brushed his thigh on the small bench. "But there's nothing I can do. Matt keeps asking me to hang out, and I can't tell him no."

"Actually, you *can*," Desmond retorted.

"No, I can't," she insisted. "He's my only friend, Desmond."

She caught the way Desmond's jaw tightened at the claim. It was as though he was frustrated that she didn't consider him her friend. A foolish flare of delight warmed Cait's chest at the thought.

"I'm alone at the school," she continued. "If I tell Matt no, I'm afraid I'll hurt him, and he won't want to be my friend anymore. Besides that . . . I think he may need me as a friend too."

Desmond frowned. "What do you mean?"

"I dunno, he just—he seems kind of lost," she said. "Like he's just as lonely as I am."

"So, you're pity-friends with him," he surmised.

"It's not pity," she argued. "It's more like—more like compassion. He's had a tough go, and I feel bad for him."

He scowled. "Compassion is the term people use when they want to sound pious. At the end of the day, pity and compassion are the same thing."

"Don't call it compassion then," Cait returned. "Call it understanding. He's lost his family—in a different way than I have, but still . . . I understand what he's going through. And I'm uniquely qualified to be his friend because of it."

"What about me?" Desmond demanded, leaning in toward her. "You're throwing me over for puppy-face-stick-figure-boy? I guess that's what I get for hanging out with a dog person."

Nose scrunched at the bizarre description, Cait couldn't help but laugh. If she didn't know better, she'd think he was jealous. She pulled her other leg underneath her, drawing closer to him. "Don't be mean," she chastised. "You don't even know Matt."

"I don't *want* to know Matt," he returned. "I have enough friends, thank you. And he seems like a handful."

With a sigh, Cait found herself admitting, "He sort of is. But . . . in a good way."

Desmond looked at her incredulously. "Can you be a handful in a good way?"

"You're a handful," she retorted.

He grinned slyly. "Oh, babe, I'm two handfuls."

The sarcasm in Desmond's tone told her not to take him seriously, yet her heart stuttered at the flirtation. She swallowed past the feeling, tucking some hair behind her ear as she turned away.

Desmond nudged her knee, where it was propped in the air between them. "You've gotta stop seeing that kid," he whispered, his hand dropping to rest by her foot on the cushion.

Cait played with the hem of her sweater. "Why?"

"Because it's getting in the way of us."

Us. Were they an "us"? Cait had always thought that impossible.

Meeting his eyes, Cait tried to detect Desmond's mood. Generally, she was good at reading him. But now, with her mind humming and her skin flushed, she was starting to question her better judgment. He held her gaze, an unreadable, steady expression on his face as his fingers rested casually against the side of her foot.

Cait's breath caught, realizing how close they were to one another. If she wanted, she could easily rest her hand on his leg. Or better yet, on his neck, drawing him across the short distance for what she really wanted.

Desmond had kissed Cait four times. Once on each of her birthdays for the last four years. First on her fourteenth birthday, then again on her fifteenth. When he repeated the now official tradition on her sixteenth, she'd expected it—hoped for it—on her seventeenth, and he'd not failed to rise to the occasion. None of them were serious, and none of them were particularly romantic. They were simple, near-platonic pecks on the lips that hardly counted. Nothing that promised anything more to her.

But this close to him, this alone with him, Cait couldn't help anticipating her next birthday. They were nearing eighteen, both of them, in just one more month. Cait was only fifteen days younger than Desmond. And while she knew better than to expect anything from their relationship, she couldn't deny that she'd been counting down the days until he would kiss her again—as platonic and simple as it might be.

The tension of their nearness on the small window seat continued to build up between them, making Cait's mind fuzzy. The hum trilled in her brain, urging her to lean into Desmond and test the boundaries of what they were to each other.

The thought kicked Cait back to reality. They were in her room. They were completely *alone* in her room. And she couldn't let dreams of what would never be get in the way of what really was.

"I'm not going to stop hanging out with Matt," she heard herself say.

Desmond turned away from her, lips pressed together in agitation.

"I'm alone, Desmond," she reminded him. "I'm always alone, and I'll always be alone if I drive away the one friend who's crazy enough to want to hang around me."

Drawing back, Desmond clasped his hands between his knees. He didn't respond, but she could almost hear the retort on his lips. *He* wanted to hang around her.

But he couldn't. They both knew that. Their secret moments together were coming to an end. Sooner than she'd hoped, it seemed. She couldn't rely on this strangely painful and wonderful relationship they had to sustain her anymore.

If Cait ever hoped to move on from Desmond, she had to have someone to move on to. And right now, Matt was her only choice.

Cait found herself vaguely wondering if that would mean something more than friendship between them. Could she ever be happy being with anyone but Desmond? Could she feel for someone else even a fraction of the emotions she felt for him? That mind-humming, heart-stilling, pulse-thrumming sensation—could anyone else do that to her? Did she want them to?

Sometimes, Cait asked herself: Why Desmond? What was it about him that made her feel those things? Was this what it felt like to be in love? She couldn't be sure. She did love Desmond; she knew that. She wouldn't be willing to let him leave her if she didn't. Sure, she hated the thought of losing him, but she knew it was for the best—for his best. And she would gladly lose him if that meant that he went on to live a full life—even with someone else. But did that mean that she was *in love* with him?

Cait rose from the bench, gaining a much-needed distance from him. "You need to go, Desmond," she whispered. "And you can't come back here."

"Is this it then?" he asked, a hollowness to his tone. "No more seeing each other. No more visits at the cove; no more meeting on the rooftop?"

Panic caused her heart to stutter. "No, that's—this doesn't have to. . . ." Cait stopped herself. Shouldn't this be the end? Wouldn't it be better for them both if they said their goodbyes now and let this all go?

"I'm not ready for that, Lewan," he whispered.

Locked in place by his honesty and adamant stare, Cait struggled to understand her internal reaction. Her chest constricted, her throat burning with fear while her skin tingled in anticipation. The hum caused her sense of reason to falter. It was like staring at Desmond, hearing that he wasn't ready to lose her, had completely broken her.

"I'm not either," she admitted.

A look of relief crossed Desmond's face.

"But I can't stop being friends with Matt either," she continued, somehow keeping a grip on her sanity if only by the tips of her fingers.

He looked ready to argue, but she spoke before he could. "We may not be able to see one another as much, but we can still meet from time to time. You just—you can't come here. And we'll have to be more intentional about finding ways to get to the cove."

With a sigh, Desmond stood. "All right," he murmured. "Well, I'm busy the next few days. Dad has got me doing stakeout duty all weekend. Which reminds me, we need to talk about some spirit-world-shit that's going on."

"Des," she chided.

He tapped her nose. "There's that wrinkle again," he teased. "You really need to work on your poker face, Lewan."

"Maybe you should work on your profanity, Simon."

"Why do you think I swear so much?"

Though Cait gave him a playful shove, she had to admit that he didn't swear *that* much. She knew he did it more out of dramatic effect than any real intention of foulness. It almost made it acceptable. It certainly made it hard for her not to laugh at it most times.

Desmond carefully reopened the window, a rush of cold air seeping through. He gave a melodramatic shiver, then grinned at her. "I wouldn't walk two miles in the blistering cold for just anyone, you know that, right, Lewan?"

Cait did know it.

Kneeling on the window seat, he scanned her one last time. "You really do look good in pink," he remarked, then began to exit.

Even as she blushed, Cait felt a tingle of joy spreading within her.

"Oh, yeah," Desmond whirled around, already halfway out the window, "I keep meaning to tell you: I'm sorry."

Surprised, Cait furrowed her brow. "For what?"

He blinked. "You don't remember?"

She shook her head.

"Never mind, then." He smirked. "Just remember that I apologized the next time I do something stupid."

"You're always doing something stupid, Des," she charged.

He winked. "It's more fun that way."

Then he was gone, sneaking across the roof of the back porch and dropping momentarily out of sight into her backyard. Cait watched, braving the frigid air to keep a better view as Desmond crept across the lawn and disappeared into the woods.

CHAPTER TWELVE

Desmond

S takeouts were supposed to be exciting, especially when you were waiting for a beast to spring up out of nowhere and attack you.

But Desmond was annoyed to discover that they were simply the most boring experience of his life.

After the Lavignes had cleared the island of the beasts' presence, the rest of the Warden was allowed to join the investigation. William had chosen to keep the number small. Each night, a band of nine Warden members were assigned to patrol the island, watching for anyone or anything suspicious. In groups of three, two regular members per singular Lavigne, they hid in the dark trees, watching and waiting.

To ensure that his son "did his part," William had assigned Desmond to each non-school night. Now, on his second stakeout, he patrolled with Brady and Garrett through the dark, thankful that he'd been paired up with his friends. Last night, he'd gotten stuck with Gary Lavigne—Brady's grandfather—and Kenneth Greene, the town doctor. The doc wasn't too bad, but he was boring, and staunch ol' Gary was on edge the whole night, jumping at every shadow.

Though Desmond had to admit, he couldn't entirely blame the old reverend. The forest was particularly eerie at night, the darkness giving the forest a spectral quality, washed out in the moonlight. And after having seen that crack in the Veil's trunk, the woods bore an extra dose of spookiness these days.

Under the tree cover, Desmond caught occasional glimpses of the night sky. The moon glowed with white silver light halfway across its face, pinpricks of stars dotting the black expanse around it. It gave the trees skeletal silhouettes. The strangely quiet forest seemed to whisper with danger.

It didn't help that Brady spent the stakeout telling them about the different beasts they'd discovered and cleaned out the last few days. True to Fish's theory, a whole consortium of scylla had taken up residence in a tree. Their sucker-covered tentacles whipped through the air with surprising strength.

"You're making that up," Garrett objected. "There's no such thing as a consorti-whatever, idiot."

Brady leveled him with a bored stare. "A consortium is the term you use when referring to a group of octopodes, *idiot*."

"What else did you find?" Desmond asked, more unnerved than the front he presented. He'd read enough Lovecraft, Poe, and King for Brady's stories to make an impressively horrific impact on his imagination.

They moved slowly through the trees, attempting to make as little noise as possible as Brady told his hushed tales. Garrett wasn't great at stealth, but he was vigilant, brave to the point of stupidity, and strong enough to back that stupidity up, so Desmond was happy to have him around.

Winding through the trees, Brady began his next story. He'd stuck with his dad on the one trip he'd joined. There were far more beasts in the woods than they'd expected. "It was like they were just waiting for the sun to go down," he whispered. "As though they could shrink themselves down and live in the shadows until night fell."

Most of the creatures Brady had witnessed Desmond knew by name if not by actual experience. His dad had made him read an essay by Henry Lawrence—grandson of the Warden founder—when he was a kid, detailing the twelve forms of beasts. There weren't any pictures, but his imagination and the aid of Cait's drawings created them on their own.

Brady, Ben, Fish, and the rest of the Lavignes had discovered nearly every form of beast within the woods of Aster Island. Scylla, arachne, hellhounds, valravns, artios, nyct, wendigos, and even sith like Hades. Though the cat-like creatures Brady described were far larger and more evil-sounding than Hades could ever be.

Desmond had never told Brady or Garrett about Hades. He sometimes thought about revealing his secret to his friends just to see how they would react. He wondered which they'd freak out over more: his use of the spirit world or his keeping a sith as a pet? Their reactions would probably be worth whatever trouble he wound up in should either of them tell on him.

Though, truthfully, Desmond wasn't worried about Brady betraying him. No matter how self-righteous his friend could act, Brady wasn't a snitch. His word was his bond, and Desmond could trust him with his life.

Garrett, however, would promise to never say a word, then blab to the first person he thought he could impress with the knowledge. He wasn't intentionally a douche, but sometimes Garrett's pride got the best of him. His cousin was a show-off—no ifs, ands, or buts about it. And while Desmond sometimes wished he could've been lucky enough to have Scott as the Edgars cousin closest to him, there was a sincerity in Garrett's reckless manner that Scott had never quite possessed.

Scanning his two best friends, Desmond found himself smiling. Garrett had his face screwed up in disgust as Brady coolly described the nest of ratatoskr they'd stumbled upon—effectively a rat king of

Lovecraftian horror, their tails and razor-sharp claws all tangled together as they roiled around each other.

At the front of the group, Brady slowed his pace, falling silent.

"What is it?" Desmond whispered. "You hear something?"

Brady shook his head, beginning to veer to the right. "Can't you feel it? We're getting near the Veil."

"The what?" Garrett asked.

"Shh." Desmond waved a hand at his beefy, blond cousin. Garrett didn't know about the Veil, and he wasn't supposed to. He turned back to Brady. "What's the problem with that? Isn't that where the action will be anyway?"

Turning toward them, Brady narrowed his eyes dramatically, making them appear shut. "It's the most *dangerous* place on this island."

"It's a tree," Desmond returned.

"It's not just a tree."

"What are you two talking about?" Garrett asked, his attempted whisper not quite low enough.

Desmond sighed. "Above your classification, bud."

"Then why am I here?"

He set a hand on his friend's shoulder, having to reach up to do it. "Because you make a great shield."

Garrett gave him an annoyed glare.

Desmond addressed Brady again. "Has anyone been assigned to watch the Veil?"

"No," Brady admitted. "It's Warden policy to keep a distance. Besides, we don't know what's happening to it. It's not a good idea to lurk near something so unknown."

"That's the whole reason we're out here," Desmond returned. "Listen, Brade—we need to figure this thing out, right? Well, the most surefire way to tell if someone is coming out here to screw with the Veil is to *be* by the Veil."

"We're here to watch for suspicious activity," Brady countered. "That's it."

Desmond crossed his arms, smirking. "You're just scared to go near it."

"I've been near it plenty," Brady replied.

"So, you'd be fine to go back?" he challenged.

"Sure, but we've got a job to do."

"Right. To stop whoever's summoning beasts."

Garrett watched the two of them as they argued, his head whipping back and forth.

With a sigh, Brady gestured away from the Veil's direction. "Let's stick to the path, Desmond," he practically begged. "We've been given a job. I don't want to screw it up."

"We could do that," Desmond said, then stepped toward the Veil. "Or we could go to the freaking Veil and solve this damn mystery."

"There's no guarantee that'll solve anything."

Garrett raised his hand, gaining their attention. "Quick thought— whatever we choose, we probably shouldn't stand in one place so long. Especially not after you two have been talking so loud."

"We're whispering," Brady objected.

"You're really not," Garrett replied.

Without knowing why, Desmond took the moment to spin on his heel and head straight for the Veil. He knew Brady and Garrett would follow. There was no reason for him to fear facing any danger alone. And worst case, he'd defend himself with the spirit world. He knew that he could. He'd even summoned a rift like the ones the Lavignes wielded a handful of times—in the privacy of his room, of course, and just for the experience of it. Still, he knew, if need be, he could draw forth the essence of the spirit world as easily as any Lavigne.

The sound of Garrett and Brady working to catch up with Desmond fell to a muffled crunch of dried leaves and grass as they approached the clearing of the Veil. Brady grumbled under his breath about this being a bad idea, but Desmond didn't care. He was bored, and they'd been out here three full nights. The longer they took to figure out who was summoning beasts and for what reason, the more danger Cait was in.

Desmond couldn't quite put his finger on what it was, but he knew this involved her. Whether it had something to do with that prophecy Hunter mentioned, or if it was simply that spirit that had attached itself to her family all those years ago, Cait was at least tied to everything happening. It scared him, the idea that it could be Cait that the monster chose. Her dreams scared him. Whatever their future brought, he knew he couldn't be with her—his looming role as her family's captor assured that. But it would be a million times worse if she turned out to be the one tied to that creature.

None of that mattered right now, Desmond reminded himself. Their future was their future, and he couldn't change that. But he could make sure this Wielder—be them Druid or otherwise—didn't draw her into their wicked scheme.

Desmond felt it—the shift in the atmosphere as they neared the Veil. The feeling was almost as though the air pressure had lightened. That supernatural sense of calm settled over him.

The giant sycamore hovered in the distance, its mottled trunk a gradient of grays in the night. Brady grabbed Desmond's arm, drawing him to a halt inside the tree line, still dozens of yards away from the Veil. "This is as far as we go," he insisted, his words a roaring whisper in the dead silence around them.

Reluctantly, Desmond nodded. He wanted to get another look at that split, but he knew Brady was right. They had no reason to get closer. They had a good enough view from the cover of the trees.

Hunkering down in the brush, Desmond kept his eyes on the Veil. He felt Garrett's breath on his face as his friend whispered, "Where's this Veil-thing?"

"I told you," he murmured, distracted by his vigil. "You're not allowed to know."

"My dad's the sheriff," Garrett argued.

Desmond rolled his eyes. "And you're his second son. Which means that you won't be getting his job."

"I'm still gonna be a deputy," he grumbled.

"Yes, and that's a very important job. Now, shut up and watch that tree."

In true stakeout form, the three boys waited. And waited. And waited. And waited some more.

After a while, Desmond's legs began to burn, squatting on his haunches. He eventually plunked down on his butt for relief. Brady begged him to go at least half a dozen times, and he refused every plea. This was how they were going to get their answers. He knew it.

The night wore on, and Garrett began to doze off. Desmond had to elbow him in the ribs every few minutes to keep him from snoring. It gave him something to do, so he didn't mind.

Desmond was beginning to see things, staring at the tree for so long. Its strangely patterned bark started swirling into the faces of howling wraiths in his lingering imagination. Its shivering leaves and swaying branches turned into drifting ghosts at the edges of his vision. If his friends hadn't been at his side, he knew he would have cut and run a long time ago.

The shadows elongated in the hollow around the Veil. At first, Desmond thought it was another trick of his imagination. Then he thought it was the clouds drifting over the moon. But when he looked up through the skeletal branches toward the sky, he found the half-moon unobstructed.

Brady's elbow jammed into Desmond's side, jolting him back to the forest. He only spared his friend a split-second glance to see him pointing straight at the Veil. Desmond jerked his gaze to the tree just in time to see the last of a strange, ember-like shimmer flaring across the bark right where the crack was located.

Desmond's jaw dropped. He rolled onto his knees, ready to push himself up. Then he froze.

The forest fell silent, the world shifting to an eerie stillness just before a shadow ripped out of the fissure and spilled down the side of the tree. It tumbled, rolling and growing, until it began to take form.

Desmond felt his throat close as Brady gripped his arm. Garrett gasped. In the clearing, under the swaying branches of the Veil, an aughisky took form—the devil-horse he'd seen Cait draw dozens of times in her sketchbook.

Muscles spasming with the urge to run, Desmond couldn't believe it. There, in front of them, a beast had simply *appeared*. It was the first he'd ever actually seen besides Hades. Afraid to take his eyes off the monster, he forced himself to take quick, darting glances around the forest, looking for whoever had summoned the creature.

But Desmond knew it was useless. He knew better than most. What they'd just witnessed—that wasn't how summoning beasts worked. When he summoned Hades, it was a simple blip of shadow and light, then *poof*, Hades was there. That strange, sparking light that had brought forth a cloud of smoke—that was *not* how beasts were summoned.

"We—we gotta get out of here," Desmond heard himself saying.

Brady rose at his side, shaking his head. "No, man, we gotta take care of it!" he exclaimed, his voice an insistent hush. "We can't leave a beast to roam the forest unchecked."

"Do you see the size of that thing?" Garrett demanded, his eyes darting nervously back to the aughisky. It began to stamp its serrated hooves, its smoky mane drifting sinisterly around its horns. Even from this distance, Desmond knew the thing would tower over Garrett's six-foot-three-inch frame.

Brady hardened his jaw, that self-righteous edge of his kicking in.

That was the problem with Brady. At the end of the day, he always did the right thing.

With long, rapid strides, Brady leaped away from Desmond and Garrett, heading straight for the aughisky. With a grimace, Desmond tore off after him.

The devil-horse was beginning to prowl around the tree, its neon eyes flashing. Brady's not-so-quiet approach drew its immediate attention, an irritated snort puffing out of its massive nostrils. Desmond always thought aughisky looked an awful lot like those horses the Ringwraiths rode in *Lord of the Rings*, the ones with nails through their hooves. They had an equally horrifying demeanor, all inky shadow and vengeful muscle. Should the thing decide to charge any of them, they'd be hard-pressed to jump out of the way in time.

Brady either didn't know about the aughisky's abilities or didn't care. He tore out of the forest, running straight across the edge of the drying grass circle. The aughisky shook its head furiously, rearing up on its hind legs at the sudden appearance of a human.

Certain the beast would clobber his friend, Desmond barreled into the clearing. But Brady didn't need his rescue. Hand raised, Brady stood unflinchingly before the beast, even as its jagged hooves came crashing to the earth, ripping the grass and dirt to shreds.

"Stop!" Brady ordered.

The aughisky listened. It snorted and stamped, but it held its ground.

Garrett caught up to Desmond, drawing up behind him. They watched as Brady, right hand held aloft, took a single step closer to the devil-horse. Desmond noted that he held his other hand down by his side, the faintest ripple of gray light hovering around it.

Desmond had always known that Brady would be a Sage like his dad. It was necessary, given the way Porthaven relied on the Lavignes. But somehow, seeing the reality surprised him. In all his life, he'd never seen anyone else summon the spirit world's essence. It was the theory that had drawn him to test it for himself. And seeing his friend manage it so easily, with such control, made his fingers tremble with the urge to draw on the essence himself.

He squashed the desire, forcing himself to watch closely as Brady controlled the beast. "You're not supposed to be here," he heard Brady saying, almost as though it surprised him. "You're—that's. . . . Whatever the case, you need to go."

The aughisky shook its head, its black, vaporous mane swaying with the movement.

"Go on," Brady said, lowering his hand with a purposeful angle. "Back in the Veil."

As he said the last part, Brady made a sweeping motion like he could shove the aughisky back into the tree. And it worked.

In a wisp of smoke and ash, the devil-horse burst apart. The tree sucked the beast back into itself until every last speck was gone.

Desmond felt his breath shudder out of him. He ran a hand over his face. "Dude, that was—" He fell silent as Brady whirled around to glare at him.

"That was your fault," he said.

"What?" Desmond gaped at him. "Why are you blaming me? We just solved the case."

"We could have gotten killed, Desmond."

"Clearly," he gestured from Brady's head to his feet, "you're perfectly capable of keeping us safe."

"Yeah, dude," Garrett added. "That was seriously awesome."

"You're both seriously idiots," Brady retorted. "I've never faced a beast on my own before. Be thankful there wasn't more than one. I'm not that strong yet."

"You seemed strong enough to me," Garrett remarked.

"That's 'cause the thing wasn't tethered to anyone else," Brady countered, then shrugged. "It wasn't aggressive either."

Desmond raised his eyebrow. "You're telling me that wasn't aggression? The thing nearly trampled you."

"It was frightened," Brady said, arms crossed. "Come on, we need to get out of here."

Perfectly happy to leave the potential threat of more beasts behind, Desmond and Garrett kept pace with Brady as he started back into the woods.

"What did you mean?" Desmond asked.

Brady glanced at him. "About what?"

"When you said it wasn't tethered to anyone else."

"Beasts tether themselves to their summoner," he explained. "Kind of like when someone tethers a ghost to a location to create a phantom. They need something to hold onto, something to keep them here in the physical world."

"Then how come this one didn't have someone it was attached to?" Garrett asked.

Brady hesitated, tucking his hands into his jacket pockets. "Because no one summoned it."

Desmond's heartbeat kicked into overdrive, his mind reeling as his suspicions were confirmed. There hadn't been a summoner in the first place, which meant no one was building an army. No one was practicing. These beasts were forming all on their own.

"Hang on—" Desmond nudged Brady's arm as they hurried through the forest. "How does that work? If they need to have something they're tethered to, how were the beasts sticking around?"

Brady shrugged. "They must've been tethering to the location. To the island itself."

"They can do that?"

"I don't see why not. If you can tether a ghost to a location, why couldn't a beast tether itself as a matter of survival?"

"Guys," Garrett interrupted, "you're losing me. We don't have ghosts in Porthaven."

"That's 'cause we don't have Druids in Porthaven," Brady said.

"What does any of this have to do with the person summoning beasts?" Garrett pressed.

Brady shared a look with Desmond. They weren't supposed to be too open with Garrett. Not when the security of Porthaven would fall to his older brother. Not when it would mean one more person they had to keep an eye on.

But in this case, there wasn't much they could do.

Desmond took the lead, guiding them toward Fish's cottage on the far side of the island. "No one is summoning beasts, Garrett," he said. "The Veil is creating them itself."

CHAPTER THIRTEEN

Desmond

The town council was, admittedly, a boys' club. In all reality, it was simply the way things worked out. And it wasn't exactly the *town* council, anyway.

The five Warden families ran Porthaven: Simon, Varon, Lavigne, Edgars, and Greene. That meant if your last name wasn't one of those five, you weren't allowed on the council purely on the basis that you didn't know the Warden existed in the first place.

The five families did their best not to marry amongst themselves. Of course, the Varons and Simons were from the same genetic heritage, automatically precluding any cross-contamination happening there. William Simon and Robin Edgars had been the first Warden couple to breach the unspoken rule in almost a century. And presently, it looked highly likely that Hunter Varon and Elizabeth Greene would shortly follow that faux pas.

Regardless, when a woman from one of the families married outside of the Warden, she made the choice to leave the organization. Not officially, but effectually. It was the responsibility of the Warden families to keep the spirit world safe. That meant keeping it unknown to outsiders. Only members of the five families even knew of the spirit world's existence. So the daughters who went on to marry outsiders kept their knowledge safe and their husbands ignorant. Which, in turn, made said daughters incapable of joining the council.

As for the women who married into the five families, they were made aware of the Warden and its responsibilities upon their marriages. After their introduction to the world, most took a decidedly neutral position on the whole subject. They weren't opposed to their husbands' dealings, but they weren't all that interested in it themselves. For those like Desmond's mother, Robin, or Fish's wife, Laurel—women who had the gumption to take a real position amongst the Warden—they were happy to make a difference with their husbands rather than sitting through laborious council meetings.

A choice Desmond *wished* he had.

He wasn't even supposed to be on the council in the first place. But none of the other members had been brave enough to argue when his dad requested to make him an honorary member while still a minor.

Sitting in the meeting room at the town hall, the council discussed the discoveries that Desmond, Brady, and Garrett had made the night before. His father had called the emergency meeting immediately following the church service that morning. It worked in their favor. The government building was completely silent, with not a single worker in sight.

Desmond swiveled in his chair like a five-year-old, immensely bored as the council endlessly debated Brady's discovery of the untethered beasts and Desmond's theory that the Veil was birthing the beasts on its own. He'd always hated the meeting room with its bland beige walls, stuffy furnishings, and cliché art prints. A ginormous, clunky table took up the majority of the space as fourteen of the other sixteen Warden members surrounded it as though they were Arthur's knights. Except this table was oval. The chairs weren't even that comfortable. Just a fancy leather that made them all look like cigar-smoking CEOs.

Glancing up the table at Dwight Greene, the oldest member of the council at seventy-something, Desmond thought that the past-retirement doctor fit the role. He had a bushy white beard that sort of puffed up when he spoke. And Desmond had most certainly smelled cigar smoke on the man before.

"Do we really believe that the Veil is . . . discharging beasts?" Gregory Varon—Hunter's grandfather—was asking, his extremely Varon-like hooded eyes narrowing.

Desmond smirked at the repulsive terminology but kept his opinion to himself.

"Are you saying that our sons are lying?" William asked coolly.

"Of course not, William," Gregory assured him. "I'm simply suggesting that perhaps they misunderstood what they saw."

"It does seem strange," Kenneth Greene agreed. "Have any of us here ever heard of a Veil producing beasts on its own?"

Most of the men shook their heads while the rest sat still without response.

Ben spoke up. "I haven't heard of a Veil doing *anything* on its own."

His father, Gary, the reverend emeritus, nodded and noted, "Neither have I."

"That doesn't mean they can't," Fish countered, stroking his plush beard.

The men all turned to him in surprise.

"What do you mean?" William asked.

Fish shrugged casually. "I simply mean, we don't know what the Veils are capable of. We like to talk a big game, but do any of us actually know anything we're discussing here?"

"Our families have been members of the Warden for centuries, Fish," Kenneth said.

"Some of us," Gregory Varon added, "for over five centuries."

Desmond rolled his eyes. Of course, a Varon would bring up their "long history" with the Warden. It wasn't as though the Simons shared any less of Gabriel Varon's blood than the rest of them.

Ignoring the obvious jab, William kept his attention on the lightkeeper. "You may have a point," he admitted. "There is certainly a great deal we don't fully understand about the spirit world. That said, if the Veils were sentient, we would have heard *something* about it through the centuries."

"Maybe we have," Ben offered. "Or at least, maybe the Warden has, and they haven't shared it with us."

Rick raised his brow. "Seems like the sort of info to share."

Ben didn't appear deterred. "We know better than most how important it is to be selective with whom we give information to, Rick. Perhaps they felt it too dangerous to make known to the masses."

"But we have a Veil," John Lavigne, Fish's eldest son, said. "If they learned that a Veil could do this, wouldn't we be some of the first people they'd tell?"

There was a collective pause as they all took this in.

Desmond looked across the table at his dad. William ran a hand over his mouth, his dark eyes on the tabletop, deep in thought.

There was a chance, Desmond thought, that the Warden had said something, and just like with that prophecy, his family had chosen to keep it to themselves.

But then, that was if he believed Hunter Varon was telling the truth. Which he didn't. At least, he mostly didn't. His plans after this meeting were purely to prove to himself that Hunter didn't know anything.

"Whatever the Warden has or hasn't told us," William finally said, "we have to handle this on our own."

Several of the council members looked at the mayor with dubious expressions. He held up a hand to still their objections. "We are a month away from the Fisher's Festival," he reminded them. "Our town survives on that festival and the tourism it brings to our shores. We don't have time to waffle on the Veil's sentience or its abilities. Our objective is to find out how to stop it from producing any more beasts so that we can return this town to safety."

"It isn't exactly unsafe as it is," Fish offered. "There were weeks' worth of beasts hidden in the island's forest. We put them down easily. It isn't ideal, but worst case, we contain the situation in the same fashion for a while longer."

Dwight Greene's mustache twitched. His old voice was gravelly as he spoke. "It's dangerous to assume that because nothing bad has happened, that nothing bad will happen."

"That's not what I'm suggesting, doc." Fish angled toward the man. "I'm simply saying that we can keep it in check for a while longer. We keep the patrols going, watching the perimeter of the Veil in particular. It appears the Veil is only summoning a singular beast each night. We can put them down as they show up. It isn't a long-term solution, but it *is* a workable, short-term one."

William nodded, looking toward the sheriff at his side. "Rick, I'll leave you in charge of keeping a team on rotation."

"We're not that big, Will," he replied. "It'll be difficult to keep up."

"With luck," William said, an ominous tilt to his voice, "it won't last long."

Desmond didn't see how they could sustain a patrol like that even for a month more. Even with the women and children, the Warden members only numbered into the fifties. That number included Desmond's seventy-five-year-old grandmother all the way to Fish's youngest grandson at six. And he really didn't think those were exactly useable candidates for running patrol.

"What if we asked the Warden—"

William cut Gregory Varon off. "We're not calling for help," he insisted. "You know how they handle situations like this. They swoop in with their teams and take complete control. We'd become bystanders in our own town. We'll handle it ourselves."

A dangerous current of tension filled the room. This always happened when a Varon tried to assert themselves over the Simons. Sometimes Desmond wished the whole thing would implode already—let the Varons and Simons finally duke it out. After more than a hundred years, you'd think someone would have come to blows already. Or that someone would have been brave enough to step up and call a truce. Yet they were still at it. So much so that Desmond and Hunter hated one another's guts over it.

Desmond found it all to be rather pathetic.

"What do we do in the meantime?" Raymond Edgars asked. The fire marshal looked just like his brother, Rick, and sister, Robin, and very little like his son, Scott.

The council waited for their leader's orders.

With his hands clasped on the table, William surveyed them all. "We keep up the patrols at night," he restated. "And in the day, we'll look through every record regarding the spirit world that we have here within Porthaven. We'll study every entry referencing Veils. We'll figure out just what these things are capable of. And we'll find out how to shut them down."

"What if we don't find anything?" The caustic question came from Hunter's dad, Brett Varon. "What if we do all this research and we come up empty? Will you agree to contact the Warden then?"

"We *are* the Warden in Porthaven," William returned. "That is the job we were given."

Brett held his glare with steady calm. "And if we fail at that job?"

A stony expressionlessness filled William's face, the calm before the storm. "Then I will resign from my position as the leader of both this town and the Warden."

Desmond felt his whole body still in shock. A tremor rolled through his hand, his fingers flinching on the leather arm of his seat. If his father resigned, it wouldn't just be his position he'd be giving up. It would also be Desmond's. Retirement would mean Desmond's instatement. A *resignation* would mean a usurpation of Desmond's future.

His first instinct was to hope they'd fail, forcing his father to stay true to his word. He knew his dad—he'd never back down from a promise made, no matter how much it hurt him. And that would mean that Desmond could be with Cait.

His second instinct was far more frightening.

Desmond glared at his father. If William *resigned*, he'd be taking away Desmond's rightful future as the true Varon. The power and responsibility that he craved just as much as he feared would be ripped from him. The hard work he'd put in to make himself the perfect heir would be gone in the blink of an eye. The chance to prove himself, to become the man he knew he could be, torn from his grasp.

They couldn't fail. Not if it meant that everything Desmond was would be taken from him.

While the rest of the council worked to cobble together the pieces of the meeting after such a declaration, Kenneth Greene spoke up once more. "One final topic to discuss on the matter," he began. "What of the Vessels?"

A different sort of silence fell.

Desmond's skin began to crawl. He tried not to draw attention to himself as he shifted in his seat.

"What about them?" William asked.

"Are we sure they have nothing to do with this?" Kenneth asked.

Pressing his lips together, Desmond wanted to snap at the man. Of course they suspected Cait and her sisters. Though, he supposed that the Faulks were included in that group, as well. Still, it didn't seem right to assume their involvement because of things they had no control over.

William held up a hand. "We have no reason to suspect them. The Faulks have always been cooperative, and the Lewan girls don't even know of their . . . condition."

"Are we sure the Lewans don't know?" Kenneth pressed.

"The block has been in place for almost twelve years," William retorted. "No one here has told them anything of the spirit world. And trust me when I say that Maeve doesn't want to lose her granddaughters the same way she lost her son. She would never tell them."

Kenneth dipped his chin in acquiescence as Dwight's mustache twitched. "I believe what my son is getting at," the old man rumbled, "is that his son is growing rather close to the eldest Lewan girl."

Unable to keep his snide grin in check, Desmond lifted a hand to cover it. There was little wonder why Ryan Greene had an interest in Therese Lewan. She was, for lack of a more creative term, hot. Like, supermodel-at-nineteen kind of hot. And she knew how to make thrift store finds work wonders for her figure. One of the reasons Desmond found her so repellent. She so obviously let her body win her attention while ignoring the fact that she also had a brain.

Quite the opposite of Cait. *She* was incredibly smart and allowed her attractive figure to speak for itself without turning it into a showpiece. Something he'd gained a fresh awareness of with the advent of those frilly pink pajamas.

Kenneth brushed off his father's comment with a delicate sweep of his hand. "I'm not worried about it," he said. "In fact, that's why he's not here today. He's going over to their place for dinner tonight."

Gary Lavigne shifted uncomfortably in his seat. "Do you think that's wise? Your son dating one of . . . *them*?"

A slightly irritated pinch pulled Kenneth's eyebrows together. "I think," he replied, a sharp edge to his tone, "that they're innocent young women. And if we're worried about their allegiance to this town, what better way to secure it than through a relationship with one of our own?"

Ben sighed, a disgruntled look on his face. "Please tell me you didn't send your son to seduce one of those poor girls all for the sake of gaining control over them."

Kenneth looked indignant. "I didn't send my son to do anything. He's taken with her. He knows what she may be, and I told him I applaud his lack of prejudice."

"Wow," Desmond heard himself say. The whole table turned to him, and he had no choice but to finish the snarky reply that came to his mind. "Aren't you open-minded?"

William glowered at him, and Desmond forced his mouth to stay shut despite the urge to keep going. He couldn't believe it. These men were discussing Cait and her sisters like they were some strange species of human. As though they were animals that needed careful watch. Alien creatures to entrap and study.

These men were who he was intended to become.

As William called the meeting to a close, Desmond glared at the tabletop. He muttered his goodbye to his uncles, Ben, and Fish, but he ignored the rest. What a joke this council was. What a joke they all were. A bunch of men with nothing better to do than find the most humane way to cage three young women, a young man, and all their futures.

While the council worked their way out of the town hall, Desmond pressed ahead, ignoring their meandering farewells. He hated them and himself. He hated what they stood for. And yet he wanted to lead them. He wanted his dad's job.

Desmond made it out of the hall before any of the councilmen. The cool breeze of the evening held a distinctive moisture that hinted at rain. He took the immediate left out of the town hall, glancing over his shoulder toward the docks. The deep purple and orange sky was thick with storm clouds.

Hurrying in the direction of their home, Desmond kept his gait confident and fast. He gave a single check to be sure no one was in sight before he looped around the sidewalk, cutting across the lawn toward the back of the hall. He hurried across the grass, straight for the back door. He slipped out the key he'd copied months ago for occasions such as this.

Desmond let himself back into the town hall, the building dark. He could still hear the last couple of councilmen ahead, their voices an ever-fading rumble of sound. He walked lightly, keeping his footsteps quiet against the hardwood, staying in the shadows. Then he heard the front door shut, silencing the last voices with it.

He stood still, listening to ensure he was truly alone. Then he moved from the shadowed hallway and to the stairs. Despite the knowledge that the building was empty, Desmond still moved carefully as he headed for the mayor's office. There were security cameras throughout the town hall, of course, but no one would have any reason to look at the tapes if he was cautious enough not to leave a trace.

Closing the office door behind him, Desmond let the latch fall back into place with a nearly silent *snap*. The setting sun cast a muted glow into the room around the closed blinds. Not willing to risk turning on a light, he moved in the dimness of evening.

Desmond took his dad's desk chair, its tufted leather comfortably plush. The government computers were never turned off, just locked for the evening. Desmond had figured out his dad's password years ago. Even with the security system's regular password update requirements, he'd deduced his dad's pattern as well—always a variation of Desmond's initials and date of birth in alternating orders. The sentiment did little to soften his heart. It was simply one more reminder of the son Desmond failed to be.

The desktop chimed, welcoming Desmond to the freshly unlocked homepage. He wasted no time. While he thought he had done a good enough job sneaking in, there was no guarantee. He had to move quickly.

Desmond doubted finding the information would be easy. However, he banked on the knowledge of his dad. If he could figure out his password, he could figure out how the man organized his most sensitive files.

Clicking through the documents and folders, Desmond zeroed in on the ones that pertained to the Warden as an obvious start. He ignored the mundane, readily available files, digging deeper into the more obscure parts of the hard drive. He reached a dead end faster than he expected.

Then, he tried a new approach. If his dad was hiding information from him, he was also hiding it from the Warden. This meant the prophecy wouldn't be sitting with other information that a Warden member might be searching for. Some of these folders were shared, after all.

No. If William was hiding something, he'd be cleverer about it.

Backing up to the central documents page, Desmond scanned the options. Boring governmental folders on budgets, vendors, employees, licenses, and proposals made up most of them. There was the Warden file, labeled "W"—as though that were difficult to figure out—and then one marked "Personal."

Desmond clicked on the personal folder. Immediately, he found family photos, records, and files. Digital copies of birth records, his parent's marriage certificate, their health insurance plan, and other typical sorts of adult-ish paperwork. And at the bottom was another folder labeled "Letters."

He moved the mouse and clicked. A box popped up, requesting a password.

"Seriously?" Desmond scoffed, typing in the same password from before: WDS100195.

The box cleared, giving a little animated shake to tell him he'd gotten it wrong.

Desmond narrowed his eyes, trying his parents' anniversary next.

Wrong.

His mom's initials and birthdate.

Wrong.

He paused, staring at the blinking cursor as it awaited another attempt. He didn't know how many tries it would allow him. What if there was some failsafe lock where if he failed too many times, it locked the file for hours? Or worse, what if it alerted his dad that someone was trying to access it? He couldn't risk trying every possible variation of their family's significant dates.

Then it clicked.

This wasn't about their family. It was about Cait's.

Recalling the information easily, Desmond carefully keyed in the date of her family's arrival in Porthaven: 101802.

The folder opened.

Predictable.

The document Desmond was looking for presented itself immediately: "Directive for Lewan Family Relocation." But there were half a dozen other files that Desmond had never heard of before.

On a whim, Desmond opened them all. It took him less than a minute to queue them all up on the printer. He quickly closed all the documents, clicked out of the folders, double-checked to be sure he left no trace, and relocked the computer.

Desmond jumped up from the desk, hurrying over to the printer on the credenza at the far side of the room. He tossed a glare at the family photo that hung on the wall there. It was a decade old. Little Desmond stood in the center of the picture with his dad on the right and his grandfather Charles on the left. The hard-fisted old man looked as unpleasant as Desmond remembered, his cold brown stare blank despite the feigned smile on his face.

No wonder his own dad was a piece of work. It ran in the Simon genetic code.

As the last of the papers spit out, Desmond quickly folded them up. He wished he had his backpack with him, but it would have been suspicious for him to carry it. Instead, he zipped up his jacket, carefully tucking the pages inside. Then he crept out of the building, locking the back door behind him.

It had begun to rain, the evening sky a blood orange wash bleeding into charcoal. Desmond walked with purpose around the back alley and onto Lawrence Avenue. His brisk pace got him to the corner easily. Then, he took a left instead of heading home. The ocean crashed with a rhythmic beat against the docks and beach. The drizzle began to weigh his hair down, so he slicked it back before digging his keys out of his pocket.

He'd come to the docks before the meeting to park his car, intent on never taking the documents back to his house. He didn't trust his dad or his mom not to search his room on some over-protective whim.

The ten-minute drive to the abandoned factory felt three times as long. The rain clouds smothered the last remaining rays of light, the sea turning steely gray in the darkness. Raindrops spattered his windshield double time, his wipers struggling to keep up with their pace. When he finally made it to the old lot, he pulled into the shadow of the building and turned off his headlights. In the storm, it was unlikely that anyone would see his car, but he didn't want to give them any extra chances.

With half a thought, Desmond summoned Hades, a dull flash of light preceding his appearance on the passenger seat. The cat-beast took up the whole seat, languidly stretching his back.

"Don't rip the leather," Desmond warned.

The sith blinked, and he could have sworn its lips turned up at the corners.

With a quick scratch under Hades's chin eliciting a low purr, Desmond pulled the papers from his jacket. He sorted through them quickly. One mentioned the Faulk family, which intrigued him. Another referenced the development of Porthaven itself. A third mentioned some woman named Elizabeth. But he passed over them all to return to the one about Cait's family. It included two pieces of paper: a letter dated just before the Lewan's arrival and the prophecy. He read the letter first.

Dear Mayor Charles Simon,

After consultation and debate, the Board of Directors at Sheraton Corporation has chosen the township of Porthaven, Maine, to take upon themselves the care of the remaining Lewan family: Maeve McCarthy-Lewan and her three granddaughters, Therese, Caitriona, and Genevieve.

It was under the urging of Sylvia Lyons that the Board arrived at this decision. Per the prophecy given to Mrs. Lyons via the spirit-being Corva, the Board believes it is in the best interest to follow her guidance.

Included is the prophecy in its entirety.

We appreciate your cooperation and care in this matter.

Sincerely,
Gregory Sheraton
Chairman of the Board

Desmond found the letter to be a tad impersonal, and he didn't get why this Sylvia chick had that much pull, but he recognized the title given to Corva. *Spirit-being.* An alternate, fancier term for the same kind of "demon" that plagued Cait's family.

Turning to the next page, Desmond overviewed the full prophecy for the first time. He reached across the console, weaving his fingers through Hades's silky blue-black fur. It helped to have some presence with him, to have a connection to someone as he read the words that might alter Cait's life.

The first lines he'd read before, naming the Simons the official caretakers of this "important task." Three simple, unimpressive lines that said surprisingly little with a date at the bottom: *September 23, 2002.* And for the first time, Desmond realized these lines were completely separate from the prophecy.

A wide gap separated the Simons' charge and the true prophecy.

"The Raven implores me to warn you: The Wolf is being hunted." A fittingly ominous start, Desmond supposed. *"The Children of Gaia will come to claim him and his Vessel, and, though they shall not succeed in full, they will end the Vessel's life. This, the premature death of Owen Lewan, will set in motion the final course."*

A cold sweat broke along Desmond's back, his mind forming suspicious conclusions before he'd finished the first paragraph. Still, he read on.

"The Vessel chosen before her time will bear the heaviest burden of us all, for this child is the only hope for true success." His eyes jumped down to the next set of increasingly menacing lines. *"The Wolf is either our greatest ally or our greatest demise. The bond of spirit and child will bring forth power like we've never seen. Together, Wolf and Vessel shall*

gather the heirs, command the beasts, and end this war: in our favor or against."

Desmond pursed his lips at the curious statement. What heirs? Surely, it didn't mean all the heirs of the spirit-beings. Those were scattered throughout the world, most of them unknown to the Warden. And everyone in the Warden knew that commanding beasts was the defining mark of the Druids. That couldn't be a good sign.

What's more, he couldn't say they were at war. He knew the Druids were out there, but were they really waging war with the Warden? He'd never met a Druid. Aside from Lilith, he'd never even been around one. And she considered the Warden to be a perfectly secure organization that could keep her safe from the cult. Didn't that mean that the Druids weren't really of that much concern?

Desmond turned his thoughts back to the page, and his stomach plummeted with the first sentence. *"The Warden's choice lay such: Save the current Vessel and prolong the war or allow his end to save our own. But be wary: Should we lose the Wolf to the Children of Gaia, we will lose the key to victory. Without the willing participation of the child Vessel, all will be lost. Our success shall come only at her great sacrifice."*

Desmond's hands began to shake. He let the papers fall as he stared at the rain rippling across his windshield. Hades let out a concerned "mew," but he couldn't respond. His heartbeat thudded in his ears as loud as the rumbling rain outside.

He forced himself to look down at the paper once more, eyes searching for the date that hovered below the prophecy: *May 28, 2002.*

They'd known.

The Warden had known that Owen Lewan's life was in danger—for months—and they'd chosen to do nothing. They could have saved his life. They could have kept Cait and her sisters from becoming orphans. And they'd done *nothing.*

It was worse than he'd ever thought.

Not only was it Porthaven's job to contain the Lewan girls, but it fell to them to groom whichever one had taken their father's curse upon herself. This prophecy tasked the Simons with preparing the Vessel for "great sacrifice."

Desmond's jaw tightened. There was no way to know for sure which daughter had inherited. Not without removing the block they'd so intentionally placed all those years ago. But *one* of them had.

The cold night air seeped through the car. Desmond shivered. His eyes drifted back to the prophecy, finding the line, *"The bond of spirit and child will bring forth power like we've never seen."*

Like we've never seen.

Like a Veil producing beasts all on its own?

Could that mean it *was* one of the Lewan girls causing the problems with the Veil?

His eyes flickered back down to the even more disturbing line. *"Our success shall come only at her great sacrifice."*

A spasm in his jaw informed Desmond that he'd clenched it too long. He struggled to release the tension.

Great sacrifice.

Whichever Lewan girl the Wolf had chosen . . . she was going to sacrifice something—*willingly*. Or the Warden would lose.

After discovering that they'd allowed Owen Lewan to become an unwitting sacrifice himself, he had no doubt they'd do whatever it took to convince the new Vessel to do the same.

Panic crawled through Desmond's chest. If this was right—if the prophecy came true—that meant Cait or one of her sisters might have to sacrifice themselves. It meant that Cait might die.

Desmond folded the letter and prophecy back in with the others. The paper creased with a ragged crinkle under his frantic movement. He opened his glove box, retrieving the plastic baggie he'd taken from the house. Shoving the papers inside, he refused to believe the prophecy was about Cait. She wasn't the one summoning beasts, nor was she the one the spirit-being had chosen. Why would the Wolf choose her in the first place? She was the quiet, timid one. The one who didn't want attention. The one who ran from trouble. Whichever of her sisters the Wolf had chosen, it didn't matter to him. It *hadn't* chosen her.

And as to the sins of the Warden—the discovery that they'd *allowed* the murder of Owen and Sabine Lewan for their own personal gain? Desmond would keep that tidbit to himself for now. It wouldn't do any good for him to tell Cait. It'd only break her heart, and he didn't have it in himself to do that to her.

The rest of the pages he'd filched—likely filled with more Warden transgressions—he'd have to come back and study later. For now, he had to get home. It was a school night. If he didn't get home in a timely manner, William would ask questions.

Rushing through the rain, Desmond carefully stashed the bag in the rusty letterbox at the front of the burned factory. Lightning flashed in the sky as he barreled back into the car. Hades hissed at the storm in the passenger seat.

The car roared with fury down the highway as Desmond rushed home. He refused to look toward the turnoff to Cait's home as he passed. The prophecy *wasn't* about her. She *wasn't* the Vessel. He wouldn't entertain the idea. Because if she was, then she wasn't just the girl he'd have to imprison. She was the girl he'd have to turn into a weapon. The girl he'd have to send to her death.

And no matter what, Desmond wouldn't do that. Doomed relationship or not, he would never let Cait become the linchpin to the Warden's victory. He wouldn't let her become their sacrifice.

CHAPTER FOURTEEN

Cait

If there was a perfect match to Rese's beauty, it was Ryan Greene. At an ideal six foot, two inches with jock-broad shoulders, his muscular physique was just the beginning of his physical recommendations. His sandy blond hair had a playful wave to it. His gray-green eyes held a mysterious sparkle. And his expression seemed perpetually locked in an amiable, charming grin.

Beyond that, Ryan knew how to get on everyone's good side. He had that "I'm dumb but funny" persona that inevitably made it impossible to dislike him. He was larger than life and sweeter than sugar.

And Cait found him to be immeasurably obnoxious.

Sitting around their tiny dining room table, Ryan smiled at the Lewan ladies. "Thank you so much for having me over, Mrs. Lewan," he said, then gestured to his plate with his fork. "My mom never makes anything half this good."

At his side, Rese beamed over at him. She'd dressed immaculately, her round eyes batting like a mad woman every time he glanced at her.

Maeve took his compliment with a grateful dip to her head. "It's our pleasure," she said, accent abnormally soft. "We don't get to entertain often enough."

That was an understatement. They *never* entertained. Ryan was literally their first dinner guest ever.

Focusing on her meal, Cait tried to stay as unseen as possible. She wasn't good at small talk, and that seemed to be all that Ryan was capable of. Genni pushed some potatoes around her plate, evidently as bored as Cait.

Crowded on a normal night, the table felt particularly small with the giant wingspan of Ryan's arms. Their utensils scraping and clattering and the patter of rain on the windows were the only sounds for a few moments. Then Rese piped up. "Did I tell you that Ryan is starting medical school next fall?"

Cait desperately wanted to roll her eyes. Of all the sons for Kenneth Greene to leave his practice to, Ryan was the worst. Not that he had any options. He didn't have any other sons. Though, she thought Elizabeth would be an excellent doctor.

"Is that so?" Maeve asked.

Ryan gave Rese a sideways glance as he chuckled nervously. "Well, that's what my dad and I have been talking about. I took a few years after high school to make up my mind about the future and . . . well, it's time to make a choice."

Cait thought it was *past* time to make a choice. Ryan had graduated three years ago. If it took him three years to decide whether or not he wanted to follow in his father's footsteps after a whole lifetime of being groomed for it, she didn't think it boded well for his ability to commit to things. Or to people.

"Where would yeh study?" Maeve asked.

"Probably in Portland," Ryan said. "It's kind of far, but it's got one of the better medical schools near us. And it's where my dad went."

"Do you really *want* to be a doctor?" Genni asked.

Rese whirled to her with a fierce glare.

"What?" Genni exclaimed. "He doesn't seem all that interested."

Ryan laughed cheerfully. "To be honest," he leaned toward Genni, "I'm not."

Surprised by his honesty, Cait scanned him with what felt like new eyes. Maybe he wasn't as vapid as he presented himself to be.

"What *do* you want to do?" Genni pressed.

"I'm not sure," Ryan admitted. "The only thing I've ever been good at is sports, but I can't really make a career out of that, so . . . it seems becoming a doctor's my only option."

"That's stupid," she returned immediately.

"Genni!" Rese huffed. "Being a doctor isn't stupid."

"No, duh," Genni retorted. "I want to be a doctor. Obviously, I don't think it's a stupid profession. I think it's stupid to do something just because you don't know what else to do."

Maeve sent her youngest granddaughter a reproving look. "*A leanbh,* yer being insensitive."

Genni rolled her eyes. "I'm just telling the truth."

Maeve prepared to correct her, but Ryan held up a hand. "Please," he interjected, voice light with amusement. "She's right. Even I think it's stupid, and that's saying something."

Cait found herself smiling at his self-deprecating joke.

Shaking his head, Ryan's grin grew. "You're a smart kid," he told Genni. "Smarter than I've ever been. The problem is—even people like me have to choose a career at some point. And in this case, the career was sort of chosen for me."

Genni screwed up her face in disapproval. "You don't have *anything* else you like to do?"

After a second of thought, Ryan shrugged. "I like studying animals."

Rese's mouth fell slack as though baffled by this. "You—what kind of animals?" she asked with something like worry in her voice.

"All of 'em," he replied. "I think if I'm gonna stick to the medical field, I'd rather work with animals than people."

"You want to be a veterinarian?" Genni asked.

Ryan pursed his lips. "Yeah, that could be fun."

"Why don't you do that then?"

He considered it. "Huh," he mumbled. "That's not a bad idea."

Blinking as she looked up at Ryan, Rese appeared blindsided by this version of him. As though she'd not realized that her not-yet-official boyfriend had any interest in animals beyond the norm. Cait supposed that he had been particularly friendly when he'd met Red. Their terrier lay in the corner of the kitchen, watching the dinner with keen interest and waiting patiently for Genni to sneak bites to him.

Cait watched as Rese picked at her food. She tried to imagine her older sister as the wife of a veterinarian. She failed. Rese didn't like animals, calling them dirty pests. She found Red annoying. She'd even disliked Conroy, their dad's massive wolfhound, and he'd been the sweetest dog alive.

No, it didn't make sense for Rese to be with an animal person. But Cait didn't think it would matter much. Rese was determined to make a name for herself. She wanted to be popular and universally adored in Porthaven. And the best means of that was through marriage to one of the founding families.

Rese hadn't always been this way, reaching for recognition and notoriety. She'd been a sweet, caring big sister back in Ireland. Cait could remember adoring Rese back then. She held infinite memories of playing peacefully in the backyard, their toes curling in the lush green grass as they ran through their nan's orchard, the scent of blossoming pear trees filling the air. They'd explored the woods around their cottage, pretending to be princesses and warriors in the fairy stories their da told them.

She missed those days, the simplicity of them.

They'd lived with her grandparents even then. Her grandda, Graham, ran the pub in Bushmills, brewing his own unique beers and ales for special occasions. His chunky jumpers always smelled of malt because of it. He'd died only weeks before her parents, a premature death. A heart attack that none of them had expected.

While their nan was still mourning her husband, her son and daughter-in-law were murdered a mere month and a half later. They still didn't know who had done it. Or why.

Cait's dreams were a direct reflection of those memories. She supposed that's why they were plagued by monsters. She'd woken to the sound of her mother's scream that night. Her bed was closest to the window, the silvery moonlight peeking through the breaks in the curtains. She'd slowly slid out from under her quilt and snuck over to the window. She could hear a commotion coming from outside. Her heart hammered through her small frame as she drew back the curtains to see the bodies of her parents lying mangled on the lawn. The shadows of their murderers whisked away into the night, unseen and unknown.

Not a second later, their nan rushed into their room, tears on her face and a strange man at her side. Smoke whorled into the room as an ominous orange glow shone behind them. The man helped Maeve snatch up the girls and spirit them away from the now-burning cottage. More strangers were waiting for them in the yard. Cait realized years later that they were from the Warden, sent to rescue the family. But they'd been too late to save her parents.

It was then they came to Porthaven. That was when things began to change. Maeve grew desolate and distant from her granddaughters; her once cheery nature dwindled as she almost regarded them with fear. Rese changed too. The relationship between her and Cait grew strained. Rese became obsessed with the town's good opinion as she readily shoved down any link to their past. Anytime Cait tried to talk to Rese about Ireland, her sister shut down the conversation. She said it wasn't worth discussing, either changing the subject or leaving the conversation altogether.

Cait forced herself back to the kitchen table, listening as Ryan charmed his way into the hearts of Maeve and Genni. She supposed he was enjoyable enough company. And Rese did seem to like him.

She didn't blame Rese for wanting a better life than the one they had. There was a part of Cait that would like to leave it behind too. She loved her nan, and something about their old house reminded her of their home in Ireland. But perhaps that was why she wanted to leave it.

Perhaps she wanted to escape the memories just as much as Rese.

When the dinner finally began to wrap up, Cait volunteered to take care of the dishes. As she began to gather the plates, Ryan tapped her arm.

"Hey, I wanted to mention," he said, that friendly smile of his turned her way. "Lizzie and I are hosting a little get-together this weekend. My parents are going out of town for their anniversary, and we wanted to have a few friends over. Obviously, Rese is invited."

He flashed that dazzling smile at Rese before turning back to Cait. "But I wanted to invite you as well," he said. "And your friend—what was his name again? Mattie?"

"Matt," Cait corrected.

Ryan snapped his fingers. "Yeah! I wanted to invite you and Matt to join. It'll be chill, just a fun little hangout."

Glancing at her nan, Cait didn't know whether to accept or politely refuse. Maeve gave her a cheery nod of approval, so she turned back and returned the smile. "Sure, that sounds fun, thanks."

"Of course!"

"Can I come too?" Genni chimed in.

Rese rolled her eyes. "It's for big kids only, Gen."

"What, like, adults? 'Cause Cait's only seventeen."

"No, like, over fifteen," Rese returned.

Genni pouted, arms crossed, and Ryan laughed. "Sorry, kiddo. You'd probably find it boring anyway," he offered by way of apology.

While Maeve and Rese walked Ryan to the door—likely forestalling whatever affectionate goodbye the couple was hoping to have—Genni sulked off to her room, and Cait began the long process of handwashing the dishes. Their dishwasher had stopped working years ago, and that was a problem Cait couldn't fix.

Hands soon soaked, Cait stared down as she worked. Inevitably, her thoughts drifted to where they always did. She wondered what Desmond was up to. He'd said he had to go on a stakeout this weekend, whatever that meant. Maybe he was doing some work with his Uncle Rick, the sheriff. He'd also mentioned weird things happening with the spirit world. And she'd promised to find a way to meet with him.

Yet they hadn't.

She supposed she should get used to it. One day, presumably soon, she'd have to live life without Desmond entirely.

The hot water grew scalding, but Cait didn't bother to turn it down. Her skin began to turn bright red as she scrubbed harder on the skillet in her hand.

Was this the end? Would she never get to spend an afternoon at the cove with Desmond again? In becoming friends with Matt, had she chosen to let go of Desmond?

Rese pattered into the kitchen, her golden waves fluttering around her beaming face. "Well," she crooned, hopping up to sit on the counter between the fridge and the sink. She tapped Cait's hip with her foot. "What do you think? Isn't Ryan charming?"

Cait wanted to say, "Not as charming as Desmond."

Instead, she said, "Yeah, he was nice."

Rese rolled her eyes. "He's dreamy. And he picked *me*. Can you believe it?"

"Not really," Cait heard herself reply. Then she looked up at Rese's wounded expression, shaking her head. "No—I—I didn't mean it like that. It's just—I just meant that it's surprising because—"

"Because what?" Rese demanded.

Cait sighed, knowing her sister wouldn't understand. "Because you're a Lewan."

"There is nothing wrong with being a Lewan," Rese retorted.

"I know that," Cait insisted. "But the rest of the town doesn't."

"Oh, come on, Cait. You have to get over that 'curse' thing. No one truly believes it."

"Yes, they do."

"Ryan doesn't," Rese insisted. "He told me that he thinks it's kind of endearing, actually. That it's a funny little quirk of our family's."

Cait furrowed her brow. "How can being cursed by a demon be funny?"

"We're—" Rese pressed her lips together. She leaped down from the counter and crossed her arms. "We're not cursed. Da wasn't a witch, he didn't deal with demons, and *we are not cursed.*"

Feeling ashamed, Cait turned back to the dishes. "I—I know," she muttered. "But—"

"No," Rese insisted. "There are no 'buts.' You have to stop caring so much about those stupid rumors. We're fine. We're all safe here. The Warden is protecting us, you know that."

"I know," Cait repeated.

"Then stop being so—" Rese struggled for the word. "Bloody *depressing* all the time. Maybe *then* you'd make some friends."

Cait thought about reminding her that she had a friend now. But she didn't care to remember that he was only her friend because he felt sorry for her. He'd chosen her for the same reason people chose dogs at the pound. She looked pitiful and lonely, and he'd picked her.

With an exasperated huff, Rese let her arms fall to her sides. "Why are you like this?" she asked. But it didn't sound malicious or cruel. It simply sounded concerned.

"I don't know," Cait whispered back.

"We used to have fun, remember? In Ireland," Rese said. "We would play in the yard and explore the woods for hours. We were best friends."

Surprised by the turn in the conversation, Cait looked up from the dishes. Rese *never* talked about Ireland. She *never* reminisced. What had prompted this?

In her silence, Rese continued. "I'm trying to take care of us. I'm trying to provide a good future for us. And you don't seem to care. You don't even try to make friends with the people in your class."

"They don't want to be my friends," Cait argued.

Rese rolled her eyes. "You don't give them the chance. You hide in the corner, ignoring everyone and blaming them for being afraid of you. While I've spent the last twelve years trying to make this town like us, you've been doing everything in your power to make them hate you."

Cait gaped at her, at a loss for words.

With a shake of her head, Rese's perfect waves drifted around her shoulders. "What happened to you?" she demanded. "You're not the girl you were in Ireland."

Hurt, Cait finally shut off the tap with a rough slap. "Neither are you," she shot back.

Rese flinched, something in her rich blue eyes flashing with fear.

Tossing the last dish on the counter, Cait moved around her sister. "I'm going to bed. Goodnight."

Nearly running through the living room, Cait made for the stairs. She fought back the tears that threatened to fall. Because Rese was right; she wasn't the same girl she'd once been. That girl had a home and a family. That girl had been happy and carefree.

Now, Cait had nothing. And she was afraid of losing even that.

~

"A party?" Matt asked after she'd told him about Ryan's invitation over lunch the next day.

Cait shook her head. "It's not a party," she assured him. "It's a get-together. Their parents are out of town, so they're having some friends over."

He narrowed his brown eyes. "That sounds like the start of a bad episode of some teen drama."

With a shrug, Cait turned back to her lunch. "I wouldn't know."

"What do you mean?"

"I don't watch TV."

Matt looked truly baffled. "Don't you have a TV?"

"Yeah," she said, gathering a cold bite of last night's leftovers. "But I only watch it when Nan makes us do a movie night. Then we just watch the classics. *Casablanca*, *Roman Holiday*, those sorts of movies."

"Weird," he mumbled. Then he perked up. "But it sounds fun. I'd love to go."

Relieved, Cait smiled back at him. She'd been concerned that he wouldn't be able to go. Or worse, that he wouldn't want to. The idea of hanging out with Ryan and Elizabeth Greene, Hunter Varon, and Rese alone sounded like a special kind of torture. One that made her both a fifth wheel and the odd man out. What could she possibly have in common with any of them? And after her run-in with Hunter, she didn't care to attempt to make a connection with him.

Cait's phone buzzed on the table. She glanced down at it and froze.

"So, what's the deal with all these 'founding families' anyway?" Matt was asking, totally oblivious to the text she'd received. "My mom said that the Simons, Varons, Greenes, and . . . oh gosh, I don't remember the rest of them. But she said they're, like, a big deal."

Casually reaching out to pull the phone onto her lap, Cait tried to formulate a coherent thought. "Uh, they just—they're just the people who founded the town," she explained lamely.

"Well, yeah, I know that," Matt returned. "But my mom said that there were several hundred other settlers that came with them. Why are *they* such a big deal and not the rest?"

"I don't know," Cait lied.

Of course, she knew. While the Simons were newer to the list, the Varon, Greene, Lavigne, and Edgars families were the original Warden families. They'd built Porthaven for Warden purposes. What those purposes were, she'd never been told. She supposed it had something to do with the spirit world strangeness that Desmond occasionally mentioned.

Thinking of Desmond. . . .

Cait chanced a look down at her phone.

"Can you disappear? " his text read.

That had always been their code. Disappear. Meaning, meet on the roof.

Back in their freshman year, Desmond had told her to meet him at the top of the staircase, next to the roof access. That's when he'd shown her the key he'd taped to the bottom of the fire extinguisher.

"In case you ever need to disappear," he'd told her.

Surprised by his kindness, Cait had looked over at him. *"Do you ever need to disappear? "* she'd asked.

"Sometimes, " he'd admitted.

And so, on the days when life became too much, Cait would disappear to the roof. And sometimes, they'd disappear together.

"They probably all have the most money," Matt concluded, still going on about the founding families. She didn't know why he was so interested, but she knew he wouldn't leave her alone long enough for her to text Desmond back right away.

Cait returned to her lunch. "I don't know what they were like back then, but they definitely do now."

"That seems kind of lame," he lamented.

"Why?" She picked up a potato with her fork. "They work the hardest and keep the town safe. Shouldn't they earn the most money?"

Matt grimaced. "That sounds like elitism."

"What's elitist?" Genni asked, plopping down into the seat next to Cait. "Sorry I'm late."

"You're always late," Matt observed. Then he gestured to her with his fork. "The way the founding families are the richest and most popular people in town. *That's* elitist. It doesn't seem very fair to me."

"You're a little too concerned about what other people are doing with their lives, Matt," Genni remarked, pulling out her own container of cold leftovers. "You should be more like me: I don't care what anyone does. As long as they're happy, I'm happy."

Matt looked at Genni like she was an innocent child who couldn't possibly understand the realities of the world. "That's nice in theory," he said. "But it doesn't hold up. What happens when what makes one person happy makes another person sad?"

Genni narrowed her eyes. Cait knew there was about to be a debate between the two of them for the rest of the lunch. She took the opportunity to reply to Desmond.

"I don't know. I'm sort of stuck."

Looking up, her eyes found Desmond on the far side of the room. His whole table was full of laughter and conversations. She often felt jealous of his friends, getting to hear all his jokes and enjoying his company all the time. As she watched, his expression shifted slightly, cued by the receipt of her text. He pulled his phone from his pocket and held it under the table, looking down. None of his friends noticed as he texted back.

Cait waited patiently for her own phone to vibrate.

"Get unstuck," he said.

She knew she had to take her time before she could respond. If she started texting regularly in front of Genni, her sister would get suspicious. There was no one for her to carry on a conversation with, after all. Their nan still had an aversion to texting, saying that phone calls were far faster. Rese was a notoriously bad texter, leaving messages unread for days with her busy social life. And the only other people she might text were at the table with her.

So, Cait waited until they were wrapping up their meal before picking her phone back up and typing, *"I'll try."*

But no matter how hard she tried, Cait couldn't find a chance to slip away. If she wasn't in class, Matt was on her heels. She attempted to dodge him by going to the bathroom, but he announced that he had to use the restroom, too, and they could continue to class together afterward. He was impossible to escape.

In every class, Desmond glared back at her when he walked in as though trying to impress on her the importance of meeting up. But there was nothing she could do.

Cait found herself chewing on the end of her pencil—something she *never* did—worrying that Desmond had been right the other night. Maybe this was the end. Maybe they wouldn't get to see each other again. No more visits to the cove, no more meetings on the rooftop. No more Desmond.

Could she take that? If it meant being friends with Matt or being friends with Desmond, could she truly choose Matt? Could she handle losing Desmond now?

He'd called them "us." Had he meant it?

Cait forced herself to pay attention in class. Of course he hadn't meant it. He couldn't mean it—not like that. Because they'd both known the truth since they were children: They weren't friends. They weren't anything. And that was all they ever could be.

CHAPTER FIFTEEN

Desmond

Half the week had passed, and Desmond couldn't decide which he found more annoying: the lack of answers the Warden had produced or the fact that he still hadn't seen Cait. He hadn't even gotten a chance to tell her about his experience on the stakeout. Not that he could tell her about the Veil, not in specific terms, at least. Nor would he dare to tell her about the truth he'd learned about her parents' deaths and the prophecy that went along with it.

Still, it irritated him that they'd found no more answers about the Veil's strange behavior. While he hadn't heard his father say it yet, he knew it was only a matter of time before the blame fell at the feet of Cait and her sisters, even though there was no way they were involved. At least, not intentionally.

One line of the prophecy kept flittering through Desmond's thoughts: *"Our success shall come only at her great sacrifice."* He'd given Sylvia Lyons a raspy voice in his head, deep, smothering, and alluring all at once. The perfect, oracle-type voice that was equal parts attractive and maniacal.

Over the past three days, that line whispered at the back of his mind every time he saw Cait. At school, from a distance around town, even when he drove past the turnoff toward her home. And every time, he wanted to yell at someone, to proclaim the injustice of it all. Of all people, she didn't deserve to be the one that the fate of the world rested upon— she didn't deserve to have to make that sort of sacrifice.

And the fact that he was part of the organization that had damned both her parents and her to death made him all the more angry. What was the point of being the ones in power if they didn't take care of the people under their charge? How could they claim to be the "good guys" and allow a man and his wife to be murdered—for a war-ending cause or not?

The way Matt kept hanging around Cait did nothing to help Desmond's mood. He'd all but given up on seeing her ever again. It disappointed him, but he supposed it was for the best. No matter how much he missed her, he'd never admit it. And in the end, they'd needed a final kick in the pants to call off whatever madness drove them toward one another.

So rather than visiting Cait after basketball practice or his internship hours, extended as they were to help with the research, Desmond went to the old factory to study the documents he'd stolen from his father's computer. The others weren't quite as interesting or condemning as the prophecy about the Lewans. Most of the articles and letters didn't make much sense to him anyway. The pages were filled with names, dates, locations, and terms that meant nothing and provided no further understanding to him.

What did become clear, however, was that his dad had been lying to him. Or whatever William Simon chose to call it: withholding information, revealing selective truths, supplying only necessary fragments.

Desmond had never heard some of the things about the Warden and the spirit world that he learned from those documents. It gave him a fresh sense of indignation. His dad wanted to "work with him," huh? He wanted them to have a different and better relationship, did he?

Well then, Desmond thought, maybe he shouldn't lie to him. Maybe he shouldn't work for a corrupt, hypocritical organization in the first place.

His conscience flagged him, labeling him a hypocrite himself. Desmond lied to his dad all the time. He had a secret, not-quite-romance-but-certainly-more-than-friends thing going on with Caitriona Lewan. He'd stolen documents from his dad's computer. If those weren't lies, what were they? And he worked for the Warden, too—in an honorary capacity notwithstanding. He was on track to lead the Warden in Porthaven. He *wanted* to lead them.

At the end of the day, Desmond knew he chose the wrong thing regularly. He wasn't a good person—that was a fact. He made the wrong choice on purpose. All so he could furtively stick it to his dad and prove to himself that he wasn't just as caged as Cait.

Liars. That was the Simon family legacy: a bloodline of liars and thieves. They'd stolen the town of Porthaven out from under the Varons. They'd taken the inheritance of Edmond Varon himself, the second son known for his dedication and devotion.

The ring his father wore, the one that bore the second Varon son's sigil, was as much stolen contraband as the liquor Desmond took from the government workers' desks.

And his family liked to pretend that *they* were the ones who'd earned the inheritance it granted.

Sometimes, Desmond wondered at that. The ring came with a blessing, the Varons claimed. A right of power and authority. Yet the Varon line in Porthaven had given up their power generations ago, letting the Lavignes bear the right to wield the spirit world.

If they truly were heirs of such great power, shouldn't they use it? What if he and his dad accepted the power granted to them? What if they used it like the Varons of generations past? Could they seal that crack in the Veil together? Couldn't they change the way the Warden ran their organization? Couldn't they make things right for Cait and her sisters?

None of his questions had any answers. He could ask them until he was blue in the face, and no one would know what to say. Because the answers weren't in Porthaven. Not to their powers, not to why the Veil was acting strangely, and not to the question that Desmond had begun to ask himself every waking moment ever since he'd read that damn prophecy.

Sitting in class, Desmond stretched his neck, then casually glanced over his shoulder. This was why he'd ordered Garrett to sit behind and to the right of him. The angle gave him the perfect vantage of the far corner—of Cait, her blonde hair glowing in the late morning sun.

"The bond of spirit and child will bring forth power like we've never seen."

"Our success shall come only at her great sacrifice."

What if the bond was broken?

That question twisted around Desmond's heart, squeezing and demanding. He had to know: If Cait *was* the Vessel, was there a way to free her of that fate?

The bell rang, releasing the students from the last class before lunch. In a flash, Garrett and Brady were out of their seats, ready and waiting for Desmond to lead the way to the cafeteria. He accepted his position absentmindedly.

With one last glance Cait's way—she was detained by Matt and his endless chatter—Desmond strolled out the door. He slung his backpack over one shoulder. It shouldn't annoy him so much, seeing Cait make friends with the kid. Even if he was a completely obnoxious stick figure.

No, he should be happy. Part of the reason he hadn't broken off their weird relationship before was because he knew Cait wouldn't have anyone else to talk to. Therese was superficial and uncaring—she forgot Cait even existed most of the time. There would be no way *she'd* lend a listening ear. And Genni was too young and carefree to be of any help. Besides, Cait would never willingly dump her problems on her little sister.

With Matt, she could find a confidant. Someone to listen to her as Desmond had. Someone who could easily absorb the pain and fear and trauma of her past, then let it evaporate off of him. Someone to put an arm around her when she needed comfort and to give her a sarcastic remark when she needed to laugh.

That was what it should be.

And Desmond felt like he had a blade jammed straight through his ribcage, into his heart, starting a slow bleed oozing down his chest.

Blocking out the pinching compression in his chest, Desmond turned the corner. Garrett and Brady were discussing something behind him—probably the travel schedule the basketball team had received this week. As the captain of both their sports teams—a role he'd acquired at the start of his junior year before he'd subsequently led them to the all-state victory in both basketball and baseball—he got one of the first glimpses of the schedule. They'd need to up their practices to five days a week if they wanted to ensure another victorious year. Normally, he wouldn't be upset about that. It would cut into his usual internship schedule, freeing him from spending time at the town hall. But with everything going on *and* his determination to "work together," William would insist that Desmond come in *after* practice.

The thought of his dad seemed to summon him. Desmond came to a near-screeching halt in front of the cafeteria doors. Dressed in his mayoral uniform of a white button down and black slacks, William stood on the inside of the entryway, arms crossed. Desmond thought the job of mayor didn't suit his dad. William Simon was far too stocky to wear slacks. His forehead was too perpetually pinched in concentration to pull off the charming town-caregiver vibe.

"Dad," Desmond said by way of greeting. Brady and Garrett muttered their own "hellos."

William gave his friends a nod before turning back to Desmond. "I've spoken to the principal," he said, tone flat and direct. "You've got the rest of the day off."

Pursing his lips, Desmond took the news in stride. "Cool. Maybe I'll hit the beach with my newfound free time."

He heard Garrett sniggering behind him. William wasn't amused. "You'll be joining me," he ordered.

"Shucks, Dad." He looped his fingers into the straps of his backpack. "If you wanted some quality time, all you had to do was ask."

Brady stepped around Desmond, giving his arm a nudge. They exchanged a brief look—his friend clearly advising him to rein in his snark. Then Brady turned to the mayor. "Have a good afternoon, Uncle Will," he said.

William gave Brady an affectionate nod. Of course, they weren't *actually* related. However, Desmond and Brady's dads were best friends, the same as the boys. It felt natural for Brady to see William as an uncle, just as Desmond saw Ben Lavigne.

Though, in Desmond's opinion, he had the better end of the deal. Even serving as the reverend, Ben was way more fun than William.

While Brady led Garrett into the cafeteria, dozens of other students funneled past father and son. "So," Desmond began. "What are our big plans for today, Pop? And please tell me it involves ice cream."

"Just come with me," William said, striding toward the exit.

Desmond knew Brady was right. On a good day, he needed to check his sarcasm. An impromptu outing with his dad required special treatment. Though, after learning that William had been intentionally keeping the truth from him all these years, he didn't particularly care to restrain himself.

Many students did double takes, watching the mayor and his son walking through the halls. Desmond was used to it. Everywhere they went, they drew attention. Another reason he and Cait wouldn't work as a couple.

William held open the main entrance door, motioning for Desmond to exit first. Immediately, he saw the silver sedan parked at the edge of the sidewalk. "Seriously?" he remarked. "You couldn't be bothered to park like a normal human being?"

Reaching into his pocket, William didn't deign to reply. He pulled out his keys, unlocking the car. In silence, Desmond tossed his backpack onto the backseat and then dropped into the front passenger seat. The car hummed to life at a respectable volume.

As they pulled out of the parking lot, William spoke again. "Curb your attitude. We have a meeting, and I won't have you making a fool of yourself."

Desmond scoffed, slouching lazily in the leather seat. "Making a fool of you, you mean."

"Your behavior does not reflect onto me," he said. "What you do is under *your* control, not mine. If you want to behave like a child, it's your own reputation you're besmirching."

"Besmirching?" Desmond grimaced dramatically. "That's quite archaic of you. Should I start using big words too? You know, to impress whoever it is we're meeting with."

William gave him a sidelong glance. He drove the speed limit like an especially boring human, turning onto Lawrence Avenue away from town. "You're in rare form today," he replied, an unusual tilt to his voice.

Desmond narrowed his eyes. Was his dad mocking him?

He sat up straighter. "Yeah, well, you made me skip lunch. I get hangry."

William grunted out an almost laugh. "You're just like your mother."

"Lucky me," he retorted. "The Varon looks and the Edgars' personality. I'm practically irresistible."

"Do your friends find this entertaining?" his dad asked, hands at ten and two. "Or are you only a smart-ass with me?"

"Hey, you like Mom, don't you?" he returned.

"She knows how to have a serious conversation."

"She also knows how to have fun."

William glanced at him. "I have fun."

"Work doesn't count."

"Do you think I tricked your mother into marrying me?" William countered, an edge to his voice. It wasn't irritation but . . . sarcasm? Was he really using sarcasm?

Turning to scan his dad, Desmond frowned. "What's going on?" he demanded. "Why are you being . . . conversational?"

Distracted by trying to figure out his dad, Desmond had failed to notice the direction they'd driven. Now, the sedan pulled into the driveway of a small house on the outskirts of town near the ocean. Built on a craggy overlook, the isolated house sat alone. Dry grass and barren trees mottled the landscape.

Desmond knew the house on sight. Every kid in Porthaven knew it. It was the house of dares and pranks. The house of the witch.

William put the car in park and turned to Desmond. "I told you," he said. "I want a relationship with you. If that means stooping to your level of immaturity, fine. I can be just as snarky as you."

Desmond shook his head, a snide grin on his lips. "Nah. No one's as snarky as me."

While William didn't reply, he did give a single, startling chuckle.

Desmond didn't know what had gotten into his dad. Their relationship had grown into a toxic indifference over the years. He knew it wasn't healthy. So did his dad. But neither of them knew how to fix it.

There had been a time, Desmond knew, when they liked each other. He remembered his kindergarten teacher asking him what he wanted to be when he grew up. His answer? "My dad."

Of course, six-year-old Desmond had meant he wanted to be *like* his dad: the mayor, happily married, respected, and powerful. But somehow, in the imagination of his adulthood, little Desmond had actually pictured himself being his dad. Looking like him, talking like him, acting like him.

Somewhere along the way, at a time Desmond couldn't quite pinpoint, the image stopped being a positive one. It became a demand, a burden, an expectation. A feared standard that he was guaranteed to fall short of.

Now, almost twelve years later, the laughter of his dad surprised Desmond. He'd grown so accustomed to being at odds with one another that he couldn't remember the last time he'd made his dad laugh. Had it ever happened?

Blinking away his shock, Desmond got out of the sedan. William was already moving for the porch, his mayoral disposition back in place. The house fit the witchy bill. Lichen and vining plant life covered its wood siding. A trellis peeked through the greenery. Windchimes plunked out their melodious tunes in the sea breeze. Strange lawn ornaments decorated the stoop, flowerbeds, and grass.

If Lilith Drake didn't want people treating her like an outcast, he didn't think she was doing a good job of refuting their claims of her dark dealings.

As Desmond wondered offhandedly what they were doing at the ex-Druid's home, William knocked on the screen door. A soft voice came from the interior, promising to be "right there." The locks snapped undone, and the door opened.

On the other side of the threshold, fuzzy from the screen door still between them, stood Lilith. Her white-blonde hair curled back from her face, cropped short to barely brush her collar. Willowy and tall, she had a sharp, square jawline, a thin nose, and round, dusty-blue eyes.

"Mr. Mayor," she said, her voice mimicking the one Desmond had given Sylvia in his imagination. Rich and husky with a cutting edge that made his skin crawl.

Lilith's piercing gaze flashed to Desmond. Her lips turned up at the corner. "And the mayor-to-be," she remarked, leaning against the door. "To what do I owe the pleasure?"

An eerie sense crept along Desmond's scalp. He shoved his hands into his pockets to keep from fidgeting. He'd never met Lilith. He'd seen her from a distance around town, but he'd intentionally not engaged with her. She always gave him the feeling that she could see into people's souls, reading them in ways he'd rather not be read.

William didn't share his hesitation. "I have some questions if you'd be available to answer them?"

"I have to be at the shop in an hour," she replied, even as she pushed open the screen door between them. "Make it quick."

With the unspoken invitation, William and Desmond entered the house. The age of the home melded with the decor to continue the witchy impression Lilith seemed predisposed to give off. The house smelled of sage and other herbs he couldn't identify. Dark paneling and rich green paint gave the space a den-like feel. Strange knickknacks littered every surface—glass bottles, dried flowers and herbs, candles, golden trays, even a skull. A staircase to their immediate right led up to what he assumed was a one-room second floor based on the exterior.

Lilith shut the door behind the men. Seeing her up close, he realized she was taller than both of them. She wore a black lace blouse tucked into surprisingly stylish gray trousers. For a woman who was clearly his mother's age or older, Desmond thought she was kind of attractive. In a spooky, pretty-sure-she-could-kill-you kind of way.

"Can I get you anything to drink?" Lilith asked, moving to escort them deeper into the house. "Water? Tea?"

"We're fine, Lilith," William said, his familiarity with her striking Desmond. His sudden awareness led him to realize other strange things, like the way his dad walked through the living room as though he'd been there dozens of times. He didn't scan the wildly decorated house in interest. And he casually stepped up into the kitchen without needing to be told to watch his step on the small lip between the rooms.

A nagging thought sprang into Desmond's mind, and he began to watch his dad and the ex-Druid even more closely.

"Well, I just made myself a cup," Lilith said, stepping around her kitchen island. A large window at the back of the room let in golden beams of sunlight, which glinted off her earrings. "So, if you gentlemen change your minds, it isn't a bother."

Across the island, William readily pulled out a barstool and motioned for Desmond to take a seat. He hesitated, growing more uncomfortable by the second. His dad was too accustomed to this house. He was too informal with this woman.

Lilith's sharp gaze drifted to Desmond. "No," she said.

"What?" Desmond replied lamely.

"You're misinterpreting things." She tipped her head toward William in an offhanded gesture. "Your father knows my home because he comes to check on me regularly. After all, I am the town's biggest potential threat."

Desmond narrowed his gaze. "Can you read minds?"

She huffed in amusement. "I don't need to when you make faces like that."

"I've been told I have an excellent face," Desmond returned, finding himself unexpectedly pleased with her banter. "Some say the best."

Lilith blinked, a slow smile spreading over her face. She turned to William. "He's your twin," she said.

"The price you pay as a parent," William replied calmly.

Desmond frowned. "We don't look *that* much alike."

Picking up the teapot on the island, Lilith began to pour herself a cup. "I'm not talking about your looks—though there is a strong resemblance. Fifteen years ago, your father had just as much sass as you." She paused, setting the pot down. "Age made him boring."

"I became mayor," William defended.

Lilith sent him a mocking stare. "And none of us can ever forget it. What do you need, William?"

Desmond had been wondering himself. He took the waiting barstool, hoping to encourage his dad's response.

William rested his hands on the counter, an abnormally relaxed quality to his stance. To Desmond's eyes, it looked as though he was trying to lull Lilith into a false sense of security. "What do you know about the Veils?" he asked.

Desmond nearly fell out of his seat. However, Lilith took a thoughtful sip of her tea as though they were discussing an everyday topic. She pursed her lips, setting the teacup down. "I was a Druid," she replied, husky voice smooth. "We practically worshiped the Veils. I know the rhetoric backward and forward."

"The rhetoric? You sound as though you don't believe it's true," William pressed.

Lilith shrugged. "Some of it's true, I suppose. How much of it. . . ." She let the thought hang.

"What do you know?"

She gave him a cynical, close-lipped smile. "That would take hours that we don't have, William." Her eyes drifted to Desmond. "Why'd you bring your pup? I didn't think you Warden accepted minors as members. Something about an age of consent."

Though Desmond bristled at the suggestion that he was too young, he kept his mouth shut as his dad replied. "Desmond is an honorary member of the Warden," he explained. "As he will inherit the leadership after me, I want him to have as much training as possible."

Lilith's dusty-blue eyes narrowed. "Something's happened," she surmised.

Now, Desmond really did wonder if she could read minds. "What makes you say that?" he asked.

She turned to him, lifting her teacup. "Dear boy, if you're here for a learning experience, there must be something important to learn."

"Maybe my dad wants me to get to know you," he countered. "You know, so I can charm you just as much as he did."

"Charm is overrated," she told him. "And if he wanted us to get to know one another, he wouldn't have brought up Veils."

"You're correct," William cut in. "Something has happened. We've been researching all week with no answers, and I felt it best to ask the one person in this town who once lived amongst those who, in your own words, worship Veils."

"I said they *practically* worship them," she corrected. "Druids worship Gaia—the mother of the Earth, and the creation birthed from her. The Veils are simply an extension of that creation."

"The Earth was created by God," William noted.

Lilith rolled her eyes. "Let's not split hairs. What do you need to know?"

"You've heard of beasts?"

She let out a derisive snort. "Once or twice."

"And you know how they're summoned."

"Yes."

Desmond couldn't help himself. He broke in, asking, "Have you ever summoned one?"

She gave him a pointed glance. "Yes."

"Have you summoned any in recent history?" William took over again.

"No." Lilith drew in a sharp breath, head tilting thoughtfully. "Someone's summoning beasts?"

"Possibly," he confirmed, then shifted to slip his hands into his trouser pockets. "Have you ever heard of any other means by which beasts might cross the line between the spirit world and our world?"

Her lips parted in surprise, a glimmer of baffled curiosity in her eyes. "William," she said as though she were correcting a pupil, "there must be a summoner for there to be a beast."

"What if there wasn't?" Desmond asked.

A long pause hung in the air. Lilith crossed her arms, lifting a hand to her mouth. William and Desmond both watched her, waiting. The tick of a clock echoed through the room, each second thumping out its rhythm.

"What's happened to the Veil?" Lilith finally asked, her voice hushed as though worried others might be eavesdropping.

William maintained his calm persona, but Desmond could see a vein in his dad's jawline pulse. "We have reason to believe that someone has tampered with it," he admitted. "Whatever they've done, whoever it is, we now have eyewitness proof that there are beasts coming through without a summoner."

A look of horror—or was it of pure shock?—passed over Lilith's face. "That's not possible."

"For someone to tamper with a Veil?" Desmond prodded.

"For beasts to come through unsummoned," she corrected, then shifted her stance to face the mayor. "William, that's not how the spirit world works. Beasts *always* have a summoner."

"You've never heard of this before then?" William asked.

She shook her head vehemently. "No!" she insisted. "No, it's—it's not possible."

"Apparently," Desmond countered, "it is."

She hardly spared him a glance before addressing William. "What makes you think the Veil has been tampered with?"

"That's classified," he replied in a dull tone.

Though Lilith lifted her eyes to the ceiling in irritation, she let it go. Raising a hand, she lifted a finger as though begging for his patience. "If someone has truly altered, or damaged, or whatever it is you believe they've done to the Veil—perhaps that's how they're summoning beasts."

"What do you mean?" William pressed.

"Perhaps they've created some tie to the Veil," she offered with a shrug. "Or maybe they took a piece of it with them. I don't know. But whatever the case, what if they're simply summoning the beasts remotely?"

Desmond frowned. "Like, they figured out some way to tell the Veil to create a beast willy-nilly?"

Lilith tossed her hand in the air, accepting it as a possibility.

"Why would they do that?" he asked.

She shook her head, sharp eyebrows pulling together. "I don't know."

"It isn't you?" William asked, his tone less accusing and more testing.

Her chin rose sardonically. "No."

Though Desmond knew there was a chance the woman was lying—after all, she *was* their best suspect—something in him told him that it was the truth. He looked at his dad, wondering what was next. If Lilith truly didn't have answers for them, this whole visit had been pointless.

"Did you—" Lilith cut herself off, wetting her lips before starting again. "Did you check on the Vessel?"

The blood rushed from Desmond's head. How did she know about the Vessels?

William didn't seem surprised. "You know perfectly well that I don't discuss that topic with you."

Lilith sighed as though he were being impossible. "I was raised by the Druids, William. I know more than you on the subject. Let me help."

"No."

She pressed her lips together, obviously frustrated. "Fine. But know this: If the Veil *is* damaged, the Vessel is going to reflect that. They are tied. You cannot separate a Veil and its spirit."

Even as Desmond opened his mouth to ask what she meant, William cut across him. "We aren't having this conversation," he objected. "I don't take counsel from you, Lilith. I came to ask you a simple question, and you gave your answer. That is all I need from you."

As William began to move back toward the living room, Lilith tightened her jaw. It was clear she wanted to argue, to speak up about something. But she kept her mouth shut.

The urge to pursue her knowledge kept Desmond rooted to his seat. What if she knew something that could help Cait? What if she was right, and the crack in the Veil could manifest itself in Cait? There was so much he didn't understand about the subject. So much the Warden didn't know. And this woman was offering to tell them everything.

William called Desmond's name, a command to get up and follow him to the door.

Staring at Lilith, Desmond nearly spoke up. The question was on the tip of his tongue, ready to beg for answers. Her dusty gaze lifted to meet his. There was a pointedness to it, a warning. And he knew, if he tried to ask, his father would shut down the conversation—by force if need be.

Gritting his teeth, Desmond rose from the stool. He wanted to yell at his father, demanding that they hear the woman out. Ex-Druid she may be, but she'd lived in Porthaven for fifteen years. If she wanted to do them harm, wouldn't she have done it by now?

As Desmond moved through the living room, his eyes swept over the witchy decor once more. He supposed he understood why people remained hesitant toward the woman. She didn't do much to garner their trust. She ran a tea and herbal remedy shop. She lived in isolation on the edge of town. She had a freaking pet snake chilling in a terrarium in the corner. The massive thing coiled around driftwood on a pebbled bed, a heat lamp over the lid.

Desmond hadn't noticed the terrarium on his way in, so focused on the weirdness of his dad and the witch's relationship. Now, he suppressed a shiver. What kind of person kept a snake as a pet? This one was ginormous too. Its scales were so dark green they almost looked black. It appeared to be sleeping, but he rushed past the cage anyway.

Once they'd walked out and Lilith had shut the door behind them, Desmond peered over his shoulder at the house. He couldn't stop his mind from running over her words and the prophecy of Sylvia over and over again. Was there any chance that this woman knew how to keep Cait safe? Would it be worth going behind his dad's back to try to get the answers? Or was the town correct? Was her history with the Druids enough to mark her as untrustworthy forever?

Desmond dropped into the car, newly determined. If he couldn't trust Lilith Drake, if he couldn't trust his own dad, he would just have to find the answers himself. Because there was one thing that he was sure of: He had to protect Cait.

CHAPTER SIXTEEN

Cait

The darkness surrounded Cait, a sentient awareness there with her.

She opened her eyes, back in her childhood bedroom. The soft yellow and rosebud quilt on each bed. The antique dresser. The bassinet. She could smell the strand of dried flowers her mum had strung across their ceiling. They'd gone to pick them together in the fields that summer—Cait, Rese, and their mum, baby Genni left home with their da.

Gleaming silver moonlight pressed against her back, casting her shadow on the door in front of her. She blinked, wondering if there was any reason to try the door this time. Did she even want to? That thing was out there, wasn't it? But the smoke would come soon, and she had to find a way out.

Tentatively, Cait stepped up to the door. The cool metal knob didn't turn. The thing on the other side began to pace in expectation.

The doorknob began to heat under her touch. Cait released her hold, shuffling backward. She clutched her hands against her chest, the soft knit of her jumper doing little to soothe the rising beat of her heart.

She hated these dreams. She couldn't understand why she had them. Or why they were always the same, their only variation in the monsters that haunted her.

The shadow of the thing pacing brought trembling to Cait's limbs. She knew it would pound against the door soon. It would try to get through. It would try to get to her.

Smoke began to curl through all the crevices of the door. The shadow kept pacing.

Cait pressed her lips together, tears coming to her eyes as she anticipated the next part of the dream.

Her mother's scream of pain rent the air. A cry of agony caught in Cait's own throat. Her tears dripped from the corner of her eyes, spilling onto her cheeks.

The smoke was rising.

An angry rumble came from the other side of the door just before the thing crashed against it. The door rattled in its frame, shaking the walls. Cait could feel its desperation to break through reverberating in her chest.

That presence—the strange other-aura she associated with William Simon—pressed onto her mind. She expected to see his likeness appear as it always did. A guard in front of that door. Protecting her from the thing trying to get in.

The presence eased, drifting away from her consciousness.

The smoke rose. Cait blinked, but William didn't appear. Her mouth dropped open in surprise, a tremor of fear racing up her spine. If he didn't come, what would stop that *thing* from breaking through?

Another crash against the door and the fissure at the hinges grew.

Without warning, a flash of black shot across Cait's vision, a rapid flurry of sound sailing past her face in a burst of wind. The smoke swirled as she cried out, whipping her head to follow the streak of movement.

She gasped, then choked on the smoke she'd inhaled.

Through teary eyes, Cait stared at the raven perched on the edge of her dresser. Glittering black eyes stared at her, its dark claws gently gripping the wood. Its feathers looked like silk, smooth and vibrant, a rich ebony-sapphire.

Taking a step back, Cait realized that the room had fallen silent. The banging had stopped, the shadow on the other side no longer furiously trying to break in. She was too frightened to take her eyes off the bird for long, but she spared the door a fleeting glance.

"Caw!" the raven cried, startling Cait.

She pulled her hands into fists. The wisps of smoke still rose, seeping under the door, working to smother her. But this bird—*this* was new.

The raven cocked its head as though considering Cait. Then it looked toward the window.

Cait didn't follow its gaze. She wouldn't. She wasn't desperate enough yet to face the torment of her parents' dead bodies. Not even as the smoke tingled in her nose.

Another *caw* came from the raven, its talons clacking on the dresser as it adjusted. It lifted its lustrous wings then took flight.

In a rapid flurry of feathers, the raven flew directly at Cait. She cried out, ducking with her arms over her head. The raven simply flew over her, straight for the window.

Heart beating erratically, Cait forced herself to turn as she expected to hear the bird collide with the glass. She didn't have to look out the window, she told herself. She only had to keep an eye on the bird. In twelve years, nothing had changed in her dream. Not a single thing. Until this raven.

But as Cait turned, she found the window gone and the raven sailing through the open air into the night sky over the beach. The cove spread out before her.

Her jaw dropped farther open, taking in the pebbled beach. The steady waves broke against the shoreline, the cliffs ranging up around her. Turning back around, Cait expected to see the pines and birches of the forest. Instead, her room remained, smoke swirling from under the door.

The shadow paced, its low rage-filled rumble signaling its discontent.

Scanning the door, Cait squinted her eyes. There, at the corner by the hinges, she saw the hairline fracture—the same one she always saw—had clearly grown. No longer could she question; a definitive rupture marred the door.

Body shaking, Cait whirled back around, half in her room, half on the beach.

And her heart stalled.

There on the pebbled shore stood Desmond, his back to her. The soft breeze ruffled his unruly hair, his shoulders drawn back and strong. He had a powerful build, muscular and defined. She'd always wondered what it would be like to be held by him. Would it feel as good as she imagined? Safe and secure.

Smoke pooled out of her room to coil across the gray shore. The sea began to swell, its gray-blue waves rising. Foam churned as they crashed, a replication of the sound of that shadow slamming against the door. The water rushed over the sand and pebbles, swirling around Desmond's feet and up to his ankles.

Smoke and water twisted together, the cold moonlight piercingly bright. Cait took a step forward, the breeze cutting through her clothes. "Desmond?" she whispered, still working to understand his presence within her dream.

Her ears pulsed with the hum of his presence, but he didn't turn.

She called to him this time, moving closer, the pebbles and sand crunching under her boots. Lightning scorched the sky, the wind picking up. Thunder ricocheted through the air, vibrating in her chest.

And then, the monsters came.

Shadows of obsidian black encroached on the cove, bleeding over the earth and sky. Storm clouds covered the full moon. Out of the darkness, beasts of wolfish form emerged. Their canines looked like fangs, their neon eyes glowing with violence in their yellow depths. Each stood as tall as Cait, their giant paws slamming into the sand as they slunk forward.

Panicked, Cait bolted for Desmond, calling his name again. His head dipped as though suddenly unsure. The waves now crashed against his thighs, and yet he stood there, unaware of his surroundings.

The hounds barreled across the beach, their massive limbs eating up the ground. Cait was too far away. Even at a sprint, she had no hope of beating the lumbering beasts to him.

"Desmond!" she screamed, desperate to get his attention. He had to turn. He *had* to see them. He was a Wielder; he could save himself. He just had to turn around and *see them*.

Desmond shifted with the next wave that crashed against his waist. He took a step back, spinning on his heel. Snuffed by the clouds, the moonlight was gone. But in the darkness, Cait could see his face. His dark eyes met hers, and he blinked. "Cait?"

But he hadn't been fast enough.

Helplessly, Cait watched as the hounds crashed in on Desmond like the waves at his back. She heard herself scream as each beast snapped its jaws, ripping into his flesh. The humming in her head rose to a howl, the sound of a hurricane whirring through her ears. She couldn't hear anything else. But she could see—in flashes of fur and teeth and flesh— as the hounds tore, and Desmond cried out in pain.

Dropping to the wet sand, pebbles cut into her knees and palms. Tears fell with abandon, sobs racking her body. This was worse—far, far worse than any dream she'd had before.

Blood mixed with water, pooling on the shore of the cove as Cait watched Desmond die.

~

"You've been especially quiet today," Matt said, drawing Cait back to the classroom. The morning sun shone through, yellow and happy. They'd gotten to school less than fifteen minutes ago, and she'd been silent their entire bike ride. In fact, Cait had been silent the entire morning.

Matt's brow furrowed when she didn't answer. "You okay?" he asked.

Forcing down the lingering memories of her dream, Cait blinked rapidly. "Yeah," she assured him, her voice thin to her own ears. She tried to sound more confident the second time. "Yeah, I'm fine. Just had a restless night."

His thin eyebrows pulled together and up, creating a sort of pyramid over his worried eyes. "Okay, well . . . if you're sure."

No more wanting to worry him than to explain her dream, Cait forced herself to smile. "I'm sure," she promised. "You still good to go to the Greenes' tonight?"

That perked Matt right up. "Yeah! I'm really looking forward to it." He lowered his voice conspiratorially. "Did you know that Ryan Greene is one of the most popular guys in town? Do you think there'll be, like, a lot of people at this thing?"

"Oh, no," Cait replied instantly. "No, he said it was a small get-together that he and his sister were having. A game night or something. From the sound of it, it'll just be us, Rese, Ryan, Elizabeth, and Hunter."

Matt glanced toward the front of the class, where Elizabeth and Hunter sat on the first row. He was leaning on his desk, facing his girlfriend. They held hands in the middle of the row, fingers playfully brushing one another's as they talked. For some reason, it made Cait jealous. Not because she wanted to be Elizabeth. Because she wished someone would look at her that way, eyes bright and affectionate.

With a grimace, Matt turned back. "Are you—are you comfortable with that?" he asked. "Like, didn't Hunter sort of accost you?"

"What?" Cait frowned at him. "No. No, he just—he apologized."

"Oh. Someone said you yelled at him."

A spark of fear rose in Cait's chest. "Who said that?"

Matt shrugged. "I think it might've been Sydney. Coulda been one of the other girls, though," he admitted, keeping his voice low. "Honestly, I can't remember who's who most of the time. They're all kind of jerks."

"They wouldn't be jerks to you if you weren't friends with me," Cait reminded him.

"Which makes them even bigger jerks," he insisted.

Though Cait disagreed, she didn't care to explain to him why she thought the people of Porthaven were right in shunning her. "It's okay," she said simply. "I'm used to it."

"Doesn't make it right." Matt rested his arms heavily against his desk. "And besides, they're the ones missing out. You're way cooler than them anyway."

Cait might have asked him how he could possibly think she was cool, but the hum sprang to life in her head, signaling Desmond's approach.

Garrett and Brady made their way into the room first, clearing the path. Desmond sauntered to his seat, dressed in his typical "cool guy" outfit. Black long-sleeved tee under his black bomber jacket, dark wash jeans, and rich brown Doc Martens. His hair displayed its usual perfected unruliness, giving him a devil-may-care vibe.

He was as he always was, and Cait's chest eased.

She had texted him first thing that morning. *"You okay?"*

Normally, she had to wait a long time to receive his response, but this morning he'd been prompt. *"Yeah. You?"*

"Yeah," she'd said.

That had been the end of it.

But now, as he dropped his backpack, Desmond glanced over everyone else in the class, meeting her eyes. A silent message that he knew there was more to say. There was more going on, and he wanted answers.

Dropping his gaze first, Cait turned to her notebook. She flipped through the pages, trying to still the torrent of relief, desperation, and desire within her. All she wanted to do was jump up from her seat, rush over to take his hand, and yank him from the room. She wanted to take him up to the roof and talk to him for hours. She needed to tell him her dream, to reveal the fear that still haunted her in the light of day.

Not only had her dream been different, he'd died in it. It had to mean something, didn't it?

Once Desmond was seated, Penny Davis started the class, and reality snapped its jaws back over Cait. There was nothing they could do. The odds of them breaking away to disappear together were slim enough as it was. Even if they could sneak away, they wouldn't have enough time to truly talk about it.

No, there was no way that Cait would get the chance to tell Desmond about her dream. Not today. But maybe—if she left early enough in the morning, she could sneak off to the cove without Matt to meet up with Desmond.

After class, Cait excused herself from Matt's company to use the restroom. She slipped into the ladies' room, hid in a stall, and pulled her phone out of her backpack. She quickly typed out her text, then slipped the phone into her jacket pocket, knowing he wouldn't be able to reply readily at school.

But it was sent. The request was out there.

It wasn't until lunch that she got her reply. *"I've got internship stuff in the morning. Tomorrow afternoon?"*

"Internship on a Saturday?" Cait sent her response quickly, knowing that it would take Matt some time to join her at the table.

"Dad's being weird. What about tomorrow afternoon?"

Cait chewed on her bottom lip. *"I don't know if I can get away."*

"What, does that kid watch out his window for you or something?"

"I can't risk it."

"What if you left in the morning?"

She almost huffed out loud. *"You want me to spend the entire day at the cove waiting for you?"*

"Do you need to talk to me or not?"

Cait rolled her eyes. *"I can't be gone that long. Nan won't like it."*

"Nan is my second least favorite person."

Though she pursed her lips, Cait couldn't help her amusement. *"Who's your first least favorite? Your dad?"*

"Mattie."

A small snort worked out of Cait. She began to text back to tell him to be nice when Genni dropped into the seat next to her. "What's so funny?" she asked, leaning over to look at Cait's screen.

Panicked, Cait shoved her phone into her pocket. "Nothing," she insisted. "I was just—just reading something."

Genni screwed up her face, dubious. But Matt showed up then, distracting them both.

Their lunch was pleasant, as usual. Genni lamented not being invited to the party, to which Cait reminded her it wasn't a party. But Genni still didn't think it was fair.

"My dad always says that life isn't fair," Matt remarked.

Genni heaved a particularly dramatic sigh. "Your dad must have a flair for understatement," she replied.

~

Matt met Cait and Rese at their house before the hangout. The Greenes lived on the far side of Porthaven on a beachfront property, so Maeve had agreed to let them take the car. Rese complained about having to show up in the old, sky-blue Ford Taurus with its rusted wheel wells and chips in the windshield. But as the other option was biking all the way there, she'd accepted the keys readily.

The sun was already setting by the time they left, casting a brownish-orange haze on the sky. Rese had coached Cait a dozen times already. "I want this to go well, okay?" she'd said while applying eyeliner on Cait. She'd insisted they needed to put their best foot forward, which meant dolling up her little sister nearly as much as she did herself. "This is the first time I'll be hanging out with his sister, and I need to make a good impression."

Cait didn't understand how *her* wearing makeup and a nice outfit would make a better impression for Rese, but she found she didn't mind. Once her sister had completed her work, Cait stared into the mirror, pleased with how she looked. She'd expected that Rese would overdo it, making her look like some overpainted doll. But the wash of pink on her cheeks paired with a rosy, shimmering eyeshadow served to make Cait feel grown up for the first time in her life.

Rese had even picked Cait's outfit, letting her borrow a pretty white dress with dainty eyelets all along the fabric. Even Matt had noticed her transformation, stuttering when she opened the front door for him. "W—wh—wow," he bumbled. "You look nice—I mean, you always look nice but—but you look especially nice. And now I think I'm probably underdressed."

Blushing as Matt scratched the back of his head, Cait waved a hand at his typical flannel and jeans. "You're fine," she promised. "Rese is just being Rese."

"Huh." Matt kept gaping at her, smoothing down the front of his shirt.

Rese padded up at that moment, calling her farewell to their nan. Matt's eyes grew to twice their normal size as he took in her flowy dress, light blue and purple flowers all over the gauzy fabric. Her golden hair draped elegantly over her shoulders; her full lips shone with gloss. "Hiya, Mattie," she crooned happily. "Glad you could join us."

"Uh-huh," Matt managed, mouth ajar.

As Rese led them to the car, her short skirt flouncing around her thighs, Matt turned to Cait. "I thought you said this was a game night," he whisper-hissed.

Cait shrugged. "I'm telling you," she whispered back. "This is just Rese. She's working really hard to impress her boyfriend's family."

That settled Matt some, but he continued to smooth his wrinkled flannel on a regular basis during their drive. They had to wind their way through downtown and to the more secluded section of town. Few people lived out this way, Cait knew. Only the wealthiest members of the community who didn't care to live downtown like the Simons.

It was only when they pulled up the long drive that Cait realized how wrong she'd been. Dozens of cars lined the driveway, some veering onto the grass. The beautiful, two-story house of the Greene family looked more like a mansion than anything she'd ever seen. Curved and squared windows covered its sprawling layout, the interior lights glowing brightly. The roof mimicked a cottage-esque style, and the soft yellow paint turned almost amber in the dim light of the evening.

"You said this was a *small* get-together," Cait exclaimed, glaring at Rese as she parked the car alongside another, much nicer, vehicle.

Rese pulled down the visor, checking her lip gloss in its mirror. "I didn't say anything of the sort," she countered. "Ryan said that."

"So, Ryan lied?" Cait challenged.

"He didn't lie," Rese objected. She closed the visor with a *snap*. "He simply stretched the truth a tad. We knew that Nan wouldn't approve of a party like this."

Cait ground her teeth, feeling immeasurably foolish that Genni had figured out this would be a party when she'd been naive enough to believe Ryan. "I want to go home," she insisted.

With a huff, Rese opened her car door. "Don't be ridiculous."

"I'm not! We shouldn't be here, Rese."

Her sister didn't listen, slipping out of the sedan to begin walking up the gravel drive toward the house.

Whirling around in her seat, Cait looked back at Matt. He was staring wide-eyed at the mansion, the bassy *thump-thump* of music reaching them in the car. "I'm so sorry, Matt," she said. "I had no idea—"

"It's okay," he hurried to interrupt. His shock was quickly melting into something that Cait could almost call excitement. "I've never actually been to a party like this."

Cait blinked. "Me either."

He shrugged shyly. "I've always kinda wanted to. It's sort of a rite of passage according to all those TV shows and movies, ya know? Could be fun."

"Fun" was the last way Cait would describe a party like this. Rowdy? Obnoxious? Unethical? Embarrassing? Yes, to all those things. But fun? Never.

"Do you really want to go in?" Cait asked, her voice weak.

"I don't think we have much choice. Your sister has the keys, and we can't leave her here anyway." He scooted forward in the backseat with a smile. "Besides, I promise to stay with you the whole time. We'll have fun—you and me."

Though Cait doubted even that, she knew he was right. They couldn't leave Rese here.

Reluctantly, Cait joined Matt, walking up to the house. The heels that Rese had forced her into, though short, were difficult to walk in across the gravel driveway. She had to focus incredibly hard not to roll her ankle in the process.

When they made it up to the door, Matt opened it himself, letting Cait enter first. Immediately, she heard Ryan's voice ring out with excitement. "There she is!" he cheered, an arm already around Rese's waist. "See," he said to her, his words more languid than usual, "no need to rush out after her."

The house blasted with noise everywhere. Cait's senses felt like they were in overdrive, trying to take in the space while also trying to make sense of the chaos. People spilled out of every crevice, most of them older than her but easily recognizable as the students who had graduated over the past three or so years. A handful were younger, though she didn't notice any under the age of sixteen.

The house felt even bigger on the inside with its vaulted ceilings and vintage chandeliers. The entry led into the giant living room, with somewhere around thirty people clustered around the space—scrunched together on the couches, dancing together in the center of the room, and hugging the walls. Every occupant held a red plastic cup in hand, the building already brimming with heat. The elegant décor hinted at a usually respectable and charming interior, but the rowdy partiers marred the effect.

Nearly all the attendees looked up to see Cait and Matt's arrival. Several of them began to whisper to one another. Her shoulders drooped, the loud music clanging in her ears.

"Come on," Ryan was saying to them, beginning to lead Rese away. "Let's get you guys something to drink."

Though Cait wanted to turn around and walk right back out the door, she followed for her sister's sake. It didn't matter that Rese was grinning ear to ear. Cait felt the need to be sure her sister didn't do anything stupid.

Moving through the living room, Cait caught a glimpse of several of her classmates. Hunter and Elizabeth were on the dance floor, seemingly unaware of anyone but each other. Packed as the space was, she couldn't fathom how they felt comfortable, staring into each other's eyes like that, sharing gentle touches.

Squeezing past a large group of people, Ryan led them into the packed kitchen, a new wall of sound slamming into Cait as he showed off their selection of drinks. Whiskey, beer, tequila, gin, vodka, you name it. The instant, familiar hum in her head overrode the need for Ryan to add, "You can thank Desmond here for most of it."

To Cait's horrified embarrassment, Desmond stood in the corner, a red Solo cup in his hand, dressed much in the same fashion as at school. On one side stood Garrett, his arm around Whitney, and on the other was Sydney, clearly trying her wiles in a low-cut blouse. There were at least a dozen others in the kitchen, all eyeing the new arrivals with a mixture of curiosity and condescension.

Desmond's dark eyes scanned Cait for all of two seconds before he lifted his cup in Ryan's direction. "Still not sure why *I'm* supplying the party when you're twenty-one, Greene," he returned.

"Because you get the stuff for free," Ryan replied.

"Oh, nothing in life is free." His gaze fell back on Cait, a small smirk tugging up the corner of his mouth. Then he looked at Matt. "Welcome to the party, Mattie. You got a drink of choice?"

Matt shifted uncomfortably at Cait's side. "Ah, nah," he muttered. "I—I don't drink."

"How honorable of you."

"Just responsible," Matt replied.

Desmond laughed softly, looking knowingly at Cait. She could feel the way he was inspecting her carefully, taking in this new look of hers.

Cait wanted to duck down under the kitchen island. Had she known Desmond would be here, she wouldn't have let Rese dress her up so much. She couldn't imagine how silly she looked to him. To all of them. The little Lewan girl, trying to make them forget she was cursed. Pretending she could ever be worthy of their attention.

Brady slipped into the kitchen behind them, pausing on his path to Desmond. He gave Cait a surprised glance before turning to see Ryan hand Rese a shot of something clear. "Real classy, Greene," Brady noted, "tryin' to get your girlfriend drunk the second she's in the door."

Though Rese hesitated, glaring at Brady, Ryan simply laughed. "It's a party, kid," he replied. "We're here to have fun."

"Oh, Brady doesn't have fun," Desmond interjected, eliciting a laugh from his posse.

As though to prove his best friend wrong, Brady snagged a beer from the counter. He tipped it in Rese's direction. "Friendly advice?" he said to her. "Try not to get plastered. Ryan's not known for his self-restraint."

"Why don't you mind your own business?" Rese retorted, then tossed back her shot.

Ryan smirked, pouring another drink. Brady rolled his eyes and moved to stand beside Desmond, pushing Sydney out of the way. Embarrassed by the whole exchange, Cait wanted to grab her sister's arm, demanding they leave. They didn't belong here. And they certainly shouldn't be drinking alcohol.

"Do, uh—do you want a water?" Matt whispered to Cait.

Cait forced her eyes away from her sister, who accepted a red cup from Ryan. "Yeah," she replied. "Thanks."

Matt grabbed two water bottles from the kitchen island. After handing one to her, he motioned to the living room. "Do you wanna . . . ?"

Nodding, Cait desperately wanted to leave the kitchen. She looked once over her shoulder, catching Desmond's glance her way. Sydney was talking, trying to catch his attention around Brady, but he ignored the redhead as he sipped from his cup.

Turning around, Cait followed Matt back into the main room. They took the first empty space against the wall that they could find. Cait clutched her water bottle to her chest, chin tucked to ensure no one noticed her.

"I'm sorry," she tried to say to Matt, but he narrowed his eyes, leaning closer.

"I can't hear you," he said loudly, pointing to his ear.

Cait raised her voice. "I'm sorry. We shouldn't have come."

"It's okay, Cait, really," he promised. "I still think we can have fun. We'll just . . . have a different kind of fun than everyone else."

Running her finger along the ridges of the water bottle cap, Cait frowned. "You think so?"

Matt smiled in his bright, goofy way. "I know so!"

CHAPTER SEVENTEEN

Cait

Why did people find parties like this fun? Cait couldn't puzzle it out. Most of the young adults were deep in their cups, readily making fools of themselves. The laughter, the music, the raised voices—the noise of it all rang through her head, overwhelming her senses.

It didn't help that Desmond's presence in the house added that constant hum to the back of her skull. Her whole body was alert, keen to his every movement. He and his posse had abandoned the kitchen, now standing on the far side of the room opposite her and Matt. Brady didn't appear to be "throwing back" as much as the rest. Garrett twirled one of Whitney's spiraling black curls around his finger over and over, the two of them visibly intoxicated. A half-dozen other young women were loitering around their party, trying to talk to both Desmond and Brady—whichever would pay the slightest attention to them.

Cait sipped from her water bottle. She swirled the lukewarm taste of nothing around her tongue. Part of her wondered what all the drinks in those red cups tasted like. Their nan didn't keep alcohol in the house. Not because she didn't approve of drinking it. Her husband had run a pub, for goodness' sake. Simply because it was an unnecessary expense, and she had three underage granddaughters.

The only alcohol Cait had ever drunk was the watered-down wine they served for communion at church and the singular sip of her grandda's beer that her da had allowed her to taste from his pint one time. She remembered the bitter tang of what her da called hops, causing her to scrunch her nose and stick out her tongue, baffled as to why anyone would drink such an awful-tasting thing.

Cait was a rule follower; she knew that. Desmond teased her about it regularly. She was too terrified of proving to be the evil, demon-cursed child the rumors said she was. If she always did the right thing, no one could truly stake that claim on her.

But at this moment, watching the gaggle of girls giggling and grinning at Desmond, she felt a sudden rebellious urge well up within her. She had to fight her own feet as they shuffled an inch away from the wall, desperate to carry her across the room. Her hands flexed with the desire to push her way through those girls, take that red cup from Desmond's hand, knock back whatever was in there, and kiss him.

The vision made Cait's throat go dry. She couldn't believe she'd thought it in the first place. Something must be wrong with her. The music, the crowd—it was getting to her.

At her side, Matt tapped his foot in time with the beat. "This is a cool house," he remarked, eyes drifting around the room.

Cait's cheeks blazed as she forced her gaze away from Desmond and his besotted fans. "Yeah," she agreed, though she stared at her shoes now. She hated them; they were cute and made her feel pretty, but they already hurt, even standing still.

"So," Matt turned to her, a glimmer of determination in his brown eyes, "I told you we could have some fun. And I think that isn't likely to happen if we just keep hanging around the wall, ya know?"

"What do you mean?" Cait asked, disturbed by where she thought he might direct the conversation.

"I mean, we could be wallflowers," he explained. "Or we could actually do something while we're here."

Fearful that he was about to ask her to dance with him, Cait took a step back. She didn't know how to dance. And she certainly didn't want to dance the way most of the others were dancing.

At least. . . .

Cait felt her eyes drift in Desmond's direction, the idea of dancing with him causing her heart rate to spike.

Matt didn't notice the heat that flushed her cheeks. "Here's what I was thinking," he said, voice raised so she could hear him over the thumping bass. "I saw an *insane* spread of snacks in the dining room on our way in here. It also wasn't as crowded in there. We should totally go and eat as much of their food as possible."

The unexpected suggestion made Cait laugh. "I like it," she told him.

"In that case—" Matt shifted away from the wall, holding out his hand to her, a big, goofy grin on his face. "Better hold on. We don't wanna get separated in all this."

Though she hesitated at the thought of holding Matt's hand, he was right. The dining room was at the front of the house. Getting through the crowd would require lots of jostling and squeezing through. And the idea of getting separated was unnerving.

Taking his hand, Cait refused to dwell on how it felt, having his fingers wrapped around hers. It didn't mean anything. They were simply being practical, she told herself. And as the process of getting through to the other side proved as difficult as predicted, she felt justified in their decision.

Matt released his hold of her the second they broke free of the crowd.

Entering the dining room, Cait found that Matt was right. There were far fewer people clustered around the space. They both grabbed a small paper plate and made a slow, meandering rotation around the massive dining table. It was chock full of snacks. A variety of chips and dip, pizza rolls, cookies, crackers, candies, and pretzels overflowed trays and bowls. There were even a couple of slow cookers on the buffet with barbeque meatballs and tiny sausages.

Taking their time, Matt and Cait claimed the room as their own. She kicked off her shoes, immensely enjoying the break from the rest of the party. They ate their fill and then some.

Eventually, Matt sheepishly pulled a deck of cards from his back pocket. "I thought we were gonna play games," he defended even though she hadn't questioned him. "And you never know when you're gonna need an extra deck of cards, ya know? So, I brought one just in case."

Though she found his over-preparedness amusing, Cait was too grateful for his forethought to laugh at him. They cleared off a corner of the table, settling in to play multiple rounds of Go Fish, War, and Slapjack. Cait couldn't remember the last time she'd had this much fun or laughed so often.

Eventually, after several games and Matt winning his third round in a row, he looked up amidst gathering the cards. "Would you, uh—" He cleared his throat, his brown eyes flickering back and forth between the deck and her face. "Do you wanna do something else?"

Unsure of what he had to be nervous about, Cait picked at the cheesy crackers on her plate. "Like, another kind of game?" she asked.

"Uh, no, I was—I was kind of thinking it might be fun to—to dance or something," he suggested, eyes on the cards as he shuffled them. They furled with a *hiss* as he bridged them. He added quietly, "If you wanted to."

Chewing carefully, Cait considered it. Did she want to dance with Matt? Not particularly. But he'd also been so kind to her. She felt guilty turning him down simply because she didn't want to give him or anyone else the wrong impression.

"Yeah, okay," Cait managed to say cheerfully. "I'll warn you, though, I've never danced before."

"What, like, *never* never?" he asked, brow furrowed. "Not even when you're alone?"

Cait found herself laughing. "I mean, sure, when I'm alone. Just not in public. And not—not with someone."

Matt nodded as though relieved that she wasn't so boring that she didn't even dance when she was alone. "Well, that's no big deal," he assured her. "I mean, you see what all those people are doing out there. It's just moving to the music."

The idea of doing what the others were doing made Cait blush. The thought had the same effect on Matt. "I don't mean," he hurried to say, "that—that—ya know, *that* kind of dancing or anything. That's not really dancing. It's more like. . . ."

Cait found herself staring at her crackers, thankful he'd chosen to trail off.

He cleared his throat again, running his hands along his jeans.

Embarrassed but sure that sitting quietly would only make it worse, Cait motioned to the other room. "Did you want to . . . ?"

Matt gaped at her like he was surprised she would still have an interest. "Uh, yeah! Sure!"

He hopped up with such enthusiasm that Cait smiled as he slipped the deck of cards into his pocket. They veered back into the living space, the party still going in full swing. They'd been on their own for almost an hour, and it showed. Most of the partygoers were plastered, their movements and voices slurring all around them. But overall, the mood was still bright and cheery.

Cait scanned the room as they walked cautiously into the throng. Garrett and Whitney were out on the dancefloor now, eyes locked as though in a trance. Hunter and Elizabeth lounged on a couch, wrapped up in each other's arms as they talked with Scott and his girlfriend, Melissa. Brady danced more respectfully with Monica, her far more into it than he. Desmond still held court, sitting on top of a sideboard, laughing as he drank and watched his friends making fools of themselves.

But it was the center of the dance floor that caught Cait's fullest attention.

Ryan had Rese in his arms, swaying to the music even as their lips found each other's repeatedly. Despite Cait's nonexistent experience with romance, she could tell this kiss involved far more intimate touching than she thought appropriate, particularly in the middle of a crowd.

Face heating with frustration, Cait tried not to let it show. Why was her sister behaving like this? Why had she brought them to a wild, illicit party? And why was she making out with a boy in plain sight of the Porthaven elite?

At the edge of the dance floor that was the Greene family's living room, Matt turned to Cait. He proffered his hand to her for a second time that night. "Shall we?" he asked.

Cait stared at his waiting palm, her heart hammering double time. What was she doing here? Why had she agreed to this? She should've refused to enter the house, even if that meant walking the whole way home.

But as Cait stared at Matt's hand, she felt her anger rising. The same flare rose within her when she'd snapped at Hunter last week. It nipped at her nerves, fraying them and sending impulsive thoughts into her head.

Cait slapped her hand into Matt's more forcefully than she needed to. He didn't seem to mind, his smile wide as he led her farther onto the floor.

He reached out and took her other hand. "Okay, like this," he said, then guided her through the first couple of steps. "Left foot, right foot. Left foot, right foot. Now, the other direction. Right foot, left foot. Right foot, left foot. You got it!"

Staring at her bare feet, Cait followed his directions. She tripped over both of their feet a few times, but he was a good sport about it. Once he got her comfortable with the basic step-step-switch, step-step-switch, he pulled back and lifted his arm.

"Now, spin!" he instructed.

Refusing to let herself become self-conscious, Cait spun, twirling under Matt's arm. He caught her hand sloppily as they laughed. He led her back through the first steps: step-step-switch, step-step-switch. When she asked him how he knew how to dance, he shrugged and said, "Mom always took me to this swing dance thing in the park every summer. We got pretty good at it."

"Swing dancing?" Cait asked. "Isn't that . . . kind of difficult?"

"It can be," he admitted. "But it's mostly just fun. Want me to show you some of the steps?"

With a little more coaxing, Matt got Cait to test out some of the more complicated moves of swing dancing. Though she executed them with mediocre talent, she found herself laughing happily, forgetting that they were in a crowd of her classmates. She twirled and swayed and lost all sense of insecurity as the dim room faded with the pulse of the music. Then, Garrett collided with Matt, disrupting the moment.

"Oh, sorry, man," Garrett yelled over the music. He held up a hand in apology, then plopped it down hard on Matt's shoulder in an attempt to keep himself upright. The oaf chuckled wildly, pointing to his head. "Getting a little dizzy."

"It's cool," Matt assured him, having to crane his neck to look up at Garrett. "You okay?"

While Garrett kept Matt's attention, Cait felt a sudden tug on her arm. She let out a small yelp as she was yanked backward into the crowd, but no one heard her in the clamor of the room.

Cait worked to keep her feet under her as she struggled through the crowd. She tried to see who had such a fierce grip on her, the crush of people making it difficult to get a good look. Then, as her arm blazed under his fingers and the hum rose at the back of her head, recognition hit. "Desmond?" she whispered.

"Shh," he hissed, drawing her through the throng. He tugged her into a hallway, glancing over his shoulder as though to be sure they weren't seen.

"What are you doing?" she demanded, keeping her voice low. She doubted he even heard her, the music still blaring as they wound through the dark hallway of the house. There weren't any people in this part of the house, a clear sense of "off-limits" radiating from the unlit corridor. "Are we allowed back here?"

"It's too loud out there," was all he said in response. He made a sharp turn, opening a door and pulling her into the room behind him. A singular lamp lit up the space. A gold-framed bed with a white, down comforter sat to their immediate left, taking up much of the room. Unremarkable paintings of the sea and lighthouses hung on the walls. Linen curtains hung open, the heavy blinds closed. A dresser with a mirror and a basket of goodies rested against the far wall.

Cait realized they were in a guest bedroom.

Desmond shut the door quietly, his movements exaggeratedly cautious. He turned back to her, his gaze unusually glassy. "You need to break up with that boy," he slurred, hand still fumbling with the doorknob.

"We're not dating," she insisted, noting the *click* of the lock. "What are you doing?"

Taking a step away from the door, Desmond smirked. "You're the one who needed to talk," he said with a sweep of his arm in her direction. Then he thumped a hand against his chest. "And I don't care to find out what getting discovered in a bedroom with the Lewan girl will do for my reputation."

He had a point, but Cait still felt her heart twist.

"Wow, my head is swimming," Desmond murmured. He shuffled farther into the room and dropped onto the side of the mattress, a hand at his head.

Annoyed, Cait crossed her arms. "Well, maybe you shouldn't have been drinking."

He looked up at her with a sardonic lift of his eyebrows. "We're at a party, Cait. It's what you do."

"I didn't drink anything."

"And are you having fun?" he countered.

"I *was*," she retorted.

Desmond blinked, his face falling strangely. "Do you want to go back out?" he asked, a tremor of hurt in his tone.

Though a twinge of guilt curled in her chest, Cait crossed her arms. "You've already got me here. We may as well talk."

Desmond sighed, scrubbing a hand over his face. "That Matt-kid is ruining everything," he grumbled.

"Why, because I'm not available to entertain you twenty-four seven anymore?"

Mouth falling ajar, Desmond stared up at her. Cait swallowed down her instant regret. She didn't know why she'd said it. She didn't think she'd said anything so rude to anyone in her entire life. But she was angry.

"What has gotten into you lately?" Desmond asked, eyebrows pinching together.

Cait didn't exactly know why she was so angry. She thought it had something to do with the fact she *wanted* someone to discover her in a bedroom with Desmond, despite knowing it was wrong in every conceivable way. She wanted him to be so desperate to be alone with her that he would sneak her away and kiss her. And maybe she was being so contrary to ensure that such a thing *didn't* happen because she knew that if it did, it would only be because he was drunk and impulsive and not because he actually wanted *her*.

Shoving down all her feelings, Cait took a step back. "Why did you bring me in here?"

"You said you needed to talk," he repeated, the words running into one another from his intoxication.

"You're drunk," she accused.

"Yeah."

She scowled. "I'll talk to you when you're sober," she said, moving for the door.

"Wait, wait, wait—" He sprang from the bed, reaching out to grab her arm again. Cait pulled out of his reach, and he stumbled. "Oh, whoa!" He set a hand on the wall next to the door. "I'm drunker than I thought."

Shaking her head, Cait struggled to reconcile this Desmond with the one she knew. She'd never seen him in this state. It wasn't all that different, she supposed. He was foolhardy and selfish on a good day. This was Desmond, only amplified.

The cruel thought made Cait feel traitorous. She knew that wasn't true. This was who Desmond *pretended* to be. He hid in bad behavior the same way she hid in solitude. The real Desmond was gentle, caring, and intelligent. He liked to read Ernest Hemingway, H.P. Lovecraft, and Frank Herbert. He daydreamed with her about traveling to Ireland so that she could show him where she used to live. He laughed easily, listened readily, and knew all the right things to say.

This wasn't him. This was some strange parody.

Working to stand up straight, Desmond met Cait's eyes. There was a desperation in his gaze, a pleading that tugged on her heart. "Talk to me, Caity," he asked, his voice soft.

Chewing on her bottom lip, Cait fought against her better judgment. She should say no. She should push him out of the way and walk out the door. She should rejoin Matt and forget that Desmond was even at the party, to begin with.

Head swirling with what she knew she *should* do, Cait couldn't tear her eyes from Desmond's face. His expression was so adamant, so tender—the real, wonderful version of him showing through—it was easy to imagine that he *had* pulled her in here because he wanted to be alone with her—because he missed her.

"I—I don't know what to say," she whispered.

Desmond's lips twitched in amusement. "You've never struggled to talk to me before."

"That was before."

His face fell. "Before Matt?"

Cait didn't have a reply. It *was* because of Matt. Not because she had a romantic interest in Matt. Because she now realized what it was like to have a real friend. One who was there, not one you had to sneak out to meet. One who took care of you at all times, not one who ignored you when it wasn't convenient.

With a sigh, Desmond slumped back onto the bed. His hands hung between his knees as he stared at the floor. "You can leave if you want," he murmured.

Though she knew she should, Cait didn't leave. She stood there, studying Desmond. "Why do you do this?" she asked.

"Do what?"

"Get drunk. Party. Act like you don't care."

He looked up at her with a false grin. "Probably 'cause I'm bored."

She set her hands on her hips. "I know that isn't true."

"Fine—" He reached down and tugged free the laces on his boots, kicking them off one at a time. "It's 'cause I'm selfish. And I'm lazy. And I hate everything in this stupid town."

Watching him cautiously, Cait stayed rooted in her spot. "I happen to know that's not true either."

With a huff, Desmond flopped back against the fluffy white pillows on the bed. His dark clothing stuck out like a shadow in its midst. He tucked his hands behind his head. "You keep telling yourself that, Lewan."

She didn't have anything to say, so she stood there, silent.

Desmond eyed her, sprawled in the middle of the bed. Then he stared up at the ceiling. "Why'd you let Therese dress you up like that?" he asked, a hint of agitation in his tone.

Shifting nervously, Cait smoothed the skirt of her dress. "What makes you think that it was Rese's idea?"

He huffed. "Like you'd ever choose it yourself."

The remark bit into Cait's pride. "You don't think I like to feel pretty?"

"I *think*," he turned his head to look at her, "that you don't want people paying attention to you."

His dark eyes scanned her from head to toe. It wasn't suggestive or mocking. Instead, it felt like a simple, admiring appraisal. "And people can't help but pay attention to you, looking like *that*," he remarked.

Though Cait didn't think it was meant to be a compliment, she couldn't help blushing. Even if it was offhanded, he'd implied that he thought she was attractive.

Turning onto his side, Desmond held her stare. "Come 'ere," he said.

Cait gaped at him. "What?"

"You're practically on the opposite side of the room." He beckoned to her. "Come. Here."

Shaking her head, Cait knew she couldn't do that. "No."

"Why not?"

"Desmond, I'm not sitting on a bed with you."

He snorted. "I do have some self-control, believe it or not. Besides," he raised his eyebrows, "I don't have any plans to touch you, Caity. I just want to talk to you, and I'm tired of staring across the room to do it."

Cait didn't move.

Desmond didn't either.

"It's not a good idea," she objected.

"Why? Because it's 'inappropriate'?"

"Yes."

He shook his head, rolling onto his back again. "I'm not gonna try anything, Lewan." His eyes remained locked with hers. "Now, get over here."

Slowly, Cait began to step toward the bed. She knew she shouldn't. If her nan or her sisters found out, they'd be irate.

Then again, Rese had been making out with Ryan in front of the whole party. Sitting on the bed next to Desmond wasn't anything like that. They weren't even going to touch. There wasn't anything romantic about the experience at all.

Cautiously, Cait sat on the very edge of the mattress.

Desmond chuckled, reaching over to tug playfully at the hem of her skirt. "You're such a prude."

Whacking his hand away, Cait failed to keep herself from smiling. "And you're a jerk."

"Yeah," he admitted, then screwed up his face as though confused. His finger brushed the eyelet fabric of her skirt again. "Is . . . is this see-through?"

Face heating, Cait pressed a hand over the tight band under the bust where the skirt met the bodice. "Just the midsection," she muttered. "The rest has a second layer underneath it."

He let out a low whistle. "Well, that's pretty hot."

Her cheeks flared another ten degrees hotter. She tried to slap his arm, but he caught her hand. "I'm teasing you, Caity," he laughed. "I knew it'd make you blush."

"You're the worst," she said, jabbing him in the ribs with her free hand.

He reached out and caught that wrist, too, gently tugging to draw her farther onto the bed. "So you've said."

Cait's heart raced at double the speed, their sides nearly touching. He wasn't flirting. She knew that. But for all the world, as his rich brown eyes held hers, it felt like he was.

Grip loosening on her wrist, Desmond let their hands fall to the blanket between them. "Are you mad at me, Caity?" he whispered.

Unable to hold his gaze any longer, Cait looked down to watch as his long fingers brushed against the backs of her hands, sending a spread of tingles up her arm. "Yes," she admitted.

"Why?" he asked, a tinge of confusion in his tone.

For all the world, Cait wanted to tell him. She wanted to open her mouth and say the things she'd always longed to say to him.

Instead, she asked, "How drunk are you?"

"Pretty drunk."

Her eyes rose to meet his. "Drunk enough that you'll forget this in the morning?"

He shook his head, a pleasant grin on his lips. "Nah. I'm at least two shots away from that. Why? Do you want me to forget something?"

She turned away. "I was just curious."

"Mm." He tapped the back of her hand. "You gonna answer my question?"

"What question?"

"Why are you mad at me?"

Staring at the far wall, Cait tried not to enjoy the brush of Desmond's fingers along hers. She wished he'd stop teasing her and hold her hand. Hundreds of times, she'd imagined how it would feel to have their fingers intertwined like that. But she reminded herself that he didn't mean any of this romantically. He was drunk and flippant, and he probably wasn't even aware of what he was doing.

Unexpectedly, the doorknob jiggled. Cait jumped, and Desmond's fingers gripped hers. Someone was trying to get in. There was a knock and then a voice.

"Cait?" Matt called.

"Occupied!" Desmond yelled, his voice more gruff than usual. It hardly even sounded like him. She wondered if he'd done it on purpose to keep Matt from knowing it was him.

There was a moment of silence, then Matt muttered an apology. The muffled beat of the music managed to cover up his retreat, and she held her breath, feeling guilty for abandoning him. He was too good of a friend for that.

"I should go," Cait muttered, scooting toward the edge of the bed.

"No," Desmond objected, tightening his hold on her.

Cait tried to pull away, but he didn't let go, leaving her practically lying across the side of the bed. Desmond's expression tugged at her heart, his face scrunched in near panic. "Don't go," he whispered. "Whatever I did . . . don't go."

As though his desperate words had locked her in place, Cait couldn't move. She couldn't speak. And she couldn't fight him as his hands slid up her arms to draw her closer. "Don't go," he repeated.

Those two words latched onto her heart, pulling and pleading with her conscience. *Don't go.* She could almost hear the unsaid meaning: *I miss you.*

Scanning Desmond's face, Cait tried to convince herself to get up. She knew she needed to leave him. But as one hand fell to rest lazily on her shoulder and the other reached up to brush some of her hair back behind her ear, her head reverberated with the hum. Some near-magical force overcame her logic, her body alert from the rumble coursing through her.

His fingers lingered on her temple, running along her hairline. "Tell me," he whispered. "Tell me what I did wrong."

Cait let herself stare at him as he stared at her. She loved his face. It was so interesting and handsome. She could look at him for hours and never get tired of it. She could never quite determine why. Maybe it had to do with the fact that those dark eyes of his weren't entirely brown— they had the smallest flecks of green around the pupil. Or maybe it was the smattering of freckles that dotted his light skin—medium and dark brown speckles that added to his carefree personality.

Two of those freckles created a nearly perfect line down his left cheek; one was in the exact center of his cheek, the other in line with the corner of his mouth. So many times, Cait had imagined running her finger from one freckle to the next, connecting those dots.

"We shouldn't be alone like this, Des," she murmured.

"We used to be alone all the time."

"Maybe that was wrong too."

Desmond frowned. "Don't say that."

"I thought that was the point of hanging out with me," she said. "It's wrong and would make your dad angry, so you do it."

"Is that it?" he asked, an edge coming into his voice. "You're upset because you think I'm only spending time with you to get back at my dad?"

"I've always known that," she returned.

"So, that's not it?"

"No."

He heaved an exasperated sigh, tossing his hands into the air around her. They fell, one landing on her waist, almost as though he was holding her in his arms. "Then, *what* is it?" he demanded. "What did I do?"

"Nothing," she said.

"Don't—don't lie to me, Cait." He glared at her. "I can't fix it if you don't tell me what's wrong."

Shaking her head, Cait shifted away from him. "Everything is wrong, Desmond," she muttered, pushing his hand off her waist. "This is wrong. Our . . . 'not friendship' is wrong. The fact that we can't spend time together because I have a real friend for the first time in my entire life is wrong. And you not understanding any of that is wrong."

As she tried to pull away, Desmond held on. "Cait—"

"Stop." She pushed his hands away. "Stop, just—"

"I know, okay?" he interrupted, panic in his eyes as he scrambled to sit up. "I know. It's screwed up and—and I'm pissed about it. But I don't know what to do."

"Then, don't do anything," she said.

"Cait." He said her name like he was begging her to hear him.

It worked. She stopped pulling away and let him draw her closer. His hands gripped her shoulders for a moment. He stared at her as though he wasn't sure what to do with her compliance. Slowly relaxing back against the pillows, he carefully tucked her shoulder into his side, guiding her head to rest on his chest.

The rumble of her senses confused so much of the moment that Cait didn't know what was happening until it was too late. Without a drop of alcohol, it was like she was as intoxicated as him. All she knew was that she wanted to lay like this with him as he swept the hair back off her forehead for eternity.

Desmond's eyes looked more at her hair than her face. She could still see the haze of drunkenness in his heavy-lidded eyes and smell the liquor on his breath. His scent enveloped her, the heady cedar of his cologne mixed with the warm tannins of whiskey. They lay there for several minutes, staring at each other. She could almost see the thoughts churning through his head as she struggled to breathe in his nearness.

Blinking lazily as though he was about to fall asleep, Desmond finally whispered, "Tell me how to fix it."

"You can't," she told him without hesitation because it was true. There was no way to fix this. No way to mend the brokenness that marred their future. No way to stop her from being the girl with a curse and him from being the boy destined for leadership.

Desmond looked immeasurably saddened by her response, but he didn't speak. His fingers brushed along the edges of her hair. The foolishness of her surrender to this moment coiled around Cait's heart like a vice. She shouldn't let him touch her this way. She shouldn't lay next to him, head on his chest.

She could hear his heartbeat, steady and sure, under her ear. The world outside the room didn't exist to her anymore. She could only hear his heart and the hum that encompassed everything inside her. And for the briefest moment of time, as Cait lay with Desmond, she let herself pretend that he loved her back.

Reality was lost to her in those moments. Her thoughts drifted into wishes. Dreams that told her foolish lies, letting her believe falsely that they belonged together. Lies that said this hum he provoked within her was destiny telling her they were meant for one another.

But Cait didn't believe in destiny. She believed in consequences and coincidences. Fate played no part in her life, only strange flukes and horrible choices.

Cait didn't stir until well after Desmond's eyes had flittered closed in sleep. His lips parted, his deep breaths tickling her forehead with warmth. The hum caused her whole being to surge with some unknown emotion. She almost called it safety. Then she chose to label it insanity.

With great care, Cait pulled out of his touch. She removed his hand from her shoulder to lay it on his chest. Then she reached up to brush back some of his unruly waves. She really was mad at him. And while she knew she should keep it inside, she couldn't help but whisper the truth to him.

"It's because it can't ever be real," she told him as he slept. "We can never be real."

Cait rose from the bed then and snuck out of the bedroom, making sure to lock the door behind her. When she entered the living room, she was surprised to find the party had dwindled. Many attendees had left, several were asleep on the couches, and a handful more were still raging on. She found Matt in the dining room, playing solitaire. When he asked where she'd been, she told him she'd needed some time alone, so she'd gone for a walk outside. She didn't think he believed her, but he didn't ask questions as she put on her shoes and requested his help in getting Rese back home.

The whole evening had been a disaster, Cait concluded. From the highly inebriated state in which she found Rese to Matt sulking on the way back home, everything had gone wrong. After sneaking Rese into the house and up to her room, Cait finally made her way to her own bed. And when she eventually fell asleep, feeling hollow and alone, she dreamed of Desmond, watching him die at the hands of monsters once again.

CHAPTER EIGHTEEN

Desmond

"So, I guess we're going on a tour of Porthaven's freak shows," Desmond remarked as they pulled into the driveway of the Faulk home. Its cheery yellow siding didn't match the emo kid he knew at school. Though, in his minimal experience with Mr. and Mrs. Faulk, he could say it fit *them*.

William leveled him with an unamused stare. "After last night, I don't suggest you start with me."

Pressing his lips together, Desmond turned away. He'd wound up sleeping through most of the night at the Greenes', only to fail at his attempt to sneak back home. It was his car's fault. The loud rumble of the engine probably woke the whole neighborhood.

When he'd walked into the house, his dad was there, waiting inside the back door. One of the perks of having a mayor for a dad and a sheriff for an uncle was that your dad had easy access to all kinds of fun gadgets via said uncle—including a Breathalyzer. Having your dad perform a sobriety test on you was a uniquely maddening experience. And while most of the alcohol had left his system during the hours of his sleep, he'd had enough through the whole party to still ping the system.

"You're grounded," William declared. "For the rest of the month."

At first, Desmond didn't think that meant much. The month was only another nine days, and his extracurricular activities were his internship and basketball. Both were important enough that his dad would never take them away from him. Not that he wouldn't happily say goodbye to his internship.

But then, his dad held out his hand. "Keys," he ordered.

"I'm not a kid," Desmond shot back.

"You're right, you're not." William's voice had been infuriatingly calm. "Which is why you should know better than to behave in such a childish manner."

"It was a stupid party. Who cares?"

"As the future leader of this town, *you* should care. It's your reputation on the line."

Desmond had scoffed at that. "Well, at least people will like me when I take office."

A thick eyebrow rose imperiously on his dad's face. "But they won't respect you."

That shut Desmond up. He handed over his keys, then shoved past his dad. The next morning, the rest of the grounding's implications set in. His dad was determined to teach him a lesson, it seemed. He'd removed basketball from his schedule, exchanging it for extra hours at the internship. "I've already called the principal," he explained at breakfast. "You'll be by my side until the end of the month."

"Is this part of your weird attempt to buddy up to me?" Desmond quipped, stabbing his fork into his eggs and sausage. He was usually quick to rally after parties, but today, he'd woken with a roaring headache, and it was affecting his mood.

"I'll be honest—" He lifted the fork, sending his dad a glare filled with every ounce of irritation he felt. "I don't think it's gonna be successful."

As he shoved the bite into his mouth, William didn't acknowledge his snark. "We'll leave for the Faulks' in twenty minutes," he'd said. "Be sure you're ready."

Desmond took thirty minutes before arriving in the garage.

Now, his head still aching as they arrived at their destination, Desmond regretted everything. Not just showing up late intentionally. That was a dick move he wasn't particularly proud of, but that was merely the icing on the cake. Because his dad was right—he was acting like a child. And no one had any reason to respect Desmond.

He'd been such an idiot last night. At the party. With Cait. He'd freaking passed out in the Greenes' guest room like a moron because he'd been so drunk. What kind of ass did that?

Yes, Desmond drank as a minor. Yes, that was illegal. No, he didn't particularly care. But he rarely drank *that* much because his dad was right—he didn't want to make a fool of himself around the people that he would one day lead.

Yet last night, he'd had more than one or two. He'd had six—in the span of three hours. Desmond had a decent tolerance to alcohol, but by how quickly he'd been knocking them back, it was a wonder he hadn't fallen flat on his face.

All because he couldn't handle the fact that Cait was there.

She never came to parties. She was exclusive to two versions of him: the public figure he displayed at school and church and the *real* him. The purest version of Desmond Simon that he only ever revealed in one place and with one person belonged at the cove with Cait. To suddenly see her there while he was playing the role of "party-boy Desmond" felt wrong. It sent him teetering off-kilter.

Then, to watch her spending so much time with Matt, laughing and enjoying herself—well, Desmond could be honest with himself. He'd been jealous. *He* was the one who made Cait laugh. *He* was the one she had fun with. This random kid didn't have the right to take his place.

But she'd been right; everything she'd said last night had been right.

And everything she hadn't said but meant—she'd been right about that too.

It was wrong, their "not friendship." The fact that he was never there for her. The fact that despite everything they meant to each other, they could never be together. The fact that for the first time in her life, she had a friend who could actually be by her side. And he was mad at her for choosing reality over impossibility.

Add to that the way she'd looked—which was gorgeous, should anyone ask his opinion—downright, freaking, upsettingly gorgeous—and Desmond had lost it.

The whole night, he'd struggled to keep it together. Even Brady had noticed, questioning him multiple times. Desmond finally snapped at his best friend, telling him to mind his own business. He'd asked Garrett to distract Matt—not that he'd explained the "why" to his cousin. He'd known even then that he was making a mistake.

He'd lied to Cait. He didn't have any self-control. And he'd most definitely intended on touching her when he asked her to sit with him on the bed. Which he'd succeeded in doing to the extent that he'd planned. Her hair felt like starlight, he'd decided. Silver strands of starlight.

He'd thought about kissing her. He couldn't say why he hadn't. Maybe he hadn't been *quite* that drunk. He'd managed to hold onto one fraction of reason while they lay next to each other.

God, they'd *lain* next to each other! The memory raised all kinds of conflicting feelings. Pleasure and regret. Victory and defeat. Hope and pain.

He was losing her. Desmond was surer of that than anything. And while he'd always known that he would, somehow, he'd never actually believed it.

"Tell me how to fix it." His own plea echoed in his head as her words ripped at his chest. *"You can't."*

The sedan's engine died, and William unbuckled his seatbelt, forcing Desmond to let go of his troubled thoughts. He hated himself—truly. He hated who he had to be. He hated who he couldn't be. And he hated that he wasn't brave enough to do something about it.

Getting out of the car, Desmond stared at the Faulk home. The quaint little house sat near Cait's neighborhood. The forest surrounded all these houses, spread out with nicely sized yards and almost two centuries of history each. Sunshine yellow siding and soft blue accents gave this particular house an extra dose of charm. A stone path led up to the bright blue door.

William lifted his hand and knocked.

"You never did tell me why we're here," Desmond muttered, trying to give himself something to focus on other than the fact that if he walked back the way they'd come and took a right, after about ten minutes, he'd run into Cait's street.

With a dismissive glance, William didn't get the chance to answer as the door opened. He plastered on his mayoral smile as Saliha Faulk stepped into view. Her thick, black-brown hair hovered above her shoulders in a neat crop. Desmond never could quite remember where her family was from originally. Pakistan? Persia? Was Persia even a real country anymore? She'd passed her golden-brown skin on to her son, making Sterling the first Faulk heir who wasn't as pale as the rest of the town.

Desmond had always liked Saliha. Not that he knew her firsthand. But being the mayor's son did put him in a unique position to observe the family from afar. And he'd noticed that the woman was kind, good-humored, and carefree.

She was the exact opposite of her moody son, who only spent time with Hunter and his pals.

Saliha smiled welcomingly at William and Desmond, pushing the screen door open for them. She invited them in, offering them a drink or some breakfast. "I made an extra pot of coffee, knowing you'd be coming by," she said.

So, his dad had filled the Faulks in, but not Desmond.

William accepted the coffee but declined breakfast.

"Tim is in the kitchen," Saliha said, ushering them through the house. It smelled of blueberries and vanilla. "He insisted on baking, but don't feel like you have to eat anything if you aren't hungry. Did you need to see Sterling too?"

As his dad assured her that a visit with their son wasn't necessary, Desmond scanned the bright house. Everything was light and cozy, a complete juxtaposition from the angst-ridden classmate he knew. Built-in bookcases, full of colorful spines, flanked a white-painted fireplace. The open floor plan led them through the living room to the kitchen.

Timothy Faulk awaited them behind the white quartz island, mint-colored oven mitts on his hands as he opened the stove. The guy was six-foot-whatever, full of cheesy dad jokes, consideration, and creativity. He had an eye for detail that made him the finest craftsman in town. He worked primarily as a woodcarver of small household goods, but sometimes, he made larger pieces of furniture that every housewife practically went to war over.

"Hiya," Timothy called when he saw them. "Hold on a sec."

There was something about the man that always rubbed Desmond the wrong way. Not that he didn't like him. He thought he was a pretty cool dude, actually. But something about the way he said things like "hiya" and "hold on a sec" made Desmond question the man's adulthood. Timothy and William were about the same age. And Desmond's dad would never say anything remotely so casual. It was as though by being easygoing, Timothy was impossible to take seriously.

But that could also have had something to do with the frilly apron the guy wore around his waist as he pulled blueberry muffins out of the oven.

"There," Timothy said, yanking off the oven mitts and reaching around to untie the apron. "Those bad boys'll have to cool for about five minutes before we dig in. Now," he turned the Simon men and held out his hand, "how are you guys? Having a good Saturday?"

William shook Timothy's hand first, then Desmond took his turn. At least the man had a firm handshake.

"I have some questions for you, Timothy," the mayor began. "Would it be possible for us to take a seat?"

With a chuckle, Timothy clapped a hand on William's shoulder. "How many times do I have to tell you—call me Tim," he insisted. He moved to the small dining table situated in the eat-in kitchen. "Have a seat."

Saliha set coffee mugs in front of Desmond and his dad, offering cream or sugar. Though Desmond would have preferred something to cut the bitterness, his dad held up a hand, refusing politely.

With their own cups before them, Saliha took the seat next to her husband. "What's on your mind, William?" Tim asked.

"Is it safe to talk openly?" the mayor asked, professionalism lining his deep voice.

Husband and wife exchanged a confused look. "Yes," Tim assured. "It's just us and Sterling here. And he knows . . . the most important things."

Desmond didn't think that exactly answered his dad's question. What the Faulks thought was "most important" could be very different from William's definition.

William agreed. "Meaning . . . ?" he prompted.

While Saliha played with the handle of her mug, Tim cleared his throat. "He knows that we have an important job," he explained. "One that is equal parts necessary and difficult. But . . . I mean, he knows what I knew when I was his age. What you told us to tell him: He's a potential Vessel, and that makes him responsible for carrying the burden well, should it fall to him. He's unaware of the complexities, but he knows that when the time comes, he may have to take up the mantle."

"Does he know about the Veil?" William asked, his voice low.

Tim glanced at his wife, then shook his head.

"Good." William leveled a serious stare at them both. "I'd like to keep it that way. So, is there any way to ensure he isn't listening in?"

"He's in his room," Tim said.

"And if he decides to come out?"

Rising, Saliha set a hand on her husband's arm. "I'll go keep an eye," she offered.

When she was gone, Tim turned back to the Simon men. His dark eyes flickered to Desmond for only a second before settling on William. "Is everything all right with the Veil?" he asked in a near whisper.

"There was an incident," William said. "We're looking into the cause as we speak. However, I need you to be honest with me, Tim: Have you connected with it in any way?"

Furrowing his blond eyebrows, Tim looked baffled. "Connected—? No!" he insisted. "No, I wouldn't even know how to begin—William, shouldn't you be talking to my father? He's still the one—"

"We don't know that," William interrupted. "Sometimes it skips a generation. Sometimes even two."

Tim froze. "You don't think. . . ." His words trailed off, and he turned to look down the hall where his wife had disappeared. "Sterling was just a baby when my grandfather passed."

"No, I don't think he was chosen," William confirmed. "But I'm not counting it out either. Not when we have a problem such as this on our hands."

Eyes narrowing, Tim glanced at Desmond again. "A problem such as what?"

Patiently sipping his coffee, Desmond didn't care to speak up in this meeting. He was happy to listen and absorb all the information that his dad might divulge. He kept running it against the documents he'd printed off his dad's computer, hoping to find something that connected the dots for him.

William always sat upright, shoulders back and chin high. In the Faulk's cheery kitchen, his posture looked bizarrely out of place.

"Someone has tampered with it," he said. "And we believe they are making a connection to wield the spirit world remotely."

Mouth hanging ajar, Tim looked truly befuddled by this news. "Can—can someone do that?"

"That's what we're trying to figure out," William admitted. "We are in the midst of investigating all possibilities. However, I need you to know, Tim, that you, your father, and your son are all potential suspects. So, if there is anything you can tell us, I'd suggest you share it."

Setting a shaking hand over his mouth, Tim's eyes dropped to the tabletop, scanning it as though hoping it could provide him with answers. "I—I don't know, William." His hand dropped limply back to the table. "I swear to you. My father is old, and his health . . . he's had a rough few months. There is no chance he could do anything like this in his state."

Desmond assumed that was why they hadn't visited George Faulk. Given his honorary position in the Warden council, he knew the old man had lost his wife a handful of years ago and that they'd moved him into a seniors' home closer to downtown for better care of his declining mental health. No one knew exactly what the cause was—some said it was dementia, but Desmond had read the secret report in the Warden files he'd stolen. They feared it had to do with the block. A potentially unforeseen side effect of repressing something for over seventy years.

"And you know," Tim continued, "I would never—I wouldn't even know how to do something like that. My father didn't even tell me where the Veil is located. I've never seen it. I don't know anything about it beyond that . . . well, that I might someday share a sort of bond with it."

"What about your son?" William asked.

Desmond thought his dad's voice was a bit too gruff, but he understood. They were running out of options. Their investigation was hitting a dead end, and the Warden was growing tired. They needed answers.

Tim shook his head furiously. "Sterling has no idea what wielding is," he insisted. "We've never discussed it. He doesn't even realize what our bloodline carries. He certainly doesn't know about the Veil."

William frowned thoughtfully. "You're sure?"

Desmond found himself agreeing with his dad's suspicions. After all, Sterling *was* friends with Hunter Varon. There was a good chance that Hunter had revealed confidential information, either intentionally or not.

With a sigh, Tim pushed his mug away from him. "Listen, Sterling didn't do this—whatever it is that has happened. I know he's somewhat of a . . . an outsider, but it isn't because he's some rebel. He's just . . . cautious."

William's eyebrows arched in curiosity. "Cautious about what?"

"He has a hard time with this," Tim admitted. "Knowing that he's required to carry on the line, that he'll never really have any control over his life. He's carrying a lot of secrets. And I think he's cautious about making friends because he doesn't want to have to lie to them."

Desmond thought that made sense. The way Sterling chose to live his life wasn't all that different from Cait's choices. And his friendship with Hunter made even more sense. Sterling had found the one friend he *could* talk to about the Warden. Just as Cait could talk to Desmond.

But Desmond had kept the truth from Cait. He hadn't told her about the Veil, Vessels, or even the reason behind her parents' murder. Hunter had shown that he didn't hold quite the same scruples regarding the Warden's secrets when he'd taunted Desmond about the prophecy. Was it possible Hunter had told Sterling about the Veil, unwittingly goading the boy into testing his powers?

Seeing the adamant and worried expression on Tim's face, Desmond didn't think *this* was the place to bring that up.

"Is there *anything* you know that could help us, Tim?" William pressed.

Scratching the back of his head, Tim wound up ruffling his feathery blond hair. He took his time, considering deeply. "There's—no, there's nothing I can think of personally," he said, then added, "However, I . . . this does make me wonder. . . ."

William raised his thick eyebrows. "Wonder about what?"

Sheepishly, Tim met William's gaze. "I know they're rumors, so it isn't confirmed, but . . . I have to assume due to those rumors that the—the Lewan girls . . . are like us?"

William didn't confirm it, and Desmond froze, dread washing over his neck in a heated flush.

"If they are," Tim continued, taking their silence as confirmation, "then I would ask: Have you checked the other Veil?"

The flush spread down Desmond's back. There was another Veil? Was this another secret his dad had kept?

The surprised lift of William's chin killed that concern. "The other?"

Tim nodded as though this should be obvious. "Yes, I mean—again, assuming the rumors are true, whichever of the girls that thing attached itself to doesn't matter. The Veils are connected to the spirit-beings. It would have come here with them."

Studying his dad more than their host, Desmond's mind raced. It was clear on William's face that he had no more awareness of this than his son. It didn't make sense. How would they have missed an entire secondary Veil in Porthaven? Was it even possible?

"How do you know this?" William asked.

Tim shrugged. "It's part of the stuff my dad told me. And what his dad told him. The Veils and our burdens are tied together. Where one goes, the other follows."

The room fell silent.

"You mean, you didn't know?" Tim asked.

William cleared his throat, adjusting to rise. "No," he admitted. "Thank you for your help, Tim. As always, we appreciate you and your family. Your sacrifice keeps us safe."

Standing up as well, Tim wasn't quite done. "Is it the Druids? Have they come for us?"

Desmond nearly lost his footing when William replied with blatant honesty, "I don't know."

Was it the Druids? God, he hoped not. They weren't prepared for something that catastrophic.

Porthaven was safe. Its secrets were well guarded. No Druid but Lilith had ever attempted to come here in the past two hundred thirty-eight years. That was part of what made the town so trustworthy, so admired by the Warden at large. Despite the Warden's vast spread across the world, Veils were rare, drawing supernatural activity and, often, Druids. But not only had they kept their Veil a secret, they'd also held a Vessel for more than two centuries without a single Druid figuring it out.

They were small, and they were careful. But they weren't strong enough to fight off a potential horde of Druids.

Following his dad out of the Faulk home, Desmond felt his phone vibrate in his pocket. He glanced up at the back of his dad's head, walking in front of him. It had been a miracle that his grounding hadn't included his phone's confiscation. A remarkable coincidence, likely only allowed because his dad had forgotten it existed.

Cautiously fishing out his phone, Desmond checked the notification. It was a text from Cait.

"I REALLY need to talk to you."

Cait

Cait tried. She really tried not to text him.

Talking to Desmond after last night felt wrong somehow. As though everything between them was now broken. Or perhaps tainted was a better word.

But after watching him die in her dreams for the second night in a row, the implications of what it might mean terrified Cait. And she didn't think she could handle it on her own. As Desmond was the only one who knew about her dreams, she had no one else to talk to.

Cait spent the whole of Saturday morning holed up in her room. Matt had clearly been upset with her for abandoning him at the party, and he hadn't asked to hang out with her that day. Which was fine with her. She didn't think she could handle being around his good-natured chatter while her head swam with fear.

She sat on her window seat, sketching as she awaited Desmond's reply. It took almost an entire hour before her phone buzzed on the cushion next to her. *"Parental interference, sorry."*

Another text followed almost immediately. *"I'm 'grounded,' so meeting will be difficult."*

Disappointed for a plethora of reasons, Cait chose to find some sense of relief in not having to face him again so soon. *"Tomorrow?"* she asked.

"Daytime's no good. I'm being watched."

Cait chewed on her bottom lip. *"Tonight, then?"*

She imagined him smirking as she read his reply. *"You suggesting a midnight rendezvous?"* His next text came through before she could respond. *"It's really our only option. Sorry."*

Sighing, Cait forced herself to abandon her scruples once more. *"The window will be open."*

With hours of daylight to burn, Cait decided to go to the cove with Red. As the terrier roamed the sandy coastline, she sketched the bear-like creatures from her dreams last night, then wrote down everything she could remember. She'd told Desmond about her dreams for years, but she'd always focused on the monsters within them. She hadn't told him that it was in her childhood bedroom or that his father made an appearance. She certainly had never told him about the thing on the other side of the door.

But the dream had changed, and she began to fear that something was wrong. Maybe it was simply watching Desmond die; maybe it was the horror that still churned in her stomach every time she thought about it. Or maybe it was the fissure that had begun to elongate on the door.

Despite her efforts to while away the day, Cait returned home from the cove well before dinner. She showered to clear the salty air from her skin, then gave Red his own bath. She helped with dinner and even offered to take care of the dishes to keep from watching the clock. Still, she returned to her room well before midnight.

With nothing to do but wait, Cait prepared her space as best she could. She cleaned up all the corners, shoved her hamper into her closet, and even reorganized her desk simply because she ran out of things to do.

She got ready for bed at her usual time to avoid suspicion, donning a more modest pair of navy pajamas.

After a quick goodnight to her nan and sisters, she double-checked the latch on the window—unlocked—then drew the curtains and turned off all the lights. She lay alert in bed for the next two hours, watching the window in the darkness. The house creaked, and every so often, she could hear the barest hum of Rese on the other side of the wall—a late-running phone call with Ryan, most likely. Cait paid careful attention, listening for the end of the call and the faint *click* of the bedside lamp switching off.

Once she was sure the whole house was asleep, Cait checked her phone, charging on the nightstand: twelve after eleven. She scrambled out of bed, knowing she couldn't endure another forty-eight minutes of nothingness.

Grabbing her sketchbook and a blanket, Cait took a seat at the window. She pushed back the curtains to let the moonlight flood in. Still large from the full moon two nights prior, it was just enough light for her to see by. The cold night air seeped through the panes as she took up her pencil.

She found herself sketching the scene in her dream—Desmond facing away from her on the beach. Shadows and waves. Cliffs and sand.

Would she dream it all again tonight?

A tingle spread over Cait's skin, and the hair at the back of her neck rose, the hum coming along with it. She looked up, knowing he was near. In the bright moonlight, she saw a figure drop onto the roof of the back porch, the maple in their backyard swaying from the release of his weight. He scrambled carefully and quietly across the slanted pitch, straight for her window.

Setting her notebook aside, Cait rushed to push the window open. Desmond climbed through without hesitation. He wore a black hoodie, the hood up to obscure his face. But she could see his grin even in its shadow.

"You watching for me, Lewan?" he whispered, giving her chin a tap before turning to shut the window behind him.

Tucking some hair behind her ear, Cait shifted away from him. Something about the hum caused her brain to forget sanity. And she couldn't go another night without telling him about the dream. "You would have preferred I fell asleep?" she asked.

Desmond removed his hood, the moon lighting up the right side of his face. He lifted a shoulder up in a lazy shrug. "Hey, I could've lived out my childhood fantasy of rescuing Sleeping Beauty."

The connotation made her blush even as she struggled not to laugh. "You had a crush on Aurora?"

"You would know her name," he retorted softly, taking a seat. "What's with all this darkness? You trying to set a mood?"

The abrupt subject change brought another wave of heat to her skin. "No, it's just—I was concerned about someone seeing any light I left on," she explained.

With the moon at his back, she couldn't tell for sure, but she thought his eyebrows rose with a dubious tilt. "Your nan do regular sweeps of the place?"

She frowned at him, taking a seat on her bed a healthy distance away. "The bathroom is right next to my room."

"I can't hear you that far away, Caity," he replied in a raised whisper.

Pressing her lips together, Cait debated joining him on the window seat. They could be quieter that way, which would be for the best. But if she did, no matter how she sat, she'd be touching him. And after last night, that felt far more intimate than she thought she could handle.

Forcing herself to stand, Cait moved two steps closer and remained standing.

Desmond scooted to the far side of the bench, clearing a spot.

With a slight shake of her head, Cait refused.

Sighing, Desmond ran a hand through his unruly hair. "Look," he whispered, "about last night—"

"That's not why I wanted to talk to you," she interrupted.

He was silent for a moment. She couldn't read the expression on his face in the dark, but he held his hands between his knees, his shoulders curving inward. "I want to apologize," he said finally.

"Don't," she returned. She didn't know if she could handle his apology. She didn't know what it would do to her. If they didn't acknowledge the night, she wouldn't have to face the truth of it. It was the same as her feelings: So long as she didn't acknowledge how much she loved him, she could pretend it wasn't true.

Desmond angled his head, looking to the far corner of the room. He wet his lips, then muttered, "Okay."

The tension in his voice drew Cait a step closer.

He turned back to her. She could barely see the glimmer of his eyes scanning her. "I like your pink pajamas better," he remarked drolly.

Smoothing down the cotton tee, Cait worked not to read into the statement. "Well, I knew you were coming this time, so I made sure to dress more appropriately."

He chuckled softly. "We slept together, Caity. I don't think you need to worry about propriety anymore."

Though she knew it was just another of his jokes, it made her feel defensive. "I never fell asleep."

His forehead momentarily pinched with something that resembled disappointment. "Huh," he murmured. His voice took on its usual snarky intonation as he added, "It was a uniquely humiliating experience, by the way. I've never fallen asleep with a girl in my arms to find her gone in the morning."

Heart twisting, Cait tried not to take his teasing seriously. She didn't like the suggestion that they'd slept together any more than that he'd fallen asleep with other girls. There were rumors around the school, of course, but she'd never heard them confirmed. And to imagine Desmond that close to anyone else made her feel sick.

She realized her discomfort must have shown on her face because

Desmond shook his head. "Don't worry, Caity," he said almost tenderly. "Call me a fraud or a coward if you like, but it's not something I've done before."

"Good," she heard herself say.

His mouth twitched in humor.

She hurried to add, "You shouldn't, I mean, with anyone."

"Well. . . ." He smirked at her. "I'd like to *someday* with *someone*."

"Of course, but you'd be married to her."

"Probably."

"Desmond—"

"Yeah, yeah, I know. And, yes, okay, I agree."

"Do you?"

He hesitated, then shrugged. "Yeah," he sighed. "I don't like it, but . . . yeah, I do."

"What don't you like about it?" she asked incredulously.

"It just . . . it's someone telling you what you can and can't do, Caity. It's annoying."

"It's God," she countered. "I think He knows better than us, don't you?"

Desmond raised a hand to rub at his eyes. "Wow, this is not how I saw this going," he muttered, then looked back up at her. "Yes, okay? I think that He probably does. But sometimes, I just wish He and everyone else would leave me alone and let me live my own damn life."

Unable to keep herself from flinching at his hard words, Cait scanned him. "You're part of the Warden," she reminded.

"And no one will let me forget it," he returned.

"You don't want to be?"

He was glaring at her now, his irritation plain in his flat tone. "You said you needed to talk."

All levity had dropped out of the room. Unsure why the topic upset him so much, Cait found herself taking a step closer to him. She wanted to press for answers and work through it with him. She wanted to understand what made his jaw clench and his shoulders hunch like that. She knew he didn't like his dad and the expectations for his future. But she hadn't realized it bothered him quite this deeply.

Without the bravery to actually help him, Cait took the opposite side of the bench. She might not be able to solve his problem, but she could sit beside him. Desmond turned toward her, the white-silver moonlight brightening half of his face.

Pulling her feet onto the bench, Cait wrapped her arms around her knees. "So, my dreams . . . ?" she prompted.

At his nod, she went on. "Well, two nights ago, I—I had another one."

Desmond frowned, resting his back against the wall. "I thought you had them every night."

"I—I do, it's jest—I don'—" Her accent slipped in, lilting in her nervousness. Desmond's brow furrowed. She never let her Irish accent slip in. He knew how hard she had worked to lose it.

Cait shoved down her emotions and started again. "I . . . I don't know what it means," she said, voice unaccented once more, "but it was different."

"Different, how?"

Slowly, stiltedly, Cait told him about her dream. Every last detail. Her childhood bedroom, the door, the smoke. The thing pacing and trying to break down that door. His father's presence and its newly, notably, missing status. The raven's appearance instead.

She told him about the window and the scene she typically saw. How the monsters formed from the smoke and crowded in around her, watching as she suffocated. Then, she described how the dream had changed two nights ago, taking her to the cove. About him, standing by the sea, the waves rising around him.

He'd kept a serious, straight face as she spoke. But at that, his expression turned smug. "You were dreaming about me, huh?" he teased.

"Desmond," she lamented. "Be serious."

"What?" He raised a hand, running it over his hair. "To be honest, it doesn't sound that different."

Knowing she hadn't told him the worst, she let herself put it off. "It's been almost twelve years, Desmond."

His face fell then.

"I've always known," she whispered to him. "These dreams started the night my parents died. It isn't a surprise, I guess. I mean, I've heard of people with PTSD having weird dreams. But . . . why change now?"

Cautiously, Desmond leaned toward her. He hesitantly reached out a hand as though asking permission. She didn't stop him, so he set his hand comfortingly on her knee. "I'm only asking because . . . because I want to be sure," he began, "but do you think it could have anything to do with this Monday?"

A cold chill swept over Cait. She cocked her head to the side. "You mean, do I think it has anything to do with the anniversary of my parents' deaths?"

He tipped a shoulder up in a shrug, his thumb brushing over the fabric of her pajama pants. His touch sent a warm spike of energy shooting across her skin. The hum rose almost in anticipation.

Fighting to keep her focus, Cait turned to look out the window. "Maybe."

"It would make sense," he said. "This is always a difficult time for you. Maybe it's making its way into your dreams now."

"After twelve years?"

"Maybe."

Knowing she couldn't keep the rest to herself, Cait grabbed Desmond's wrist. "I watched you die."

His expression went blank. "What?"

"In my dream," she explained, "you were standing on the beach in the cove, and then the monsters showed up. The massive wolfish ones the first night. The death-bears last night."

"Wait, what?" His face paled, and his hand tightened on her knee.

Cait felt the same. "I couldn't stop them. I couldn't—both times, I couldn't get to you. And they killed you."

Jerking back, Desmond rubbed his hand across his mouth. She could see his chest expanding with deep, nervous breaths. He kept blinking as though trying to clear his vision. His jaw tensed, the veins in his neck pulsing.

Then he spoke. "It's just a dream."

Frowning, Cait knew he couldn't mean it. He wouldn't be this bothered if he truly believed it.

"What if it's not?"

"Caity," he shot her a fierce glare, "it's a dream."

"Is it?" she heard herself hiss back.

He stared at her, a knowing glint in his eyes.

"What if it's the curse?" she demanded, saying aloud what she knew they were both thinking.

Desmond let out a weak scoff. "There's no curse, Cait."

"Isn't there?" Cait returned. "There's a reason everyone is afraid of us, Desmond. The town accuses us of being witches and being cursed by a demon. What if they're right?"

"They're not."

"What if they are?" she insisted, letting her legs drop to the side as she leaned closer.

Desmond hesitated as though he knew she was right but didn't want to admit it. "You aren't cursed," he said, though she could tell he didn't mean it.

"Then why do you have to sneak into my bedroom to talk to me?" she asked, calling his bluff.

His dark eyes narrowed. "What are you talking about?"

"If there's no curse—if none of the rumors are true," she whispered fiercely, "then why do we have to be a secret? You told me when we were eight that we could never be friends. If there's no curse, then there's no reason for that."

Desmond stared at her, silent, confirming her suspicions. Their faces were inches from one another now, both of them adamantly defending their side. Cait could see the barest tinge of green flecked in his rich brown eyes, his pale skin glowing in the light.

Head spinning and heart pounding, Cait pushed off the bench. She couldn't be that close to him. She couldn't think that way. And she had to win this argument. She had to get him to take her seriously. Because Cait knew—no matter what anyone else said—she knew the truth.

"There *has* to be a curse." She whirled to face him, tears of anger, fear, and shame burning her eyes. "Because you're just as afraid of me as the rest of them."

Without a second's hesitation, Desmond leaped up from the bench. He grabbed her arms, leaning down to stare directly into her eyes. "I'm not afraid of you, Caity," he insisted.

"Yes, you are," she argued, her chest searing with the need to cry. "It's the reason you spend time with me. I'm cursed, and you want to pretend that makes you some kind of rebel by being around me. But it doesn't, Desmond. You keep me as your secret, proving to yourself that no one controls you, but you're so afraid of me that you won't even call me your friend."

"That's not—" He tightened his grip on her. "We *can't* be friends, Cait. You know this."

"Why not?" she demanded, the tears slipping.

He didn't have an answer, his eyes locked on the tears sliding down her cheeks.

Cait felt her lips twist in a bitter grin. "Because it's me, isn't it?" she asked. "Rese and Genni? They have friends. Rese is dating Ryan-freaking-Greene. But me?"

The door in her dreams became suddenly clear in Cait's mind. The shadow of the thing pacing behind it. She knew the darkness that shadow represented.

"It's me," she repeated. "I'm the one who inherited my da's curse. I'm the one the demon chose."

Desmond began to shake his head, but Cait knew he was only lying to himself.

"You know it too," she whispered. "And it's why *this*—" She foolishly placed her hand on his chest. She could feel the heat of him even through his hoodie. "Will never be real."

Before she knew what was happening, Desmond jerked on Cait's arms, pulling her to his chest. His arms wrapped around her, and he buried his face into her neck. His breath burned her skin, his fingers digging through her pajamas and into her back.

The hum became a bay of sound, thrumming in her skull.

"I'm *not* afraid of you," he promised, his words muffled against her neck.

She didn't believe him.

Cait leaned into his embrace anyway. She rested her head on his shoulder, reveling in the hum that reverberated in her core. Her arms worked around him, and she realized this was the first time they'd ever hugged. At least like this. They'd shared side hugs a handful of times. He'd draped his arm across her shoulders in that lazy, teasing manner of his. Even last night, he hadn't put his arms fully around her. Until now, he'd never held her, and she'd never held him.

Now that it had happened, Cait never wanted to let go.

Desmond's hand twitched on her lower back, pressing her ever so slightly closer. She had to adjust her stance, taking a step into him so she wouldn't lose her footing. It felt so good to be held by him—as though they'd always been meant for it.

With her cheek resting against his neck, she could hear his pulse beating rapidly. She felt her own heartbeat rising. If she turned her head, her lips would be on his neck, right where that vein was thrumming so strongly.

As though he'd been thinking the same thing, Desmond shifted, drawing back until his nose brushed her jawline. Her breath hitched as his lips parted, his exhalation tickling her collar. Eyes closed, she didn't know whether to feel hope or fear. She wanted him to kiss her—her neck, her cheek, her jaw, her mouth. She was desperate for him to kiss her. But if he did, she didn't think she'd be able to stop.

With a shaky breath in, Desmond's hands flexed against Cait's back. Then they were gone, his arms releasing as he pulled back. Head still dipping low, his eyes met hers. He reached up to brush at the dampness on her cheeks. "You're not cursed," he whispered.

Cait didn't reply, too caught in his stare to form words.

"And it is real," he promised, his voice husky and tense. "It just can't happen."

"I know," she murmured.

He cleared his throat, motioning to the window. "I'd better go," he said, stepping away from her. "I've got a long walk back."

Cait nodded. "Thank you—for coming."

"Always, Lewan," he said but didn't move.

They stood there, staring at one another.

There was too much between them. Too many feelings that they could never act on. And she didn't think she could bear it anymore.

Even as fresh tears came to her eyes, Cait chose to do what they should have done years ago. "We can't see each other anymore, Desmond," she whispered. And somehow, it didn't hurt to say it. They were only words. Words she didn't believe even as she said them.

He looked like she'd slapped him. "Wh—what?"

"With everything that's happened, I think it'd be best if we just . . . took it as a sign." She drew in a deep breath before continuing. "You don't have to worry about me being alone. I have Matt now."

He practically scowled as she kept going. "I don't need you anymore," she lied. "And you've never needed me."

"Stop it," he snapped, his voice thick with agitation.

Cait blinked in surprise.

"You're not—we're not doing this," he insisted.

"It's for the best."

"No," the anger hissed out of him, "it's not."

She stared at him, and he glared at her.

Desmond rolled his shoulders, shifting back toward the window. "I'm going home," he whispered. "And *this*—" He motioned between the two of them, "is not over."

Unable to speak through her emotions, Cait watched as Desmond spun on his heel, pushed open the window, and crept out. She saw his shadow move across the roof, dropping out of sight. She stared at the silver-tinged darkness for several minutes, knowing that despite what he'd said, he was wrong.

Cait moved to the window, locking it.

He was afraid of her. She was cursed. And it was over.

Because no matter what, Cait wouldn't draw him into this curse with her.

CHAPTER TWENTY

Desmond

I t was her.

Cait was the Vessel. Desmond had no questions anymore. And the lines of the prophecy kept ringing in his head, over and over.

"Our success shall come only at her great sacrifice."

That wasn't acceptable. No matter what good it brought—no matter if the loss of Cait's life meant the salvation of every other life in the world—Desmond refused to accept it. Ever.

Desmond had planned to tell Cait everything that night. For almost two weeks, he'd held it all in. He wasn't used to that. Sure, he had secrets. He kept things from Cait. But it was because of those secrets that he liked to share everything else with her. He already carried too much for him to hold anything else inside. And this was more than simply withheld information about the Warden and the spirit world.

He'd planned on telling her everything: about the Veil and the beasts, about the truth behind her parents' murders, about the Warden's part in it. She deserved to know.

Then she'd told him about her dream.

About the beasts.

The hellhounds and the artio.

He'd known then.

The next morning at church, he'd asked Brady to be sure. "Hey, what were the beasts that came out of the Veil over the past few nights?" He'd prodded as nonchalantly as he could when everyone else was distracted.

Brady didn't hesitate. "I haven't heard what it was last night yet. But Friday night it was one of the bear-beasts. An artio," he confirmed, then grinned. "The night of the full moon, it was a hellhound, though. Dad said it looked like a wolf. Ironic, right?"

Desmond laughed it off with his friend, but he hadn't felt it. He couldn't.

It was her. Not just the Vessel, but she was the one connecting to the Veil. The one summoning beasts.

What he couldn't figure out was how.

Desmond had taken all of Sunday to develop his plans. His grounding helped with that. After church, it didn't weird his parents out that he spent the rest of the day in his room. They weren't suspicious of his reclusive behavior, and they left him in peace to work through the problem.

He needed answers; that was the conclusion he came to. Answers for both Cait and the Warden.

The Warden was growing desperate. They were tired and spread thin, and they had no more answers than when they started. William had chosen to scour the peninsula for a secondary Veil on his own, not prepared to worry the council over it yet. They didn't have the manpower to watch one Veil, let alone two.

Desmond knew that if he took the truth to the council now, they wouldn't hesitate to take Cait into custody and interrogate her. It wouldn't matter that she had no answers for them. She had no clue what was going on, but they'd insist on questioning her anyway. And he couldn't entirely blame them. There were so many questions that they needed answers to:

How had this happened? When had it begun? Was the Wolf breaking free?

None of those answers mattered to Desmond. All he cared about was figuring out how to stop it.

No, he couldn't tell the Warden. He couldn't let them know that Cait had anything to do with it. He just had to solve the problem himself.

Desmond had made his plan late in the night. He would go back to the Veil. He would study the fissure, and he would figure out what had caused it. Then, he would find a way to seal it back up.

The problem? His grounding meant that his dad watched him like a hawk. And even if he offered to go on the stakeout as a "recompense," his dad would never approve of letting him join on a school night. He couldn't wait an entire week or hope his dad would believe in his attempt at restitution.

He had to get answers now.

So, he came up with what might be the dumbest plan he'd ever made.

~

At school Monday morning, when Desmond and Brady were alone at their side-by-side lockers, he turned to his friend.

"I need a favor," he said quietly.

Brady didn't hesitate. "Sure, man. What's up?"

Shutting his locker, Desmond turned to him. "I'm gonna lie, and I need you to back me up."

Brady raised an eyebrow. He was almost as much of a prude as Cait.

"Look, I gotta get on the island," Desmond explained. "I have a theory, and I'm not ready to run it past my dad yet. But I've got to get out there to gather more evidence. So, I'm gonna tell Uncle Rick that Dad wants you and me on shift tonight to help out."

Brady looked incredulous. "Dude, it's a school night."

"What are you, eighty? You can't handle one all-nighter?"

Brady didn't reply, clearly disinterested.

"Come on, man," Desmond begged. "You're the only one I trust. I need you there to keep watch for me."

Brady spun his lock. "Aren't you grounded?"

"What about it?"

"How do you plan on getting there?"

Desmond raised his eyebrows. "Does that mean you'll help?"

"No," Brady returned. "It means that *if* I help, I want to be sure we're not gonna get caught."

They began to move toward their class, keeping their voices low. Garrett could join them any second, and Desmond didn't want to include his cousin in this venture. Garrett was a loyal friend, but he couldn't keep his mouth shut.

"We won't get caught," Desmond promised.

Brady wasn't convinced.

"And even if we do," he added, "we won't have to worry about consequences after we give them the solution to all their problems."

"You're that sure you know what's going on?" Brady asked.

Desmond could see Garrett making his way down the hall toward them. "Yeah," he assured him. "I just need to do some recon to be sure I can fix it."

With a sigh, Brady glanced in Garrett's direction. He dropped his voice and murmured, "It's stupid to include your uncle. I'll call Fish."

Brady and Desmond developed their plan in spurts of conversation and texts, keeping Garrett clueless.

Late in the night, Desmond and Brady would sneak out of their respective houses and meet at the docks. There, Fish would be waiting for them. The lightkeeper held no qualms about helping the two of them. Brady said that when he called his great-uncle, the man accepted minimal explanation with the promise that they were doing something important.

"I trust the both of you," Fish had told him. "Whatever you're up to, I've a feeling it'll wind up working in our favor."

From the dock, Fish would port them across the ocean and to the island, where he'd guide them to the Veil. That was his stipulation. If he was going to help them do something potentially dangerous, then he was going with them to keep them safe. Desmond had readily accepted that condition.

The rest of the school day dragged on endlessly. Every class, Desmond found himself regularly checking in on Cait and Matt. For some reason, the kid was abnormally quiet. He still stuck with Cait the whole day, but something was definitely off.

Either Cait didn't notice herself, or she chose to ignore it. Desmond thought it might be the latter. She was probably too absorbed in her own thoughts to care about that sort of thing now.

He'd texted her earlier in the morning. *"How are you?"*

It wasn't the sort of question he would normally ask, but this day—September 23—was always a difficult day for her. The memories of her parents plagued her each year on the anniversary of their deaths. The day she'd lost everything, and the Warden had taken her from Ireland. And he was worried for her.

She hadn't texted him back.

At first, Desmond thought it was because Matt was around. Then, at lunch, he'd noticed that Cait was sitting alone at the table, phone in hand. He kept expecting a text to come through. None did. And he realized she was intentionally ignoring him.

Sudden understanding came to Desmond. She'd meant it the other night. She was ending things between them. And now she was blocking him out to prove it.

Desmond clenched his hands under the cafeteria table. His body felt hollow and heavy all at once. He wasn't losing her anymore. He'd already lost her.

"Tell me how to fix it."

"You can't."

Desmond wanted to flip the table. He wanted to throw the stupid aqua-blue lunch tray against the wall. He wanted to hear the clatter of the plates and utensils as they crashed to the floor. He wanted to see the stains of food smeared on the dingy white walls. He wanted some physical manifestation of his anger, of his pain.

But most of all, Desmond wanted to go to Cait. To take her hand and pull her out of her seat. He wanted to guide her to his table, tell Brady to scoot over, and hold the chair for Cait as she sat down. He wanted to show her just how wrong she was about everything.

"You're so afraid of me that you won't even call me your friend."

She didn't know.

She didn't understand.

And Desmond couldn't tell her.

If she was right—if they were both right, and she was the Vessel, they'd been doomed from the start. She wouldn't want him if she knew. She wouldn't even want to be his friend. Not when she found out it was his job to keep her chained up. To lead her like a lamb to slaughter.

For years, Desmond had been able to pretend. He'd tricked himself into forgetting what she might be. But now, he knew once the truth came out, she'd become a true captive of the Warden. Just like the Faulks, the Warden would place her under custody and careful watch, the entirety of her future dictated—by Desmond.

That was the mayor's job. Keeping Porthaven safe revolved around keeping the Vessels under control. And that meant he would be her overseer, her captor, and her controller. Whatever he felt for her now, whatever desires he carried, he'd have to forget them all. Because it would be his job to ensure three things: that the Warden maintained control of Cait, that the Wolf never broke free, and that she produced a singular heir to carry on the bloodline before she sacrificed herself for the sake of the prophecy.

Of course, that meant Desmond would have to find Cait a husband. Probably some devout Warden member from another town willing to give up his own life for the sake of the cause. Someone like Saliha Faulk.

That's how they kept the Faulk bloodline going. If there was no Warden member in Porthaven willing to marry into the life of service and captivity, they searched for a member elsewhere. It was almost certainly how they'd find Sterling a spouse.

Could Desmond do that to Cait? Could he give her to someone who didn't love her? Who didn't even want her? His skin crawled at the thought. But he knew there was no other choice.

It couldn't be him. He'd always known that. As the Varon heir, his child couldn't be a Vessel heir too. The Warden would never accept it. There'd been a blip of hope within him all these years—a lingering optimism that if Cait wasn't the Vessel, then, perhaps, they could have a future.

Since Desmond was thirteen, he'd known what he felt for Cait wasn't as simple as friendship. He'd always thought she was cute. But it wasn't until then that he realized how much he felt for her. How much he desired her. And it had only grown over the years.

Doomed. From the start, they'd been doomed.

"It is real." His words haunted him as he stared across the cafeteria at Cait. *"It is real."* Everything between them, everything she felt for him, and everything he felt for her. It was real. Everything they both wished they could be. It was real. Every dream they both carried. It was real.

They were real.

And Desmond wasn't ready to give that up yet.

He'd lied to Brady. He wasn't going to collect evidence. He was going to fix the Veil. Whatever was wrong with it, if he could seal it back up, he could buy himself more time. Then he'd find a way to save Cait.

There were rumors within the Warden. A secret like the Vessels and the spirit-beings tied to them couldn't help but leave legends in their wake. And while most people relegated those rumors to superstitions, Desmond knew of a handful that were true.

One rumor whose validity he had yet to determine was the one he clung to now: A Vessel could be freed from its spirit.

Once he fixed the Veil and the beasts were stopped, Desmond would have time. He could find out how to free Cait of the demon plaguing her nightmares. He could save her from the fate of the prophecy. And she never had to know.

Then, they could be together.

That was all Desmond cared about now, selfish as it might be. He wouldn't lose Cait. No matter what.

~

The black sky surrounded Desmond as he waited in the shadows by the docks. Brady was late. He kept checking his phone, sure he'd see a text from his friend warning him that he'd been caught. But no text came.

Shivering in the cold, Desmond zipped up his hoodie. He'd layered up. Even in early fall, Maine grew winter-cold at night. Over the hoodie, he wore his bomber jacket, and under it, he wore a tee shirt and a thermal. Still, the breeze off the sea cut deeply, biting at the skin he hadn't managed to cover up.

"Come on, Brade," he muttered. He could hear the motorboat coming along the sea. Fish was near, but he couldn't see the lightkeeper from his vantage, crouched by the legs of the docks.

Suddenly, a shadow dropped down in front of Desmond. He jumped. "Looking for someone?" Brady asked, a playful grin on his face. Even more bundled up than Desmond, he wore a knit beanie over his swoopy bangs.

Desmond slugged his friend's shoulder. "Where were you?"

"Sorry." Brady gestured back toward the town. "Jenna kept asking me questions."

Furrowing his brow, Desmond stared at him. "Tell me your sister didn't find out about this," he begged.

"Nah, she has no idea," he promised. "She just—she's got a thing for Garrett, and she was wondering if I thought he was serious about Whitney."

"Garrett? Seriously?" Desmond snorted. "I hope you told her to seek help."

Brady grinned lazily. "Pretty much."

They both fell silent as they watched the small motorboat glide into the dock. They crept out from the shadows, hurrying along the weathered planks. Desmond kept an eye out for anyone in the area. The docks remained silent. The few night fishermen would be well out to sea by now, and there was no real need for guards around the wharf.

The lighthouse's beam flashed over their heads as they approached Fish and his boat. "Evening, boys," he called, hand on the tiller.

Climbing in, Desmond was thankful to find the water gentle beneath their feet. The small boat was simple and old. It bobbed pleasantly in the current, the motor rumbling steadily. He and Brady took a seat on the bench facing Fish.

The old man's bushy gray eyebrows rose as he appraised the boys. "You promise this is on the up and up?"

Desmond held onto the side of the boat, stomach unsettled, knowing the journey they'd have to take across the sea. He had never liked sailing of any kind. "You wouldn't be here if you didn't think it was, Fish."

"Sure, I think it." His bright eyes twinkled in the moonlight. "But I'd like to know it."

"I promise," Desmond said. "We're doing this for the right reasons."

Fish gave a slow blink as though assessing if that was a good enough answer. Then he let out a huff. "All right," he mumbled and turned the boat around.

Despite the gentle rock of the boat in the harbor, the minute they got up to speed, it began to jump and crash through the waves. Desmond's stomach rolled. He really didn't like boats.

Butter-yellow light flashed over their heads again. They neared the lighthouse, the sea spraying through the air. It dampened Desmond's jacket, splattering his cheeks. He gripped harder onto the side and the bench. His fingers burned by the time they pulled into Fish's personal dock.

Once they were walking up the wooden staircase to the island's beach, Fish glanced over his shoulder at them. "There's a patrol out tonight," he informed them. "All of 'em a hundred paces away from the Veil per your dad's orders. We'll have to skirt around them to get there. You sure this is necessary?"

Desmond reflexively checked in the pocket of his jeans for his phone, wondering if he'd need the flashlight in the dark forest that loomed ahead of them. "Yeah," was all he could say. Now that he was here on the island, he was beginning to second-guess himself. Not the importance of his mission but his ability to complete it.

How was he supposed to fix the Veil? They didn't even know what was wrong with it.

But he had to try.

Carefully, Fish led them through the forest. "Keep your eyes peeled," he warned them. "We're pretty sure we cleared out all the beasts, but you never know if one gave us the slip."

In the darkness and the wind, the trees rustled, their skeletal branches almost empty of all leaves. Only the pines retained most of their needles. The drying leaves crunched under their feet, and Fish took care to lead them in a wide berth around the path of the Warden members' patrol.

The silence of night pressed in on them. Whatever animals remained on the island were either hibernating or hiding.

"What happens if another beast comes out while we're there," Brady whispered, walking by Desmond's side.

With a shrug, he tried not to let his friend know his fear. "Then you kill it like last time."

Brady pressed his lips together nervously.

"I'll handle it," Fish said, voice a low growl.

Though Desmond hadn't originally liked the idea of Fish joining them, afraid that he might rat them out in the end, he was thankful to have him with them now. If a beast *did* appear, he had no worries that the two Lavignes could readily control it.

After the near-hour hike through the forest, Fish had them slow their pace. They moved as stealthily as they could through the patrol grounds on the way to the Veil. They didn't know the Warden watchmen's exact location, so they had to take extra care not to stumble into their path.

They were nearly spotted when two men stalked through the trees. Fish grabbed hold of Desmond and Brady's collars, hauling them behind a tree to duck out of sight in the low bushes. Kenneth Greene and Brett Varon came into view, talking in hushed voices.

Immediately, Desmond knew something was wrong. The patrols were meant to have three members, always including a Lavigne. So why were Kenneth and Brett walking alone?

"You shouldn't have done that," Kenneth was saying.

Brett shook his head, his light brown hair taking on a deeper shade in the dark. "It's for the town's own good."

"I understand that," Kenneth returned, though he didn't sound understanding. "But William is our leader. We have to trust him."

"Trusting the Simons is what got us into this mess."

Desmond ground his teeth, watching the men move away at a slow pace.

"Don't do that," Kenneth objected. "Don't take up the anti-Simon agenda because your family lost control. They're good people."

"They're narcissists and thieves," Brett shot back. "And I don't trust any of them. Least of all William."

"So you're going to force him into resignation for a grudge?"

Dread spiraled through Desmond's chest.

"That's not what this is," Brett argued.

"You called Jeremiah Rhader," Kenneth exclaimed, voice an angered hush. "That's like contacting internal affairs on a cop."

"And I've got a feeling that William is dirty."

"Brett—"

"The Simons have put us in this place, Ken. We aren't a Warden town anymore. We're a sideshow."

The men walked far enough away that Desmond couldn't hear their words clearly. Their voices still grumbled in the distance, going back and forth on the validity of investigating his father for negligence. He wanted to slam his fist into the tree to his right. But he flexed his fingers, forcing himself not to care.

It wouldn't matter after tonight anyway.

Desmond knew the name Rhader. He was the man the Warden sent when things went wrong. He was the one who'd brought Cait and her sisters to Porthaven twelve years ago. If Brett Varon had called Rhader, it meant he was working to usurp his dad's claim on the town. Finally, the Varon-Simon feud had reached its peak. It was headed for an all-out war.

Desmond didn't know whose side he was on.

Once the men's voices faded away, Fish pushed the boys up. "Hurry," he instructed. "We don't want to risk running into any others."

They rushed as silently as they could, drifting from tree to tree as the forest grew thicker. They didn't run into any more Warden members. Nor did they hear any movement through the forest. It was still, aside from their own presence.

When they neared the Veil, Fish slowed them. Gooseflesh spread across Desmond's skin, sticky with sweat from their activity and the adrenaline rushing through him. He sensed the stillness the Veil brought to the air. It washed over him with a strange mix of peace and unease.

The clearing came into view, the sycamore's leaves a golden-brown blanket on the ground now. Several branches hung low, the rest rising into a twisted web above them. Taking a step into the clearing, Desmond wondered if only his imagination created figures of beasts in its mottled bark.

"I'll stay here," Fish said, an unusual thinness to his voice.

Looking over his shoulder at the lightkeeper, Desmond frowned. "Why?"

"One of us needs to watch the perimeter," he suggested, gaze sharp as he scanned the area. "I don't want anyone—or anything—sneaking up on us."

Desmond nodded, then gestured for Brady to join him. They approached the tree cautiously as though a beast would spring from that crack so far up on its trunk.

That's when Desmond realized the crack had expanded.

He cursed under his breath, hurrying over. What was once five feet long was now ripped at least two feet lower.

"What is it?" Brady asked at his side.

Desmond gaped up at the tear. With its extended reach, the tear was low enough that he could see it clearly for the first time. He set his shaking fingers on the corner. The jagged ridge rubbed his fingertips raw, but the interior was smooth under his touch. Or perhaps not smooth as much as solid. The texture felt like wood.

In the dim light, he struggled to get a clear grasp on what he was looking at. He pulled his phone out of his pocket, turning on the flashlight.

"Dude," Brady gasped, "that's creepy."

Desmond agreed. Under the LED light of his phone, he could see into the fissure in the Veil. He'd been right before; something was trying to get out. But it didn't make any sense.

"Is that . . . birch?" Brady asked.

Touching the white and black bark, Desmond nodded. "I think so," he said. He shifted his hand to the other side of the crack, to the gray-brown bark with diamond-like ridges. "But what is this?"

Brady stepped closer. "I—I dunno," he replied. "Some other kind of tree?"

It was clear to Desmond now. Two additional types of trees grew within the sycamore. It was as though they'd been planted inside and were tearing their way out. The two woods twisted together, bulging out of the sycamore. The trees were fighting for freedom. *They* had caused the rip in the Veil.

"How?" Desmond wondered aloud. He looked up to see budding

limbs sprouting from both trees. Branches of the darker, ashen tree reached up to tangle with the sycamore. The spindly branches of the white and black-striped tree filled in the gaps, a handful of leaves clinging to their ends. "It doesn't make any sense. How does something like this happen?"

The better question, Desmond realized, was how would he fix it?

Brady shook his head. "I don't know, man. But this is freaky." He took a step back, motioning to the tree. "Just—do whatever you need to do, and let's get out of here."

Forcing himself not to wimp out now, Desmond nodded. He took a picture of the fissure for later study. Then he returned his phone to his pocket.

As Desmond stepped closer to the tree, Brady whispered, "Be careful."

"Sure," he muttered, setting his hand on the sycamore. Its uneven bark was rough under his palms. He didn't entirely know what he was trying to accomplish, but he closed his eyes and focused on the tree. It was stupid, he knew. What, did he think he could simply will the tree to close back up? But what else was he going to try?

Desmond took a deep breath. He knew the spirit world. He'd wielded it. He could recognize it. And this Veil was a direct link to that world. If he focused enough, maybe he *could* close the tree back up. He *was* the Varon heir. Power and connection to the spirit world flowed readily through him.

He could hear Brady shifting behind him, likely wondering what Desmond was doing.

What *was* Desmond doing? Standing here, pressing his hands against a tree, that's what. And making no headway.

Adjusting his stance, Desmond placed his hands nearer the crack. He closed his eyes again, screwing up his face in concentration. He could do it. He'd close the tear, save the town, and buy himself and Cait more time.

Reaching out with everything in him, Desmond tried to grip onto the will that he used every time he summoned Hades. He searched his whole being for that knowing—the part of him that *knew* he could wield.

The branch above them rustled, and Brady yelped.

Leaping away from the tree, Desmond stared up, expecting to see a beast swooping down on them. His pulse pounded in his ears as he searched the branches. Then he relaxed.

"What's going on over there?" Fish called.

"Nothing," Desmond replied.

Brady grabbed his arm. "That's not nothing," he hissed, pointing upward.

Desmond knocked his hand away. "It's a cat," he grumbled, then glanced at Hades, perched on the branch above his head. The sith's eyes glowed a golden-neon yellow, his dark fur coiling like smoke at the edges.

"It's a beast," Brady countered. He raised his hand toward Hades. His eyes went wide. "It's tethered to someone."

"Yeah, you idiot." Desmond gave him a shove. "He's tethered to me."

"What?" Brady gaped at him.

"He's my cat."

Brady looked like Garrett when their math teacher called on him in class. "What?" he repeated.

Without warning, a loud *crunch* sounded behind them, leaves breaking under the weight of something heavy. Desmond and Brady whirled, both of their hands alight with rifts of the spirit world's essence, ready to face whatever beast was coming their way.

On the forest floor, soft amber wisps of that same essence swirled around a figure, and Desmond's breath caught in his throat.

CHAPTER TWENTY-ONE

Cait

Cait wished that—for *once* in her life—she could have a night's rest without her dreams interfering. After the long day, she needed sleep. Deep, blissful sleep. Something she couldn't remember experiencing.

The whole day, she thought about her parents, remembering life in Ireland. Life before Porthaven.

Owen and Sabine Lewan were lovely. Everyone in Bushmills had said so. He was friendly and wise; she was considerate and intelligent. No one knew a better-suited couple. No one found a happier family than theirs.

Memories of walks in green grass, visits to their grandda's pub, and the warm scent of bread baking in their cottage filtered through her mind. She could still feel them—her parents. She remembered the gentle touch of her mother as she braided Cait's hair. She remembered the strength of her father's arms as he held her, telling one of his fantastic bedtime stories.

If her melancholy state wasn't enough to make the day difficult,

Desmond had texted her. She almost cried when she read it. As simple as it had been, she knew what he was asking. She knew he was checking on her because he cared. And that made it all the worse.

On top of all that, Matt was still mad at her. She could tell, even though he didn't say anything about it. She considered broaching the topic with him at lunch. He'd been abnormally quiet as though trying to decide if she still deserved his friendship. After making her decision to end things with Desmond, she knew she couldn't afford to lose her only real friend.

But knowing that Genni could interrupt them at any time, Cait kept her thoughts to herself. She'd resigned herself to hoping that things would sort themselves out, that she wouldn't lose Matt's friendship over something she had no control over in the first place.

On their ride back home, Matt spoke up. "I'll only ask you once," he muttered, voice taut. "Then I'll let it go forever. What happened Friday night?"

Cait forced herself to consider it a good thing. Genni was spending the afternoon with Alexis, so there was no chance of interruption. If they could get this over with, they could go back to normal.

"I'm sorry, Matt," she said honestly before she began to lie. "I know it was rude of me to leave you like that, but . . . I—I get kind of overwhelmed sometimes. And I just . . . I needed to be alone for a moment."

"Was it something I did?" he asked, eyebrows pulling together. "'Cause I thought we were having a good time, and then you were gone."

"No," she assured him. "No, it wasn't you."

Matt pursed his lips, his whole face quirked with worry. "I mean, I guess this isn't the first time you've disappeared."

Cait thought back to her escape to the roof. She'd been with Desmond then too. "Like I said, I get overwhelmed sometimes."

"Why?" He sounded genuinely confused. "What makes you feel like you have to run away?"

Peddling through the streets, Cait stared at the road ahead of her tires. The answer to that question was too complicated. It was too fraught with things that she could never even begin to explain. Things like Desmond Simon and the Warden, things like dreams and monsters, things like curses and demons.

So, Cait simply said, "I don't know."

Matt accepted her answer. He told her that he didn't hold it against her. And just like that, he was back to his usual self. He started gabbing about the projects he had at school and how his mom wanted him to see about joining some extracurricular programs to help him socialize more. He lamented that he didn't need more friends. He had Cait.

She offered him a half-felt smile at that. She liked having Matt as a friend; he was a sweet, endearing guy. But no matter how hard she tried, she couldn't help comparing him to Desmond. And no one could compete with him.

Shoving down the thoughts, Cait spent the rest of the evening with her nan and sisters. Once Genni returned home, they had a somber dinner. None of them wanted to talk about Ireland or their lost loved ones. And yet, none of them could think of anything else to talk about. Instead, they sat in silence.

As Cait lay in her bed that night, she cried, knowing that she would dream. Knowing that no matter what, she couldn't escape the past. Knowing that *she* was the one the curse had passed to.

Then she was dreaming, standing in her childhood room. She looked at the bed where her father once held her. She saw the hairbrush that her mother used to run through her hair. Everything was as it was twelve years ago. Except for one thing: The locked door now bore a distinct crack.

Cait had thought she was imagining things the first few times. She'd *hoped* she was imagining things. Now, she knew she wasn't.

There, by the upper hinge, the wood door was beginning to splinter. The thing behind it was breaking through.

The dream sped by as it always did. The smoke came. The shadow paced. The raven flew in, crying to her before flying away into the cove at her back.

Cait turned to see the cove, the smoke curling around her figure. Desmond stood on the surf, waves licking at his feet. Her heart lurched, knowing he wasn't real and knowing, despite that fact, she couldn't watch him die another time.

Sprinting forward, Cait forgot about the empty room, the cracked door, and the pacing monster on the other side. She called to Desmond, and his head turned. Lightning flashed, a jagged white line in the sky. Thunder snarled in its wake. The inky black waves rose, crashing onto the shore.

"Cait?" Desmond shifted as the water rolled around his calves. He turned to her. "What are you doing here?"

The wet sand gave way under Cait's feet. She slipped, and Desmond reached out to steady her, his grip strong on her arms. Alert of the impending monsters, she didn't allow his presence to distract her. She scanned the beach, though nothing yet appeared from the shadows.

With a moment of hope, Cait looked up at Desmond. "We have to get out of here," she insisted, taking hold of him too.

She began to pull him away from the ocean, but Desmond held his ground. "What's going on, Caity?"

"Des, we don't have time." She pulled harder, her footing failing as the waves slammed into her knees.

Desmond held her upright, his arm slipping around her waist. He held her against his chest, both of them struggling to stay on their feet. "Cait?" He whispered her name, his face so close to hers.

Shaking her head, Cait couldn't let them stay there. They had to get away before the monsters came. "Desmond, please," she begged.

Another wave pressed against them, hitting their thighs now. Desmond was taller than her, though only just, and he managed to keep them strong against the force of the waves. He held her closer, unconcerned by the rising water and her panic.

Staring down at her, Desmond's hand rose to cup her cheek. She could feel his breath coming out ragged from the fight with the waves. His head dipped toward hers.

Clutching onto the front of his jacket, Cait stared up at him. This was a dream, she reminded herself. This wasn't Desmond; it was her imagination. "Stop," she said, the order coming out weak and hollow.

His thumb brushed her cheekbone. "I can't."

"You're not real," she objected. "None of this is real."

"I told you, Lewan," he whispered, his rich brown eyes locked with hers. "It *is* real."

Though Cait knew he was wrong, though her mind was playing cruel tricks, she couldn't make herself move. She couldn't bear to pull back as he leaned in. The water rushed in around their waists, but it was as though nothing, not even the ocean, could stop them.

Gently, Desmond's lips brushed hers, their breath mingling. Then he kissed her. Really, truly kissed her. Her mind reeled with sound—the hum rising, rising, rising within her. It slammed against her chest, pulsing within her limbs and reverberating in her skull. And she was lost to it.

Arms finding their way around his neck, Cait kissed him back as she'd longed to for so many years. Real or not, it *felt* real. And it was exactly what she'd hoped for. His hand on her neck, his arm around her waist, and his lips on hers—it all felt *so* real.

The sudden break of a wave slammed into them, crashing over their heads and plunging them under the water. Cait tried to tighten her grip on Desmond, but her fingers dug into a crumbling softness rather than the firm muscle of his body. In her shock, Cait opened her eyes, the saltwater stinging. She gasped, choking on the sea.

Dissolved into sand, Desmond's form disintegrated in her grip. She tried to scream but only took in more water as another wave picked her up. End over end, it threw her onto the shore.

Cait sprawled onto the pebbles and sand of the beach, coughing and soaking wet. Her body shook, tears coursing down her face. She rose to her hands and knees, spitting out the sand and water stuck in her throat. The hum was gone, and Desmond with it.

A sob choked out of her.

Desmond was gone, and she would never get him back.

A low rumble reached Cait's ears. She froze, her mind going still. She knew that sound. She'd heard it in her dreams many times.

Raising her head, her body went rigid in fear as she saw them. All of them. Every beast that had ever been in her dreams lined the shore. Smoke, shadow, and darkness. Neon eyes of slitted, beady, and hollow design. Feathers and fur and scales. Hooves, paws, and tentacles. Each of the monsters stared straight at her. Waiting.

Then, the earth dropped out from under her.

~

Cait hit the ground hard. It was as though her bed had suddenly disappeared, sending her plummeting to the floor.

Startling awake, she rolled onto all fours. Dried grass and leaves crunched beneath her, dirt crusting her nails as she curled her fingers. Cold night air prickled her skin. Dressed only in her navy pajamas, she shivered.

Why was she outside? How had she gotten there? Wherever "there" was.

"Cait?" a voice called to her left.

Whipping her head toward the sound, Cait found herself staring at Desmond and Brady, a large tree behind them. They gaped at her in shock, strange wisps of light drifting around their hands. Brady's was a soft gray, Desmond's a rich blue-black like the night sky.

Cait blinked, trying to make sense of the scene. She didn't recognize this place, and her brain couldn't quite comprehend those spiraling rifts of light.

As he took a step forward, Desmond's rifts extinguished, Brady's following a second after. "What are you doing here?" Desmond asked.

Startled by hearing the words he'd said in her dream, Cait scrambled to her feet. She wrapped her arms around herself, still shivering in the cold. "I don't know," she admitted.

With a sigh, Desmond rushed forward. He quickly worked off his black bomber jacket, wrapping it around her shoulders. "How did you get here?" he demanded.

The hum thrummed through her as he adjusted the jacket collar around her hair. "I don't know," she repeated. "Where are we?"

"You don't know?" Brady asked, still several feet away.

Looking over at him, Cait caught sight of that tree again. It was giant, as big as her house. There was something soothing about it. She took an involuntary step forward.

Desmond's hand clamped onto her arm through the jacket. "Don't," he ordered.

Only sparing him a glance, Cait found herself unable to keep her gaze off the tree. "What is it?" she asked. A flicker on one of the branches drew her attention. A black cat perched on the bough, its dual-tail swishing happily. Hades.

Desmond was saying something to Brady, but the hum within Cait grew to an almost deafening howl. Something about the tree called to her. She tried to take another step toward it.

"Cait—" Desmond tightened his grip, keeping her back. He grabbed her shoulders, stepping into her sightline. "Stay here, okay?"

"Where are we, Desmond?" she asked, her brain too fuzzy to be concerned by Brady's presence.

Wetting his lips, Desmond seemed to struggle with words. "We're on the island," he said, then turned back to his friend. "We've got to get her out of here."

"No shit," Brady returned.

Cait blinked in surprise. She'd never heard Brady swear before.

"How'd she even get here?" he exclaimed.

"I don't know," Desmond replied. His voice was tight and worried, his grip still firm on her.

Gaze drifting back to the tree, Cait frowned. "Is it . . . is it supposed to do that?" she asked, pointing to the smoke drifting out of the tree. She thought she should be afraid. Something inside told her not to be.

Whirling around, Brady and Desmond looked at the tree. "Oh, God," Desmond muttered. He jerked back around to face her. "What did you dream about?"

"What?" she gasped.

"What did you dream about, Cait?" he demanded again, his voice low.

An old man stepped into the moonlight on the far side of the clearing. "What's going on?" he called.

Brady began to respond to the man, saying something about a beast. His hand had that strange light around it again. The dark smoke was growing as it tumbled onto the grass at the base of the tree.

Desmond tightened his hold. His eyes bored into hers adamantly. "What monster was in your dream, Caity?"

"All of them," she said, her gaze constantly drifting back to the cloud of smoke.

"What do you mean 'all of them'?"

"I mean, all of them," she repeated, scared by the ferocity in his tone. "What's going on, Des?"

"Desmond!" Brady called, the old man now at his side.

The smoke—which Cait thought of more as a shadow—was taking form. Massive, frightening form.

Cait's jaw dropped, recognizing the process. It was them, one of every monster in her dreams. Twelve in total, they solidified into reality.

Desmond had dropped his hold on Cait, standing before her like a guard. She could see his hands shaking even as he raised them, those strange dark blue rifts rippling around his skin. "Stay behind me," he whispered.

Brady and the old man backed up to stand by Desmond. "There's never been more than one," the man said.

"Are we strong enough to take twelve?" Brady asked.

"I hope so."

Desmond never took his eyes off the monsters, but his head angled toward the men. "Fish," he said, words rushing out. "If it looks like we're gonna die, get Cait out of here."

"I'm not leaving you boys," the old man—Fish—said.

"Shouldn't we call for the others?" Brady asked, his voice shaky.

"No!" Desmond insisted. "We can handle this."

Eyes locked on the shadow creatures forming, a tremor rolled through Cait's body. She knew all these monsters. She'd sketched each of them in her notebook hundreds of times. The twelve creatures lined up before them, their neon yellow eyes fixed on her. And yet, she couldn't feel fear as she scanned them. They were all so different. Feathers, fur, hide, scales, and skin. Beaks, jowls, and fangs. Antlers, tendrils, tentacles, and claws. They should be hideous; they should be terrifying. But she knew them.

"Why aren't they attacking?" Desmond whispered.

"They aren't tethered," Brady said. "There's no one to tell them what to do."

"Then . . . we just bring them down?"

Fish stepped forward, his hand lit by his own arc of soft gray light. The whole crowd of beasts shifted aggressively at his movement. "I think they might fight back then," the man offered. "They're docile so long as they don't perceive a threat."

"Desmond," Cait heard herself whisper.

He spared a glance over his shoulder at her. "Yeah?"

"What's going on?"

"It—it's gonna be okay," he said, one hand reaching behind him. She took it on instinct, surprised by the blue-black rift that circled around their hands without feeling. "Just stay back, all right?"

Cait didn't reply, unable to think of what else she would do. Things were starting to make sense to her. Desmond had told her about the beasts of the spirit world in small, unspecific terms. He'd had to explain Hades to her, informing her that Wielders had the ability to summon the beasts from the spirit world, but it was a generally frowned upon practice.

Seeing the beasts now, she didn't know how she hadn't realized it years ago. The monsters of her dreams were the beasts he'd talked about. And Cait realized he must have known that too. Yet he'd kept it to himself.

The beasts were growing restless. The wolfish one began to pace. The devil-horse pawed at the ground. The bird-like one fluttered its wings.

"The first volley together," Fish said. "We take down three all at once."

"What if our arcs aren't strong enough?" Brady asked.

"Then throw another one," the man ordered. "Ready?"

Desmond let go of Cait, holding his hands in front of him. "Ready."

"On three," Fish ordered.

The tentacled beast coiled a limb around a branch. The antlered one hunched low as though ready to spring forward. The bear-like beast lowered onto all fours.

"One."

The beast with bat-like wings rose into the sky.

"Two."

The rat beast sniffed the air greedily.

"Three!"

As one, Desmond, Brady, and Fish let their rifts of light fly. Gray and blue streaked through the air, hitting three separate beasts in unison. The snake-tendrilled one, the panther-like one, and the devil-horse. All three beasts cried out in rage. The tendrilled beast hit by Fish's arc burst into shadow and ash.

Cait's head exploded with the beasts' wails of pain. Her hands flew to her ears as though she could block them out. But they echoed within, reverberating off her skull, crashing into the hum that resided there.

The attack had been a mistake, Cait thought. For in the instant that those arcs hit their companions, the rest of the beasts burst forth in a frenzy. They charged, their claws, fangs, and tentacles flying.

Pressing back in retreat, the three men continued to send arcs of light toward the creatures. Another two beasts disappeared—the devil-horse and the arachnoid one this time—but the rest were on top of them by then. Desmond ducked beneath the slash of the panther's huge paw. He crashed into Cait in his retreat. Fish threw out a wall of gray light, saving both himself and Brady from the attacks of the scaled and antlered beasts.

Dark blue light flared from Desmond's hand, the panther disappearing in a puff of smoke. "Finally," he muttered, then whirled on the next beast in line. A larger, more powerful rift exploded from him, heading straight for the bear-like beast that charged them.

The light enveloped the bear, turning it into smoke that evaporated back into the tree.

Seven beasts were left.

Brady's bursts of light were weaker than Fish's or Desmond's, and he was struggling to keep his own. Fish spent most of his time defending Brady rather than going on the offensive against the beasts. The rat-like one slipped around the barrier that Fish had thrown up and leaped straight for Brady.

Cait watched in horror as the beast knocked Brady to the ground, tumbling as he grappled with the thing. Its razor-sharp claws slashed at whatever it could hit, Brady crying out in pain with each swipe. Desmond and Fish took a step toward the boy, desperate to help him. But they were fighting off beasts of their own.

The tentacled beast snapped out a limb, wrapping it around Fish's leg. The bat-like creature swooped over the old man's head, landing at his back. It reared a fearsome, clawed hand preparing to strike.

The wolfish beast hounded Desmond, herding him back farther and farther from the tree. The antlered beast charged, a dark blue arc striking to blow it into ash. But the scaled beast, like a wingless dragon, pressed in on his other side.

The dragon beast crashed into Desmond, driving him to the ground. Like a bull, it dipped its head, ready to gore him with the sharp spines lining its face.

And as all that happened at once, Cait heard herself bellow a single word. "NO!"

The hum exploded out of Cait's body in a wave of sound, rippling through the air. It rammed into each of the beasts, knocking them away from Desmond, Brady, and Fish. Something like electricity sparked through Cait's body, sharp and alive. It snapped, arcing across her skin, bringing her every sense alight.

Heads bowed, the beasts backed up, away from the men. Desmond pushed himself up, gaping at her. Brady held a hand to a bloody gash on his side. Fish watched, his hands still bright with rifts.

A strange sense of control took over Cait's mind. She couldn't quite explain it, but it was as though she wasn't herself anymore. Something else had taken hold. Something confident and steady. Something powerful.

Taking a step forward, Cait surveyed the remaining seven beasts. Their forms radiated a slight haze like they weren't fully present. Or like they didn't belong in this world.

Cait moved closer, not entirely sure what provoked her to do so.

Desmond reached out and caught her hand where it hung by her side. "Cait," he whispered, in a tone that begged her not to go nearer.

She didn't pull away but kept her eyes on the beasts. They all waited. For what, she didn't know.

"Leave," Cait ordered, and they all took an instant step back.

Seeing that it had worked, Cait put more force into her will. She commanded them again, "Leave."

A sudden pulse worked its way through Cait's body. She heard Desmond gasp, and he dropped her hand. The energy rushed out of her into the earth. A surge of light rippled across the grass and leaves. Flashes of amber light dotted the clearing like sparklers, striking each beast and dissolving them into embers that joined the ripples. The energy converged on the tree, shooting up its trunk.

Cait could feel it, that energy racing through the bark. Somehow, she felt connected to it. She saw the strange fissure in its trunk and focused on it. *"Leave,"* she told it in her mind.

The energy united around the tear, a web of light glowing a bright amber with a creamy halo. It rippled and grew, weaving over the protruding growth of branches. It formed a shell over the rip, fusing, bonding, and hardening to encase the tear in amber.

The light went out.

The clearing was still.

The hum filled Cait's mind. Her body felt full to overflowing. The night air nipped at her arms, and she realized she'd lost Desmond's jacket in the scuffle. Yet she felt warm on the inside. Almost too warm.

"Caity?" Desmond whispered somewhere behind her.

Cait blinked at the tree. It still called to her, drawing her another step toward it.

But as she took that step, Cait collapsed.

CHAPTER TWENTY-TWO

Desmond

Surging forward as her knees buckled, Desmond caught Cait. The brunt of her dead weight struck him. He hadn't fully gotten to his feet by the time she collapsed against him, dropping him to his knees.

Fish and Brady stared at them, but Desmond was too worried about Cait to care. Carefully adjusting her in his arms, he supported her back and lifted a hand to feel for her pulse. He found it in less than a second, allowing him to relax. She felt warm to the touch, almost hot, her veins beating furiously.

Relieved, Desmond found himself brushing those silvery-blonde strands from her face. His breathing eased. She was safe. Whatever she'd done, whatever had happened to her, she was safe and alive.

Fish cleared his throat, crouching in front of Desmond. "That's one of the Lewan girls, right?" he whispered.

Desmond instinctively drew her closer. "Yeah," he admitted.

A clear glimmer shone in Fish's bright eyes. With a sigh, the lightkeeper brushed a hand over his beard. "Does your father know—"

"No," Desmond cut him off, not caring about the specific question he was asking. The answer to them all was the same.

No, William didn't know he was spending time with Cait.

No, he didn't know what Desmond felt for her.

No, he didn't know that she was the confirmed Vessel.

And if Desmond could help it, his dad never would.

"He can't know," he told the lightkeeper. He looked up at Brady. "No one can."

A grimace contorted Brady's face. He wasn't prone to lying. He'd do it for those he cared about, but he wouldn't like it.

Fish set a hand on Desmond's shoulder. "We need to get her out of here," he said, his deep voice a comforting rumble. "We'll keep this quiet for now. But I want you to come by tomorrow and explain exactly what is going on."

The unspoken alternative was clear. Desmond would either give Fish the truth or Fish would reveal him to the Warden.

With a nod, Desmond promised that he'd tell him everything.

"Good." Fish squeezed his shoulder. "Do you need help carrying her?"

Desmond shook his head. He took his time, carefully adjusting his hold on her to replace his jacket around her shoulders. Keeping one arm on her back, he slid the other under her knees. Then he widened his stance to lift her.

The hours in the gym paid off. No matter how much Cait weighed, it didn't come near the weights he lifted each day. Carrying her through the forest would be cumbersome but not difficult.

Fish took the time to inspect Brady's injuries, healing the direst ones. "I don't have the skill to handle them all," he apologized.

Brady shrugged it off. He could explain a few scratches. Taking care of the life-threatening gashes was all that mattered anyway.

The whole walk through the woods, Brady stuck to Desmond's side. His friend regularly glanced over at him. Cait's head lolled against his shoulder, and he could feel Brady's inspection drift to her just as often.

Desmond didn't doubt there were questions his friend wanted to ask. The familiarity and protectiveness he'd displayed with Cait couldn't have escaped Brady's notice. He wondered what sort of damage control he'd have to do tonight.

In addition, how would the Warden explain the amber that now covered the tear in the Veil? How soon would they find out? The patrols were keeping their hundred-pace distance under his dad's orders. He didn't want them getting close to the Veil. How much time would that order buy him? Would they ever find out?

That was a stupid question. Desmond knew they would. If Cait had done what he thought—if she really did seal the Veil back up—no more beasts would come through. And without some explanation as to why the beasts didn't appear anymore, William Simon would go out to the Veil himself to get the answers.

But how long until then?

Desmond calculated his odds the entire walk back through the trees. They managed to skirt around the patrol without incident. They made their plans the minute they broke free of the tree line. Fish would take them back to shore and stay with Desmond and Cait until Brady could make it home, grab his car, and join them back at the docks.

Fish led them straight to his boat. Desmond laid Cait on the bench beside him, resting her head on his lap as he gripped firmly to her and the rail. Brady sat across from him, jaw tight as he stared at the sea.

Once ashore, it took Brady almost half an hour to return with his car. They gently slid Cait into the backseat, still sound asleep. Desmond had regularly checked on her, fear nagging at the back of his mind that her condition might be more dangerous than it appeared. But her pulse remained steady, her breathing deep, and her countenance peaceful.

Sitting in the front seat next to Brady, Desmond forced himself not to constantly look back at her. Tension filled the silent car. Brady held the wheel at a white-knuckled ten and two, his eyes glued to the road. He kept flexing his jaw as though swallowing an impossibly large pill.

Tired of waiting, Desmond spoke. "If you have something to say, say it."

Brady spared him a glance. He shifted in the driver's seat. "I'm not sure what to say," he replied dully.

"No?" Desmond scoffed. "Then why do you keep giving me the side-eye?"

Pursing his lips, Brady looked annoyed. "Maybe it's because we almost died tonight," he retorted. "Or maybe it's 'cause you apparently wield the spirit world. Could be because the freakin' Lewan girl appeared out of nowhere. Or *maybe* it's because you seem to know her far better than I would have ever guessed."

"It's not a big deal," Desmond muttered, trying to deflect.

Brady let out a huff. "Which part exactly? The dying part? The wielding part? Or the you being in love with the Lewan girl part?"

His head whipped to the backseat to be sure Cait was still unconscious. Then he whirled to his friend. "I am not!"

With a nonchalant shrug, Brady kept his eyes on the road. "Dude, I don't blame you. She's a Lewan. She and her older sister have been all the guys could talk about for the last four years."

Containing a snarl, Desmond crossed his arms. "I'm aware," he grumbled, then added, "I'm not in love with her. I don't even know her."

Brady didn't believe him. "How long have you two been—what, are you dating?" he asked, surprisingly chill about the question.

"No, we're—we don't hang out."

"Why are you lying?"

"I'm not!"

Brady chuckled sardonically. "I don't care, dude. Just don't do anything stupid."

An instant swell of indignation rose within Desmond, both for his sake and Cait's. "I'm not Garrett, okay? I do have *some* common sense."

"Good," Brady replied calmly. He pulled over onto the shoulder of the road. They were outside Cait's neighborhood. Within a ten-minute walk, they'd return her to her home.

Turning off the car, Brady angled to face Desmond. "Why are you keeping your relationship a secret?"

"Because—" With that one word, Desmond realized he'd admitted to having a relationship with her.

A smug grin pulled up the corner of Brady's mouth.

Desmond sighed, running a hand over his face. "We're not dating," he said. "We spend time together . . . in secret. That's all."

"For how long?"

He pretended to need to think about it. "Ten years."

"Ten years?" Brady gaped at him. "That's—that's like the whole time she's been here."

Desmond shrugged, mentally correcting his friend that it was two years shy of that.

"So, what? You guys are . . . you're not just friends." He said it like it was a fact—like the idea itself was ridiculous.

"Yeah, we are," Desmond countered.

"No way."

"Why not?"

"Dude, I'm not an idiot." Brady frowned at him. "I don't know how I didn't see it before—the way you've been protecting her all year. The way you look at her. It's—well, it's kind of creepy."

Desmond shot Brady one of his fiercer glares.

"Hey," Brady laughed, "she saved my life tonight. If you aren't dating her, I might take a shot."

Now, Desmond scowled at him.

Brady smiled. "That—" he pointed to Desmond's expression, "is how I know you love her."

"I don't."

"And Sydney's hair isn't red," he mocked.

Staring out the windshield, Desmond shook his head.

"Why are you so against it?" Brady asked.

That was the wrong question. Because Desmond wasn't against it. He wanted it. He felt it. He just couldn't allow himself to admit it.

"Nothing can come of it, Brade," he muttered.

"Why not?"

"She's a Lewan."

"Don't be stupid," Brady shot back. "If you love her, who cares what her dad was."

"That's not—" Desmond was about to say that that wasn't the point. But it was the point. It was the *whole* point. Because he did care, and it did matter who Owen Lewan had been. He cared because it made Cait the one girl he *couldn't* be with.

Not unless he found a way to free her from her father's affliction.

Sighing, Desmond refused to entertain the conversation anymore. He opened the car door, the night air instantly sending chills across his skin. "Come on," he said, climbing out of the sedan.

The walk to Cait's house gave Desmond time to work out how he'd get her back into her bedroom without waking the whole family. He handed her over to Brady, his friend waiting in the woods lining their backyard. Then he dashed across the lawn, straight to the enclosed porch. It was dangerous to enter the house. Despite the late hour—or early, depending on how you looked at it—there was a chance that her nan or one of her sisters would be awake. Red might even be on the prowl, prepared to alert the family to any intruders. But hoisting Cait onto the roof while unconscious wasn't exactly an option.

Desmond opened the screen door with care. The faint creak of its hinges made him grimace. He slipped past, walking across the porch to the back door. Porthaven was a small town. Many residents left their doors unlocked. He couldn't leave out the possibility the Lewans did too.

Unfortunately, they didn't.

Backtracking, Desmond made his way to the maple tree nearest the house. This was the same path he'd taken both times he snuck into Cait's room. He climbed the tree easily, then carefully scrambled along the limb that veered closest to the roof. It wasn't particularly thick, and it wavered under his feet. But that wound up helping more than hindering, its unsteady waver drifting him even closer to the roof of the covered porch.

Desmond slipped from the branch, landing lightly on the roof. He crossed the black shingles on the balls of his feet, keeping one eye on the window to his right—one of her sister's rooms, he thought. Cait's room was the window to the left.

Angling that way, Desmond breathed easier when his hands pressed against the glass. He tried opening it, but it was locked, as he'd suspected.

Closing his eyes, Desmond imagined the room. Purple walls lined with sketches, dark wood desk littered with schoolwork and cosmetics, light blue bench seat where they'd sat together. He willed Hades to appear on that bench and push back the curtains.

Desmond opened his eyes to see the blue-black cat staring at him from the other side of the panes.

Smiling, Desmond mentally instructed the sith to unlock the window. Hades rose on his hind legs, massive front paws deftly handling the latch. The sill shifted under the cat-beast's weight, allowing Desmond to open it.

Pushing the curtains wide, Desmond climbed through. He took the time to sit on the bench seat and remove his boots to lessen the odds of making noise as he worked through the house.

In his socks, Desmond crept out of Cait's bedroom, the door giving a soft *squeak*. He stood in a narrow hall, remaining still and listening for any sign that he'd woken the family. The hall, L-shaped and lined with doors, remained quiet and full of shadows.

Secure that he'd caused no disturbance, Desmond left Cait's door wide open behind him. He didn't want to get it wrong when he returned.

A staircase led down to the first floor. He took each step slowly, flinching with every small *creak*. He tried to memorize the location of each creak so he could try to avoid them on his way back. Desmond had no clue how Cait had managed to appear out of nowhere on the island, but he desperately wished he had the skill to teleport her back into her bedroom now.

Desmond made it downstairs, finding himself in the tiny living room. There were two doors: one right before him—the front door—and another to his immediate right. He ignored them both, following the clearer path past the worn-in couches and mismatched decorations toward the soft glow of the kitchen range. In the corner of the room, he saw a dog bed and Red's wire-furred figure curled up.

Moving cautiously, Desmond tried to sneak past when a floorboard groaned. The dog's ears perked up, and he lifted his head. Desmond froze, breath caught in his lungs. Red stared up at him, then stood. The tags of his collar jingled as he trotted across the short distance between them. He sniffed Desmond's pant leg, his tail beginning to wag.

Releasing a sigh, Desmond crouched down to pat the dog's head. "Good boy," he whispered.

Continuing his journey with Red now at his side, Desmond peered through the doorway into the kitchen. He found it empty, the light from the range casting a pleasant golden glow over the room. Part of Desmond wished he could take his time exploring Cait's home. He wanted to know every space, every scent, every detail of where she lived. He wanted to take it home with him so that when he thought of her, he could see her life perfectly in his mind's eye.

Instead, he crossed the faded linoleum floor straight for the back door. Then, he was out on the porch once more.

Holding the screen door open, Desmond beckoned toward the woods. Brady emerged, carrying Cait with even more ease than Desmond had. That was the benefit of height and extra muscle, he lamented internally.

"You got her?" Brady whispered as he transferred Cait over to Desmond.

Draping her over his shoulder this time to make it easier to maneuver, Desmond bent his knees to absorb her weight. "Yeah," he confirmed. He let Brady take hold of the door and began to back away. "I'll meet you at the car."

Brady shook his head. "I'll be in the trees," he insisted. "I want to be sure you make it out."

With a nod of thanks, Desmond turned. He moved back into the kitchen, extra aware of Cait's head hanging against his back as he turned to shut the door. Taking every step with care, he moved with as much speed as he felt he could, Red padding along beside him. He felt like a burglar, sneaking through a house at night. Except in this case, he was returning something rather than taking it.

When they reached the staircase, Red took a seat to watch as Desmond sucked in a nervous breath. He began the treacherous journey back up to the second floor. His heart thudded in his ears, on high alert as he listened for the creaks. He managed to escape a few, but others whined at the weight of both him and Cait. He tensed with each sound. He couldn't decide whether he should move with a steady gait for the sake of speed or if he should slow to make it seem more like the natural, random creaks of an old house.

After what felt like an eternity, Desmond made it to the top of the stairs. He doubled his stride, hurrying into Cait's room. He risked leaving the door open in exchange for setting her on the bed first. Then he rushed back to close it silently.

Leaning against the door, Desmond released the breath he'd been holding since he started up those stairs. His lungs burned, and his shoulder screamed at him. Tomorrow would be hell at school, his body exhausted and sore from all the events of the night.

Desmond regained control of his breathing and turned back to Cait. He'd rested her rather haphazardly, though gently, on the twin-sized mattress. Now, he returned to correct his sloppy care.

Pulling back the layers of blankets, Desmond prepared as clear a spot as he could on the small bed. Everything she owned was small, he decided. Small desk. Small bed. Small clothes. Small trinkets.

Gathering her back into his arms, Desmond realized the room fit the girl. Though Cait pushed the average height for a girl—only a couple of inches shorter than him—she was definitively *small*. Her shoulders were trim, her figure narrow. She felt fragile as a seashell in his arms. Light, breakable, and unfathomably precious.

Desmond deposited Cait on the spot he'd cleared. He carefully placed her head on the pillow, brushing the hair out of her face. He tucked the blankets up to her chin. Then he paused. Did she like the blankets pulled this high? He knew he didn't. What if it was too warm for her? She did have several blankets, though none were as thick as the comforter on his bed.

Nervously deciding, Desmond pushed the blankets back a fraction. He guided her arm out over the covers. The moonlight streamed through the window, turning her pale skin to porcelain.

Desmond heaved a sigh. She was gorgeous. She looked like an angel with that silvery hair splayed across her pillow.

Rolling his eyes at himself, Desmond whirled toward the window. Hades waited there, his fluffy fur given a halo in the moonlight. He sat next to the cat as he put his boots back on. His eyes kept drifting to Cait, still sound asleep in her bed.

Desmond paused as he finished tying the laces. He couldn't leave her here without an explanation, could he? What if she woke up and thought it was all a dream? That would be good, wouldn't it? Maybe the best possible outcome would be her believing it never happened.

Staring at the peaceful expression on her face, he knew he couldn't do it. He already had enough secrets that he kept from Cait. He couldn't lie to her about this. It would come out eventually, anyway. Better to get it over with now.

Desmond hurried to the nightstand and opened the sketchbook there. He flipped through the pages to find a blank one but stopped when he found a picture of the cove. He immediately knew it was the scene from her nightmares. The one she'd recently begun to have.

The stormy skies were almost black, a single, stark strike of lightning piercing through the scene. The sea churned, and smoke coiled across the sand. She'd captured the moment with frightening realism. Perhaps it was because he knew the cove so intimately, but he recognized every detail. The craggy cliffs, the thick woods at the edges. And himself, standing in the water, facing the horizon.

Knowing there was no better page to leave his note, Desmond picked up the pencil and wrote, *"I'll explain everything – Des."*

Propping the sketchbook open for Cait to find in the morning, Desmond didn't know which he hoped for more: that he'd be able to explain or that she'd let him in the first place.

CHAPTER TWENTY-THREE

Cait

A cold, harsh breeze nipped at Cait's cheeks in a rushing whorl of sound that startled her awake.

She still stood by the tree; she could tell that much. The sky had darkened, the moon shrouded by heavy gray clouds. She could hardly see the behemoth of a tree before her. Black shadows reached across the clearing, so thick she only knew the tree by the slight tug in her gut to take a step closer. Her head pulsed with that steady thrum so familiar to her. But this was different from the hum that accompanied Desmond's presence. This hum was sharper, firmer, and strangely empowering.

The sycamore's branches creaked, fighting the furious wind's demands. Why was she still here? Had Desmond left her on the forest floor to fend for herself? She'd saved him, hadn't she? She thought she had. He would never leave her like this . . . would he?

Fear welled up to clog Cait's throat. The monsters she'd faced earlier—the beasts of the spirit world—would they come back?

Even now, Cait's skin tingled with the unusual energy she'd felt when she'd commanded them. She had no idea how she'd summoned those sparks of light that had turned to amber on the sycamore's trunk. Could she control those beasts again if they came for her now? Alone, was she strong enough to protect herself?

A flash of lightning split the sky. White blanched the clearing for one second, giving Cait a glimpse of the sycamore before her. She startled at the gnarled sight of it.

This wasn't the same tree—it couldn't be. Yet she felt that same pull. She'd moved an unconscious step forward in that lightning flash.

But she'd seen it. The tree was different. Something had happened to it. Its twisted branches now spiraled into an arthritic maze, tangled up in itself. The trunk, with that strange tear, now bulged to twice its size. Something was desperately wrong.

The wind blew fiercer, angrier. Cait looked up at the sky just as the first raindrop fell, an icy, salted splash on the bridge of her nose. The clouds churned, roiling like a mass of smoke above her. Their wisps thinned, revealing the full moon above her.

Cait tipped her head to the side, curious. Had the moon been full that night?

Rain crashed to the earth, splattering and tumbling through the leaves to soak the dirt under her boots. Cait frowned. She'd been barefoot when she'd woken on the island. Her hands went instinctively to the thick knitted sweater and denim jeans, little droplets of rain clinging to them. She could have sworn she was wearing her navy pajamas too.

Looking back up at the tree, Cait realized that Desmond hadn't left her—it was all a dream. She should have known. He'd never abandon her, not even after she abandoned him. She knew she'd made the right choice, ending whatever warped thing was between them. But her heart grieved the loss of him still.

Cait's eyes filled with painful tears. Alone on the strange island, cold from the wind and the rain, she felt like a shell of herself. She didn't want it to be like this. After only two days, she missed him. Desperately. Seeing him tonight, it felt like someone had ripped a piece of her soul from her chest and shredded it in front of her. She'd been so confused, too overwhelmed by the chaos around her—the tree, the beasts, the presence of Brady and Fish—that she hadn't been able to process what she felt in the moment. But Cait knew now with absolute certainty: If she was going to survive life without Desmond, she couldn't be around him. She couldn't let herself cling to that false dream of her youth any longer.

White-hot lightning burned three jagged lines in the sky above Cait. The clouds kept swirling like a hurricane, the eye of this storm the silver-white moon. Its light washed over the clearing, casting a pale hue over the tree as the shadows fought to maintain their hold. The branches of the tree were so thick that its trunk still eluded the light. But amid the tangled limbs, Cait spotted a shimmering flash of movement.

Eyes locking onto the sudden movement, Cait braced herself for a beast. Instead, beady black eyes met hers, jewel-like blue-black feathers sleek amongst the branches. "Caw," the raven cried. "Caw, caw."

Cait tightened her jaw, nervous at the sight of the bird. It was the prelude to a change in her dreams. An omen of danger, she decided.

The bird took flight, the gleaming moonlight catching on its wings as it flew through the tangled branches. In a swoop of shadow, the raven descended to the far end of the clearing. It tucked its wings, landing gracefully on the shoulder of a young woman. Her pretty blue sweater brightened the somber forest. The wind played with her hair, the moonlight gilding her coppery red waves. She looked only a couple of years older than Cait, a soft expression on her pale face as she looked up at the tree thoughtfully. The raven perched comfortably on her shoulder, but the young woman paid it no attention.

Cait began to call out, then thought better of it. Whomever this woman was, she'd never before encountered any strangers in her dreams. And after her experience with the beasts earlier in the night, she found herself even less trusting than usual.

The raven had other ideas. It crooned a gentle "caw," drawing the woman's attention. She looked at the bird, the elegant features of her face drawing together for a mere second before her gaze shot across the clearing, straight for Cait.

Cait took a step back, wondering if she should run. But there was something about this woman that couldn't quite inspire fear in Cait. Perhaps it was her youth or the gentle, curious smile that tugged at the corner of her lips. Whatever instincts warned Cait, they weren't strong enough to combat the woman's seeming harmlessness.

Lightning flashed again, and the raven let out another cry.

The young woman responded, turning away from Cait to look to her left. Directly across from her, Cait followed her sight line. The moonlight's silvery glow cast spectral shadows through the tree's limbs. Cait had to squint to get a clear sight of the boy who stood there. The hum increased, the hair on her arms rising with it.

On the edge of the tree line, staring up at the hulking sycamore, the boy took a step forward out of the murky shadows and into a stream of light. His thick black hair whipped around his face, just beginning to dampen from the rain, and his bushy eyebrows pulled together to crease the warm brown skin of his forehead. Cait gasped, recognizing Sterling Faulk. The puff of sound from her surprise didn't carry across the distance between them, and Sterling just kept staring at the tree, confusion marring his features.

Cait glanced back toward the redheaded woman. She remained on the far side of the clearing, eyes narrowed and lips pulled down as she stared at something on the opposite side of the tree from Cait.

Curious at the cause of the woman's reaction, Cait shifted, trying to peer around the side of the tree. Her heart beat in time with the hum coursing through her body. She needed answers. Everything that had happened to her that night sat like a fishing hook lodged in her chest. It tugged at her, forcing her a step forward and to the right.

Whatever the redhead was looking at was important; Cait could feel it. And she was tired of being in the dark. She was tired of being the only one without answers—tired of standing back and letting people lie to her. Tonight, she'd experienced the spirit world as she'd never known before. She'd felt power she never knew existed. And while fear twisted around her spine, after facing down beasts and getting a glimpse at her own power, Cait refused to stand in the shadows anymore.

Taking another step closer to the tree and to the left, Cait strained to see around the sycamore's giant, warping trunk. Lightning cut through the air, fiery-white lines streaking through the clouds. Rain soaked through her clothes, chilling her to the bone. Hollows of light and shadow obscured the other side of the clearing. But there, amongst the darkness, Cait could see a fourth figure, shrouded by night.

And then, she woke up.

Cait & Desmond will return
in book five of Archives of the Warden

Also Available from V.K. Dixon

ARCHIVES OF THE WARDEN
Lake of Glass
Vault of Stone
The Raven's Cry
Veil of Mist (Coming 2025)
Book Five (Coming soon)

WARRIORS & MAGES
Fire & Night
Sword & Shadow
Relics & Thrones (Coming soon)

Follow the QR code below
to sign up for V.K. Dixon's Newsletter:

Newsletter: vkdixon.substack.com
Instagram: @v.k.dixon
TikTok: @vkdixon

Glossary of Terms & Names

arachne — *[ar—ack—nay]* — Spider-like beast from the spirit world

artio — *[ar—tee—oh]* — Bear-like beast from the spirit world

beast — A creature summoned from the spirit world to work on behalf of a Wielder

Benjamin Lavigne — *[Lah—veen]* — *aka 'Ben'* — Reverend; Brady's father; Warden member

Brady Lavigne — *aka 'Brade'* — High school senior; son of the reverend; best friend of Desmond

Brett Varon — Hunter's dad; Warden member

Caitriona Lewan — *[Kuh—trina Lew-en]* — *aka 'Cait'* — High school senior; originally from Bushmills, Ireland; middle Lewan daughter

Cleric — Classification of Wielder, able to speak to ghosts and summon beasts

Corva — Prophetic spirit-being

Desmond Simon — High school student and honorary Warden member

Druids — *aka 'Children of Gaia'* — A cult of Wielders intent on releasing the spirit world upon the physical world

Dwight Greene — Retired doctor; Elizabeth's grandfather; Warden member

Elizabeth Greene — High school senior; daughter of town doctor

Fischer Lavigne — *aka 'Fish'* — Lightkeeper; Warden member

Gabriel Varon — The first Varon connected with the Warden; considered the father of the Varon line

Garrett Edgars — High school senior; second son of the sheriff; cousin of Desmond

Gary Lavigne — Retired reverend; Brady's grandfather; Warden member

Genevieve Lewan — *aka 'Genni'* — High school sophomore; youngest Lewan daughter

ghost — The lingering spirit of a dead Wielder with unfinished business in the physical world

Gregory Varon — Hunter's grandfather; Warden member

Hades — A sith beast; summoned by Desmond Simon

hellhound — Hound-like beast from the spirit world

Howard DeGarmo — Matt Davis's grandfather

Hunter Varon — High school senior; Desmond's rival

hydra — *[hi—druh]* — Snake-like beast from the spirit world

John Lavigne — Eldest son of Fischer Lavigne; Warden member

Kelly Davis — Sister of Matt Davis

Kenneth Greene — Town doctor; Elizabeth's father; Warden member

the Leviathan — A spirit-being under the guard of the Warden

Lilith Drake — Owner of the tea shop; ex-Druid

Ludus — Cait's dog in present day

Maeve Lewan — *[May—vuh]* — Grandmother of the Lewan sisters

Matt Davis — High school senior; new to Porthaven

nyct — *[nicked]* — Bat-like beast from the spirit world

Owen Lewan — Father of Cait; Warden member; deceased

Penny Davis — History teacher at Porthaven High; Matt's mom

Peter Varon — Writer and Warden member from DeVerre, WA

phantom — A ghost that has been tethered to a specific location in the physical world

Porthaven, ME — Small, Warden-run town in northeast Maine

ratatoskr — *[rah—tah—toss—ker]* — Rat-like beast from the spirit world

Raymond Edgars — Fire marshal; Scott's dad; Warden member

Red — Lewan family terrier

Richard Edgars — *aka 'Rick'* — Sheriff; Garrett's dad; Warden member

Robin Simon — Wife of William and mother of Desmond; Warden member

Sabine Lewan — Mother of Cait; Warden member; deceased

Sage — Classification of Wielder, able to speak to ghosts, summon beasts, and wield the essence of the spirit world.

Saliha Faulk — Mother of Sterling; Warden member

Scott Edgars — High school senior; son of fire marshal; cousin of Desmond

scylla — *[sky—luh]* — Cephalopod-like beast from the spirit world

sith — Cat-like beast from the spirit world

spirit-being — A creature of the spirit world with unknown qualities and abilities

spirit world — A parallel world that exists alongside the physical world

Sterling Faulk — High school senior

Sydney Bellerose — High school senior

Sylvia Lyons — Prophetess of the Warden

Therese Lewan — *aka 'Rese'* — Barista; eldest Lewan daughter

Timothy Faulk — *aka 'Tim'* — Carpenter; father of Sterling; Warden member

valravn — *[val—rah—ven]* — Bird-like beast from the spirit world

Veil — Specific locations around the world where the boundary between the spirit world and the physical world is thin

the Warden — An organization of Wielders dedicated to protecting the spirit world from the control of the Druids

wendigo — *[when—de—go]* — Deer-like beast from the spirit world

Whitney Toussaint — *[Too—sawnt]* — High school senior; Garrett's girlfriend

Wielder — A human with the ability to wield the spirit world

William Simon — Mayor and leader of the Warden in Porthaven; father of Desmond

Acknowledgements

Cait and Desmond's story has been sitting with me for well over a decade now, and it was the origin of the Warden before I even knew what the organization was. I'm so glad I finally get to tell their tale.

There are always so many people who help writers through their journey to a completed novel. This journey was no different.

First, thank you to my readers. Writing would be a lonely affair without you. Each and every one of you make my heart so full with your love and support.

To my husband, Josh: Thank you for being the best friend and manager I've ever had. You made all of this possible. You will always be my favorite.

Thanks to my family and friends for being my biggest fans and encouraging me to pursue this dream of mine.

To my editor, Brittany: As always, you helped turn this story into everything it could be. Thank you for always knowing just what I'm trying to convey, for cheering me along every step of the way, and for teaching me to be a better writer.

Thank you to my beta reader, Jennie, for all your advice and for reminding me to finish out Cait's arc. Chapter Twenty-Three is for you, friend!

And thank you to God for giving me this wild story and helping me to write it. I pray that my work may bring you glory forever.

About the Author

V.K. Dixon writes fantasy and romance novels filled with found family, lasting love, and unique magic. She believes that the extraordinary gives us a deeper desire for the things beyond us; for the things of God. Faith, art, and community are her guiding values as she pursues the vision on her heart.

www.ingramcontent.com/pod-product-compliance
Lightning Source LLC
Chambersburg PA
CBHW022007310726

48972CB00006B/1557